CHARA

PATTERNER'S PATH, BOOK 3

STEVE TURNBULL

TAU PRESS 2020 LTD

AUTHOR'S NOTE

If, in starting this book in the series, you have not read "The Dragons of Esternes" series, this might be a good time to do it.

There are events in this book that could be considered "spoilers" for some of the events in that story. Although nothing important or that spoils the ending.

If you just want to carry on anyway, that will work too. There is nothing in "The Dragons of Esternes" series you need to know to continue with "The Patterner's Path".

I just thought I would mention it.

CHAPTER 1

The first thing she noticed was the stench of rotting vegetation and flesh. Then voices in the distance. Women shouting their conversation at one another as if they were spread far apart. Raucous laughter.

She was lying face down in mud or sand, or both. The surface was gritty against her cheek but her right hand was plunged into slimy cold that slid and clung as she tried to extract it.

Her face must be in shadow, she thought, but her right leg was hot as if the sun beat down on it. Damp seeped through her clothing and she thought the voices might be coming closer.

The power of a big ley-circle throbbed gently nearby. It was quiet and there was no hint of a feeding. But she could draw on it if she needed.

She managed to get her hands under her and pushed herself up, pulling in her legs as she did so and getting into a half-sitting position. The blast of sunlight blinded her. She shaded her eyes and was rewarded with a shower of clotted lumps of sand across her cheek and down inside her clothes.

The coast of Mirriasmia had taught her how treacherous sand could be, and how difficult it would be to get it cleaned away.

Her eyes adjusted and the world came into focus.

The wet sand and rocks with drying weeds made her think she must be on the coast somewhere, but as she scanned from right to left all she could see was a line where the dark damp changed to green grass. She looked past the figures of women teetering across the stones all staring down as if they were looking for something. There were so many, they were uncountable. Hundreds spread out across the strange landscape.

Then there were boats, all high and dry as if the tide was out but these were not vessels with tall masts and steep sides like those at Avakending. They were low and flat, a few of the larger ones did have masts but even they looked flimsy.

She finally found water, with barely a ripple reflecting the blue sky like a mirror. It was wide but she could see the far side as if it was no more than a poor excuse for a lake.

The sun was setting and was to her left, that meant she was facing north. She scrambled to her feet and turned round.

"Oh no."

A great citadel of white stone, half of it shimmered in the sunlight while the other half was in shadow. It was similar to Avakending, made as it was by the hands of the Taymalin. It stood like a diamond on the shores of what had been a great circular lake. She knew this place; her greatest shame had been wrought here at the wedding of Drahail and Hope.

Canvor. The great capital of Faerholme. The seat of the Dragonblade.

And she had drained the lake as she destroyed the Fastness of the Emperor, or the Empress. Or Jaymis.

The memory punished her. She shook her head trying to dislodge it but it sat there festering in the back of her mind.

The *Kisharuk* was real and it wanted to kill her. Yet she had beaten it, for a time at least. She needed to hide and a city was a good place for that. People would not recognise her. She touched her hand to her scarred face. Even those closest to her would not recognise her now.

But her damaged face made her memorable, the fewer people

who saw her, the better it would be. She needed to find somewhere to rest and decide what to do next.

She set off across the exposed bed of the lake towards the nearest grass. There were pools here and there, one had a fish still flapping about in it. She understood then the women were looking for fish like this one, or perhaps lost treasures.

The creature gasped for air and tried to hide its glistening, multi-coloured skin. She knelt down, picked up a rock, yanked the fish from the water by its tail and dashed its head in. It wriggled and flopped a few times before it went still.

"Sorry."

She was curiously surprised to find that not only was she clothed but still had her bag. There was money in her purse and her knife. She made quick work of the fish, topping and tailing it then slicing it through to scrape out the guts. There were seabirds here but they had a glut of food without having to fight for it.

Elona wrapped the fish in her cloak and continued heading for the steep climb up to the grass line. She almost didn't see the sudden drop off and only saved herself from toppling in by leaping awkwardly across the gap. It was a great crack in the ground almost as wide as she was tall. The sides were smooth as glass and water flowed along the bottom of it like a river.

The great ley-circle of Canvor might have been underwater but that did not prevent it from distorting the landscape. It explained why the women had not come down here, closer to the city. That and perhaps the proximity of the ley-circle itself.

She moved on, taking more care now, until she was distracted by the sound of men's voices ahead. She glanced up and then turned away immediately, pulling her hood over her head.

Armsmen, patterners, and nobles in their finery. They surveyed the landscape. They did not shout and laugh like the women. Their voices were quiet and sombre. The patterners would understand what had happened even if they did not know how it had been done.

Elona continued towards them, as if she were not concerned if they saw her, but kept her eyes to the ground. She aimed for a point off to the side as if she intended to bypass them. Then she heard a voice she recognised and glanced up again.

Drahail.

Not a single emotion stirred in her as she watched him. She thought he looked older. Perhaps it was the weight of the kingdom on his shoulders. He conversed calmly; she could not catch the words but his tone conveyed a questioning. And they answered him, first the armsman, perhaps a general, and then the patterner. It was not the Arch-Patterner for which she was grateful since she was not sure she could control herself in the presence of the man who had destroyed her life.

She was passing closer now, the lake bed rose slowly but the steep incline ahead meant they were high above her. She was forced to turn in their direction by a boulder blocking her way. She kept her head down.

"You! Woman!"

"Master calls, hey?" Elona did not look up but mimicked the accent of the Kadralin traders as best she could, though her skin—where it was undamaged—was far too pale to be mistaken for one.

"What are you doing?"

Still without looking up she unwrapped the fish and held it up. "Home to family, hey. Masters." She risked looking up hoping that the distance and the damaged skin would make them think she was Kadralin.

"This is your King!"

That voice. *Oh no.*

She dropped her head and went down on her knees so fast that if the ground had not been mud, she would have bruised them. She dropped her head low and dug her free hand into the mud then brought it to her cheek. Hidden by her hood she worked as much of it across her pale skin as she could.

What twist of fate brought both Drahail and her father to this place here and now? She sighed. She had done it herself by draining the lake to destroy the Fastness.

"Lord Corlain, I am not a despot. Woman, get up, get your fish out of the mud, what is your name?"

She did as he said but made sure she kept her face hidden.

"Parthia, Lord King."

"That is an unusual name for a Kadralin."

She cursed her stupid mistake. "I was not born Kadralin, Lord King."

"Come up here."

"Lord?"

Elona cringed this was going from bad to worse. Drahail liked to think of himself as a King who was happy to speak to any of his subjects. She should have gone off in another direction the moment she realised who he was.

"I want to talk to you."

"Yes, Lord King."

There was no way up to him from here, her only choice was to follow her original path to where the slope was less and she was able to climb slowly keeping the fish in one hand as she did so.

As she mounted the final ridge and came out onto the grazing land around the castle, she saw the rest of Drahail's retinue. At least a hundred armsmen keeping a watchful eye on both the land around them and the sky. In addition, the patterner had another half-dozen attendants of lower ranks.

She kept her hood up and her head down as she walked across the cropped grass, avoiding the dung of the *kelukisa*. Their patterns stood out to her, as they grazed in large groups.

The men were talking and she caught fragments about *fish* and *opening a path*. She stopped a good distance from Drahail, close enough that they could converse but far enough that neither he nor her father could see her face properly.

Drahail did not attempt to close the gap. Beside and behind him were two *zatasa*, large and lithe. Their skins glowed in the evening sunlight as they lounged comfortably beside their master. But even without making direct contact, she could feel the wariness in them. They knew their duty was to defend Drahail and they did not know her.

"So, Parthia, how is it that you are a Taymalin adopted by Kadralin?"

The walk and climb had given her an opportunity to think about how she was going to answer this question. "I was cast out for my deformity, Lord King, and taken in by Kadralin, hey."

"Deformity?"

Elona raised her head a little and drew back the hood but only on the side where her face was scarred. She was satisfied by the indrawn breaths, mutterings and even someone making the sign to avert the *Kisharuk*—if only they knew.

She let the hood drop back and lowered her head once more.

"Even so," said Drahail, "it is a terrible thing to abandon a child in such a way. Can it not be healed?"

She shook her head. This was a dangerous subject, if someone should take it into their head to try, it would not be long before everything was exposed. She spread out her senses and made contact with a herd of *kelukisa*, they were not large like their cousins, but there were about fifty of them.

"Have you travelled far?" It was her father and in the instant, he spoke she realised she was still wearing the travelling clothes she had bought with Jaymis in Glytheni. The grazing animals were easy to control and it took barely a moment before she had them heading towards the group at a slow trot.

"A great distance, Lord, hey."

Elona encouraged the *kelukisa* to a run and turned her attention to the *zatasa*. At heart, they were hunting animals and they loved to chase. A herd of stampeding grass-eaters were just the sort of thing they liked. But they resisted her.

"Well?"

She realised her father had asked a question and she had missed it. She flung herself to the ground.

"I am sorry, Lord."

"I asked if you came with your Kadralin people?"

"No, Lord. I travel alone."

She could sense a stir among the armsmen, some of them had noticed the moving herd. She drove them into a full gallop and the sound of their hooves drifted over the group. She forced an awareness of the running prey into the minds of Drahail's *zatesa*. Finally, they latched on.

She realised her father was walking towards her.

"Your clothes are dirty but they are quite new. And your boots look expensive. Are you a liar? Or simply a thief?"

His shadow went over her.

As the thundering of the *kelukisa* blotted out all other sounds, the two *zatesa* hooted in unison and bolted away from their master.

Drahail shouted. She lifted her head just enough to see and watched him chasing after them. Her father headed away too, along with Drahail's body guard trying to keep up with them.

Elona stayed just where she was for a count of twenty then stood carefully, in an effort not to attract attention. She allowed herself a quick glance around. No one seemed to be looking in her direction. She turned away and headed towards the city. She forced herself to walk slowly fearing at any moment that they might come after her.

The city was still the best place to hide though she knew her father would be relentless in trying to find her if he decided he needed to, but she was sure she could elude him and his men.

Then she heard a woman scream in the distance behind her as if it had come from the dried-up riverbed. It was not a cry of pain but more of horror. She did not turn. There were more screams and shouts, some of them from men now, and someone giving orders. The desire to turn and look was strong, but she had to keep moving forwards.

The castle gates loomed before her. They were not as large as those at Avakending, and at this time of day the entrance was not crowded. She had to turn now, which gave her the opportunity to look back towards the empty lake. There was no pursuit that she could see, quite the contrary there was a stream of armsmen moving out towards a large clot of women making a circle around something.

Whatever it was, Drahail and his entourage were far more interested in that than they were in her. The relief gave her confidence. The guards did not give her a second glance and she was inside quickly.

Like Avakending there was a killing ground just the other side of the massive gates but it was not as extensive as the southern city. She knew the road to the right was the one that led up to the palace, so she went the other way.

It did not take her long to find a small and cheap hostel clinging to the side of the hill in an area that was just the wrong side of good quality. She paid over the money for a night then extra to have her fish cooked and delivered to her room for both evening and morning meals.

She was starving. It felt as if she hadn't eaten for days and when she thought about it, it probably was at least a full day. From the moment she and Jaymis had left the hostel in Glytheni, done their shopping, gone to the ley-circle and jumped to the Fastness. Followed by the hours there before the battle with the *Kisharuk* and then arriving here.

She washed off the mud but kept her face covered when her food was delivered. She ate slowly trying not to think about Jaymis, then lay down and fell asleep even as the tears came.

CHAPTER 2

'So, you're *fahain*?' the *Kisharuk* had said. 'Always the rebellious ones, a troublesome lot.'

Elona opened her eyes and the sun was pouring in through the window. She did not know how long she had slept but the day was well advanced.

The monster had been speaking through the mouth of Lord Nemon's wife, Hilaneena. People talked about the creature, and they used his name in their curses but they did not know what it was.

She thought back to the mummer's play she had seen when she was young. The very first time she had met Drahail, the man she had been betrothed to. He had been obnoxious but she had not been much better. She shook her head. Now he was the King with a wife and son, while she was a fugitive with half a face.

The play had told the story of the escape of the Taymalin from their enslavement by the Slissac—and the retribution of their masters in creating the *Kisharuk* to hunt them down and kill them.

But the monster was not doing that. At least a thousand years later and not only had it not killed them all, it had been trying to rule them instead. Did that mean anything? Was that simply the way it had chosen? Or, after all this time, did it want more?

It liked hurting people, she knew that, whether it was physical or through their emotions. She had seen the delight in it when it had taken Jaymis and was able to taunt her with the secrets it learnt. But it said Jaymis was still there, did that mean he was alive?

She sat up.

The past did not matter, she was still not safe. Her father had not seen her face but Drahail had. They would be looking for the woman with scars, dressed in traveller's clothes.

Breakfast was delivered as arranged and she made her plans while she ate cold fish soup.

So, she needed to get new clothes and a new place to stay—not in an inn because that was where they would look but proper lodgings.

She went through her things. She had enough money to last for a while and some jewellery from Faerholme which would fetch a reasonable price if she needed more. From her selection of clothes, she managed to put together a costume that did not look too much like a traveller but she still needed to wear the cloak so the hood could hide her face.

There was nothing she could do about that. This time there was no chance she could pretend to be one of the Sisters of Taymalin. They would be sure to hear about the woman with the scarred face and she would be a newcomer among them.

She gathered the rest of her belongings, asked for directions to the street of clothiers and headed that way. There was no point trying to be clever and not going there, since that was the only place she would be able to find the sort of person she needed.

The day was, as she suspected, well advanced and the streets were busy. In the mountain village, everybody knew everybody else. But in cities, especially one as large as Canvor, no one knew anyone outside of their circle of family and acquaintances. And here, unlike Avakending, she was a native. She spoke the language the same way as everyone else and she understood, at least in theory if not from experience, how everything worked.

If it had not been for her face, she could have blended in perfectly and vanished.

The cobbled length of the Clothiers Street was wide and airy. It ran along the lower slopes of the mount on which the castle stood. The day was sunny and fabrics were on display outside each shop. Elona felt more comfortable here, since the people about her were almost all women.

The quality and prices increased the higher she went so once she had reached the end, where the street debouched into a square with the metal-workers quarter continuing up the hill and woodworkers down to the right. She bought a honey roll and *tasa* in a wooden cup for an outrageous price then leaned against a wall, in the shade.

It was almost as if her life was normal as she stood and sipped the aromatic liquid to wash down the sweet dry bun.

Normal like those people around her. Mothers, wives, maids, children, young men, old men, armsmen all going about their lives as if nothing that happened in the outside world could touch them here.

But their cocoon had been pierced. Even if they did not realise it, she had changed their lives by draining the lake that protected them.

That could be why Drahail and his people had come to look. They were deciding what steps they must take now that the great ley-circle was exposed. Her father might have been summoned for the task, since the ley-circle at Corlain was almost as powerful but completely exposed—as most were.

Canvor had never had to guard its ley-circle before.

She finished her food and handed the wooden cup back to the merchant who rewarded her with a tenth of a tay, a tiny chip of a coin easily lost.

Elona made her way back down the hill, still pausing at the shops here and there. Reminded of that moment, back at the fair when she had been examining the rich clothes of a stall when she first experienced the hateful nature of Krazak, Nursey's son.

"Hello, pretty."

Her blood ran cold. She turned slowly towards the voice on her left, expecting to see the dark moustached face of Krazak, though worms had been eating him for many years.

It wasn't Krazak, of course not, the man did not resemble him at all. Where Nursey's son had been hard and lined, this man was soft with the rounded edges of someone who had never lacked for food. But there were still similarities, and she could see the violence lurking beneath his skin just as she had in the other man—though she did not recognise it then. And he grinned like a wolf.

She realised too that this man was shorter than she was, but he had arrogance to compensate. So, she laughed.

The fake smile on his face dropped away, to be replaced with the red of anger. The man grabbed her bicep and gripped painfully hard.

"For that, pretty, you will feel pain and not pleasure."

She had not turned her face fully towards him, and she still hid beneath the hood.

"You think I am pretty?" Her controlled voice upset his barely maintained calm even further and he was hurting her arm a great deal. But she did not show it, her life had contained far worse pain than this.

Instead, she turned to her inner sense and saw the violent rhythms of his barely controlled anger and lust.

She wanted to infuse him with fear. She wanted to cause him the mental pain that he tried to inflict on her, and had certainly done to other women. She wanted to crush him. To kill him where he stood.

But she dare not. Instead, she controlled herself in precisely the way it seemed that he could not.

He could not have seen what passed through her mind but the fact she did not show any fear caused his passions to waver. Which gave her what she needed. It was almost like a healing, binding together a pattern the way it should be. She saw his wavering patterns built upon it and fed it back to him.

She smothered his lust. Every tissue, every muscle, every bone. And with it the violence dissipated.

"What are you doing?" he said in a voice that had lost all its menace.

His hand fell away from her and he just stared, his mouth open.

"You need to go home and rest," she said.

There was a delay as if the words had difficulty penetrating his mind. "Yes, I will."

He turned away and was soon lost in the crowd.

Elona glanced around. There was a woman, on the other side of the street, looking on with undisguised curiosity. Elona pulled her hood forward and headed down the hill.

She stopped looking at the hanging fabrics and clothes, but continued down to the second-to-last shop on the street. It was a small narrow building pressed between much larger ones, it had no racks of cloth on the street, there was simply no room for it.

Without hesitation she plunged into the dim interior. A bell over the door jangled to alert the owner of her presence.

The place smelled pleasant enough, if a little musty. The scent of fresh *tasa* tickled the back of her throat.

The light from the street window only illuminated a short way, and beyond that were oil lamps. She appreciated the darkness, since it hid her face.

"Can I help, goodwife?"

The voice came from a thin pole of a man who stood considerably taller than her, it seemed curiously fitting to have someone like this in charge of a tall and thin shop.

"Do you sell completed garments?"

"I do have some but nothing like the selection available at other establishments higher up the street."

"I also have things to sell. Perhaps exchange?"

"That is not my usual mode of business, goodwife."

"It's all good, bought recently. Travelling clothes mostly but I do not need to travel any more. I need replacements."

"I will be honest, goodwife, if I agree to this trade it will be strongly in my favour."

"I understand."

The bell jangled again.

Elona turned with a jump and saw the woman who had been watching her come in and begin to examine the rolls of cloth in the light by the door.

"I should perhaps mention," said the shop owner, "that I do own a *zatek* who will protect me and my property. Talon!"

A long and low growl rolled through from the back of the shop.

Elona's pattern sense found the creature in a moment.

"He sounds a strong beast," she said. "But if you think this woman is my accomplice and that we intend to steal from you. I don't know her and I just want to do business as I explained."

"One cannot be too careful," he said, "and besides, you would say that regardless."

"Does the King not maintain order?"

"He is as good as his father was," said the shopkeeper, "but these are difficult times. And I ask myself why a woman who speaks like someone born to the upper echelons of Faerholme society would be trading travelling clothes for something simpler."

"I have been away."

"And you have returned."

Concerned that their conversation was being overheard she lowered her voice. "Must I pay for your silence too?"

He raised his hand. "I'm sure it is none of my business, goodwife."

"Can we just get this over with?"

"Please to follow me."

He led the way further into the back and a storage room. She was not concerned since she felt no unpleasantness from the man. He had a right to be curious and his words simply demonstrated how hard it was for her to fit in even if she had not been scarred. Even her voice betrayed her.

"I have no room set aside for trying on clothes," he said. "So, I am afraid this will have to do. *Oh, Taymar's teeth.*"

She had thrown back her hood and turned her face towards him.

"I do apologise, goodwife. It was simply the surprise. I hope you can forgive me for such common rudeness."

Elona could not help but smile. She reached out and placed her hand on his arm. "Thank you, your response has been one of the kindest I have received."

"May I enquire what happened, was it a fire?"

"An accident, yes. Fire? Yes." *It might as well have been.*

"But you have not had it healed?"

"The fire distorted the patterns beyond healing."

He shook his head. "I have never heard of such a thing."

"Neither had I."

"Let me fetch you some *tasa*, while I collect together what I think will fit you and you can spread the items you have on the table there."

He left leaving the door open as if he were thoughtful enough not to worry her that she was trapped. There was a chair and Elona sat down. It was strange, she felt safe here. Like it had been in Usala's house.

Suddenly the only thing she could see was Jaymis's face and she cried.

She tried to stifle it but there was too much and each breath was a sob of pain and loss. Her sleeve became soaked with her tears until all she was doing was wiping the wetness across her cheeks. She gave up, put her head down and sobbed until her chest hurt and her throat ached.

The muzzle of a *zatek* suddenly rested on her thigh and it made little hooting noises in sympathy. She let her hand drop on to its scaly head. It reached up and a rough tongue lick her cheek.

"He's after the salt."

Elona jerked upright. The *zatek* licked her sleeve instead.

"I'm sorry."

"No need to apologise. You take as long as you need." There was the chink of a proper *tasa* cup being set down beside her. "Drink it while it's hot. That's when it's best for tears."

"You're too kind."

"It has been said. Anyway, this other woman who is not your friend also heard you crying and was concerned I had upset you."

Elona wiped her eyes again trying to focus through the blurry tears. The woman was in the doorway looking between them.

"I'm all right, really. He didn't do anything. He's been nothing but kind." She felt like she owed them an explanation for her lapse in good manners. "I lost my—" she hesitated not sure what to call

Jaymis when she didn't really want to lie, "—man a couple of days ago."

"Oh, you poor thing," said the woman and now came into the room as if that were her cue. She pulled up a second chair beside Elona and sat close, taking her hand.

The *zatek* gave up on her sleeve and lay down at her feet.

"I'll get another cup of *tasa* then. Two perhaps."

"I'm Makeela," she said. "Was he an armsman? Mine was. Died last year in Esternes."

"Armsman? No, fifth son of a minor lord. We were coming back. Attacked by brigands." She hated lying but the truth was unbelievable. "You followed me. Why?"

"I'm sorry, yes, I did. I saw you with that man, I was worried for you."

"Do you know him?"

"He is known to the women here, but he left you alone. You were lucky."

"He saw my face. It's usually enough."

The shopkeeper returned with two more cups of *tasa* with some sweet cakes on a small tray, and a chair in his other hand.

"I haven't this many people in my shop for such a long time that I thought we should celebrate."

The cake was delicious, though Elona had only one hand since Makeela was still holding her other one.

"I'm Parthia," she said. "This is Makeela."

"Kendreth."

She was glad he didn't want to hold her hand as well because then she would miss out on the excellent *tasa* and sweet breads.

"These are delicious, did your wife make these?" she asked.

"Certainly not," said Kendreth. "I made them myself. And I am not married." He seemed quite proud of that fact so Elona did not pursue the point.

They ate and drank in silence. Elona felt it would be rude to take her hand out of Makeela's, and it reminded her of the times she and Savi had played together and held hands—when she could get away from Nursey.

"Well," said Kendreth standing up. "We can't be sitting around all afternoon; I have customers to deal with."

"Where?" said Elona.

"Oh, Mistress Parthia, I believe you are trying to be funny. But you cut me to the quick. You are my customer, of course, as I do not think this other lady has any intention of buying anything."

"I am helping Parthia."

"And when you entered my establishment you did not even know one another. Perhaps I should forget my poor father's legacy and become a match-maker instead."

"This is your father's shop?"

"It *was* my father's shop. He has joined the Tahulin, or his pattern has returned to the World, or whatever you care to believe. He is no longer here, so now it is *my* shop. There was a time it was busy dawn until dusk. No longer, as you can see."

He cleared away the cups, plate and tray while Elona, with Makeela's assistance put out the clothes.

"These are certainly good quality," she said. "But where did you get them?"

"Taltia." It wouldn't do to suggest she had come from Tirnia. They seemed kind people but it would be very easy for them to assume she was a spy.

"Such a long way."

Elona did not answer. It was a very long way but no more than a breath in and out when she could use her power. Better that they did not enquire which path she had taken to bring her here.

Kendreth returned with his selection of second-hand clothes.

"I have selected those which I believe will be closest to your height and size." He piled them onto the chair he had vacated and examined those that Elona had brought.

"Hardly any wear in these at all."

He spoke half to himself so she did not comment on that. "What about shoes? Do you have any?"

"There I cannot help you, my dear."

"You don't want to change them," said Makeela. "No one will be able to see them under a long dress and why exchange them for ones less sturdy?"

"Well, I shall leave you two. Perhaps the arrival of the person who is not your friend is fortuitous, since she will be better able to assist you."

He left and closed the door leaving them with the oil lamp.

Elona stood awkwardly on one side of the table while Makeela sorted through the clothes. She rejected some items without even consulting Elona, most of the others she put on the table and very occasionally held up an item for Elona's decision.

"Why are you helping me?" said Elona.

Makeela has been examining a heavy rust-red skirt but let her hands fall.

"Widows have no one to help them but each other."

"You didn't know I was a widow."

"You were a woman in trouble."

"But I wasn't."

"I thought you might be."

Elona said nothing and Makeela looked embarrassed.

"You reminded me of someone."

"Someone you did a harm to and now you're trying to make up for it?"

Makeela nodded.

"It doesn't work."

"Then let me help you because you are someone who needs it, and I will bring you to the Widow's Court and you can stay there until you choose what you intend to do next."

"Very well, Makeela. But please remember I am not the person you wronged, and I owe you nothing."

"I am the one with the debt, Parthia."

Elona looked her in the eye. "In my experience that is not the way these things work out."

CHAPTER 3

It took a good piece of the afternoon to go through all the clothes, try them on and make her selection. When Elona stripped, Makeela was horrified at the scarring across Elona's shoulder and arm, as well as the strangeness of the knife wound.

"And no healing works?"

Elona shook her head. "It has been tried. It must have been a magical fire."

"It is a worrying thing to think that there are wounds that cannot be healed."

"But we are not always near a healer." Elona thought of her mother, killed by wolves. Metrid had been a healer too but her intent had not been to save.

Once over her initial shock, Makeela did little more than stare. And not all of the time.

Kendreth brought them more *tasa*, which had been a moment of extreme embarrassment for him. Elona had been in a state of partial undress but when he knocked, she invited him in without a thought.

Makeela was embarrassed for the two them. But while Kendreth might have focused on her exposed chest, it was the extent of the scarring that drew his eye and it was a moment before he even realised, she was half-naked.

He managed not to drop the tray and left quickly, averting his eyes. Makeela burst out laughing but Elona did not join her.

Once the final selection had been made, Kendreth gave Elona a price which did not seem unreasonable and she did not haggle but just paid it over. He stared at the coinage for a few moments and bit into one of them.

"A private word if I may, Parthia?" he said.

Makeela gave him an odd look but continued through the shop and went out into the late afternoon.

"Let me change your coin for you."

"What? Why?"

"I understand you might want to keep secrets, Lady Elona, but these coins are from Tirnia, and I recognised the clothes immediately. I think perhaps you would not want the wrong person to know you had been there recently."

"How do you know?"

"The coins have Myrlask's head on them, and the *nachak* on the reverse. Only a fool would not recognise them—"

"I meant…"

"I know. Come."

She followed him into the furthest room at the back where he matched her purse coin for coin and then pulled out a muslin cloth and piled sweet cakes into it.

"Here is your excuse for me bringing you into the back. For you to share or not, as you will. But as for who you are? My father supplied cloth for the King for many years, which is why we were always in favour. It was as a result of that that I was able to attend the wedding of Drahail. Not that I had a good position but how could one not forget the mad daughter of Corlain?"

"I'm sorry."

"What for? You were promised to him and treated very badly. I was, however, terribly impressed with the way they had dressed you to disguise the manacles and chains. Forgive me if it seems uncaring.

It is the liability of knowledge that one sees deeper than the ignorant."

She put her hand on his arm. "You are good man, Kendreth, if it is ever in my power to reward you for your kindness then I will do it. And I will not forget."

"WHAT DID HE WANT?" asked Makeela as soon as Elona appeared through the door, and pulled a shawl over her head.

"I'm not sure I should tell you. After all, I might not want to share."

Elona was amused by the look of indignation on her companion's face.

"Tell me. He did not make any lewd suggestions, did he?"

"He wanted to give me more of his sweet cakes in secret just in case I wanted to keep them all for myself."

Makeela laughed again. "For one of those I will show you the way to the Widow's Court."

"You were going to do that anyway."

"That was before I knew you had proper payment."

THE WIDOW'S Court was on the far side of the city to the main gates. It was located on the north side of the citadel where green moss seemed to cover everything. The city wall overlooked part of what would have been the lake and there was a dank moistness in the air.

Elona followed Makeela as she turned into an alley going downhill.

"It's probably not the sort of thing you're used to."

"I have stayed in worse places."

Makeela laughed. "This side of the castle is almost always in shadow. And we're close to the lake."

Elona thought a lack of curiosity would be strange. "What happened to the lake?"

"Nobody knows," said Makeela, she dropped her voice as if they would be overheard. "I mean, everyone knows it was a path, but where to? And why did they do it?"

"Perhaps it was an accident."

"How?"

Elona shrugged. "What if a patterner opened the path meaning to connect to to somewhere else?"

"Is that possible?"

"I don't know."

"Someone said that one of the Brothers said it was the *Kisharuk*."

Elona pursed her lips deciding how to respond but it seemed a reply was not required because Makeela laughed again.

"But nobody believes that." She stopped. "Here it is."

It looked as if the Widow's Court had once been an inn. The main entrance and the arch for riding animals had been blocked up with stone, except for a narrow gap in the latter. All the windows on the ground floor were covered with planks of wood while metal bars covered the ones above.

"I know it doesn't look friendly on the outside," said Makeela, "but we can't be too careful. There's a lot of men that think a widow is anyone's property to do with as they wish."

"I know the sort."

The gap was barely wide enough to squeeze through, and there was a door just inside. Elona did not fail to notice the metal grid in the ceiling with a trapdoor beyond it. The Widow's Court was its own little castle with a killing ground to dissuade unwelcome guests. Makeela pulled a cord and there was a jangle of a bell inside.

"Who is it?" shouted a voice from inside.

"Makeela and a guest, Parthia."

"I'll open the first door, you know how it works."

Makeela turned. "I go through and they'll shut the door. I can tell them whether I was being forced to bring you. I won't say that, of course. Then they'll open the door for you."

Elona nodded and wondered how it could be this bad so close to the Dragonblade's castle. A bolt on the door ahead ground open and Makeela went through, pausing only for a moment to turn and say "Don't worry."

The door closed again and the bolt slid back into place.

There were sounds of hushed discussion. Another door opened and closed. Then the bolt was drawn back again.

"Come through," said the distant voice and Elona pushed through into a second small space. The door was closed and barred again, then the door ahead opened by a smiling Makeela.

"Come on. I want to introduce you."

Another dark corridor, on side of which was the original wall of the arch and the other made of roughly built stone. It might not have been skilled work but it looked solid enough and there were small gaps for weapons to poke through even here and a metal net across the top. But ahead was a door outlined in daylight while the sound of children screaming and laughing penetrated it.

"This is a lot of protection," said Elona as they came out into what would have been the inn's courtyard. Half a dozen children aged from perhaps three to ten were rushing about chasing one another in some frantic game.

Three old women sat at one side, talking and watching the children. Several others watched cautiously from a doorway. And when it was clear it really was just Makeela and her guest they went back inside.

"Let me introduce you to Avalia, she's the mother here."

Elona had been expecting someone much older than the woman who, she guessed, was no more than ten years her senior. She was also surprised to see that she was at least partly of Kadralin descent. They always seemed to keep themselves to themselves. The room was simply furnished with old chairs with padding that no longer provided much support but Elona was happy enough to use them. Sunlight filtered through the gaps in the barricaded window.

The woman poured a cup of water for each of them then sat opposite.

"I am Avalia. They like to call me the mother, because of my skin."

"Parthia."

"Is that your real name?"

"Does it matter?"

Avalia smiled. "Not really. And are you a widow?"

"My Jalka is dead though we were not officially married."

"And who are you hiding from?"

"Does that matter?"

Avalia leaned forwards. "Of course it does. Do you want to put these women in danger? The children?"

"No, of course not, but you already have a lot of protection—for widows."

"In some cases, the husbands are still alive. We do not harbour women who have deserted their husband for another man, but if they have left out of fear then we will not deny them. If those men discover where their wives and families have gone…I'm sure you can imagine."

"Has that ever happened?"

"Yes," said Avalia. "They were persuaded to go elsewhere."

Elona nodded.

"I did not lie about Jalka, he is gone. There are those who would have chased me but they are a very long way from here and do not know where I am."

"And what of your family in Faerholme? Don't be surprised, you are clearly a native by your speech."

"I thought that would help me fit in."

"It will but since you are from here, is there family who would recognise you?"

Elona touched her hand to her scarred face. "They are unlikely to know me at a distance. My face was whole when I left, it is not known what became of me."

"Can you not be healed? We have skilled women here, some of them know the patterns."

Elona wondered how many more times she would have this conversation but shook her head patiently. "It has been tried."

"Very well, and you want to stay here?"

"If I may, at least for a time, I have money."

"If you can contribute to the pot then that is good, but do not feel compelled. There is a period in which, if you commit any misdemeanour or it is clear you cannot get on with the majority, then we will ask you to leave."

"I understand."

"We bring in work for those who cannot or dare not leave. Some of the others earn their money outside in various ways but none of them dishonest. If you find there is work you can do that brings income then all to the good. If not, we will be happy for you to help. Anyone who commits a crime is sent away immediately. We cannot afford to be a thorn in the side of authority, they could destroy us."

"I understand," said Elona. "And I am not afraid to work. I have some skills that may help. I can always clean."

"Are you good with children?"

"I—" An odd feeling came over her. "I don't know, I have never known any."

Avalia got to her feet, followed by Makeela and Elona. "Makeela can have the responsibility of looking after you during the probationary period. And you can stay with her for the time being, unless that is a problem?"

"No, I don't mind."

"Very good, the evening meal will be soon."

CHAPTER 4

Makeela's room was on the second floor as were all the bedrooms. This one was on the outside and faced the mount on which the citadel sat. The streets and buildings mounted higher until the slope was too steep and the walls of the castle began.

The height was dizzying and Elona became convinced that the tower she could see poking up beyond the walls was the one she had fallen from. She lost her balance and ended up on the floor.

Makeela was there in a moment and helped her to the bed that was to be hers. Then she sat on the mattress too, their hips pressed together.

"Are you all right? What happened?"

"Sorry, I'm not very good with heights."

Makeela laughed. "But we're only on the second floor."

"I wasn't looking down."

"You got dizzy looking up?"

Elona shrugged. "I don't like heights, it affects me badly."

"Sorry."

Makeela continued to sit at her side. She was staring at Elona's face, the damaged side.

"Can I touch it?"

Elona hesitated, then nodded. The woman reached out and gently touched the cheek.

"Can you feel my fingers?"

"Not on the skin, but deeper in yes."

She could see rather than feel Makeela running the tips of her fingers from the cheek up to Elona's scalp then down again to the neck. As if she was fascinated but why shouldn't she be? People simply did not have injuries like this. She was a freak.

"Stay there," Makeela said suddenly as she got up. "I'll be back in a moment."

"Why—?" Elona started to pull herself up.

"No, just lay there. Please."

So she slumped back and stared at the mottled ceiling and beams. There were no cobwebs, Elona could imagine that Avalia was strong on cleanliness.

Elona was beginning to think Makeela was not returning and had decided to get up anyway when the woman came hurrying back through the door. She carried a large jar cradled in one arm.

"I had to promise Efley I'd do all her cleaning as well as mine for a five-day. I hope this works."

She put the jar down heavily on the floor with a thump and then peeled off the sealed lid. The smell of oranges filled the room.

"Efley makes scented unguents for sale. She's very good at it. I think she knows some patterning because it always comes out very smooth. Here you feel."

Makeela reached down and came back with an orange cream on the tips of her fingers. Then she touched the end of Elona's nose, leaving a spot and bursting out laughing again.

Elona could not help but smile this time as she wiped the cream away and noted that Makeela was right. It had a very fine texture.

"All right, but what did you get it for?"

"You, of course."

"Why?"

Makeela shook her head in disbelieving wonderment. "For your scars."

"It won't heal them."

"Of course not, but perhaps it will soften them."

Elona managed to suppress the words *but what good will that do*. Makeela was being very kind and it would be churlish to criticise.

"Well, we can try," said Makeela as if she had heard the words anyway. "If it doesn't help, we can just use it on our proper skin."

THE OINTMENT WAS pleasant enough but Elona couldn't feel any difference though Makeela insisted it looked better. When questioned further this apparently meant it looked less cracked.

The hammering of a gong announced the serving of the meal so Elona took a scarf she had acquired from Kendreth and wrapped it round her neck to hide her scarred face.

"Don't," said Makeela as she placed her hand gently on Elona's.

"People shouldn't be forced to see this."

"They shouldn't judge."

"They always do."

"But that's them, not you."

Elona was not in a mood to argue though she thought it was a bad idea. They would all stare at her.

The eating hall was on the ground floor, and given its proximity to the kitchen, Elona assumed it must have been the main room of the inn. There were stains in the wood flooring, and a place where she guessed the bar would have stood.

Everything had been ripped out some time in the past and islands of furniture were spread about. The two women followed several others into the hall, one holding the hand of a child, and passed half-unoccupied tables but Makeela headed for a particular one. There were places for ten, of which all but three were occupied.

Elona sat quietly as Makeela introduced the other women, one of them was Efley, her hair greying but her eyes were bright. The women stared, of course, but then very deliberately looked away. The room filled with the bustle of conversation intermingled with scraping chairs and the whining of a child for whom everything was wrong.

The sound levels increased and Elona felt as if she was drifting, her mind wandering but to nothing in particular. Then she felt a tug in the direction of the present and realised someone was saying her adopted name.

"Parthia?" It was the large ruddy-cheeked and red-headed woman who seemed to have better quality clothes than most. Zoralie?

"Sorry."

"Can you believe it? People are saying it was that monster that drained our lake. People are going to starve if we can't fish. How long do you think it will be until it's full again?"

Makeela laughed and put her hand on Elona's. "Stop it, Zora. Can't you see she was miles away."

"But, I mean, one of them here, if there's one there'll be more. This is an invasion, mark my words."

The gong sounded again and the talking died away. Elona was left with the feeling she had missed something important.

She looked around and realised the place was full. There were a few empty chairs but most were filled, and Elona estimated the Widow's Court must provide a home and living for perhaps sixty women. The irritated child was still whining.

At the table nearest the kitchen, Avalia stood. Elona and Makeela had chairs facing that way but other had to turn in their seats to see her, including Zora.

"Good evening ladies. We have a new guest, Parthia, who will be rooming with Makeela for the time being."

Someone giggled. But Avalia ignored it.

There were announcements about duties and rotas. It seemed each table defined a group within the Court and the chores they were assigned. Although they listened it was clear this was something that happened every day and their full attention was not on it.

Elona found Zoralie to be fascinating, although fully Taymalin by her bones she had the tanned skin of someone from the south. There had been no hint of an accent. But these things were all superficial, and there was something else. Zoralie was intensely sensual, as if her every move, every look was intended to lure. Elona had never seen such a thing in anyone before.

Then the announcements were over and Avalia offered a prayer of thanks to the Mother and also Taymar. She sat and on that cue the doors to the kitchen burst open and three women pushed and pulled a large trolley into the room.

"I think the new girl should do it," said Zoralie.

"Come on," said Makeela, "the head of the table has spoken. I'll help."

"Do what?"

"We have to fetch the food for the others."

Others in singles and pairs were getting up and heading through the room.

Elona desperately wanted to pull the scarf over her face but instead she stood with Makeela and followed her to join the rest.

They brought back bowls of stew on large trays and, in the meantime, someone had fetched water.

"Nothing stronger?" asked Elona, more out of curiosity than any desire for anything alcoholic.

"Expensive," said Makeela. "And Avalia doesn't want it in the Court."

"But purifying the water can't be cheap."

"Avalia knows the patterns, and she's taught the women in the kitchen."

Zoralie raised her cup. "Best water this side of the mountain. Not a patch on a good Mirriasmian wine though."

"You should know," said Makeela.

"One of my regulars bought me a lovely meal today," said Zoralie. "Knocked back a bottle between us."

Efley turned to the younger woman. "You drink too much."

"Life's short, Efley. Even shorter if that monster is anything to go by. We'll all get slaughtered in our beds at this rate."

A couple of the women at the table dropped their spoons. Makeela was one of them.

"Zora!" said Efley.

The red-head looked at what her words had done and the smile on her face evaporated.

"Mother's tits. Sorry. Sorry."

"You have no control when you've been drinking, Zora."

Then Makeela stood up. "I—sorry, I need to go." She headed away as if in a trance.

Elona stood up as well, unsure what to do. The meal was only half-eaten.

Efley smiled. "Go with her, take the bowls and some water."

At her word, one of the other women lifted a tray onto the table and moments later both bowls were on it along with a flagon of water and their cups. Elona grabbed it up and hurried after her room-mate.

Back in their room, she kicked the door shut with her heel and put the tray on her bed. She refilled Makeela's cup with water and handed it to her as she stood in the middle of the room.

"Zoralie's a prostitute?"

Makeela nodded.

"And thoughtless."

Makeela glanced at Elona and nodded with the faintest fleeting smile.

Elona gestured at the bed. "Sit down."

Makeela did as she was told. Water spilt on her fingers and she stared at the cup as if she didn't know how it had got there.

"Avalia doesn't mind having a prostitute in here?" said Elona.

"Zora had the same troubles we all did. She's not better than us, she's no worse either."

"Sounds like she was gossiping about nothing."

Makeela looked up and there was fear in her eyes. "Oh no, it's true."

"What's true?"

"They found a Slissac in the lake."

Makeela said more but this time it was Elona who wasn't listening.

Even though she had ended up at Canvor, Elona remembered

distinctly, at the moment when she thought she was going to be drowned, thinking about Chara.

She must have brought Chara to Canvor as well. There had been the screams and shouting as she had left the lake bed. And she had seen the lords and their armsmen heading in that direction

Death was following Elona again, and stalking those she loved.

She would not let it claim her sister.

CHAPTER 5

"*P*arthia?"

She realised Makeela was trying to attract her attention. She forced a smile on to her damaged face. "I'm sorry." She sat beside Makeela and placed her hand on the woman's arm. "It can't be a Slissac."

"No one wants to believe it. But one of Zora's gentlemen is high up in the guards. She says he told her everything, and not the gossip, it was the truth."

"As he knew it."

"Zora was full of it when she came in. They only found one and they think it's a woman. But they have armsmen scouring the countryside in case there's more hiding. They think the Slissac drained the lake deliberately to send an army."

Elona didn't think it made much sense. If they thought an army was coming through a patterner's path, why search? And if an army was coming, why wasn't it here? They would have needed to have used the surprise, so it was already too late.

"But you're all right now?"

Makeela nodded. "I was just overwhelmed."

Elona wondered what had done the overwhelming, it sounded like Makeela had already heard all the news from Zora earlier.

But everyone has their demons.

They ate the rest of the meal then Elona piled the crockery on the tray and headed for the kitchen, leaving Makeela darning one of her stockings by the window.

The building wasn't quiet. The sound of the children playing filtered in from the courtyard and women talking came from every direction, some loud, some whispered. None of it made individual sense but it gave the place the feeling of being home. And comforted Elona the way she had felt in Usala's house.

She passed two women on the stairs who nodded and smiled. Although she returned the acknowledgement, she saw how one looked away quickly and the other's eyes lingered a little too long. She did not blame them.

"How is Makeela?"

Elona had just turned into the dining area where several women were clearing and cleaning. She turned to see Efley with a mop and bucket soaping the floor.

"I think she's all right."

Efley smiled. "This was one of the tasks she had promised to do in my stead for the cream."

"I'm sorry, I can do it for you when I've taken the tray through."

Efley shook her head. "She can start tomorrow. Though if I had known the seriousness of your problem, I would probably have given it for free."

Elona shifted the weight of the tray awkwardly in her hands.

"Off you go now, but if you want to come back and help. I'll appreciate it."

"Is Zora around?"

"Oh no, she has clients most evenings—if you want to talk to her then the best time is mid-morning."

"Thank you."

～

THE ELONA of three years ago would not have considered helping to clean but things were very different now. Besides, wiping down tables and mopping the floor gave her time to think.

The idea that she had somehow brought Chara to this place weighed her down but she had to think about it logically. It would involve Drahail, of course, because nobody had even seen a Slissac in over a thousand years—except for her. And they represented everything bad in the past of the Taymalin.

It was what they were taught: Slissac were evil.

She had to dismiss the idea of simply heading up into the castle, saying who she was and getting an audience with Drahail. Nobody here would trust her. It had been easy for Jaymis, he had been accused of killing his father but everyone was happy to blame his mother Metrid instead once her true intentions were revealed.

Elona did not have it so easy. Even if anyone accepted that her perception of reality had been distorted by Metrid's magic, people had still died by her hand. And now the incurable scars on her face made her ugly as well. There is no sympathy for those who are not beautiful.

No, she could not approach them directly.

What if it was not Chara? Would she leave them to their fate?

She paused, leaning on the mop handle and staring at the boarded-up window. Even if it was not Chara, she could not leave the Slissac rotting in a dungeon, not when Elona herself had been the cause. Communication would be difficult because their language was very hard to speak for someone with a soft mouth but she had learnt some of it.

The biggest problem was what the Taymalin would choose to do about it. This was not something that only affected Faerholme, every kingdom would react once they knew—and they would find out no matter if Drahail tried to keep it secret.

"Off with the Tahulin, Parthia?"

Elona jumped, Efley was right beside her and she had not even noticed.

"Tahulin?" Elona remembered the ghostly powerful creatures in the heart of the Tirnian Fastness. "Not at all."

"It's nothing to be embarrassed about, it's the same for everyone when they first arrive. We all have things to worry about."

"I'm all right."

"You're stronger than most, I can see that. But there's no shame in tears, when you're ready to shed them."

"Thank you."

"Are you finished here?"

Elona looked at the damp floorboards drying in the warmth of the evening.

"I think so."

"Well, empty the bucket outside and then put things away in the cubby by the door."

"I was thinking of going out."

Efley studied her for a long moment. "Is there anyone you might not want to meet out there?"

Elona shook her head. "No one here knows me. Even if someone was visiting, they wouldn't recognise me," she brought her hand to her face, "not with this."

"Still, it's better you go with someone who knows their way about."

"Perhaps Makeela."

Efley paused. "Perhaps it would be good for her to get out a little."

"I don't understand why she reacted so badly to what Zora said."

"If she wants to tell you then she will. She needs someone who will be a friend to her."

"What about everyone else here?"

"Makeela can be difficult to be friends with."

"Then why me?"

Efley grinned. "Because you're the new girl, and Avalia knows what she's doing."

That comment did not impress Elona. "I have been manipulated all my life, I don't see why I should stay here if the same thing is going to happen."

"There is no malice in what Avalia does and I doubt her actions were only for Makeela."

"Very well. I will see if Makeela wishes to accompany me."

She emptied the bucket in the courtyard where the children still laughed and ran as if their life depended on it, then stowed the equipment where she had been told.

Makeela was where Elona had left her, by the window and still darning though there was now a small pile of garments. Without asking permission, Elona picked up the finished items and folded them. Then sat on her bed looking at what Makeela had done and the quality of the clothes she was working on.

"This is neat work," she said examining where the strong *kelukisa* wool had been sewn in tight weft and warp across the holes. "These are not all yours?"

"I take in darning work," said Makeela. "It doesn't make as much as Zora's trade but I do not need to put myself at risk every day."

"How many of the children are hers?"

"None," said Makeela. "She deals with those little accidents in her own way."

Elona absorbed that information, it was something she knew very little about though she understood that she was at risk of one of those accidents herself just now. Whoever it was that had decided to make the act of love so pleasurable that children could not be avoided was very clever.

That was something else she might want to discuss with Zora.

"I wanted to go out. Did you want to come?"

Makeela paused in her work and looked up. "Have the others been talking about me? Is this pity?"

"I have no idea what you're talking about. I was just saying so to Efley, she thought it would be better if someone accompanied me."

"And she didn't say anything?"

"You mean that you can be difficult to get on with? I think I could guess that from the way you are behaving now."

Makeela went back to her darning, but one did not need the power to read patterns to feel the anger flowing from her.

Elona tried again. "Do these clothes need to go back to their owners?"

"I was going to do it tomorrow."

"All right. I'll go on my own." She reached for the scarf to disguise her face, and hide her shaved scalp. She wrapped it around her neck three times and pulled the cloth up and over her head, favouring the right side. Hoping it looked casual, and hid the worst of her scarred cheek.

She had her hand on the door latch.

"Wait."

She turned back. Makeela was gathering the finished items into a bag.

"I'm sorry."

"I'm not your enemy."

"I know."

She was ready in just a few moments more. And approached the door.

"Don't move."

Elona frowned but Makeela adjusted the scarf, pulling it forwards a little more.

"There."

THE AIR OUTSIDE was warmer than it had been in the Widow's Court. It wasn't long before they were away from the dark part of the town and into the sun-filled lanes. Makeela guided her back to the street of clothiers but they did not stop there.

"They can all do their own darning."

But they continued up hill, arm-in-arm, through the street where the ringing of hammers on anvils filled the air, along with chants and songs of apprentices pumping the furnaces. Elona could feel patterns being worked here. And beyond that through the quiet jewellery quarter constantly patrolled by armsmen, to where residential buildings began. These were stone-built but had seen better days.

"The street of broken merchants," said Makeela.

"Really?"

She laughed. "No, that's what I call it."

"The ten turns of famine?"

Makeela nodded. "Yes, this was once the street of wheat and flour merchants, they did not do well. So, you know history."

"I was forced to study."

"I knew you were noble by birth."

Elona stayed calm. She knew she could not really pretend to be anything other than what she was born into. She did not expect to be around people long enough for them to realise.

"I was, but not anymore. Besides this is a history you know too."

"My people came from Pavag. My grandmother never ceased to use the threat of going back to persuade the children to behave."

"I never knew any of my grandparents." *Or my mother.*

"Count yourself lucky then."

Elona followed Makeela into the grounds of first one house and then another, at each she went to the servants' entrance and selected clothes from the bag and handed them to either a maid or house-keeper. Then there would be a delay and she would be given some tays in return. Elona always stayed back and kept the good side of her face turned towards the people in the house. Better if she was not noticed.

They left the street behind and continued upwards. Now they could see out across the black scar that was once a lake. Patches of water still gleamed here and there, where they had been caught by a dip in the lake-bed.

"Looks awful like that," said Makeela.

No women searched for fish now, or scavenged whatever else they might find of value. Instead, armsmen were encamped on banks and patrols moved across the uneven landscape. They were preparing for an attack, though Elona did not think there would be one. She had destroyed the Fastness even if she had not killed the *Kisharuk.*

She was sure she had managed to eliminate most of the patterners who served the creature. He would need time to rebuild and re-establish his control of Tirnia. Even assuming that was his intention, with Jaymis's body could he convince people to follow him?

Or would he simply discard Jaymis and take someone more important? Perhaps some lord who could be seen as a successor to the armies.

And would Jaymis then be truly dead?

"Parthia, what's wrong?" said Makeela.

Elona realised she had stopped in the middle of the street. She moved forward again and wiped a rebellious tear from her eye.

"Memories."

Makeela put her arm through Elona's and pulled her close.

"It's all right to cry."

"Do you know what a *fahain* is, Makeela?"

"Sounds like an ancient word."

"It's a curse."

They walked on in silence. Elona pulled her eyes away from the drained lake and looked up instead, at the gleaming white of the castle. From here she could not see the tower from which she had fallen. But that did not make the view any more pleasant. A wave of nausea went through her and she brought her eyes back to ground level, there were buildings on either side now and if she didn't think about the hill down to the lake, or the cliff up to the castle, she could imagine they were on flat ground.

"Only one more delivery."

They turned into an alleyway that ran down the side of a nondescript building of grey stone. Makeela went through her usual process and returned with an empty sack.

"That's good, I can do collections tomorrow."

"It never stops."

"People wear clothes, and they get holes in them. Mostly it's darning because the feet wear through the fastest. Sometimes it's mending tears. Adjustments too if I'm making something down to a younger child." She shrugged. "It's not exciting but not the worst job in the world. I get to talk to people who don't know anything about me except that I can mend their clothes." She sighed. "Better than the Widow's Court most of the time."

The sun still had a good way to go before it set.

"Come on," said Makeela, "I know a place we can sit. Not as pretty with the lake gone but it's private and we can buy something to eat and drink."

CHAPTER 6

The place Makeela had in mind was even further round the castle mount. Shortly before the street joined with the main thoroughfare that climbed up to the castle gates, Makeela led them off up a steep climb of steps.

Elona was not keen, particularly when coming down would involve facing towards the drop, but she did not want to spoil Makeela's gift. There was a small square where a stall sold cakes and wine. Elona bought them because she didn't want Makeela to waste the money she had earned.

Then there was another alley that zig-zagged in short flights of stairs. Elona worried that the place they were heading would be somewhere she could not manage and she would panic. As it turned out, while the place was very high, it was a wide expanse of grass that ran up against the cliff on which the castle stood. The smooth carved stone of its walls began here.

Makeela held her hand and pulled her up the final gentle slope and they sat down with their backs to the wall.

The roofs of the city were laid out below but far enough away that Elona did not feel as if she was about to fall. And not a single window could be seen, the place was as private as any place could be. The sun was to their right and its warmth penetrated her clothes.

Makeela giggled and Elona turned to see her stripping off her clothes.

"What are you doing?"

"Nobody can see."

"But—why?"

"It's freedom, Parthia. We are told what we must do with our lives. The men tell us what to do and beat us when we disobey. The Widow's Court isn't much better, we must work and pay to be there, we must follow Avalia's rules." She had untied the bindings of her dress and in one shrug it fell to the ground. And the sun made her skin glow—everywhere except for scars that covered her legs, belly and breasts in pale criss-cross lines.

She stepped out of the clothes and turned round with her arms outstretched as if she worshipped the sun and the sky. The stripes across her back, behind and thighs were even more numerous and there was barely a single patch of skin that was unmarked.

Every injury Elona had ever had was healed. Not a single scar marred her body until the void ate the patterns of her skin. And seeing the harm that had been done to Makeela, Elona felt the guilt in her perfection. Even the scars that now scored across her perfect skin had been self-inflicted. No one had done this to her but herself and there had not even been any pain.

Makeela lay down on her back in the soft grass with her arms still outstretched soaking up the rays. Then she rolled over, propped up her chin on her hands and smiled at Elona.

"Your turn."

Elona gave an embarrassed smile and looked down at her feet. "I can't."

"You were not shy when you let me use the unguent."

"That was different."

"Yes, then we were indoors and anyone could have come in. Now we are outdoors in the sun and nobody will see but you will feel the sun on every part of you."

Elona stared into Makeela's eyes. There was a strange person staring out of them: frightened, angry, lost.

It felt like the hardest decision she had ever made but she stood, unwound the scarf from her head, then loosened her belt and let it fall.

Makeela bounded to her feet. "Let me help." She untied the cords that held the dress tight to Elona's body and as the tension went from the cloth Makeela took hold of the shoulders and pulled it down over Elona's arms. The dress slipped past her hips to the floor.

But Makeela did not let go of Elona's shoulders, instead she pulled her close and kissed her. Her lips were softer than Jaymis's and there was no prickly beard but nor was there any emotion.

Then her arms slid round Elona and their bodies pressed against one another. Makeela's cheek against Elona's neck.

"Please do not push me away."

Elona was confused by this turn of events, though she realised Makeela's earlier hand-holding and touching had all been a precursor to this. She had not pushed the woman away then, she smiled to herself. She would not push her away now.

She felt awkward standing there naked above the city and sank down, almost carrying Makeela with her.

The grass was dry though the soil beneath it felt cold with dampness. The sounds of the city drifted up to them. Hammering in the distance. Shouts. The grinding of iron-shod cartwheels on cobbles. And the sun hung above the hills in the west casting lengthening shadows in the slowly cooling evening.

Makeela's head rested on Elona's right shoulder though she could not feel it, nor the woman's hair that would have tickled. All she knew was the pressure of weight. But her arm curled around Makeela's back and by touch Elona could make out the ridges on the woman's body.

Makeela did not seem to want anything from her, only to hold and be held. Her breathing steadied and she lay still. Perhaps the lack of clothes meant more trust.

Elona lay back and looked up the rising cliff that leaned out towards them. The sensation of falling surged through her yet she lay there every part of her legs back and head touching solid ground, with Makeela anchoring her.

Something to the left, embedded in the cliff, glinted in the sunlight. She tried to twist her head to see better but it didn't help. Was it a grill? Beneath it hung a heavy strand of damp moss that dripped constantly.

Jaymis had mentioned the spaces beneath the castle.

If she could get in secretly, she might manage to find Chara and rescue her.

She gave her companion a gentle squeeze and started to sit up. Makeela pushed away and they both sat. Makeela kissed her again. Elona knew it was not mere sisterly affection since it contained the same passion that she had felt from Jaymis. She wished she could return the feeling but how could she when she had only known the woman for less than a day. And lost Jaymis barely a two-day ago, though it seemed like a year.

"Thank you," said Makeela.

"I haven't done anything."

"You didn't push me away."

If only my life had been that.

"Couldn't you have had your skin healed?" asked Elona.

Makeela's hands went to her stomach and traced a mark.

"They are too old, they are part of me now, part of my pattern. It could be done but it's too expensive." She took a deep breath. "My husband did this. For years."

"You ran away?"

"I poisoned his beer."

"Oh."

"Don't worry it wasn't quick. I punished him for a long time. Just a little at first and he became weaker. He paid for healers of course, but sometimes there is nothing they can do." She reached out and touched Elona's blackened cheek. "You know that. And finally, he was in his pallet all the time. I was the dutiful wife. I tended him, cleaned him and fed him. He had no more money for healing. I started taking in darning work so we had money for food."

"But you kept poisoning him."

"Oh yes. I had thought it would make me happy to see him wasting away after all he had done to me." She shook her head. "But it didn't. There came the time he was too weak to do anything for himself and then he begged me to kill him. And I said 'I have been'." She sighed and ran her fingers along one of the marks. "Then he knew and there was nothing he could do about it. He tried to tell his family when they came, but they thought he was raving. I could have ended his life easily but I made him last as long as I could. So, he knew finally that I was the one who had the power over him."

She went silent.

"And he died."

She nodded.

"But you could still be made complete again."

"I will never be complete. If I were to remove the marks he made on me, how would I know that what I did had been just?"

Elona could not claim that she did not understand.

"I could heal you."

Makeela jerked away. "No, you do not have the right."

Elona sighed and put her hand on Makeela's arm. "I won't, unless you ask me otherwise."

The sun was touching the hills and would soon be gone.

"Perhaps we should go back?"

"I want to stay here forever," said Makeela.

Elona smiled, she had known that feeling too. "Come, let me help you into your dress."

They slowly covered themselves as the light went. Fires were being lit across the lake bed. And armsmen patrolled.

Once she was fully clothed Elona went around the side to look at the dripping moss which hung from a metal grill covered in spikes with iron struts as thick as her wrist. Below it was a damp runnel that looked like it carried a lot more water at other times.

"Castle sewer," said Makeela beside her. "I think that's why people stay away from here."

"It doesn't smell at all."

"Does it matter?"

Elona weighed her options, she felt she needed to talk to someone but how could she trust a person she had only just met? That Makeela had killed her violent husband did not bother Elona, who had murdered enough people of her own and some of them had been innocent.

"No, not at all. I was just curious."

A change in the patterns trickled the back of her neck and she spun round to stare out across the lake. The arch of a patterner's path had taken shape in the lake but even at this distance it looked huge.

"*Kisharuk.*"

"What is it, Parthia?"

"Something's coming."

A bell jangled out on the lake bed. Moments later, a bell above them rang out, its clamour echoing across the city.

"The alarm?" said Makeela in horror. "The city is under attack?" She stared wildly across the expanse laid out before them. From the city came a rising tide of shouts and screams. "You knew!"

"My curse," said Elona. "Come on, we need to get back."

She took a long look at the fortified grille. She knew she could get through it and now there would be even less time. If they thought Chara was somehow connected with the attack that was coming who knew what they might do?

Makeela was already starting down the first flight of steps and Elona hurried after her, but as soon as they opened up before her a wave of horror swept away her focus.

"Makeela, please, wait!"

Elona sat down. Makeela came back slowly. "What's wrong? You said we should go."

"I forgot about the stairs."

"I don't understand."

"I have a mortal fear of falling when I am in a high place. It freezes my limbs and I can barely move."

Makeela cast a scared look over her shoulder at where she

thought the attack was coming from. "But you said we have to go down."

"I need your help. I have to close my eyes."

Together, with Makeela in front an Elona's hand on her shoulder they made their way down slowly. Makeela called out warnings when the steps were particularly uneven.

At first, they were alone and the tumult from the city was in the distance. But as they descended, people would brush past them from time to time, making Elona jump when she wasn't expecting it. The frequency of impacts increased and the noise was becoming deafening.

Someone was calling for all able-bodied men to muster in the fields outside the walls. And there was shouting and weeping from the women, pleading for their men not to go.

Finally, Makeela turned and took Elona's hand. "We're here."

Elona opened her eyes onto a chaos worse than she had imagined from the noise. Together they made their way carefully back. The street of blacksmiths was opening up once more and the furnaces being pumped hard. Men and boys travelled in groups heading downhill to the main gate.

It was only when they were approaching the Widow's Court that the mad rush died away.

"Makeela!"

Elona turned and saw Zora almost running their way. They waited.

"Lose your client?" said Makeela.

Whether Zora recognised the harsh tone, or simply did not care, Elona wasn't sure,

"Lordling. Had to go off to be an armsmen."

"Did you learn anything?" asked Elona as they hurried towards the Widow's Court—Elona tried to remember the route but it was now too dark to see landmarks.

"A patterner's path has opened. Nobody was expecting it, I mean we never expect it do we. It might be nothing."

It isn't nothing.

"Parthia felt it open."

"You're a patterner?"

"No, I just have a sense."

"Ha!" said Zora. "Like one of those Kadralin witches."

Elona didn't think it was wise to respond so she changed the subject. "Did you hear anything more about the Slissac?"

"She's not talking but everyone thinks it's them coming."

"They'll be torturing her."

"Good."

Elona was saved from any more conversation by their arrival. Zora went first, Elona last.

The other two were accosted by the women inside desperate for news having only heard the alarm bell.

Zora said something about a curfew as soon as it was dark for any ordinary citizen.

Elona headed to the room.

CHAPTER 7

She was in the middle of packing her bag, and wishing she hadn't got rid of her travelling clothes so quickly, when Makeela arrived.

"You're leaving?"

"Just preparing. You should get a bag ready as well. Everyone should. You don't know what's going to happen."

"You think the Slissac will win?"

Elona sat on her pallet. "I don't think it's Slissac, Makeela."

"But who else would it be? The war with Tirnia is over." She hesitated. "Isn't it?"

"I don't think so." She stood up again. "I need to talk to Avalia."

With Makeela trailing behind—her worry almost palpable to Elona—she headed along the corridor and then down to Avalia's room. There several other women already in there.

Elona had not put her scarf back over her face and she knew she made an ominous figure in the light from the lantern. She stood in the doorway. The women closest to her noticed first and attracted the attention of the others and eventually the talking stopped. They parted giving her a view of Avalia, the light reflecting from her dark skin.

"Parthia?"

"I think you would be best preparing for all the women and children to leave the city."

"I would be interested to know your reasons."

"She knew the path was opening before the patterners did," said Makeela breathlessly. "I saw her turn and look, though there was nothing to see. And it was after that the alarm sounded. She knows."

"Is this true?" said Avalia.

"I can sense patterns."

"Any healer can do that," muttered someone in the group.

"We are half a league or more from the circle," said Makeela angrily. "She saw it from just below the castle wall."

Avalia looked from Makeela back to Elona. "And what was it you saw?"

"The portal for a path big enough to pass the red moon through it," she said. "And I know what's coming."

"Slissac," was whispered by several making a sibilant hiss in the air.

"No, not Slissac. Men. An army and great flying beasts that make the walls and cliffs of Canvor worthless as defence. They will rain fire on the city and its defenders. If you do not escape, the crimes committed against you personally will be nothing to what these men will do to the city and all those who live within its walls."

"You have seen them."

"With these very eyes, and escaped with my life but without my Jay-Jalka."

"You are scaring them," said Avalia.

"They should be scared."

The women had been staring at Elona but now they were turned to their leader.

"Yes. Even if you are wrong—" she nodded at Elona. "—there can be no harm in making preparations. Have the women prepare for a journey. Only as much as they can carry, but we will also need to make provisions. Cook everything we have so that we can take it with us. If nothing happens, our rations may be a little bland for a few days but we are used to hardship."

The women took that as their dismissal and Makeela went too, leaving Avalia and Elona together.

"Let us go to the roof."

THOUGH COOLER than it had been in the heat of the day's sun, the roof was still warm. The stars were twinkling pinpoints of brilliant whites, yellows, reds, and blues. Colimar was in the sky but its red light did not illuminate the landscape.

The noise from the city below had quieted, perhaps with the curfew, or the realisation that nothing had happened.

To Elona's senses the huge portal remained.

"What do you see?"

"A patterner's path, big enough to bring an army."

"You think it will?"

"Yes."

"Is it Tirnia?"

"Perhaps."

"Slissac?"

"I don't think so."

"How would you know, Parthia?"

"I have seen many things and been to many places. Slissac are the least of our concerns in this world."

"I think you are not yet twenty turns but you speak like someone with three times that age."

Elona shook her head but realised Avalia would not be able to see it. "Not quite twenty, no, but sometimes I feel as old as you say."

"The loss of one you love brings a great weight with it."

And I have lost more than one. Then aloud. "The weight of the living can be a greater burden."

Avalia laughed. "Don't I know it."

The portal rippled as if the pattern of the world was ripped apart and she perceived a dense pattern emerging.

"They're here."

"They will have trained guardsmen to contend with."

"Unless they learnt a lesson from what happened in Esternes last year, Canvor does not have the weapons to deal with this."

A second dark shape slid into the world. With her real eyes there was nothing to see under the dark of Colimar as the invaders were travelling with doused lights. But stars were eclipsed by the bulk of the oncoming *tekrasa*.

"You were in Esternes?"

"No, but the attackers there flew in giant *tekrasa* perhaps fifty armsmen in each. And they are coming now."

Another broached the portal.

There was the distant winding of horns as the alarm went up.

Avalia's calm voice had become agitated. "The biggest *tekrak* could not even carry a single man."

Elona grew impatient and grabbed Avalia's arm. "Look! See the shapes as they block the light of the stars."

At that moment one of the *tekrasa* fired up their flame tube and illuminated half a dozen of the monstrous beasts with their cargoes of death. The first of them had already crossed half the distance from the portal.

"There," said Elona, "that is what you must fear. The walls will not save you."

As she spoke fire arrows arced upwards from the defenders in the lake bed, barely reached the height they needed and fell back.

"The defenders cannot prevail, Avalia."

The bell in the castle high above them rang out again shattering the semblance of peace.

Elona stepped round and grasped Avalia by her shoulders. "The women must flee, Avalia."

She seemed to focus now, a reflection of the *tekrasa* fire tube in her eyes. "But where? The gates will be closed."

"Perhaps on the lake side where before there was water? Speak to them; one of them will know of a way. Men may talk but women listen. If there is a way someone will know."

"Why do you care so much for us? You do not know us."

Because I brought this on you. "Because there is little I can do, but however little it is, I will still do it."

That seemed to satisfy the woman, at least for now and they headed back down.

∾

ONCE DECIDED ON HER COURSE, Avalia acted quickly and positively. She gathered the leaders of each unit, described what was happening and her intentions, then had them go to their groups and ask if anyone knew of a way out of the city.

It was Efley who had the answer. In her youth she had been a maid in the household of a city engineer. It seemed that building the castle on top of all the previous incarnations that had stood here was not without its problems. The cliffs—which were not natural but simply an earlier building—had to be checked constantly and reinforced where they threatened to give way. There were areas inside the castle too that were not safe and in a constant state of almost collapse.

But Canvor was Canvor, and it must stand.

There was a drain on the west side, similar to the one Elona had seen with Makeela, which went down through a tunnel where water from the lake came in through a natural cave in the original bedrock under the wall. But if there was no water in the lake, the tunnel would be empty.

The only problem was that while she knew it existed, Efley did not know anything more, such as how passable it might be. But they would prepare for that.

Beyond the walls of the Widow's Court came the flickering lights of fires and the castle bell continued its clamour.

Efley's description of the castle pleased Elona since she still had to find Chara. She spoke to Avalia again quietly.

"I have another task."

"You are deserting us."

"I have another duty to fulfil and it cannot wait."

"Despite all this?"

"Because of it."

"Did you know it was coming?"

"No. I had hoped for some peace." *But wherever I go, death follows.*

"You should not go alone."

"It is better if I do. I do not want to put anyone else at risk."

"You're going into the castle. Who are you?"

Elona sighed. "I am Elona of Corlain."

Avalia gasped and brought her hand to her mouth.

"I knew it," said the voice of Zora from the other side of the door, she slipped inside. "I saw you at the wedding. You didn't have the burns but I never forget a face."

"Zora, that is an extremely bad habit."

She shrugged without even a hint of shame. "Information is power, Avalia."

"And what do you intend to do with this power?"

"It has no value just now. You never know what it might have in future."

"Will you take our Parthia into the castle?"

"You mean I wouldn't have to crawl through dirty tunnels? I'd be happy to."

"How?"

"Easy. I'm a courtesan and you can be my student."

Elona thought about it, it was a better choice than burning her way through iron bars which was what she thought she would have to do. And if they failed to get in, she still had that choice.

"Only one thing though," said Zora. "Why?"

"My sister is there."

Avalia frowned but Zora was already answering. "Elona of Corlain had no brothers or sisters."

"We are like sisters."

"Oh, really?" Zora grinned. "Of course you are. That's why you were happy to room with Makeela."

Elona opened her mouth to object but realised it was easier to let Zora believe what she wanted.

"You two should get dressed immediately. The sooner you go the better. We will prepare to set out as soon as we can. We will not wait on your return."

"If I can get in, I won't be coming back out," said Zora. "The castle's the safest place I can be."

Elona turned to Avalia. "Don't wait for me at the tunnel. I don't know how long I will be." *Or whether I will escape at all.*

"Very well, may the Mother guide you."

ELONA RE-DRESSED QUICKLY CHOOSING ONLY the clothes that would serve her best. Makeela brought enough freshly baked bread and smoked meat to last a few days. Zora turned up a few minutes later and tossed Elona a cloak and hood made of very fine cloth.

"Keep that in a bag until we get close then use it to hide your face. The thugs and ruffians are bound to take advantage to ply their trades on a night like this when the guard are all elsewhere."

"Aren't you concerned?"

"If we run into trouble, let me do the talking."

"And if talking doesn't work?"

A long-bladed dagger appeared in Zora's hand. "Then I will use extra persuasion."

Then they were ready.

Makeela surprised Elona by kissing her full on the lips again as she said goodbye. Zora gave a short laugh and Makeela glared at her.

"Oh, don't mind me, I've kissed plenty of women myself. You're just easy to tease."

Zora gave short goodbyes to all as they headed down to the courtyard, Elona answered those that were given to her though she did not know any of these women. Instead of going to the main exit, someone pulled up a trapdoor and handed a lit candle to Zora who headed down the steps.

Elona followed and moments later they were in a tunnel that took them under the building.

"Avalia always knew there was a chance the place might come under siege—some stupid husband or father. She has a lot of plans and this was part of them."

"Where does it come out?"

"The warehouse across the street. There'll be no one there at this hour."

An iron gate barred the way further in but it was unlocked. The hinges opened smoothly and without a sound.

Down here, in the dark and silence, it was possible to believe that nothing was happening above ground. But Elona pushed that seductive thought aside and instead tried to imagine what the attackers' plan might be.

The first step was a surprise. They were unable to disguise the opening of the portal but they knew the defenders would not be expecting *tekrasa*. They would send them through to spread fear and confusion, and drop sufficient armsmen to be able to defend the path so the land-based forces could get through.

Canvor was simply not equipped for this battle. And she was the one who had made it possible by draining the lake. Trying to destroy the *Kisharuk* was a worthwhile reason, but who would believe her? Who would even believe she could have done such a thing?

They reached a solid wooden door. Zora took a little while getting it open, but finally the lock clicked and it swung back on oiled hinges.

"Have you done this before?" asked Elona, her voice barely audible.

"There's no need to whisper," came the quiet reply. "Once someone's been accepted, they are taught all the escape routes. We have to practice even without light." She sounded as if she thought it was pointless, but Elona saw the wisdom of it.

Elona shut the door behind her and the lock clicked again. There was no handle or keyhole on this side, nor were the hinges visible. If you did not know it was a door you might not even notice it.

There was not a lot of space and they seemed to be in a room with an assortment of wooden boxes that smelled of damp. The candlelight faded as Zora headed through an opening. Elona followed along a short corridor and up some steps.

The sound betrayed the size of the room they were now in,

though it was filled with boxes and jars in groups and covered with cloth. Flickering yellow light came through the openings that served as windows high up on the walls. And the smell of burning drifted through the air.

Zora stood still and stared up. "What's happening?"

"They are trying to raze the city."

"But why?"

"Because it scares people, destroys the food and makes the place unlivable. It causes problems for the King in addition to the need to defend the city. War is chaos."

"How would you know?"

"Because I was forced to read history books."

"I can read."

"The longer we wait, the harder it will be to get the safety of the castle."

Zora seemed to find herself again. "This way."

She had the key to a small door close by which exited on to the street on the opposite side to the Widow's Court.

Outside there really was chaos. Smoke drifted through the streets and across the buildings, people were running in different directions, shouting and crying. Some carried buckets.

"Which way?" said Elona into Zora's ear.

The woman nodded directly at the castle mound. "That way."

Looking up Elona felt her stomach turn over. It made sense. The road up to the castle encircled the hill on which it stood. The fastest way to get there was to climb directly to the road from here. The fires were in the direction of the city gate and there was nothing but buildings between here and the road.

It meant a precipitous climb.

"I am not good with heights," she said. "But you are right."

CHAPTER 8

The first stage was not hard. Zora knew the way and led through streets and passages leading upwards. It wasn't tiring but Elona stopped from time to time and looked back over the increasing expanse of the city.

White light on the eastern horizon heralded the arrival of Lostimal, and the red light of Colimar was already gone from the sky. But the city was burning and the buildings were highlighted in the yellow of its own light.

The constant yells and screaming were a counterpoint against the constant thunder of burning buildings. The crackling of wood like some giant bonfire, and the thunderous roar of a wall collapsing, sending fountains of sparks into the air.

And the *tekrasa* continued to turn and twist in the sky, she counted at least twenty now. They were all high up, she knew they dared not risk coming too close to the flames and sparks. And if the defenders of the castle had attempted to fire on them, they must be too far.

In the light of the burning city, Zora's face had lost its usual condescending expression. She too watched in horror while they caught their breath.

Out on the empty lake bed, there were more lights, lines of armsmen carrying torches and, on the shore, a growing encampment. The portal was gone, at least for now. The invaders had gained a foothold and could defend it against any support for Canvor coming that way while using it as their supply line.

There were few historical precedents that she could remember. But why was she even trying? Every battle was different.

She turned to face the climb and her stomach turned over. It looked vertical. Once again she bemoaned the strange desire of the Taymalin to build their castles as high as they could.

"Come on," said Zora in a voice that was strangely flat.

She started up the steep steps and Elona followed.

AT FIRST THERE had been metal rails along the side of each flight but they only lasted as long as there were buildings around them. They passed people who must have lived in the houses, staring out at the devastation being wrought on their city. Some cried but most watched with empty eyes, as if they had lost the capability for emotion.

This was not supposed to happen to Canvor. It had always been taught the capital of Faerholme was impervious to attack. That truth had been made a lie with an easy speed that carried all rational thought and emotion before it.

But Elona had no time to worry about these people or their pain. Chara was waiting for her.

She focused on each step, one at a time. and when there was no longer a rail to hold on to, and the steepness of the stair made it more like a ladder, she went on all fours, clinging to the stones.

Zora stopped on a wide ledge and sat down heavily with her back to the cliff.

"Passing place," she said in a hoarse voice before she pulled out a flask, took a swig and offered it to Elona. She turned and peered up as Elona pulled herself into the corner and half sat-half crouched against the wall, looking along it rather than out.

"Not far now."

"You can't see how far it is."

"I used to do this all the time when I was younger."

"I'll be glad if I never have to do it again."

"You do get it bad."

"Yes."

"At least we haven't run into any trouble."

"Didn't you ever learn not to say things like that?"

Zora gave a short laugh. "Mother's tits, I don't believe in that nonsense. You're probably right though."

She stood up and Elona panicked as she seemed to lose her balance and had to move her foot to the edge.

"Nothing to worry about," said Zora but there was a tremor in her voice as she started on the next set of stairs.

Elona made no attempt to stand. She crawled to the first step then made her way up at a slow and steady pace.

"Stop right there! Who are you?"

Zora's feet disappeared from view as the man's voice burst unexpectedly from above them. Elona did not dare to stop climbing and finally managed to pull herself over the top. She rolled over twice, away from the edge, ignoring the stones that dug into her and then lay on her back staring at the sky.

Her arms and legs ached from the exertion.

Zora was talking to the armsmen. Elona still had the cloak in the bag but there was no way she could put it on without attracting attention. She would have to make do with the scarf and hope they did not look at her too closely.

The need to cover herself energised her enough to roll on to her knees and get herself into a standing position. She brought the scarf up and then stood so her scarred face was away from the armsmen. It was a patrol of five.

The road was too high to be lit by the flames of the burning city, but Lostimal had breached the horizon and her full white face lit up the world, bright enough to cast shadows.

The haze of smoke rising from below glowed silvery and moved in great clouds. The *tekrasa* were gone. They normally flew only during the daytime so keeping them active must be a trial for the patterners. They would let them land and dig their roots in for the rest of the night.

"What's her name then?"

"Parthia, my maid and protégé."

"How much for her if I can't afford you?"

"You are a naughty fellow," said Zora and sighed dramatically, "but sadly, you see, she is virgin and my lord has already paid a great deal to take it from her. It is a thing that cannot be replaced."

"She looks too old to be a virgin."

"Very strict upbringing by an overprotective father." Zora moved closer to him. "She's desperate to be made a woman of the world, but we must wait until her training is complete. Unless you want to argue it out with his lordship?"

She said the last thing as if it were a real decision, and up to the man himself. But his friends laughed and he declined.

"If you have any trouble with any other patrols just mention my name."

Zora went up on tiptoe and kissed him on the cheek. "Take that as a promise."

The two women moved on accompanied by a chorus of disgusting comments and whistles.

"Hope that didn't upset your sensibilities."

"I'm not a virgin."

"I can teach you a few tricks if you ever want to pretend you are."

"No, thank you."

They continued to follow the road as it wound slowly around the high mount and up toward the main gates.

Elona pulled on the cloak and covered her face with the hood.

The sheer stone walls of the castle took over from the whatever material the hill was made from—all the earlier buildings and constructions going back before the Taymalin invaded this land.

They encountered no more patrols and approached the gate openly, not wanting to be mistaken for the enemy.

They were stopped of course, the gates were closed and barred. Elona could feel the magical barrier that had been put into them. Similar to the one in the walls of the Fastness that she had broken so easily. But this one must be held by living patterners, not maintained through the power of a ley circle.

It could not stand for long against a determined force.

Zora performed her own magic. It was apparent she was well-known to at least some of the armsmen and it did not take long for the two of them to be allowed inside the gates where they were told to wait while Zora's gentleman friend was summoned to decide what should be done with her and her maid.

Elona looked at the shadowy buildings illuminated by oil lamps mounted at intervals in wall sconces. She recognised the building opposite as being the main hall in which she had watched Hope marrying Drahail. The final victory of Metrid against her.

The tower from which she had fallen was not on this side and for that she was grateful.

It took a considerable amount of time before the young Lord Darrien appeared. He wore light armour with his sword at his side. For some reason, Elona had expected Zora's beau to be much older, but this man could have been half her age. He reminded her of Jaymis.

He gave her a quick bow and she curtsied. Elona followed suit though she knew it was not very smoothly done. But that would help to confirm her position as someone of no importance.

"Zora? Why are you here?"

"I feared for my life. The city is burning."

"We know. We are busy, there is an enemy at the gates."

"I wanted to be close to you. I can make the nights more pleasant."

Barely suppressed laughter came from the armsmen at the gate.

"I'm not sure what to do with you."

"Find us a place to stay, I will be there when you need me."

"And who is this girl?"

"She is Parthia, my servant."

He frowned at Elona and seemed as if he was trying to see into the shadowy depths of her hood.

As he did so, the back of Elona's head itched.

She reached back to scratch it and realised she was seeing something tiny and magical up and behind her. Closing her eyes, she focused on the source and saw immediately it was a copy of the one that hung around her neck.

Walking forward she fell to her knees in front of the lordling.

"Forgive me for speaking out of turn, sire, but there are Farahalek in the castle, I think the King is in danger." She spoke quietly and in earnest, praying that he was not a fool. She might not have any loyalty to the Crown of Faerholme anymore, but she did not want the forces of the Kisharuk—or whoever they were—to bring any more chaos. Besides she had a debt to repay since she had made it possible for them to appear.

"Farahalek? How do you know?" Thankfully he also spoke quietly, rather than alert the one behind her.

"I have seen it. Ask Zora if I am right."

"What's this about?"

"It's true, she can see magic."

"And with that voice, she is no servant of a courtesan."

The Farahalek was moving away along the wall and would not see as she pulled back the hood a little, just reveal the left side of her face. Lord Darrien's eyes widened as he took in her features.

"My name is not Parthia. I am Elona, the mad daughter of Corlain, and I can see the magic that some of the Farahalek carry with them. I know it because I have seen it before." She took a breath. "If you care for the life of your King you must warn him. The attack on the city must have been a distraction."

Darrien hesitated for only a moment. He summoned two of the guards and had the women follow him, with the guards behind.

"At any sign of treachery do not hesitate to strike them down."
"Darrien!" Zora was outraged.
"We will determine the truth, Zora."

CHAPTER 9

$\mathcal{E}$lona was not familiar with the castle and their guide/captor led the way through numerous passages, across squares open to the sky then down several flights of stairs before eventually stopping in a corridor without any doors nearby.

"Guard them until my return."

Zora did not look happy; she had probably been hoping for a pleasurable night in a good bed with a paying customer to keep her company. Elona just stood quietly waiting for the inevitable return of Darrien. It was not something she was looking forward to.

When he did return, he was alone, much to her surprise. He told the guards to take Zora to his quarters—which brought a smile back to her face—while Elona he beckoned to follow him.

It was another long walk. Darrien had clearly brought them only part of the way. Just in case they were traitors. The door they ended up at looked perfectly ordinary but Elona could feel the power in it, in the form of a pattern she did not recognise. Without even thinking she reached out to touch it in a desire to learn more, Darrien's cry of "Don't!" reached her ears too late.

Her body exploded with pain radiating through her from her

fingertips and her head struck the opposite wall violently as the power of the pattern flung her away.

She lay there with her eyes closed.

Darrien shouted something and, after a short delay, the door swung open.

"I couldn't stop her in time."

Elona felt the power of the ley-circle and pulled it to her. It flowed through her. She had not been damaged but the magic in the door had somehow created confusing swirls and eddies in the patterns of her muscles. She focused on them until the churning stopped.

She sat up and rubbed the back of her head.

There was a man standing directly in front of her. Patterner robes, beard and a wide-brimmed floppy hat in his hand. He was leaning over and peering at her.

"Florian," she almost snarled. "Should have expected you to be here."

He held out his hand and she let him pull herself up.

In his touch she detected another pattern she did not know, nor could she divine what it was for. But a glance with her inner eye told her that it was woven into every part of his skin.

He stared at her face and without a by-your-leave stretched out his fingers and touched her scarred cheek. She batted his hand away.

"Elona?" It was Drahail, his voice as soft as she remembered it.

"Stay out of my way, Arch-Patterner," she said. "Understand that I hold you responsible for everything that has happened to me. And I may not be able to keep my temper."

The man said nothing but stepped away from her and to the side. The young King stood in the doorway silhouetted against the room's bright lights.

"Florian, you told me that your pattern would strike down any enemy who touched it—and they would stay down."

Elona went into the room, brushing past the patterner and the king. "But I am not your enemy, Drahail."

The dark mass of her father loomed at one end of a large table.

She ignored him. The door closed and the pattern once more flared into life.

"What has happened to you, Elona?" said Drahail, he was staring at her face.

"That is a tale for another time. There are Farahalek in the castle, Drahail. No doubt come to kill you, and your council of lords. And, with any luck, the Arch-Patterner."

Her father moved. "Is that a threat?"

She turned on him. "Do not think the crimes you committed against me can be assuaged by turning me into the enemy, father."

He moved forwards. "You are a murderer."

"Who I pardoned," said Drahail, his voice hard now and tinged with anger. "All that was done was caused by Metrid. Your response, Corlain, was understandable but it was not *just*." He took a deep breath and returned to his gentler self. "Elona saved my life and for that alone I shall be forever grateful." He turned back to her. "How do you know it was Farahalek?"

"I am familiar with them and their ways. They tried to kill me in Mirriasmia and also in Glytheni in Tirnia."

"And yet you live," said her father.

"Yes, I live but many of those around me did not and I am no friend to these monsters." *Though I have a blade that is a brother to all of theirs.*

"But you saw one and my men did not?"

"I only caught a glimpse but who else would be skulking in the shadows?"

Drahail nodded and turned to Darrien. "Go quickly and warn the guard, make sure all the council are well defended."

Elona nodded. "The Farahalek will not attack unless they have a clear advantage, staying together in large groups and well-lit areas is wise."

Florian let the man out.

Elona took a deep breath. "Drahail, I require something of you."

"I am forever in your debt, just ask."

"Give me the Slissac woman you hold in your dungeons."

THE SILENCE that followed her words felt deeper than the void that had eaten her face. The surprise and shock on Drahail's face would have been comical if the situation had not been so serious. And though he neither moved nor spoke she felt the looming presence of her father becoming more dangerous.

The only one who seemed unsurprised was the Arch-Patterner.

"How do you know about it?"

"Everyone knows about it, Drahail, did you think you could keep it a secret when she was discovered in broad daylight in the lake bed?"

"It was you," said her father abruptly.

Elona felt a wave of guilt. "What do you mean?"

"Yesterday, by the lake, the woman in the travelling clothes. It was you."

"Yes."

She could see him struggling with the idea of blaming her for the draining of the lake but that would need her to have so much power that he could not accept it. She knew she would have to lie again but, as she had thought before, the truth would be impossible for them to accept.

"How do you know it is female?"

"Her name is Chara and she is my friend. She saved me when I was on the verge of death." She did not know for certain it was Chara, but she was certain it was.

"Why are they attacking us?" demanded her father. "Where are they from? We must take the fight to them."

"The attackers are not Slissac, probably Tirnian. They are taking advantage of the disaster. This Slissac was alone, a foundling, she had been raised by a human woman in a village in the mountains. Has she not spoken in our own tongue?"

"She has said nothing," said Drahail.

"Let me see her, let me talk to her. Let us leave here, Drahail, please."

He gave her a long look. "That may be difficult."

Elona's heart turned to ice. She could barely speak. "Why?"

"Because she is a Slissac, Elona, the enemy of the Taymalin. This is bigger than just being a Faerholme matter, Elona, this is a concern to the entire Conclave."

"But she has done nothing."

"The lake."

"It wasn't her. She doesn't even know any patterning."

"You do," said her father.

"I can talk to wolves and heal—like my mother."

"And survive a particularly unpleasant pattern," said Florian.

"Just healing," she said. "At least let me see her and speak to her."

Drahail suddenly looked tired, he sighed and nodded. "In the morning."

"Now. Please."

"Yes, all right. Now if you must."

"We shall accompany you," said her father.

Elona would have preferred to be alone with Chara but if this was the only way then it would have to be sufficient.

THEY HAD ACQUIRED a guard of twenty armsmen as protection as they climbed back out into the open again. The air smelled of smoke and, above them, the stars were smudged.

It was another long walk through the castle courtyards and then down even more flights than before. Eventually they came to the first locked door with its own guards. It was opened for the King and his party but their escort remained behind as they descended further. Apart from Drahail's occasional orders, no one had spoken the whole time, but Elona could feel her father's looming presence and the strange pattern that enveloped Florian.

As they descended, fear welled up inside her. What if she was wrong? What if this wasn't Chara? What if the attack was from the Slissac after all?

She shook her head. *I can't be wrong.*

Even her fear of falling was overwhelmed by everything else.

There were pairs of guards on the next two sets of doors, passages went off on either side and the smell was now overwhelmingly urine and excrement. She was disgusted with it, but remained silent.

They reached the bottom where the floor seeped with oily water and while she expected it to be silent, she could hear curious knockings and echoes coming through the walls.

Drahail, it seemed, possessed the final key and used it on the one door remaining. It led through into an antechamber where two guards were standing to attention as they entered.

Opposite was a door made of iron. Without being instructed the two armsmen left and closed the outer door after them.

"Word might be out about what they think we found," said Drahail. "But none of the men are allowed to see her."

"If she were to disappear, the story would just wither and die."

"I cannot do that, Elona."

She had been about to comment on his promise to give her anything when there was a sound and a movement from beyond the door.

"Elona?"

She flung herself to the door. "I'm here, Chara." She turned to Drahail. "Open it!"

He hesitated.

"You have your precious Arch-Patterner to protect you, and my father. Thirty guards between here and the surface, just open it! For the life you say you owe me, give me this at least!"

He walked over and unlocked. She brushed him aside and pushed the door back. The cell was in complete darkness. Elona hurried in and stopped, unable to see anything beyond the light filtering in from the doorway.

"Chara?"

"Is it truly you?" Her strange clipped words caused tears to well in Elona's eyes.

"It's me, Tek."

A shadow moved swiftly from the darkness and threw its arms around her. Elona embraced the thin frame of her sister.

"I thought I would ne'er see you again."

Shouts and cries filtered through from above.

"Elona, come on, you've seen her."

Without releasing her sister, Elona turned her head. "I will stay here."

"I will lock you in."

"Do it."

It was the shadow of her father that moved to the door and slammed it closed.

The key turned in the lock. The outer door opened and closed soon after followed by the murmuring of the armsmen talking. No doubt noticing that they now had two prisoners. Elona could imagine how happy that made her father.

Elona remembered the pattern that had been used to light in the room where she had first been taken. She moved away from her sister.

"Elona, what are you doing?"

"Give me a moment, where's the wall?"

Chara took her hand and pressed it against damp stone. Elona focused for a moment, being very careful not to put too much power into it, and the stone beneath her hand lit up with a white glow that filled the room.

Chara blinked.

"You're naked!" said Elona.

"It's how I arrived." Chara looked at her sister for a moment. "The story you told me, the first time, did you do it? Why did you bring me here?"

"It was an accident."

Elona was busy with her bag and pulled out some of her clothes.

"And what is wrong with your 'ace?"

"Long story, no time." She lifted her head and looked towards the door. "Can you hear that?"

"Sounds like 'ighting."

"I think they're trying to kill Drahail."

"Your king? Who?"

"Two days ago, I would have said the *Kisharuk*, but I'm not sure. There are assassins in the castle."

Elona took Metrid's knife from its sheath that hung around her neck and attacked the door hinges while Chara put on the dress.

"This is not 'ractical."

"It's all I have." The hinges had been sliced through and she stood beside the lock. "Can you hold the door in place when I cut this?"

Chara smoothed down the dress, which was not her shape at all, tightened the belt, then went to the door.

"Have they been feeding you properly?"

Chara clicked in quiet laughter. "They gave 'e raw 'eat."

"Did you eat it?"

"I needed to kee' my strength u'."

Elona's knife sliced effortlessly through the lock.

"'Ut what a'out the guards?"

"When the door falls, just hide in the shadow. I can deal with them."

"No shadows, sister."

Elona glanced at the glowing hand print on the wall and it went out.

"Let it go."

She heard Chara move away but the door remained where it was. There was no handle on this side but she managed to get her fingers round a protruding iron band and yanked it hard.

The door moved a short distance and jammed.

"Will I never learn?" she muttered to herself. "Next time just cut the lock."

She hacked at the side of the door to create a handhold, pushed the top back in place and pulled at the door as if opening it. It came free, overbalanced and fell with a crash.

The first armsman came at her with his sword at waist level. Drawing on the power from the nearby ley-circle, a blue barrier materialised in front of her. The man struck it twice but gave up and took a step back when realised there was no way he could get through it.

"Come on, Chara, we're leaving."

The Slissac woman stepped into the blue light.

"You couldn't do that 'efore."

"No."

She focused and the wall of blue moved away from her pushing the armsmen backwards until she had them jammed into the corner.

"If you don't cooperate, I will crush you against the wall. Do you understand?"

They said nothing but looked from Elona's half blackened face to the Slissac's dark reptilian skin.

"They look very 'rave, sister."

"Yes, they do. I don't think they believe me."

The two women stepped into the room and Elona raised her hand and with the flat facing the men she "pushed". The wall crept forward pressing them tighter into a shrinking space.

"Yes!" said one of them quickly.

"That's good, because the King might need help and, as you can see, I could provide it. Chara, take my knife and unlock the other door. Be careful it could take off your finger and you wouldn't even notice."

"I ha'n't 'orgotten."

Elona brought the barrier back a short distance and turned it so that there was some space. "Drop your weapons, leave them in the corner, and move away from them." They did as instructed. "Now you, tie his hands with your belt. Do it tight, I'm watching."

"But—"

The blue barrier ground towards him. "No buts, your King needs help."

Finally, they were as safe as she could manage, she forced them into the cell and extinguished the lights. Chara gave her back the little knife.

"Only trouble with not being a patterner," said Elona to Chara quietly. "Is that my magic disappears when I stop concentrating on it. We need to move fast once we're out of here."

"Are we really going to help your king?"

"If it's not too late."

The sound of fighting had stopped.

They extinguished the lights and slipped out through the door.

CHAPTER 10

They climbed through the levels of the dungeon, Elona's knife making short work of the lock on the first door. She was prepared to fight the guards but the ones that had been here were gone. And the next sets of doors were unlocked.

They came across the first bodies at the first door that led down.

Several armsmen, swords in hand lay dead. And there were two in dark mottled cloaks with their faces masked too.

"Farahalek," said Elona. She looked with her inner eye but they did not have the magical blades. Perhaps it was an honour given only to a few, which made her wonder how Metrid had got hold of one.

"What are these Farahalek?"

"Assassins."

Chara clicked disdainfully. "We have those too."

Elona looked up. "Did they try to kill you?"

Chara gave a very human shrug. "I have stories long in the telling also."

Elona nodded as Chara picked up a sword and balanced it in her hand. Then they moved on, following drips and trails of blood.

"I spotted the Farahalek when I arrived and warned the King."

"That is the one called Drahail?"

"Yes."

"The one you were 'etrothed to."

"Yes."

"He did not see' that 'ad," said Chara. "For so'eone who was terrified and fascinated at the sa'e ti'e, and who wanted to force infor'ation fro' 'e."

"Did they torture you?"

"They had not got to that stage although the other, older man wanted to start straight away."

"My father, I expect."

At each corner they stopped and listened before creeping forward once more.

"My a'ologies for insulting your kin."

"Don't, you know what my father did to me, but Drahail is a good man," said Elona. "Being king must be hard."

"It is."

A raw and raucous scream echoed down the passage, and it was difficult to tell if the one who uttered it was even human. They stopped in the passage with its paved slabs worn smooth by a thousand years of feet. Opposite them was a wide staircase heading up.

"What is your 'lan, sister?"

Elona sighed and leaned back against the wall. Its solidity reassured her. "Before the attack I was going to sneak into the castle and escape through the passages underground. There are a lot of them, Jaymis told me."

"Who is that?"

"He called himself Jalka."

"Oh, that one, so he was a friend?"

"A good one."

"'Ut he is not here?"

Elona hesitated. "He's dead—I think, I'm not sure. He's part of the long story but he had been in the passages below the castle and told me about them."

"But there was an attack and we are going up instead of down. What is the 'lan now?"

"Protect Drahail and then escape."

"Why 'rotect hi'?"

"Because this attack is my fault. It wouldn't have happened if I hadn't drained the lake."

Chara put her hand on Elona's arm. "There is too 'uch I do not know."

Elona covered Chara's hand with her other one. "I know, I'm sorry, we just don't have time now. It's my duty to ensure this attack fails, if I can, because if it had not been for my actions, there would be no danger. At least no more than usual."

"I trust you," said Chara, "but you cannot make a good decision unless you have all the needed information." She looked across at the staircase. "We must go u' and look down on it all. Learn what can be learnt."

For Elona, height had its own cost but she knew Chara was right and together they started up.

"You know this is hard for me."

"I have not 'orgotten."

And they kept going up until there was nowhere left except to follow the passage that went off to the right.

"No, please!"

Elona sucked in a shocked breath at the voice echoing from one of the rooms further down.

Then a cry and a whimper that spoke of terrible pain and clawed at her mind

Elona broke into a run. The doors were closed except one near the end. Light from Lostimal shone through the window but it was too bright and made dark shadows.

Her shoes slapped on the stone.

She slammed open the door at the end and it crashed against something behind it. The noise startling and loud.

An uncaring fire glowed and crackled softly in the hearth. She was in a suite of rooms, adequately furnished for visitors and guests. There was no one here but the rasping of someone trying to breathe pulled her into the next room.

A dozen lit candles on wall sconces, showed her the naked body on the bed. Her red hair like a halo round a friendly face. And sheets beneath the body glistening with red from a body sliced into pieces.

"Zora! Oh Zora!"

Elona flung herself at the woman, desperately trying to sense all the damage.

She was still alive, her eyes open, her face distorted with pain. Elona took her hand and tried to focus.

"I'll help you, I will. I'll heal you. Stay with me."

But there was so much damage she did not know where to start.

Behind her came the clash of steel.

Elona closed her eyes, tried to find the pattern that was the most disrupted. But there was too much wrong, and she found a wound on Zora's arm and tried to heal it. But it wouldn't mend.

"No!" She recognised the damage. Touched by a blade tainted with the void, like her face and she slumped back in the horrific realisation there was nothing she could do.

"Zora, I'm sorry." Her eyes filled with tears and she wept for the dead.

"Ssister!"

She felt him coming, as the patterns that made up Zora's life dissolved before her. Elona gathered up the energy of the dead woman's life and half turned. Flinging out one arm as the Farahalek ran at her.

He crashed into a wall of blue. Elona stood and turned.

Moments later he had pulled out his tiny void knife and sliced at the barrier. It vanished.

Elona gathered the power of the ley-circle to her and created a new barrier but halfway along his outstretched arm as he tried to cut her just as he had cut a woman, she had known for less than a day, and yet had died because of her.

The knife was barely a finger's breadth from her face but stuck.

He could move everything except where his arm was gripped by the blue patterning. And unable to do anything about it.

"Tell me your mission," said Elona, "and I will kill you quickly."

"Never."

His accent was not one she recognised.

"Very well."

Elona walked around the end of the patterning she had created so neatly and went to the door where Chara waited. She had a cut on her arm.

"When did you learn to fight?" said Elona.

"When did you learn to do that?"

"I haven't finished," she said with a calmness she had never felt before.

She turned back to the bedroom and looked at the candles. Closing her eyes, she felt the pattern of the fire, so chaotic and different to that of life or something simple. But she saw it and understood it.

Gathering the power of the circle once more, she opened her eyes.

Every flammable item in the room caught fire.

The Farahalek screamed as his clothes erupted in flame. But she still held him in place.

"You!" he screamed. "We are here to kill *you*."

Elona took a step back as the heat increased.

"Who sent you?"

But his body slumped and burned, still held by the pattern she had set on him.

Annoyed with herself she let him go and he fell.

Elona put a barrier across the doorway and focused her power on the bed to ensure everything that had been Zora would return to the World's Pattern. The flames roared and even behind the barrier she could feel the heat. The bed was consumed and the body of Zora rendered into nothing.

"Elona, will you burn down the castle?"

She took a breath. The fire was eating through the floorboards now. She stopped feeding it and took away all of its heat until there was nothing but a smoking ruin.

When she finally turned around and let the barrier across the door fall, she found Chara staring at her with wide eyes.

"What are you?"

"*Fahain.*"

Elona stalked out of the room and found the flight of stairs that led on to the roof. *People are dying because of me.*

⚬

As she came out, a streak of golden light shot across the sky—like the one she had seen in the hills near the village in Taltia. She still had no idea what it was.

But her precarious position grabbed her attention. Unlike the flat roof of the Widow's Court, this one had a tiled and slanted one with only the smallest gap and a crenelated wall that did not look big enough to stop her falling over the edge.

She knelt behind one of the higher sections and peered out.

Two *tekrasa* were hovering over a tower, away from the front entrance. The tower itself made her queasy as she was certain it was the one, she had fallen from. But she kept her mind on what she was doing.

"You could ask me for help." Chara was standing casually behind her leaning on the stone.

Elona rolled back so that she was sitting and facing towards the roof.

"Two *tekrasa*."

"Yes, I can see them."

Elona did not watch as Chara leaned over the wall to look down.

"I can see a lot of dead 'odies, but Drahail's forces are the greater, and they are 'ressing their attack against the invaders who are trying to withdraw. Oh wait, what's that?"

"What?"

"Is that a *zirichak*?"

Warm damp and smelly air wafted down on Elona. She threw herself to the side and flung up a barrier.

Through the blueness she could see a huge bulky shape. A sinuous neck lifted a wide face which looked over the barrier and down at her.

"Taymar's teeth, it is."

"What's it doing here?"

"Looks like it's attacking the *tekrasa*, so'eone ju''ed on to the first one and is cutting the ro'es. It's a very small 'erson."

Elona managed to pull her gaze away from the beast looming over her and looked at Chara who was facing away and looking out into the dark.

"There's one here."

The creature gave a grunt and bumped its nose against the patterning.

Chara turned her head and stared beyond Elona. "It's so big, and beautiful. And feathers, 'other used to talk a'out them." She turned back. "The first *tekrasa* has 'roken loose and is 'oving off. That small 'erson is on the second one now doing the sa'e thing."

"How can you see so well?"

"Underground dwellers, we see in the dark."

"You never said."

"You did not ask."

Elona sighed and turned away from the beast at her side. She stared at the roof in front of her and the image of Zora's body hung in front of her. *I avenged her*, said one side. *I killed her*, said the other.

Drahail doesn't need me. He's a king and has everything he needs, including a wife and child.

A blast of wind broke her out of her reverie.

Something huge was bearing down on them.

Elona caught the magic gleam of a Farahalek blade.

"Slissac!" shouted a voice from the direction of *zirichak*, and a tiny figure leapt from the winged monster as it flew overhead.

"Farahalek!" warned Elona as she threw up a second barrier on the other side of Chara.

The *ziri* behind her roared and reared up. It towered above the wall she had made. She flung both her arms outward. The blue defensive walls shot away from her in both directions, ripping the masonry and roof tiles to shreds.

The first ploughed into the *zirichak* and forced it from the roof. It turned in the air as it tumbled away and the huge wings snapped out.

The wall on the other side tore away an entire section of the tower which went crashing down to the courtyard below. Elona prayed that only the Farahalek would be hurt then a movement caught her eye. The tiny figure swung up on to the parapet beyond the hole she had made.

Elona made to create another wall but the … girl? … dodged back and darted out of sight behind the slanted roof. Elona closed her eyes and focused on the dagger the girl carried and watched as she—

"Elona?"

"Ssssh."

—climbed the roof so swiftly she might have been running on flat ground.

"Elona!"

The girl topped the ridge and threw herself over, aiming directly for Elona herself. The protective wall appeared as a solid flat surface beneath her and she landed hard. Elona forced it upwards fast, taking the girl with it.

"If I get it high enough, she won't survive the fall."

"I wouldn't be too sure, but if you hurt my daughter I'll kill the Slissac," said a new voice with a strong accent but her words were clear. "Come out where I can see you."

Elona looked at where Chara stood with her hands held out from body in a gesture of helplessness. Thudding wingbeats filled the air, Elona crawled forward and turned so she was sitting on the roof tiles, which seemed much less solid than the stone of the parapet.

Another huge *zirichak* was beating its wings hard on the other side of the wall and on its back, between the wings, sat a young Kadralin woman. The short bow she held was drawn and the arrow was pointing at Chara's heart.

"If you hurt my sister, you will die painfully," she said. The stones of the parapet, torn away on either side of them, groaned and another piece fell away. Elona's heart jumped. Chara moved closer to the middle. The tip of the arrow followed her.

"I believe you are outnumbered," said the woman. And as she spoke half a dozen more of the flying beasts swooped across the sky above them, hooting eerily. Elona had not missed the power that flowed through this other woman.

The roof tiles beneath her shuddered as the entire wall in front of them collapsed, Chara barely managed to fling herself back in time.

"I can't save us and your daughter!"

There was another surge of power—it wasn't like a pattern being cast.

"Let her go, and save yourself," said the rider

"I can't let her fall!"

"You were ready to kill her."

The stones where Elona had been sitting, slid noisily into oblivion.

"We are not fighting now!"

"Elona, she has sent the *zirichasa* up, you can let the girl go. I do not wish to die here and now."

"Save yourselves, witch."

The whole tower shuddered this time. Elona closed her eyes to the terrible drop that lay in front of her and pulled power from the ley-circle.

I will not make a path. I must stay here. I must save Chara.

She reached out her hand and grabbed Chara's arm.

And conjured a protective sphere around them both. Its skin cut the tiles and joists holding up the roof, and they crashed through into the room below. Landing among the wood and stone that they brought with them was painful, but she let go of the sphere immediately.

At least she no longer felt as if she was going to fall—

The wall behind them collapsed and the floor tilted—

Chara scrambled to her feet and pulled Elona up the slope towards the door. They got through it as the floor gave way completely.

"Esternes!" said Elona suddenly as they ran as fast as they could away from the collapsing tower.

"What?"

"I know who she is."

"I do not care who she is. She and that devil daughter of hers are dangerous."

They reached a staircase and ran down it as fast as they could. Descending levels settled Elona and she could focus better.

They reached the ground.

"We must leave," said Chara. "The arrival of this woman turned the tables on the attackers. Your Drahail is safe enough for now."

"Let me think."

They walked along a corridor in silence, Chara with the hood pulled over her head to hide her skin. Elona had nothing to hide hers. But there was no one to see them, only armsmen would be about, all the rest would be hiding. And the battle was elsewhere.

Dawn was tinting the windows with its light and while no one was out and about just now, it wouldn't be long.

"You're right."

"I know."

"But you will not like my plan."

CHAPTER 11

Chara did not like the plan.

They found another set of stairs going up and climbed, eventually making their way to the roof again.

Once there, they found a place that was a long way from the edge but where they could see across the empty lake to where the enemy had made their camp.

Sleep came too easily for Elona and judging by the position of the sun when she finally awoke it was past midday. Chara lay beside her, her eyes still closed. Elona smiled at her sister and gently stroked her cheek, feeling the strange hard texture.

"Time to wake up."

"Not now," she murmured. "A little more time."

Elona broke the crust of a hard roll and munched it noisily.

Chara finally came awake. "I dreamt we were at home."

"I wish we were."

"Wishing doesn't get the milking done."

It had been a favourite saying of Usala. Frequently aimed at two lazy girls. Elona smiled and passed the remainder of the bread to Chara who munched her way through it and drank some of the water to wash it down.

"Are you ready?" said Chara.

Elona nodded. "I've never done anything like this before."

"I' ne'er seen you do e'en half the things. You ha'e changed."

"I have done some terrible things."

"My story is not 'uch 'etter, sister. We ha'e to do what we can, and so'etimes people are hurt."

"Yes, well, this shouldn't hurt."

She closed her eyes and focused on the *zirichak* that the woman had been riding. This was a little bit like the control that she could exert on animals, especially the ancient ones, but she was not trying to control this time and she felt the same difficulty with them as she had with the *sikechasa*. Anyway, she did not think the Kadralin woman would like it very much if she forced her will on them.

No. She found the beast in question and sent him—it was a male —a picture of where she was and an invitation to come to them.

She opened her eyes. "It's done."

THEY DID NOT HAVE to wait long. First one *zirichak*, grey and black, shot across them at a considerable height but Elona could see it turning its head to look down. Then another, green and yellow, streaked past them much closer but still looking down.

They remained sitting. Elona was sure she could repulse an attack from them but she needed to talk.

Then the child appeared, standing on a roof ridge as if it was solid ground.

Four more *ziri*, without riders like the others, flew in and landed in positions around them.

Chara and Elona stood up but kept their hands down and in view.

Finally, the Kadralin woman arrived. The beast she was riding looked even bigger in daylight and its feathers glowed in brilliant iridescent colours under the bright sun.

She slid off its back in a move that was so graceful she looked like a dancer. She walked forwards beside the creature's neck and gave his head a hug before muttering something to him and coming forwards.

"You can talk to animals?"

Elona assumed it was a rhetorical question.

"Does anyone else know where we are?"

"I did not tell them, I am not beholden to any Taymalin."

"I want to talk but I'm not sure we have a lot of time." She glanced past the woman to where she would see the patterner's path open, when it did.

The woman turned and looked too. Then back at Elona. "You're waiting for it so you can return to your friends. You and your Slissac."

"My sister's name is Chara and those people are not my friends."

"I find that hard to believe."

Elona changed tack. "I've heard about you. You're the Kadralin from Esternes who defeated the Tirnian invaders."

"I didn't do much in the battle. Saving my people was more important."

"I want to ask a favour."

The woman burst out laughing and did not quiet for some time.

"I am not the enemy of Faerholme or the Conclave. I destroyed the castle of the emperor in Tirnia."

"And yet here they are." Kantees swept her arm to take in the horizon. "When they have control of the air they are strong, but we stop them."

"We have a common enemy. We should work together. You have seen so'e of the 'ower my sister can wield. When she says she destroyed the castle you know she has the strength."

"I see a Slissac and a Taymalin. You have enough power to bring down a tower and put yourself in mortal danger."

Anger boiled up in Elona. "Then why did you let me escape yesterday? Why did you come here without telling anyone? Why are you behaving like this? You are *fahain*, we are both *fahain*, we should not be fighting."

At that moment, the patterner's path opened, once more big enough to accommodate *tekrasa*.

Elona's eyes were drawn to it as the arch etched the sky and the Kadralin woman turned to look.

"They're coming," said Elona. "And if they bring enough *tekrasa* through even you won't be able to deal with them."

The other woman turned back. "I know. That's why I shall destroy them before they even get here."

Every one of the *zirichasa* ruffled their feathers and moved backwards and forwards impatiently.

Elona took a step forward. "Please, you have to take me and Chara."

"Take you back to your leader?"

"They are my enemy just as they are yours!"

Chara took several steps forward. "This is going nowhere. If you didn't 'elieve her, you would ha'e left—you would ne'er ha'e come! I a' not *fahain*, I ha'e no 'agic, but I know when so'eone is talking *lukisa* shit!" She took a deep breath. "Take us or don't take us, but sto' with this nonsense!"

The Kadralin stared at her for a long moment and then burst out laughing again. "I like you, Chara, my name is Kantees. I don't like your sister very much."

"Your 'rejudice does you no favours."

"Yes, well, I have met some decent Taymalin, but most of them judge me by my skin."

"You think that is so'ething I don't understand?" Chara dropped her hood just to reveal her dark reptilian features. "At least you are, 'y your standards, attractive. You think there is no 'rejudice against Elona with her face?"

Kantees held up her hand. "I give in. You win."

Elona turned to Chara. "How would you know there was prejudice?"

" 'Ecause I a' not an idiot, Elona. And you two are just as 'ad as each other. This arguing has wasted too 'uch ti'e already."

Elona turned back. "When do we leave?"

"The path is open, we will go now."

"What about Drahail? I expect he wants to talk to me."

"He's not *my* king."

Chara picked up Elona's bag and they followed the dragon woman along the valley between two roof tops, towards the edge of the building.

Now that the discussion was over, Elona became very aware of the course she had agreed to take—had *decided* to take. It had been bad enough aboard the *tekrasa* on the occasions she had done it. But at least it was possible to keep her eyes shut or stare into the distance.

On the back of one of these monsters, there would be no way to hide. Even closing her eyes would not save her from the fact she was sitting on something that was flying with nothing supporting her.

"Chara will ride with me," said Kantees as the young girl, her daughter she claimed though the child's skin was as pale as Elona's, arrived at her side. "This is Ulina, she will ride on her own."

"I can't ride," said Elona abruptly, the words spilling out of her mouth in terror.

"Of course not, you'll ride with Darrien." She nodded to her left without looking and Elona saw another *ziri* coming in. This one was equipped with straps and a saddle, and Elona recognised the rider. Zora's client.

Guilt overwhelmed her. As the beast alighted on the edge of the parapet, she could see the hardened face of a person who had suffered. He knew.

"Come, Sheesha," called Kantees and the beautiful beast of blue and gold waddled across and settled ready for her to climb up. The child ran up the slope of the roof and threw herself on to the back of one of the brown *zirichasa*.

While Chara went over to Sheesha, who spent some time smelling her before Kantees gave him a clout and he let her get closer.

Taking care not to get too close to the edge, Elona walked to Darrien's mount who, in contrast to Sheesha, seemed indifferent to her. The saddle was longer than expected and clearly designed for two. Elona glanced back at Kantees and shook her head.

All that wasted time when she had already decided.

"I am scared of falling."

"I will not let you fall, Lady Elona."

"You don't understand: I have a mortal terror of falling."

"Tuleesha is a perfect mount. She is strong and will fly safely."

"I'm sorry I am not explaining myself, Lord Darrien. There are no words that can calm this fear. Assurance that the beast can carry me easily will avail nothing. I must force myself to climb up, simply grit my teeth and bear it because there is nothing that will take this from me. I may cling to you very hard. I may also throw up."

"I see," he said very stiffly as if her words were some sort of affront to his mount. "Then I hope nothing happens to worsen your fear." He put out his hand to help her up.

She gave him a humourless smile. "Where we are going, Lord Darrien, I expect the very worst."

Taking a deep breath, she stepped forwards raised her hand to his and he caught her about the wrist.

"You were on the tower that collapsed last night, do you know what happened to Zora."

She looked up into his eyes. "I do know, but it is too long a story to tell now."

"Tell me this, Elona of Corlain, did you kill her?"

"It was because of me that she died—" his grip tightened "—but I did not do it. That was a Farahalek, I was too late to save Zora but I revenged her, he died in great pain."

His answer was to pull her effortlessly up and back. She did not want to hurt the *ziri* but had to put her feet on the wings. Her stomach turned over because there was nothing on the other side of the beast except a long drop. Darrien still had her wrist and was gripping it painfully. She managed to pull up her long skirt and sink into the saddle. Coming down on it hard and convulsively gripping as if she were on horseback.

"You'll need both hands to belt yourself in," said Darrien over his shoulder.

She whimpered as he let go, she desperately searched for the ends of the belt finally locating it and buckling it as tight as she could. She shut her eyes.

"Get your feet in the grips. And hold on to me if you need to."

She did not care who he was, she threaded her arms beneath his and clung on to him as her feet found solid leather holes which provided at least a semblance of stability.

Then she was falling to the right. They were all falling together. She felt Tuleesha's wings flick out. She was forced into the saddle as they came out of the dive and the strong wingbeats carried them upwards.

Then she felt the magic.

And opened her senses to it.

There was a pattern forming between the *zirichasa* and they moved to align themselves with it. They became a pattern moving in the air. She felt it, and she understood it. The heart was Sheesha, the others spread out in a diamond pattern. This was why Kantees flew with so many *ziri*, it was clear that the bigger the pattern the more power it could generate—though she had no inkling of what it was supposed to do, she was not a part of it yet it gave her a form of comfort.

"Archers below!" shouted Kantees.

Elona kept her eyes closed but she perceived the shape of things. The *ziri* pattern, the *tekrasa* in the air and on the ground, and the gate of the patterner's path already close ahead.

So easily it was barely even a conscious thought, she conjured a defensive wall beneath the formation of *zirichasa*.

"Kantees!" she shouted above the wind but her voice was stolen away because she was behind her.

"What's wrong, Elona?" said Darrien.

"We should take down the *tekrasa* before we go."

"There are thirty of them, Ulina can't do all of them."

"Why must she do it all?"

"I cannot break from the formation."

I could break it, Elona thought to herself but did not know what the repercussions would be on the *ziri* themselves, and she was certain Kantees would be very displeased.

They were heading for the path.

Elona had done it before so she tried it again. Pushing an image to Sheesha of them turning away and not entering the path yet.

As if they were a single entity, the *zirichasa* veered to the left. The tightness of the turn kept Elona forced into the seat so it felt as if the rest of the world was changing rather than her.

They flew out across the dried-up lake bed and the formation's pattern disintegrated. Elona let the protective spell go. Moments later, Kantees' voice came from their right side.

"What in the name of the Mother are you doing?"

"I had to stop us." Elona turned her head in the right direction but kept her eyes closed.

"Do not ever do that again! Do not ever interfere with my *ziri*."

"We have to get rid of the *tekrasa* here or there will be nothing to protect by the time you get back."

There was a long pause as the *ziri* glided through the air. Elona could feel them continuing to move away from the gate.

"Yes. You are right. Do you have any ideas?" A cold calm exuded from Kantees now, and Elona found it more disturbing than the anger.

"The golden lines in the sky, that's you, isn't it?"

"Might be *ziri*, might be *melinasa*."

"But it's the pattern made by the formation of *zirichasa* that does it."

The hesitation from Kantees told Elona the Kadralin did not know about the pattern.

"You're *fahain*, Kantees, like me. Just look at them when they're flying. You'll see it."

The wings of Tuleesha beat hard suddenly and the creature dived then came to an abrupt halt. Elona opened her eyes and was grateful to be on the ground again. Kantees had already dismounted, so Elona undid the buckles and let Darrien help her down. Then he dismounted too.

Ulina stayed on her *zirichak*. "Armsmen are coming." She pointed in the direction of the ley-circle.

"We have time," said Kantees then turned to Elona who was relishing feeling the solid ground underfoot. Even if it was mud. "You have a plan?"

"What would happen if you went into the golden light through their camp?"

"Too dangerous."

"That's what we'll be doing along the path," said Darrien. "It will kill everything we pass."

"But the path is straight and flat," said Kantees. "Out here, one mistake and we'll all be dead. Even if we succeeded, the next wave would take its place and we would not be here to stop them."

"Your Ulina is very dangerous," said Elona.

"She was trained by the Farahalek, they take children very young and make them into assassins."

"But you rescued her?"

"We don't know what happened, we found her free. But she cannot fight an army alone."

"I *can*."

"You *won't*."

"Yes, mama."

Darrien cleared his throat. "We cannot take too long over this. The second wave is coming."

Elona thought about the *tekrasa* then said. "I know what we can do."

CHAPTER 12

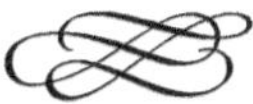

The second time of being in the air did not make things any easier for Elona. She clung to Darrien with her eyes shut. At least it was faster than a *tekrak*.

By the time they had taken off, there were three *tekrasa* heading their way but it made no difference for what Elona had planned, though she had no idea whether she could do it. And there were risks—but that was all right because she had brought this trouble to her own land and if she gave her life protecting it, that was fair.

The gate of the patterner's path was her point of reference with her eyes closed. She wondered in passing if Kantees was seeing the *zirichasa* pattern now it had been mentioned.

As they approached the enemy encampment, she placed the defensive barrier beneath them once more. Only moments remained.

They streaked across the waiting army, they were defended from below but not from the sides. The *tekrasa* had been deployed around the gate and their bowmen were loosing arrows.

Elona had mentioned she might be able to put a sphere of protection around them but Kantees was uncertain what effect that might have on the formation, so they decided against it.

Kantees directed them even lower and they skimmed the surface in order to get beneath the floating monsters.

They pierced the gate and everything changed. All sound from the outside, the shouting and animals, stopped abruptly.

"There's one in here!"

The *ziri* formation broke apart.

Tuleesha turned on a pin, making Elona's stomach heave, and shot back towards the gate.

"Say when," called Darrien.

The exit back to the army was coming at them fast. "Now! Stop!"

Elona unbuckled herself and fell awkwardly on to the World's Pattern. The strange surface gave at her touch. She opened her eyes to the shifting patterns that seemed to twist under her fingers.

"I'm all right."

Ulina landed beside her as Darrien turned away. She heard screams of agony. After their earlier aborted run for the gate, they had guessed the enemy might have placed a *tekrasa* here to wait for them. Kantees explained it wouldn't be a problem. Elona glanced up and could see *ziri* tails sticking out of the gondola and whipping left and right.

Ulina hit her on the arm. "Your turn." She pointed at the gate.

Elona took a deep breath and conjured a blue barrier across the entire opening. It was no harder than she expected, which meant magic did work the same here, just as Kantees had said.

She walked to the wall and let it drop before stepping through.

SHE BLINKED in the brilliant sunlight which always seemed so wrong after being in the perpetual night of the path—even for such a short time.

The air was filled with sound again. The roaring of the *tekrasa* fire tubes as they manoeuvred round. The shouting of the army, hundreds perhaps thousands of men. Of which a large number were plodding through the sucking mud towards her, banging their swords on their shields.

A single cry went up and the air was dark with arrows arching towards her.

She threw up a defensive dome and through its blue surface she watched the arrows bounce and break. The men approaching hesitated.

I wish there were two of me, she thought as she expanded the dome. It had been easy in the Fastness, but here the area she was covering was so much bigger. She could feel the intensity of the barrier fading as it grew. But the *tekrasa* around her were pushed away, the advancing ranks of armsmen thrust backwards into the archers behind them.

They were in disarray when she let the barrier go.

Now she had to rely on Ulina to protect her.

She let her senses reach out into the air and the ground around her, as far as she could, taking in the lake and the enemy encampment, and as much as the air above as she was able.

She pulled the heat from it, channelling it into the ley-circle beneath her. She held her breath. Nothing seemed to be happening. Then the ground around her frosted over and a mist formed as the air cooled.

She focused on the air around the *tekrasa* and drained it. Men swore in the distance, their curses turning into cries of pain and then screams of agony as the frigid air cut into their skin and their feet stuck in the frozen mud.

One of the beasts fell from the sky, the gondola crumpled when it hit the ground and was crushed as the weight of the dead plant landed on it. She heard the same happening further out in the mist which was turning white as the tiny drops of water froze.

Two frost-covered armsmen battled through the frozen waste, tripping on the folded mud that was now as hard as stone. Ulina stepped forward though she too was covered with a dusting of frost.

Elona pulled in her power and turned her attention to the ground beneath her, she could feel the heated turmoil below. The ground trembled.

She forced her cold joints to stand.

"Ulina? Please leave them."

Even as the men came on, they fell again.

Ulina turned to Elona with a look so lacking in emotion it made her shiver with more than the cold.

They hurried back through the portal gate and into a strange mist that seemed to pour from the gate into the tunnel like a waterfall. It flowed along the ground until it finally dissipated.

"It worked?" said Chara.

Elona nodded. Not only did death follow her, it went before her.

"Mount up," called Kantees, already on the back of Sheesha.

Elona was the last to be ready, and she did not think she was dawdling intentionally. But once she was buckled in, the *ziri* took off in a storm of wings that stirred up the mist.

The pattern of the *ziri* formed quickly and their speed increased.

There came a moment when a new pattern of great complexity took shape around the formation. Golden light shone out behind Elona's closed eyes and, if she hadn't been aware of the truth, she would have sworn the *zirichasa* had become motionless.

The World's Pattern blurred.

It was impossible to judge their speed but it was now so quiet she could hear Kantees and Chara talking. Her life had given her very little practice in casual talk with other individuals. It had all been study alone when she was young—and, after that, everything had been about survival. She corrected herself: except for the winter with Usala. And the time when she and Jaymis had been walking away from Avakending.

"I did not know you rode a *ziri*, Lord Darrien."

"No reason you should."

"There are so few Ziri Towers in Faerholme."

"Two."

"Yes."

The conversation lapsed.

"Why is Zora dead?" he said suddenly.

Elona sighed, it was a conversation she had been expecting and more like the ones she always seemed to end up having. "I do not know precisely why. The Farahalek were trying to kill me, and she was the one I was with. Perhaps they thought I would be in the room. Perhaps they wanted information—though there was nothing Zora knew that she could tell them. I'd only just met her."

"Did she die quickly?"

"I'm sorry, but no. I tried to heal her when I found her but I could not do it in time." She waited for him to say something to that but he did not. "The assassin came after me and I burned him alive as I made a pyre for her."

"Did he suffer?"

"A great deal."

"I am glad of that at least." He took a deep breath. "I didn't love Zora, but she was a friend who made a good companion at night."

"Even though you had to pay her?"

"You think it strange?"

"I don't understand how a woman could sell herself like that. I don't know how you could like a woman who did it." She shook her head against his back. "But I know it happens, I am not a fool."

If Darrien was going to explain more, he did not get the chance.

More power fed into the golden shell around them and their speed increased further. The entire formation swung left as if it were a single creature. Elona clutched Darrien tighter.

"Don't worry you're perfectly safe."

I don't feel *safe.*

"We did this in Esternes, when we were first introduced to Kantees. Beyond the golden light, we are forcing the very air out of our way. And anything we pass is, at best, buffeted, but within the path there is nowhere for the air to go, and it wrecks anything it touches."

There was no sensation Elona could detect, only the feeling of movement as the *zirichasa* forged ahead.

"You could open your eyes."

"No, thank you."

The golden light cut off without warning. The *ziri* broke formation and landed. When her feet touched the surface of the path she sank to her knees and gathered what certainty she could from the curious surface.

She opened her eyes and watched the shifting patterns. She did not know their meaning or purpose and that gave her strength. She knew she was becoming too strong, any pattern she cast could kill someone, just as she had almost killed Chara and herself on the parapet the previous night.

Perhaps there was sense in the patterners having proper training.

Eventually she pulled herself together and climbed to her feet.

Perhaps I should cease to use magic altogether.

She could smell something burning. In the far distance, from the direction they had come, the flames of a great fire reflected from the path's walls and floor.

"That was the second wave," said Kantees. "They won't be hurting anyone now. I think we can call that a success. We'll be heading back."

"You promised to take me to the other side."

Kantees shook her head. "I can't do that. If we continue on, they will close the path and we'll be trapped on the other side. I've been stuck nowhere before without a portal to bring me back. It's dangerous."

"You 'ade a 'argain," said Chara.

"I can't take the risk," said Kantees, though her voice wavered.

Elona shook her head. "Why did you even agree if you had no intention of going through with it?"

"I will take them," said Darrien.

Kantees frowned. "Tuleesha cannot carry three."

"Give me one of the others then, one of the wild ones."

Elona looked up, something was tickling the back of her mind—or something behind her. A golden light. *More zirichasa?*

The Kadralin woman sighed. "Very well. Kashit is dependable and ranks lower than Tuleesha in the formation. He'll follow you." She raised her hand and one of the dun-coloured beasts looked up and waddled over. "But you have to give us time to reach the end of the portal. Once you exit and they realise who's come through, they will—"

"Mama! *Melinak!*"

Elona jerked her round as a tiny flash of gold shot past them.

She saw Ulina throw her Farahalek dagger, but it did not even come close as the bird streaked by. Elona doubted the girl could throw as fast as the creature was moving.

"Mount! Mount!" shouted Kantees as she turned and pelted across the path, as Sheesha dropped his neck and she threw herself on to his back.

Ulina was running for her dagger and her *ziri* loped after her.

Darrien grabbed Elona by the waist and tossed her onto Tuleesha's back. "No time to buckle up," he said as he climbed up after her.

Elona saw Chara hesitate then Sheesha was already beating his wings. Chara put her arms around Kashit's neck and as he stood straighter managed to get her leg over his back and sit herself between his wings.

The other *ziri* were already in the air as Tuleesha drove her wings hard and lifted off. Chara's mount followed and Elona could see the look of panic on Chara's face.

Ulina had retrieved her weapon and was getting into the air as Elona passed her. She realised they were heading away from the army the *ziri* had crushed. They were moving towards the place she wanted to go.

"Formation! Now!" cried Kantees, though Elona knew that it had made little impression, this was a thing the *ziri* did without help or instruction. But the pattern coalesced and the creatures were once more back in exactly the same positions relative to one another.

The golden light enveloped them and they powered forwards through the dark of the World's Pattern.

"I don't understand," said Elona more loudly than she meant.

"Nor do I," said Chara from behind.

Elona could feel Kantees forcing the *zirichasa* to fly faster.

"If that *melinak* gets to the beginning of the path before we do, they will close it."

"What's so special about it?" Apart from being a small bird with the same magic as the *zirichasa*.

"The Tirnians use them to carry messages."

"The final act of a defeated general."

"Or 'erhaps, it got 'ree on its own," said Chara.

Kantees was urging the *zirichasa* even faster. The golden light of the *ziri* wasn't constant, she noticed, it ebbed and flowed, glowed more than faded in some unfathomable pattern.

"I haven't closed my eyes," she said to no one in particular.

"Or put on the buckles," said Darrien. "And I find it easier to breathe at present."

The realisation that she had been too busy to be afraid annoyed her. The last thing she wanted to believe was that this was something she could overcome. It was the only thing she had to give to people to show she was like them.

She settled her position, slid the leather straps through the metal clasps and made sure they were firm before laying herself against Darrien's back, wrapping her arms around him and closing her eyes.

"Does that 'eel 'etter?" said Chara.

"Yes, it does."

"I have nothing to hold on to."

"You'll be fine," said Darrien. "Kashit is more like a comfortable chair."

"I do not think you and I have 'ones in the same 'lace," said Chara.

"In all my life, I never thought I would ever have a conversation with a Slissac."

"And I ne'er thought I would have a con'ersation with a Darrien."

"To be fair," said Elona, "if it had been any other Slissac, there would be no conversation, and probably a great deal of blood."

"I can see the portal," called Kantees from the front of the formation.

She felt Darrien's body become tense.

"That means it's out," he said.

"We'll make it," said Elona. *We have to.*

❧

Elona felt it before anyone else.

A patterner's path was a tunnel made through the World's Pattern. It was shored up by the symbols created by the mage at one end. So much power was needed it could only be done from one ley-circle to another.

And when that power was taken away., the walls collapsed. And anything that remained inside the tunnel vanished forever, they said it was absorbed into the World's Pattern but no one knew the truth, because no one had ever survived.

Elona heard Kantees swearing defiantly, refusing to permit the destruction of her family. Chara's surprise and Darrien's noble defeatism.

She felt the golden light around them fading as the walls closed in and the *ziri* slowed down.

But she could not let it happen. There was too much still to do. The *Kisharuk* was not defeated and she had not yet told anyone the truth of what was happening in the world.

She must not die.

CHAPTER 13

Chara stared down at her sister, lying as if asleep on the floor of the golden ball that trapped them. And through that wall, as they could occasionally see, was the infinite emptiness of the World's Pattern as her mother had taught her to call it. Her own people referred to it as the Mother's Blood.

The name did not matter, it was death if it reached them.

"The *ziri* aren't doing this," said Kantees.

Things were not very comfortable. The sphere was quite large but the curvature meant everything wanted to fall down to the bottom. And the bottom was always wherever Elona was, apparently. They tried moving her but it made no difference. She was the centre of their world.

"But it is the same magical and protective wall that they make when we fly fast. Damn her."

Darrien looked up. "Damn her? She saved our lives. Honestly, Kantees, if you hadn't argued about bringing her, we would not be here now."

"So, it's my fault?"

"No, of course not. I'm just saying…" he finished weakly.

"If you want me to say I was wrong, then yes, I was wrong," she said. "But we were so close, another few moments and we would have been out."

"This is not hel'ing," said Chara. "I' you are *fahain* what are you doing to hel'?"

Kantees sat down beside Elona's prostrate figure and took her hand. "I am not like her, I can't do this," she gestured to the walls, "All I can do is talk to the *ziri* and help to work patterns sometimes."

"Help win a battle, free your people, and be a great leader," said Darrien.

"Nothing that helps here. Even if it was true."

"Don't you know any magic that could help, Chara?"

She shook her head. "I do not have skill with 'atterns."

Kantees looked around again. "We will run out of air if nothing changes."

"Run out of air?" said Darrien.

"It's happened to me before. We nearly died."

Chara nodded. "This is something the Slissac know too."

Darrien sniffed. "How long have we got?"

"The air will get stuffy and hot. Then you will feel tired and want to go to sleep," said Kantees.

"But you will never wake u'," said Chara.

"Well, at least we saved Canvor," said Darrien.

Chara stared at Elona. "Why is she like this?"

Kantees glanced up. "What do you mean?"

"In the time I knew her 'efore, she ne'er was like this when she did her 'atterning or whatever it is she does. She was always awake. What does this mean?"

"She's maintaining the golden sphere against the World's Pattern, that must take a lot of strength," said Kantees.

"Isn't there 'ower here then?"

"No, the *ziri* draw theirs from within when they're flying fast along a path."

"She's doing this on her own?"

"Unless she has some other source of power. Does she have a *chilafrah*?"

Chara looked at her. "You know a'out those?"

"I have one—unfortunately not here."

"I see. No, I don't think Elona has one."

"All right, if she is maintaining the protection, we may have even less time. I will have to see about our escape."

"How?"

But Kantees did not reply. Instead, the *zirichasa* stirred, Sheesha moved until he was standing in a line with the way Elona's body lay. The others positioned themselves in roughly the right places for their formation.

"Elona told me something I had not seen, even though I experienced it every day. The *ziri* formation is a pattern, of sorts. It's how they create the golden light."

Kantees climbed up on to Sheesha and sat as if he was going to fly. She went silent. As far as Chara could see nothing happened, she looked at Darrien and he shrugged.

Then Elona breathed deeper. The skin on the undamaged side of her face, grew pinker. But the walls of the sphere, also imperceptibly at first, began to shrink around them.

"There!" shouted Kantees in triumph.

She was pointing directly ahead where the sphere was distorting as if someone was poking a finger into a damp cloth but the hole was away from them.

"Darrien, you go first."

"Go? Where?"

Then the scent of trees and damp warmth wafted past him. There was a hole through which fresh air was filtering.

He did not need further encouragement, with his sword in his hand he scrambled up the slope, squeezed through the gap and disappeared.

"I'm sorry, Chara, you'll have to come last with Elona. And she must come last of all."

"You think she's made a path?"

"It must be something like that but you know what happens if she goes before you."

Kantees did not wait for a response. The *ziri* broke their rough formation and one by one—apparently under tight control from

Kantees—they made their way through the hole which expanded to let them through before closing down again.

It was the strangest thing Chara had ever seen as their bodies and wings squeezed through until their tails disappeared.

The sphere was shrinking faster now. On the one hand, it made it easier to drag Elona to the exit but Chara had to go through feet first while hanging on to Elona's wrists. The sensation of the hole wrapping around her body was like water—but less willing to move in response to her movements.

She flailed through backwards until she felt hands grab her ankles. They yanked her hard. It was as if she was being pulled from the gullet of a giant bird. She squeezed out on to a stony surface, and Elona came after her. Chara managed to get her hands under Elona's head before it struck the stones. All Chara saw on this side was a strange distortion in the air which instantly shrank and vanished the moment Elona was out.

"'Other's 'ilk," she said as she breathed in the warm air. A roar told her there was a waterfall close by and a big one judging by the fine mist. All she could see in front of her were huge trees filled with leaves, with hanging creepers, and birds giving voice.

She crouched over her sister and felt her hands. "She's cold."

She had expected some sort of response but none came, turning she could see Kantees and Darrien staring away from her. Ulina crouched behind Sheesha's leg, staring up at her mother with a fierce expression, and the tiny blade she carried clutched in her hand.

Kantees shook her head slowly and held her arms out to show she was not armed. Darrien followed suit. Chara peered between the bodies of the *ziri* all of which were lying down—their heads either out or curled round—and she could see many armsmen. From their stance, it looked like at least some of them had bows.

If Kantees wasn't fighting, and restraining that murderous child, it probably meant they were heavily outnumbered.

But the armsmen were only on the side away from the river and bushes. And since they had not attempted to kill them, it suggested they probably wanted to capture them instead. In turn it meant Elona would not be harmed, and possibly helped.

Kantees and Darrien will look after her.

She knew she was trying to justify her next actions but the fewer of Elona's people who knew that the Slissac were more than just legends, the better. And she had a better chance of helping if she were free.

The dress she was wearing was a problem. She wished she had the clothing Usala had made for her from *lukisa* hide. But there was no time to worry about that.

She leaned down so her mouth was next to Elona's ear. "I will return."

Glancing back one final time, she saw Ulina looking at her. Chara pointed at herself and then the bushes about twenty paces away. Ulina gave the tiniest of nods, stared back at her mother and then jabbed Sheesha with her elbow. The beast grumbled and moved a little.

Chara saw Kantees nod, then jerk her head backwards. If Chara did not know what that meant it seemed that Ulina did, and she was not pleased about it. The girl untied a purse from her belt and put something into it.

Then Sheesha raised his huge head and emitted a burp worthy of his belly and neck. Laughter rippled through the armsmen. Ulina threw the purse with surprising accuracy and it landed directly in front of Chara just as she was pulling up her skirts. She grabbed it up and moved directly towards the bushes, keeping as low as she could.

One of the other *ziri*, slightly further away, burped too, though it lacked the resonance of Sheesha. More laughter and sounds of derision followed. Then one of the others farted explosively.

In the midst of the joking, and complaining, Chara made it into the bushes.

As soon as she had gone far enough that the *ziri* were no longer visible she stripped off the dress. She was not happy about being naked but now she was little more than a shadow. The river was deep and fast moving, the place where it tumbled over to become the waterfall was not far.

She tossed the dress into the water and watched it drift away.

The undergrowth was thick here and it would be easy to disappear, her scales were tough enough to protect from most insects, thorns and stinging plants. The soles of her feet were less well protected but she could manage.

What she wanted was a weapon. Her time among her own people had been difficult, not least because she had not been brought up with their customs. She kept thinking like a human instead of a Slissac. She remembered how odd it had been that Elona had understood her people better than she had.

Her mother Usala had not taught her politics or how to be the matriarch of a Slissac family. Elona at least understood how cut-throat it was.

Among the humans, Chara had hunted to keep her and her mother well-fed so she was not concerned about finding food. And, in the time since Elona had left, she had been trained in combat, as well as the more common methods of assassination so she could avoid them.

But it was her tracking and stalking skills she put to use now. Not that a troop of *ziri* was hard to follow.

She took a circular route back to where they had emerged from the—she had no idea what they had been in. A bubble? The patterner's path had collapsed and Elona had managed to save them. From what the others had said, that was impossible.

But then her sister commonly performed the impossible.

The cold mist that had flowed into the patterner's path at Canvor was a testament to the statement Elona had made when she claimed she could turn a spring morning into winter.

There were thirty armsmen surrounding the group as they began to move, Chara frowned, how was it possible they had just happened to be at this place in particular?

Kantees and Darrien were walking at the front under guard. Elona was lying on Sheesha's back while Ulina made sure she did not fall off. The rest of *zirichasa* were following in that curious ungainly walk they had when they were on the ground. But they too were being flanked by armsmen. She realised one of the *zirichasa* was moving more slowly than the others. And leaving a trail of blood. She frowned. They had attacked the *ziri*.

No doubt Kantees had been told the *ziri* would die if she attempted to escape. Chara was sure the nine beasts could easily deal with that number of men. But they would not escape without further harm, and perhaps death.

The track the armsmen followed passed between two hills.

Kantees went over the ridge instead, moving deftly among the trees. When she reached the other side, she discovered why the armsmen had been so close by.

Over the hill was a wide river plain. Trees had been cut down and even roads made between them. At its centre was a ley-circle, with four *tekrasa* floating above it while tethered to the ground by huge ropes. There were enough tents for an army, no doubt the one that had invaded Canvor.

But there were still hundreds of men here. Away on a hill, perhaps a league in the distance, stood the massive defensive walls of a huge castle.

But it seemed Kantees and the *zirichasa* were not being taken to the castle, instead they turned along the ridge of hills towards a group of substantial buildings. She wouldn't be able to reach it in broad daylight without being seen.

A patterner with his own two guards was hurrying from the ley-circle towards them. He talked to the sergeant, looked at the members of the group one by one then gesticulated in the direction of Elona. The sergeant's reply was short and angry. Moments later they continued on towards the buildings. The patterner followed slowly.

Once she had confirmed the armsmen were stopping at the building, Chara slipped back into the woods. The air was filled with the buzzing of insects and some that seemed intent on landing on her, though she batted them away. She knew from experience that it took something bigger than these to be able to get through her skin. The trees were not of any sort she recognised, and she was aware they must be far across the world now. The sun had moved significantly from when they left and it was evening.

She briefly contemplated the fact that Elona had got them out of the bubble away from the ley-circle. But then she knew, from Elona's story when they first met, that she had been able to create some sort of instant path when she fell from the tower at Canvor.

Chara looked around for inspiration, she still needed clothes and a weapon.

The pouch from Ulina hung around her neck. She opened it and clicked her tongue in surprise and pleasure. It was the girl's knife.

She drew it carefully from the sheath. It was similar to Elona's but with patterns cut into the blade itself. Chara held a twig and pressed the edge of the blade against it. There was barely any indication she was doing anything further than slicing air but the twig came away in her hand.

A more substantial branch came next. Moments later, it fell to the floor, cut through clean and perfectly smooth. She clicked again, and searched around for stone in the mossy undergrowth, disturbing myriad of unpleasant looking insects. The knife made short work of a small rock—now two smaller ones.

She located a relatively straight branch, made it smooth with a few deft strokes, then brought the end of it to a sharp point. She now regretted getting rid of the dress, she could have cut the hem back and used that length as a belt.

The sun was going down.

She didn't hurry as she went further back along the track and crossed it so she could approach the buildings from the forest.

Night caught her by surprise. There was very little twilight which she had planned to use for travel. Wherever this was, it seemed that the sun moved below the horizon faster than she was used to.

The animal sounds changed too as the day creatures found somewhere to be safe, and the night beasts came out. The air seemed alive with a sort of bug that glowed blue. And there was something else flying through the darkness that was attracted by them.

Her eyes adjusted but it was now all heat and shadows. Most

insects were invisible to her now. The upper parts of trees still glowed with the heat of the day, and glowing shapes moved in and out of the undergrowth.

Something stopped to look at her. About half the size of a *zatak*, it was on four legs moving smoothly and unconcerned through the dark. It had paused and turned its head in her direction, contemplating her for a few moments before deciding to continue on, in the same unhurried way.

She kept moving, avoiding the larger patches of warmth she came across, on the basis that it might decide she was a threat. Those ones probably had enough teeth and claws to cause her harm.

After a while she reached the point in the woods closest to the buildings. There were guards on the doors and the fire at the front made her eyes switch back to normal vision. The place had barred windows.

She climbed a tree and peered out. The *ziri* seemed to have been put in some sort of an animal corral at the back of the buildings. Which made little sense since they could easily fly away but the guards did not seem worried about that. They had their prisoners locked up.

There were no patrols that she could see. The ley-circle must be the only way to get here, and they were confident there would be no attack from the land.

No Slissac would have made that mistake, she thought. Every family was an identity to itself and they trusted no others. There were alliances to achieve certain goals and they lived in towns for better general security. But betrayal was inevitable.

She found it hard to live there. Her mother had taught her to be trusting, and the Slissac ways did not suit her. As a result, she had stayed quiet and small, not entering any alliances—apart from that first one which had brought her property and some staff—and did not present herself as a threat.

There was no getting away from the fact she was not a good Slissac. That, however, led to a further thought, there was a feast day coming up and if she did not attend, she would lose everything again. This time it would be permanent. She wasn't entirely sure how she felt about that.

Time wore on and Lostimal broached the horizon casting her white light across the plain. And silhouetting the castle on the hill. There were no lamps or fires she could see from any part of the buildings. That did not necessarily mean anything, they might be in the parts she could not see. But still, it seemed unusual.

There was no shortage of lights closer to the ley-circle. From her vantage point, she could see collections of fires and lamps stretching out all along this side of the river.

It was then she realised, she had not seen anyone leave the place in the direction of the castle to alert their leaders. No one had left at all. The patterner had gone inside.

When she judged it to be past midnight, and the temperature began to drop significantly, she moved again. She descended and followed the tree line round to the rear then crossed the open space to where the *zirichasa* slept.

She slipped inside. Her night vision showed her which hot and smelly patches on the ground to avoid as she moved between the feathered beasts. She wondered what it might be like to sleep curled up with one, even to have that special connection Kantees had.

One of them stirred and lifted its head. She could see its open eye as a brilliant hot spot. It stretched close to her and sniffed. Then it grumbled like an old woman and curled back up again.

It seems I am not an enemy.

But she had seen the size of the teeth and talons, and what they could do to someone they didn't like. When they attacked the *tekrasa* just inside the path—was it only today?—body parts had rained down.

Kantees had these beasts and she had her strange daughter. She needed no other protection. But apparently, she had seen the opportunity for Chara to escape and instructed Ulina to give up the dagger to maximise their chance of success.

She reached the far side of the corral and slipped between the logs. If there had been horses or *kichesa* here they were long gone.

They certainly would not have enjoyed being so close to such powerful predators.

Chara sat down and focused on the walls. She knew from experience that if humans stayed still long enough, they heated the walls around them—unlike Slissac who, it seemed, had cooler blood.

She remained motionless as if she was hunting a *sikechak*, and watched. Her eyes adjusted and slowly shapes appeared in the walls. Someone lying there. Another over there, one of them small, and someone standing up. Further over a shorter person standing—no, someone in a chair. But just next to that one, many people merged into one big blob of heat.

So that would be the guard room. A single person in a chair, perhaps with a view of the cells. Then a cell with perhaps Elona, Kantees and Ulina, then another with Darrien.

Entering the cell furthest from the guards seemed the best approach. The windows on this side were just bars and they would not be able to resist Ulina's knife.

CHAPTER 14

She couldn't reach the bars and the only thing she could find that would get her up to the right level was a small barrel which had probably contained beer or wine. It smelled very bad but was not too heavy and she was able to roll it over to the wall.

Once on end, it served well enough to get her up to the window. She carefully extracted the knife. The sheath itself must have its own magic since the blade had no effect on it. There were stories of blades that could cut through anything—in both human and Slissac stories, some of them were the same story—but the weapons were always cursed in some way. Elona's had certainly been cursed but the child did not seem to be affected by anything bad.

Chara gripped the first bar and slid the blade through it. A high-pitched whining came from it as it cut. Thankfully it was not loud.

Having done the bottom, she cut through the top and the bar came free. It was surprisingly heavy. Taking a chance, she tossed it into the mud and grass behind her. It landed with a low thud.

The second went just as easily, and she sent that down to join its brother. Then the third and that finally came away too. She carefully aimed the third one into a different place than the other two. She dare not risk them striking one another. It might only make a slightly noisier thud but she did not want to take a chance.

"Darrien?" she said quietly.

She heard a slight sound of movement and jumped as his pale face popped up at the window.

"Chara, at last. Kantees said you'd be here to cut through the bars."

"How could she know that?"

"She said she's been here before. She wasn't pleased. They had to take the long way home."

"I don't know what you're talking a'out," she said. "Can you get out?"

"Yes, but Lady Elona is still unconscious."

"One thing at a time." She jumped down from the barrel and kept a watch as he pulled himself up and squeezed out head first. She couldn't imagine what he thought he was doing. He'd crack his skull open that way.

But he whistled quietly and a flurry of feathers brought Tuleesha up and out of the corral and down beside the window. Darrien tumbled out and landed on the back of his mount who still had the saddle on her back.

He walked Tuleesha to the other window and held out his hand for Chara to climb up. "Are you sure you want to touch a Slissac?"

"I have lived a dangerous life," he said quietly. "And I follow a Kadralin."

Chara wished her face was as expressive as a human so he could see how disgusted she was at his words. She did not doubt that he meant well, and that he was incapable of understanding how he insulted both Kantees and herself in one short sentence.

Instead, she took his hand and let herself be drawn up.

"Are you unclothed?"

"Hush."

She attacked the bars. Moments later Ulina's face appeared at the window. Chara lay the knife down between them, and pushed the hilt round towards the child but she pushed it back, so Chara continued to cut through the bars. This time she handed them to Darrien who disposed of them just as she had.

Once the bars were gone, Chara took the sheath from her neck, put away the blade and handed it back. This time Ulina took them. There was a flurry of activity in the corral, some of the *ziri* jumped the fence and waited a short distance from the buildings.

Tuleesha made an odd hooting noise, so Chara got off while Darrien climbed in through the window. His mount moved away from the wall to be replaced by the much larger Sheesha, whose back was almost up to the level of the window. But he ducked down with his head and neck in front of Chara.

She took that to mean she was supposed to get on his back, though she was facing a mouth that could eat her down to her waist in one gulp. But he did not protest and once she was kneeling on his back he lifted back up to the window where Kantees and Darrien held Elona awkwardly between them.

Chara reached in and supported Elona's head as they passed her out through the gap. Until Chara was taking all her weight and half collapsed onto Sheesha's back. He grunted but did not move.

Once Elona was on the ground, things moved quickly. Ulina, Kantees and Darrien climbed out. Then with Darrien on Tuleesha, they got Elona up behind him and strapped her into the saddle.

Chara and Ulina found their mounts. Sheesha and the rest of them took to the air, moved into their formation and flashed away on a thread of gold.

"IS SHE ALL RIGHT?" said Chara to the others when they came down in a clearing a good distance from the castle and ley-circle. Elona had been laid out on the close-cropped grass.

"The patterner said there was nothing wrong that he could see," said Darrien though Kantees scoffed at that. "He said she had exhausted herself maintaining a pattern. Then he was very curious about the scarring on her face, and he also wanted to know how we had escaped from the path."

"What did you tell him?"

"We had no idea so we said that. Why is her face like that?"

"I don't know. She didn't have it the last time I saw her."

Darrien looked at Elona. "She's the most powerful patterner I've ever seen."

"*Fahain*," said Kantees. "If she had not been with us, we would have gone back towards Canvor, then they would have collapsed the path on us and we would have joined the World's Pattern."

They settled back into silence in the dark. Around them the sounds of the forest continued the same with the occasional louder cry from some hunter or prey.

"Should we set a watch?" said Chara.

"No need. Sleep under your *ziri*'s wing, they'll alert us if anything threatens. But no sane creature would attack a group of *zirichasa*.

Chara looked for the one she had ridden here.

"That one," said Kantees pointing, "her name is Sulassa."

"Do you give the' these na'es?"

"They don't name themselves but seem to like having them. Ulina was the one who named Halenth, he has a lot of fire just as she does."

Chara walked cautiously towards the animal she had jumped on without a thought when they needed to fly. She held out her hand as she would if it was a *zatesa* giving it a chance to smell her. Which the creature did. Sulassa's big head, while only half the size of Sheesha, was still enough to bite her arm off at the shoulder. Instead the *ziri* sniffed her hand thoroughly and then all the way up and down her body.

Oh no, I'm still naked.

"Have you got any spare clothes, Kantees?"

"What, oh, yes we're about a size I suppose—though you don't have anything up top."

"Slissac don't."

"Wasn't a criticism, just saying about the fit." She found a bag. "You don't mind wearing men's clothes?"

"I 'refer them."

"Good because I don't have any skirts or dresses. Waste of time in my opinion, and you can't fight in them."

Chara pulled on the clothes and felt better for having herself covered.

"Time for a slee', Sulassa."

The creature grunted as if she understood and settled down where she was, stretching her wide wings then bringing them in with a shake.

"Just give her a kick if you need her to move," said Kantees.

"I would ne'er kick a creature so 'eautiful."

"You think that now, you'll learn."

With Darrien's help, Chara brought Elona over to the *ziri* who lifted a wing and let them both rest against her warm feathered body. Her wing came down over them both and blotted out the world. It was the strangest and most comforting experience Chara had ever experienced.

~

"Where are we?" said a voice in Chara's ear.

She opened her eyes. It was still dark and she could see Elona's warmth only as part of the *ziri* but their bodies were pressed together. She put her arm across Elona and squeezed gently for reassurance.

"Slee'ing under a *zirichak*'s wing."

"Of course."

Chara went back to sleep.

~

The next time she opened her eyes, sunlight was trying to penetrate the close packed feathers. Elona was still nestled into her shoulder and asleep. Chara wasn't entirely sure whether she had dreamed the part where her sister woke up. But on balance, she was fairly sure it had happened.

Then she realised she could smell cooking meat.

"Are you awake?"

It was Darrien's voice.

"Yes," said Chara. She pushed at the feathers in front of her. The wing twitched but didn't lift. She thought of Kantees' promise of the previous night and resolved not to kick. Instead, she slid out from underneath Elona and made sure she was resting safely against the gentle rise and fall of Sulassa's body then squeezed out into the open.

She squinted for a moment against the dazzling daylight before her eyes adjusted. Darrien held a flat stone on which there were several thin strips of meat. They had been thoroughly, if not overly, cooked on the fire burning a short distance away. Ulina was slicing through some animal and draping the pieces over a construction of wood next to the fire.

"Not much variety, I'm afraid. We had to make do without any utensils or pots. But it tastes alright."

She took the stone plate from him, and he handed her a skin of water.

"Thank you."

"You speak our language very well."

"I was 'rought u' 'y a hu'an."

"That explains it then."

She forced herself not to say *explains what?* And reminded herself that Darrien served Kantees and belonged to her family. Chara only had her sister. She just wished he was less arrogant, less … human.

Sulassa did not want to move her wing.

"Give her a kick," said Kantees watching from the fire.

"I won't."

Kantees shrugged. "That's how they treat each other. You're part of the family now, if you don't show her who's in charge, she'll run you ragged and so will the rest of them. I've worked with them for years, and I love them dearly, but they don't really understand kindness and consideration, even if they do things that seem kind. It's wrong to imagine they think like you and me, they think like *ziri*."

Chara realised that was the longest thing she'd ever heard

Kantees say. And it did sound like she knew what she was talking about.

She looked down at Sulassa's head where it was circled round and faced her. Her great eyes were open. Chara gave the wing a kick, not hard but firm enough to be noticed. The wing promptly lifted making enough space for Chara to move inside and sit down beside her sister.

"I can't deny it's comfortable," said Elona.

"You're awake."

"That Kantees is very full of herself."

"She's right though."

"Probably."

"Food?"

"Water first, I'm parched."

Chara passed over the skin which Elona unstoppered and drank from in long regular gulps.

She let it drop and corked it. She took a deep breath. "Better."

Chara offered the meat and they both ate for a while in silence, regularly washing it down with more water.

"Oh well," Elona said finally. "I suppose it's time for talking."

Chara helped her to her feet. She was unsteady. "I feel like I've run from Corlain to Canvor without a break."

Chara struck the wing with her elbow and Sulassa let them out.

THE SUN WAS BURNING down and they were in the open. Chara found it pleasant but the humans felt the need for shade. Kantees had the *ziri* move around until they created a space with a couple of the smaller browns stretching their wings to protect them from the sun.

"Will the *ziri* be all right?" asked Chara.

"They'll be fine. The feathers work both ways, they keep in the warmth when it's cold, but keep it out in the heat."

They all sat on the grass.

"I am going to tell you what is happening," said Elona when they were settled. "And you probably won't believe me. I will start from the very beginning, parts of the story you will know. Darrien will have heard the stories of Elona the mad daughter of Corlain. Chara knows what happened when I disappeared. But there are some things none of you will have heard."

So she told them, skipping the unnecessary or too personal details. Her betrothal to Drahail, her descent into madness under the enchantment of Lady Metrid. Her escape into the mountains and meeting Chara.

Chara was uncertain whether it was wise telling Darrien about the Slissac but she did not interrupt, since it was clear she existed as one of them.

Then came the part she knew nothing about. The battle at Apra, killing Metrid, and returning home. Then Elona's travels and adventures with Jaymis, Lord Nemon and this place.

"You've been here before as well?" said Kantees.

"Lord Nemon is in that castle," said Elona. "But you were here?"

"Brought by the Dunor's errand boy."

"What's the Dunor?"

Kantees hesitated, seeming surprised Elona did not know. "A council of Taymalin lords who decide that your precious Conclave no longer had value or meaning—led by Myrlask in Tirnia."

"Myrlask is dead," said Elona. "And so is his successor—I killed her myself."

The humans fell silent at this news. Chara felt strangely separated from it, she knew what her mother had taught her about the Conclave and the Taymalin. She had spoken of the Kadralin though she did not really know much about them. But they had been so far from that world, it meant little.

And then, returning to the place of her birth, and where she had some power, she had been removed even further from the Taymalin.

"So, is this Ne'on still here, is he 'art of this Dunor?"

"I know that Nemon was betrayed by Myrlask, and turned on the Emperor," said Elona. "But this where my tale becomes strange and where you may think the mad woman has returned."

She told them of how they had been finally caught by Nemon and he had talked about the ancient evil that the Slissac had created to destroy the Taymalin. And when she spoke the name of the *Kisharuk*, Chara found herself forced into the story, no matter how incredible it seemed.

Elona told of how they had entered the Fastness and come face to face with the creature inhabiting Lord Nemon's wife's body. The battle in which Elona had killed her and how the Slissac monster had taken Jaymis. Chara saw the tears in her sister's eyes.

She had destroyed the Fastness by opening a path to the lake at Canvor, and drained it. Then arrived there having, it seemed, dragged her sister too.

Kantees did not say anything for a long time. "It is difficult to believe."

"I know."

"Then let me tell you my story."

And so, they learnt how a slave on the Isle of Esternes had risen to where she was now, and how Darrien, who had been living at Canvor, had sent a *melinak* to Kantees to ask for her to come when the lake drained. He had been one of those recruited to fly with her at the battle of Jakalain and he was well aware that an attack could cripple Canvor that had lived so long with the arrogance that it was untouchable.

"You had a prophecy as well, Kantees?" said Elona, not keeping the hard edge of anger from her voice.

"Yenteel was sent by someone."

"The Arch-Patterner," said Elona and it wasn't a question. "He was the one that set Bejeren to guide me."

Chara knew the names, Elona had mentioned them more than once on those long winter nights, she blamed Arch-Patterner for ruining her life. Chara was not certain it was true, but it was not something she would argue over.

"Yes, it was him. I cannot say he ruined my life though it was difficult for a long time."

"He manipulates us to do his dirty work."

"I've never met him," said Kantees.

Nobody asked Chara to tell her story. Even though it seemed the Slissac were tied into this tale. Instead she chose to try to move the story into the future.

"What do we do now?

CHAPTER 15

Chara knew the answer would not be quick in coming, so she settled down to wait for the humans to talk through their thoughts and their prejudices.

"I have to kill the *Kisharuk*," said Elona.

"How can you do that if it can simply possess someone else?" said Kantees. "Though I do not think I believe in your Taymalin demon used to scare children into obedience."

"I do not know how I can do it. I just know it must be done. The monster said it 'You are mortal, I live forever'. If it's not stopped it will just keep attacking."

"I know the story. It was created by the Slissac to destroy Taymar and his followers when they escaped from their slave masters." Kantees looked hard at Elona. "Your people enslaved mine, you should be grateful I do not want to destroy you."

Darrien gave her a sharp look but Kantees just shook her head. "I'm just making a point, my friend. This monster, if it exists at all, only wants to kill the Taymalin."

"I am Taymalin," he said.

"And do you believe her?"

"The stories go deep. I cannot say that I do not believe, no matter how unlikely it might seem."

Elona stood up and stared out across the landscape.

"Do you truly think the *Kisharuk* will stop at the Taymalin? How will it even tell the difference? Our blood has been mingled? No matter how much the aristocracy of my people claim to be pure—and perhaps they are—we both know that the blood of the Kadralin and Taymalin has been mixed again and again.

"Who are you to say you are without Taymalin blood? Can I truthfully say I do not have Kadralin in my ancestry?" Elona turned to look at Kantees. "We are *fahain*, and the one thing the monster said was that our kind have always been a thorn in its side."

She stopped suddenly and turned to look behind her.

"Of course. I have been a fool. The Arch-Patterner *knows*."

Kantees got up and went to stand beside her, staring in the same direction as she was looking. "What are you talking about?"

"Don't you see? Florian *knows*."

"Florian?"

"That's his name, or that's the name he uses. He knows about the *Kisharuk*, that's why he's been interfering in our lives."

She went silent and stared into the distance.

Kantees looked again and then turned away. "I need to think."

She headed down the slope, Sheesha loped after her while the others remained close by.

Darrien stood as well. "I have an errand to run." He jumped up on Tuleesha's back, was in the air and gone.

The remaining *ziri* showed no sign of leaving so Chara decided they were not being abandoned and the others would return eventually. But that suited her, it meant that they were finally alone.

"Elona?"

Her sister turned and finally looked at her properly. There was an awkward moment and then they were in each other's arms.

"I missed you so much," said Elona. Her voice almost a whisper in Chara's ear. "I'm sorry I left you. I shouldn't have."

"No, you had to go. I know. We had our own 'aths to follow. If you had not gone Lady 'Etrid would have succeeded."

"Perhaps."

"It is the truth, and you know it."

Chara did not want to break their embrace but it was getting difficult to stand. She pulled away but let her grip slide down Elona's arm until they just held hands. They sat, legs touching and Chara looked at the terrible scarring on her sister's face.

"I'm still sorry I left. Anyway, did you not have male Slissac to entertain you? I remember your staff were keen for a liaison."

"The 'ales have two functions, and are only skilled at one."

"They are no good in bed?"

"I have nothing to co"are it to. 'Any of the 'atriarchs bed one another as 'art of their alliances. I hear that's 'ore 'leasant."

"But you didn't do it?"

Chara hesitated. "I am not good in that world, Elona. I do not truly understand it and I feared to make alliances. So no, I did not discover if the wo'en were 'etter than the 'ales." Then she clicked. "And was your experience good?"

Elona gave a sad smile. "It was getting better. Then I lost him."

"Do you think he's still alive?"

"I can't think that. If I hesitate when the time comes to destroy the *Kisharuk* all will be lost. No, he is dead and gone."

Chara squeezed Elona's hand.

"You did not say how your face was scarred."

"No, that too is unbelievable."

"Not to 'e."

So Elona filled in parts of the story she had missed. The visit to the Mother's Kitchen, the attack that left her dying and the use of the strange void to heal herself. Then when Jaymis was about to be destroyed by the feeding how Elona had used it again to protect them both.

This time Chara was truly impressed. "You warded off a feeding?"

Elona shrugged. "For all the good it did me. That's what scarred half my face and my right side."

"But you survived a feeding. Nobody can do that."

"My mother did too," said a small voice behind them.

They had forgotten Ulina.

"She did not mention it," said Elona.

"You did not mention yours."

"But Kantees carries no scars."

"Do you disbelieve me?"

Chara squeezed Elona's hand and her words died in her mouth. "I do not disbelieve, but I do not know how it is possible."

"If she did not tell you, I cannot. But I will tell you that she did stand in the white light of a feeding and did not die." Then she turned to Elona. "You are not Farahalek but you have one of their blades."

"As do you, and you are not Farahalek anymore."

"I earned my blade, what did you do to get yours?"

"I was given it by a woman who wished me dead. I believe she intended me to take my own life."

"But you live."

"And she is dead."

Ulina nodded. "Then you earned yours too."

"Thank you," said Elona. "Do you intend to tell your mother what you heard us discussing."

The child seemed to consider that for a moment. "I will not, unless I think it's important for her to know and you are not here."

"That is fair."

The girl looked as if she was going to leave them but then turned back and hesitated.

"What do you want to ask?" said Chara.

"The *Kisharuk* is real?"

Elona nodded. "It is."

"You fought it?"

"Yes."

"You defeated it?"

"You heard my story. I was the victor but only in that encounter. It lost the Fastness, but it still lives and can still command its armies."

"We are not safe here," said the child.

"No."

"The Farahalek worship the *Kisharuk*," she said.

"They serve it?" said Elona in astonishment.

Ulina shook her head then nodded. "It is their god. It is the reason they kill. I had to worship too."

"I'm sorry."

"I would like to plunge my knife into the *Kisharuk*'s heart and tear it from him."

Elona turned away, and Chara guessed she was imagining this small girl doing that to the body of the one she had cared for.

"Ha'e you told anyone else this?" said Chara.

She shook her head. "My mother did not tell you but it is the Farahalek who had the skill to use *melinak* to send messages."

"Is that im'ortant?"

"I thought you should know."

The girl turned abruptly and walked away as if she had used up the number of words she was permitted for the day.

"Chara, I feel sick—" Elona's voice sounded distant and uncertain.

Elona's legs gave way. Chara jumped forward and managed to get her arms round her before she hit the ground, but they were both dragged down and landed on the damp grass.

Elona was breathing normally but her heart was beating fast and she seemed to be asleep, or unconscious. Her skin was pale.

Just exhausted, thought Chara. She found Sulassa, fast asleep, and propped Elona up against the soft brown feathers of her body so her sister was in shade.

She went to the fire and found the water skin. It was empty. She looked back at Elona in between five *zirichasa* and decided she would be safe enough. The stream was not far.

It was hot here but she barely noticed it, not like the humans. Darrien in particular sweated noticeably, Kantees very little, but Elona was sweating a great deal though not where her skin was damaged.

Chara was not familiar with human illnesses, Usala had been a healer and a very hardy person. The other humans in the village tended to stay clear except when they needed something. Her mother had explained why but that did not make it any easier.

She filled the water skin and brought it back. Elona did not wake up but gulped down the water anyway. Chara poured some over her head just to be sure. Then went back for another skinful.

~

KANTEES RETURNED HALFWAY through the afternoon. Chara could not help but be impressed at the sight of Sheesha's glistening feathers of blue and gold.

"Is she all right?"

"All that talking this morning exhausted her, she's not fully recovered from saving our lives."

Kantees had nodded and moved away.

Later, Darrien returned with a wide selection of clothing both male and female.

"Should I ask where you stole this?"

"We assumed there must be villages, someone has to keep the castle and its men fed. We were not wrong."

Chara sorted through what he had brought and found a shirt and pants that fitted her quite well. She selected some items for Elona.

~

ELONA WOKE AGAIN when the sun had set and the air becoming cooler.

Kantees came and sat with her. Chara stayed to make sure she did not upset her sister, or tire her.

"How did you save us?"

"I used the golden magic of the *zirichasa* to create a barrier that prevented the skin of the path from collapsing in on itself. It is a very strong pattern."

"Were you doing it or the *ziri*?"

"I did it."

"I couldn't do that."

Elona shook her head. "And I cannot ride."

"It's not the same."

Elona gave a little laugh. "It is to me."

"And have you decided what you need to do, Elona of Corlain, bringer of winter, witch of the waters, and protector of *zirichasa*?"

Chara stared at Kantees for a long moment and then realised the woman was smiling. So she started to click her own laugh, which made Kantees stop and stare.

"Don't be surprised, Slissac have a sense of humour too," said Elona.

"I do," said Chara. "I a' not so sure a'out 'y Slissac sisters. I ne'er heard one o' the' tell a joke. Least not one that was funny."

"The clicking?"

"The clicking," said Chara.

Kantees turned back to Elona. "Well?"

"I have no choice, Kantees of the Ziri, I have to pursue the *Kisharuk*, stop it where I find it, and discover a way to destroy it." She paused. "And what will you do?"

"I will assist you with everything that I have to offer."

Chara stared at the Kadralin woman.

"I would be grateful for your help."

"There are conditions."

"Name them."

Kantees counted them off on her fingers. "You will listen to my council. You will inform me of everything relevant to our quest. You will never harm a *ziri* and, if I decide our ways should part, you will not argue or try to stop me. Finally, we are equals."

Elona nodded. "Listening to your council is not a hardship, I welcome it. I will tell you everything, when I know it is relevant. I would never intentionally harm a *zirichak*, I have never seen anything that is so beautiful in the air—especially as I hate flying." She sighed. "And no, I would not prevent you from leaving if that is your will."

Chara realised she was trying to get up, and jumped to help her. Elona did not argue though she seemed stronger and steadier now.

"But," said Elona. "It is not all my decision. My sister has her own mind too."

"I 'ill go where you go," said Chara quickly.

"No, Chara ko-Tek Tegina ar-Tek Guala ar-Gey Aytrueth, you are the matriarch of a Slissac house, not some younger sister in a Taymalin household. You have your own life and you must decide properly."

"I ha'e 'een away 'or only a three-day, though it 'eels like three ten-days." Then she remembered. "The Feast of S'ring! All the 'atriarchs must 'e 'resent. I have to return."

"Or what?"

"Or I lose e'rything."

Kantees shrugged. "Is that so bad? Seems like you prefer to be with your sister."

Chara turned on her. "'Eople died to give me back a family. And 'y 'arents were killed 'y some of them. I cannot give them what they want. Not without a fight."

Elona nodded. "Of course, we have to go."

Kantees looked at them. "I did not think our pact would be this short."

"What are you talking about?"

"I can't go. I'm not a Slissac."

"Neither am I," said Elona.

"No, but you're her sister and they tolerated you before, from what you said. And you even look a bit like them now with—" she ran her fingers down her own right cheek. "They might even believe you were half-Slissac."

"No, this is 'erfect," said Chara. "I vanish for days and return with a show of 'ower. It's what Elona said."

"Did I?"

"You told me it is a game of 'ower. I did not have any, and I do not want to 'lay their games of alliance and 'etrayal. 'Ut this would 'e unex'ected."

Elona nodded slowly. "I could even make my threats come true this time."

"Threats?" said Kantees.

"When we were there before I had to threaten the elders with my great magic power to make them do what we want."

"But you are powerful."

Elona smiled. "I wasn't then." Then she seemed to shake herself. "Kantees, you must become our sister, if you want to."

"This sounds like a child's game."

"No," said Elona, "it's a patterning."

Now Chara was the one to stare at her. "You know the pattern of the sisterhood?"

"I was there when it was used, and it sits inside us even now. I know it, I can extend it to Kantees—but only if that's what she wants."

"And if I don't?"

"Then it won't take. It's very subtle and besides, Kantees, you have already experienced it."

"What are you talking about?"

"The *zirichasa*, your bond with them is similar."

"You can see that too?"

"Only when I looked."

"But I have to take your word for that?"

"If you don't want me to do it, I won't."

Kantees hesitated. "But what does it mean? What's the point of it?"

Elona shook her head. "I have no idea, but it didn't stop me from leaving Chara and going my own way. You'll know it's there but it won't make any difference to you, but it will to the Slissac."

"They will hate it," said Chara. "That one of the slave race 'erformed their 'recious 'atterning."

"Seems reason enough to do it then."

"We'll do it under the light of Lostimal," said Elona. "It will have more meaning, and you can decide whether that's what you want."

"And tomorrow?"

"We'll pay a visit to the castle and find out who ordered the attack on my life," said Elona.

CHAPTER 16

*E*lona slept again as Chara spent some time combing the area for things to put with the meat. Darrien had also collected a cooking pot on his raid. With an evening meal being prepared, she felt a good deal better than she had, even if she felt sorry for the people who had lost their clothes and kitchenware.

She was also concerned that they had spent nearly a day here, and discovery was inevitable.

But evening became night and a couple of the *zirichasa*, she wasn't sure which ones, had returned carrying a pair of dead *kelukisa* one of which was devoured by the *ziri*, while the humans hacked at the other and cut meat from bone.

The Slissac consumed vegetables, fruit and fungus in preference to meat, and she had become used to the new diet easily. Her mother had always just fed her normal human food. Chara couldn't say that she preferred one over the other but her body felt calmer when she ate as a Slissac.

They were different creatures, though she had more sharp teeth for tearing at meat than the humans. But also more for grinding. Her mother had found the differences very interesting and Chara had

143

acquiesced to her investigations. There had been questions about reproduction too.

Chara knew more about that now. She suspected her human mother would have been horrified, and she was not sure how even Elona would react if she knew that Chara could become pregnant whenever she chose. That had been another part of her training in becoming a matriarch.

She had been brought up by a gentle and good human, but she was not a human, and never would be.

It did not mean she loved Elona any less.

But Kantees was right, her sister really did look almost Slissac-like on one side of her face, but without the iridescence.

THE SUN WAS GOING down as Elona woke again, Chara was by her side.

"I'm probably going to be awake all night now."

"You sound like a spoilt child."

"I wish I had been."

"Hungry?"

"Very and that smells delicious."

They ate quietly. Kantees explained to Darrien and Ulina that she, Elona and Chara would be performing a patterning a little later under Lostimal's light.

"It will be full tonight," said Darrien. "Does that auger well?"

"I'm sure it does," said Elona.

"Now you are being condescending," he said.

They laughed. "Yes, I was, I'm sorry. Truth is I just don't know if it makes any difference."

"It is good to think it will," said Chara. "And we would not 'e here without your hel'. I would still 'e naked."

The laughter broke the seriousness even though what she said wasn't even true.

Lostimal was huge in the sky and its light painted the world in silver, casting deep shadows.

"Look," said Ulina. She was pointing at the horizon from which Lostimal had risen which now glowed red with Colimar's light.

"Is it a feeding?" said Kantees.

Elona stretched out her senses towards the ley-circle far away and felt it trembling in anticipation.

"The circle thinks it is."

"You talk like it's alive," said Darrien. "And that's a thought I care not to have."

"I can't say whether it is or not, but they react when a feeding is due. They begin to boil. It's how the patterners know."

Kantees interrupted. "No, your precious Taymalin patterners have devices that can predict when a feeding will happen. Yenteel said they also know how to predict the location as well. They just don't want *us* to know."

Chara stood up and watched the red curve of the smaller moon as it climbed above the horizon. A thousand-thousand stars filled the sky as if a giant hand had been sprinkling flour across the great dark dome.

The *zirichasa* were awake and restless. They knew something was happening, and felt the tension of their mistress.

Darrien stamped out the fire then poured water across it. He didn't say anything but pointed back the way they had come from the ley-circle.

Floating close to the ground, perhaps two leagues away, its top half highlighted by the silvery light of Lostimal, was the vast curve of a *tekrasa*.

"Move down the slope slowly and towards the trees. Stay close to a *ziri*," said Kantees. No one argued. "Elona, can you hide us?"

"Hide us?"

"Yes, there's a pattern that can make things invisible."

"I know something like that but I can't do it while doing something else."

"But you could protect us if it attacks?"

"Yes, but we can just fly away."

"But you wanted to do the sister pattern."

"Binding?"

"You said it didn't bind."

"I said it doesn't stop you doing what you want."

They made it to the trees and pushed into them. Ulina climbed quickly and was lost in the shadows in moments.

Elona could feel the power building in the ley-circle even at this distance.

"It's going to be a powerful feeding." She remembered the one at Corlain when she had been chained in the tower. Watching the brilliant white light from the Mother's milk filtered through the shutters making bands of light across the walls.

"How soon?"

"Very."

Ulina reappeared.

"The *tekrasa* has turned and is coming this way."

"How much time have we got?"

"Not long."

"Pity I don't have my bow," said Darrien. "Take out the patterner and the creature has nothing to control it."

"Chara, Kantees, to me now please," said Elona standing in a space between the trees, where the branches above were a little thinner and painted with the light of Lostimal, with a hint of Colimar's blood.

She held out her arms at shoulder level. Chara moved closer and intertwined her arm so each had their hand on each other's shoulder. Kantees joined them and they made a circle of three.

The light of Lostimal dimmed as Colimar's smaller disk crossed it.

"Relaxing is better," said Elona. "Close your eyes, too."

"I've never done this before," said Kantees. "And neither have you."

"You 'ust trust your sister," said Chara.

"I wouldn't be here if I didn't."

Elona tutted and they fell silent.

Chara could feel her reaching through them with the power. Sensual and deep.

Kantees' grip on Chara shoulder tightened, she must feel it to, perhaps more because she was *fahain* as well.

Then the world turned white, even behind her closed eyes. She heard both Darrien and the unflappable Ulina gasp as one.

The power from the Mother overflowed the circle and poured across the landscape. It touched and flowed through everything. Even to Chara it was as if she could see the patterns with a crystal clarity.

But as suddenly as it had come, it was gone again. Replaced by an utter blackness.

Chara felt Kantees stretch out her mind to the *ziri* and they moved almost as one back towards the edge of the trees.

"I don't feel different, is it done?" she said to Elona.

"It is done," said Elona rubbing her eyes.

They separated.

"Then let's move before the men in that *tekrak* recover, find us and decide to attack."

"The castle?" said Chara.

"The castle," said Kantees and Elona together.

CHARA FOUND her mount and mounted its back.

Then watched Elona climb up behind Darrien, buckle herself in and put her arms around him with her cheek against his back. Her eyes tightly closed. It was strange to see someone so powerful become a frightened child.

But there was no time to be lost.

The *ziri* crashed upwards through the trees, a branch scraped Chara across her arm and it stung as they wheeled away from the dark shadow of the *tekrak* hanging above the dimly lit gondola attached beneath it.

Chara dug her fingers into the neck feathers of her mount and let it follow Sheesha. The formation assembled and they accelerated. Then the *ziri* became rigid, their necks and tails pointing straight forward and back. And, as the golden light took form around them, even their wings stopped beating, yet they arrowed forwards into the night.

Were they really going to seek out the *Kisharuk*?

Usala had talked about the history of the Taymalin, and had mentioned their slavery under the Slissac along with their escape. But the story of the *Kisharuk* was something else, after all no human had been there to witness its creation. She shuddered and wondered whether perhaps there had been slaves present, perhaps they had been needed in order to create this demon pattern.

But it was still just a story. The story of the Taymalin did include strange happenings as they fled the Slissac lands—but they could be invented, or misunderstandings of what truly happened.

Since she had been back among her people, she had heard not a single word about the creature, as if it didn't exist in their history.

Before she could think on that further the *zirichasa* started to flex their muscles, the golden light evaporated as if it had never been and a wall of air struck her as they slowed down.

And there before her was another great castle. The hill it was on was not high but the buildings spread over a much wider area than the one at Canvor. She guessed it was large although she had no real experience on which to judge it.

Much of the place was dark, all except the central towers and those seemed to be lit by great fires—was the castle *on* fire?

A vast ball of flame burst up from behind the inner walls. Chara stared in fascination as it flew with terrifying accuracy towards them. It did not seem to be moving quickly and she felt the formation twist to one side, then the burning sphere seemed to accelerate towards them.

"Elona!" Chara screamed. "Help us!"

It was if her sister had been asleep and she moved with such slowness as the flaming ball came at them. She had been facing the wrong way and she had to turn her head.

Then she gestured. A wall of blue light materialised between them and the fireball. A drumming like the collapse of a thousand stone towers thundered across them as the fireball struck the wall.

The ball disintegrated into a shower burning branches—to reveal a second one coming in, and a third behind it.

Not directly behind one another, but spread out as if to intercept their line of flight.

The *ziri* went into a dive. Elona screamed as she flailed in her seat—but the straps held her in place as she clutched at Darrien.

They accelerated towards the ground. The second fireball, as big across as Sheesha was head to tail, shot over them and she could feel the intense heat of it. Char could sense this was just burning wood, they had a pattern holding it together and something intensifying its heat.

As she watched it seemed to falter in the air as if it had decided to change direction and its curving trajectory became a simple collapse as it plummeted earthward.

It must be under control of patterners even in flight.

The black and silver of the fast-approaching ground grabbed her attention, she stared at Kantees' back, it was not that she didn't trust her, after all Darrien followed her without the slightest doubt. And she had fought in battles. But this seemed like suicide.

Then she felt the formation dissolve and each broke out of the dive in its own way and its own direction.

She realised she was now in charge of her mount.

"Above!" called Darrien. Tuleesha was already twisting away as she pulled out of the dive. Chara glanced over her shoulder. The third fireball was on its way down but Chara understood why Kantees had headed downward. The great outer walls now blocked the rest of the castle and whoever was controlling the fireballs could no longer see them.

Her mount was pulling out of the dive, but lacking instructions from her rider had continued in the same direction. The ground below them reflected the fire from above. Chara leaned to the left, the direction Tuleesha had gone. Her *ziri* followed her movement and its shape became a curve from her head to her tail with her wings in a V shape. The castle wall was coming up fast lit by moon-light and fireball.

Chara leaned back and the turn became tighter.

The fireball crashed behind them. A giant shadow of Slissac on a *ziri* flashed across the old and broken surface of the castle wall.

Chara wished she had the flexible face of a human so that she could smile as her mother had so often done for her, and with her. There was an emptiness in her heart and she was not sure which mother she longed for—the one who had borne her, or the one that raised her.

It doesn't matter.

She searched the ground and skies for Elona. She saw Tuleesha flying fast at ground level following the outer wall. A couple of the other rider-less *ziri* were following Darrien.

She focused on Elona and leaned forwards. Her mount accelerated. Chara patted its neck.

"You may not be a gaudy show-off like those pedigrees, but I think you are wonderful."

As if it had understood her words, the *ziri* managed to put on even more speed, with its wings beating hard and fast. They gained on Tuleesha.

CHAPTER 17

After a short time, Chara's *zirichak* came up beside Darrien and Elona. Chara was pleased to see that her sister was forcing herself to keep her eyes open although she was still clinging very hard to Darrien. One could only hope he did not mind.

Darrien glanced over and waved. Chara felt confident enough to wave back. Elona was not looking, instead she pointed up.

Immediately Tuleesha climbed then, moments after reaching the top of the wall, she slipped over and down into the space on the other side.

Chara had not followed immediately so had to take a long turn away from the castle, before returning and gliding over the wall. It was thicker than her cell had been in its longest dimension—seventeen of her paces. There was not a wide gap on the other side and she had to lean forward to make her mount go down. The beast raised its wings into a V and they descended frighteningly fast. A sudden flurry of wing beats had them land lightly on the stones of its floor.

Moonlight did not reach this far down and it was all black shadow but Chara could see Tuleesha, Darrien and Elona standing a short distance from them. The thudding of wingbeats heralded the arrival of two more *ziri*.

Chara dismounted and hurried across the cobbles to Elona. They hugged even though it had only been a short time since they left the forest.

"I like *ziri*," said Chara.

"I do not," said Elona with a sigh. "And I can't defend us if I'm too terrified to even look. I can't do *anything*."

"You defended us 'erfectly well."

"Only because you shouted at me."

Chara realised Elona was trembling.

"Don't you see? You could have been killed, and all because I'm scared."

"Or me," said Darrien.

Chara clicked and the sisters separated. "You are right, Lord Darrien, whatever would we have done if that ha''ened. What would Elona ha'e to cling to?"

Elona didn't laugh. "Where's Kantees?"

"She went in the other direction, it's just us and the *ziri*." Chara looked around. "It was cle'er to co'e inside the castle, Elona."

"We can't find out who's here if we're outside."

"We should rest," said Darrien.

"I'm not tired," said Elona.

Chara turned to her. "You were aslee' a lot of the day. We weren't."

"Yes, but we should try and get closer to the centre. I know from when we were here before, these outer parts of the castle are empty."

Chara knew Elona meant when she and Jaymis had been here before. The Jaymis who was now the *Kisharuk* if she was to believe what Elona said—and how could she not? Elona had lived through so many horrors, why invent one?

But it was more than that. She knew with a clear certainty Elona was telling the truth. Perhaps that was an effect of the binding—but did the binding mean you could tell if something was true, or that you believed whatever the other said?

"If there's no one here, it will be as safe to travel in daylight as night," said Darrien, "and the *ziri* need sleep even if you don't."

Elona held up her hand, although Chara knew she was the only one who saw it.

"Very well, you can all have your sleep. I'll try."

"Are you able to make a light? We should try to get undercover if we can."

A light glowed from Elona's raised hand and Chara recognised it, it was like the mosses that shone with magic.

They could see each other and the shapes of the *ziri*. The walls rose up on both sides and there was not a great deal of space between them. Perfect for trapping attackers if they managed to breach the first wall. And not enough room to wield a ram against the inner one.

"You don't need moss anymore?"

"Seems not."

There were no entrances here, just sheer walls and a dead-end in one direction.

"Let's see if we can find somewhere," said Elona.

Chara clicked. "So, we all have to stay awake after all?"

"Darrien said you wanted to get undercover, there isn't anything here. Or you can just sleep here in the open under a *zirichak*'s wing."

That thought appealed to Chara, but they could compromise. "We should search for a little while, in case there is so'ewhere 'etter close 'y. Otherwise, we can just camp out."

Neither of the others objected, so Darrien took the lead with Elona and Chara behind him. The *zirichasa* followed. It was impossible for them to travel quietly as their talons scraped on the stones and their feathers rustled. Not to mention their occasional bodily noises.

"They're digesting," said Darrien after a particularly loud stomach gurgle. Chara thought it might have been Sulassa.

The gap they were in took a sharp right and then right again. And they realised they were on the other side of the wall to where they had been before—although it was still quite thick.

After they had gone another ten paces it branched with an opening to the left while the one they were on continued forwards.

"It's a maze," said Elona.

Darrien turned and looked. "I've never heard of a castle having a maze in the outer parts."

"It would certainly cause difficulties for an attacker," said Elona. "They would be running around trying to find the way through."

"No use if you can fly," said Chara.

Elona stared around. "Also, no use if you can't bring death to the attackers."

"What are you thinking, sister?"

"These walls must be more than they appear. They'll have passages inside and ways to get up to the top."

"Nobody has a castle like this," said Darrien again.

Chara noticed Elona glance at her as if there was something she knew but wasn't saying. It didn't seem to make sense keeping things from Darrien, but she must have her reasons.

"There will be traps," Elona said.

"'Ut will they still work?"

"I'm not going to walk around here hoping that they don't. We need to get out of here and if we can't walk, we need to fly."

It was then Chara smelled it—and this time it wasn't a *zirichak* fart.

"Can you s'ell that?"

The other two sniffed the air.

"Only smelly feathers," said Elona.

Darrien shook his head in the dark. "What?"

"'Urning. A wood fire."

Chara stuck out her tongue to taste the air better. "It's co'ing fro' that direction." She pointed into the passage that led off their one.

"Might be Tahulin," said Elona suddenly.

"Do ghosts need to make fires?"

"I haven't told you some of the things I've seen."

"Tahulin don't exist, they're just more stories to scare children," said Darrien.

Elona gave a short laugh. "And you've seen everything."

"Hush," said Chara. "Stay here."

She didn't wait for them to respond but moved off in the direction of the burning wood. Elona's light faded rapidly and she saw small warm creatures infesting the walls.

The stones were warm from the day and showed her the ground and the walls, as vague haze. It occurred to her if there were dangers lurking here, she should have let them continue arguing, it would have covered any sound she might make.

The scent she was following increased in intensity and it wasn't long before she saw the glow of a fire reflecting around a corner—and heard snoring. She could not determine how many were here. Only one was distinguishable by sound.

A quick look at the walls showed they would be of no help to her. It was at a time like this she suspected the physical abilities of Kantees' daughter, and her complete lack of compassion for enemies, would have been useful.

There was only herself and she was not armed.

However, she could follow the trail of any animal without its knowledge, until that fateful moment she killed it.

She crouched down and placed her hands on the ground. A *chikik* fled from her when it realised how close she was. Feeling her way, she moved forward on all fours. At the corner, still in shadow she put her head close to the ground and let herself rock forward.

A large pair of boots and the mound of a body were silhouetted against the low flames of the fire but he wasn't the one that was snoring. There were two others, one propped against the opposite wall with the firelight bright on his face, he too was asleep and was the one from which the noise emanated. The other was smoking a pipe and staring into the heart of the burning wood.

She drew back almost immediately and froze, waiting to see if the awake one had noticed her. But there was no sound beyond the crack of splitting wood—

The skin of her back and neck tingled. She let herself go limp and flattened against the ground as a weight landed on her legs and something heavy went over her head. It crashed into the wall with a solid crunch. She twisted her body so her shoulders and head faced upward while the rest of her was still held down by the weight.

The faint light from the fire and her perception of heat revealed another man drawing back his arm for another swing at the enemy he had somehow managed to miss with the first stroke.

If the human realised his enemy was now facing him, he did not get a chance to react as Chara's rigid fingers jabbed viciously into his neck. The strangled sound was satisfying. He was off-balance and distracted now, she grabbed the hair at the side of his head and slammed it sideways into the stones. The arm holding the metal mace jerked to the ground to support his weight as he tried to understand why he could no longer breathe.

Chara saw shadows moving across the opposite wall. She twisted back, placed her palms against the ground and levered herself up, throwing off her choking attacker. She grabbed up the mace, it was heavy but she preferred to have a weapon than not. As her legs pushed her up and forward, she swung the mace.

The oncoming assailant came into view just as the path of the mace intersected with his stomach. He doubled over with an agonised groan. Sparks showered from his pipe as it flew from his mouth and struck the ground.

When outnumbered, bring chaos. The words of her Slissac battle teacher came back to her.

She spun away from the one she had just hit and took in the scene. He was the one that had been awake. The one on the floor in front of her was rousing and the other climbing to his feet.

Taking no time to think about it, she took a stride toward the fire and stamped hard on the groin of the one lying down. Her teacher had not taught her that one, it would not have been effective against a Slissac male. That was from Ulina.

Ignoring his pained cry, she took another stride and leapt over the fire. She twisted in mid-air, bringing the mace down in a long swing that struck the embers and sent them raining down on the man getting to his feet. She landed neatly, turning her head and shoulders to look directly behind.

And was face to face with the oncoming figure of the one she had struck in the stomach. His look of anger dissolved into shock and perhaps fear as her face was revealed in what remained of the fire's light.

The knife in his hand glinted as he too leapt the embers—if he had thought she was just a simple enemy in need of killing, she was now a nightmare from his childhood, an impossible monster from ancient tales. It did not appear to sway his resolve to kill her.

Chara jumped, even while she was twisted in that strange inhuman configuration. The knife sliced her leg sending a stunning wave of pain through her. Then a hand grabbed her clothes. He weighed a great deal more than she did, and he jerked her from the air as he landed.

She could not deny he was quick. The knife penetrated her side sending another excruciating wave of pain through her. And his free arm was around her neck, closing off her wind-pipe while holding her ready for another knife blow.

If she had been a human, she would be dead.

She could not turn her neck fully backwards without her shoulders moving, but she could get most of the way. Moments later his savage look of satisfaction, turned to horror as she bit into his face, feeling the strange sensation of the poison pumping into her prey.

It acted fast and she could see the terror in his eyes as his body ceased to respond and went limp, his knife clinking on the floor as his uncontrolled hands dropped it.

But she had no time to pause. The one she had covered in embers was coming at her with his knife.

She relaxed every muscle and slipped to the ground. The blade flashed past her cheek and embedded in the one she had poisoned. She dropped the mace and lifted the dagger as she launched herself sideways, slicing the blade across her attacker's unprotected stomach.

He screamed in pain.

But she didn't pause. The one that had been on the ground was disappearing round the corner. She bounded after him, taking the corner fast but he was already out of sight around the next bend. She charged after him only to run straight into him standing stock-still just past the bend. She hefted the knife and thrust it hard into his back.

He groaned and staggered forward. She stayed with him and twisted the knife, driving it deeper until even her hand was half buried in his skin.

She let go as he toppled forward and slammed into the ground.

A snuffling sound ahead made her move into a prepared position though the pain from her leg and side were demanding her attention, and she could feel her clothes wet with blood. There was something huge in the dark ahead of her.

"Chara?"

The mass that she saw resolved into *zirichasa* and people.

"Elona—" She dropped to her knees. "—I got them all."

WHEN SHE RECOVERED HER AWARENESS, she found them in the place where she had the fight. The fire had been rebuilt and the *ziri* were a huge pile of feathers snoring just beyond the firelight.

Elona had her hands on Chara's side with her eyes shut. She was muttering something. A short time later she opened her eyes, realised Chara was awake and smiled.

"How do you feel?"

"Aching."

"I'm not surprised."

Chara's right hand felt strange, once glance told her it was encrusted with blood.

"We haven't had time to clean you up."

"Was it 'ad?"

"It's all right now but you might have died. What possessed you to take them all on? How did you even do it?"

"One of them surprised me, I didn't have a chance to avoid it."

"You must be a formidable warrior," said Darrien. "To kill four armsmen when they surprised you."

"Only one did that, the others were resting, two were asleep."

"Even so. You must tell me how the battle went, when you are sufficiently recovered."

I probably won't. The less people knew about the strengths of the Slissac in combat, the better it would be. As for having a poison bite, it had never come up even with Usala, and Chara hadn't known until she had been told. Not that it was any use against other Slissac, they were immune to its effects.

She now knew that humans were not.

It had been explained to her that using her bite in any fight with her own people would make her no better than a *xililik*. She had no idea what that was either, and had been informed it was a very small parasite of *kikisa*, which had no value whatsoever.

She did not think that using her bite against humans would be considered that way, however. Since all humans were supposed to be killed on sight by whatever means were available.

"I didn't think the one with the knife in his chest should be dead though," said Elona. "Doesn't seem to be anything else wrong with him, and I wouldn't judge it to be a fatal wound."

"We haven't made any progress if they're all dead," said Chara, wishing she'd had the foresight to keep one alive, or at least not kill the one that had stopped when confronted by *zirichasa*.

"I wouldn't say that," said Darrien. "They have food, a fire, some weapons and a map."

"What map?"

Elona smiled. "This one." She pulled out a folded sheet and handed it over.

Chara turned it to face the light as she opened it. It showed the whole labyrinth on this side of the castle in detail and the entrances to the castle proper.

"Do we know where we are?"

Elona reached over and pointed. "I think we're here. It looks to be quite accurate."

Chara lay back suddenly overcome by exhaustion.

"So tomorrow," said Elona. "Once you're properly mended, we'll move in."

CHAPTER 18

EARLIER

Kantees veered away to the right as the fireball plummeted to the ground behind her. She did not need to see the *ziri* to know Darrien and three others had shot away in the other direction. She was being followed by the remaining five.

Another fireball came down, casting fast-moving shadows on the outer wall. They needed to get away from the area but out of sight.

After Elona had shown her the formation pattern, she could see it clearly, and had been furious with herself for not noticing it before. She had plenty of experience with patterns, it simply had not occurred to her to look.

They stayed low with the *zirichasa* forming a simple triangular pattern behind her. She could have forced them to fly fast but that would have defeated the object of not being visible.

Now she cursed for not having paid more attention to the castle the last time she was here. But it had not been important, they had been escaping from the very same prison close to the ley-circle as they had the night before.

She did recall that it was very large—compared to those she had seen—and it did not have a Ziri Tower.

Moving swiftly and staying low, they headed around the

perimeter until they reached the river. The wall went over it and there was a heavy metal gate going down into the depths. Kantees decided this was far enough, and headed away to the north with the light of Lostimal illuminating the world with its silver light.

Hills loomed ahead and she groaned at the sight of a forest at their base.

The reflection of yellowish light caught the corner of her eye just as Ulina called out again.

Another fireball was coming. They must have had lookouts on the tallest towers, and they had been seen as they broke free of the walls. She urged the *ziri* faster and their wings pummelled the air as they accelerated.

She knew how impenetrable the *ziri*'s golden light was, she also knew that the enemy thinking they had been killed would give them an advantage. She looked behind at the approaching ball of flame. There was one thing she had never tried, because there had never been a need, but Elona's use of the golden pattern when the path collapsed gave her the idea.

They could, of course, simply switch to the *zirichasa*'s magic and be far away in less than a heartbeat. But the ones who had created and controlled this weapon would know they had missed.

The fireball was coming in fast and there was no more time to think.

She commanded Sheesha to create the golden pattern and somehow tried to make him remain in place.

The air around them changed. The *ziri* became rigid. And the monstrous fireball struck them. Exploding in a blinding flash that made the world outside the shell vanish into reds, yellows and blacks.

It faded as fast as it had appeared and Kantees told Sheesha to let the pattern go, there was another fireball coming in but she had the *ziri* simply fall out of the sky. If anyone could see them at this distance the explosion would have been obvious and the second incoming fireball would have hidden any sign of the golden sphere. Now they would just see the bodies falling.

There was the risk the second weapon would be directed at the place they fell but at this distance it would be hard to judge where that was. Kantees spotted groups of white fluff scattered across the terrain. The *kelukisa* would make good meals for the *ziri*.

Then the second fireball went over them and simply winked out of existence, apart from falling embers. Kantees considered that to be interesting, these weapons were a creation of patterning and it appeared could only exist as long as a patterner focused on them.

The *zirichasa* pulled out of their falls at the last minute and Kantees had them land in a small dip in the landscape where they would be invisible to anyone trying to see them from the castle.

She and Ulina slipped off their mounts and climbed to the top of the ridge where they lay looking back the way they had come. The castle was a slab of carved stone in the undulating terrain. Lights glowed among the central towers but no further fireballs were sent in their direction.

They turned and slipped back down to where the *ziri* were making themselves comfortable on the cropped grass.

"The Dunor have been busy trying to create a defence against us," she said to Ulina. "This is a good thing to know."

"It is a good weapon," said Ulina. "It can be used against *tekrasa*, and men on the ground as well. A king on the battlefield could be killed easily by this."

"Then we must make sure the knowledge of it is destroyed here before we go on a *sikechak* hunt to the Slissac's home."

"I did not think the Slissac were real though we worshipped them."

"Seems we were both wrong."

"Will we help the others?"

"Yes, of course," said Kantees and she was suddenly surprised at her own words. Was that a result of the binding spell? Or did she truly want to help them?

The Taymalin *fahain* had said you could not take part in the binding unless you were truly honest in wanting to be part of it. She had been without family for so long, longer than she could even remember. Even though she had somehow created her own with Ulina, Gally and the fussy old uncle, Yenteel.

But this felt different.

This was similar to how she felt about Ulina, though she was never sure the girl was the same. Ulina had suffered strangely and her thinking was unnatural for a child of her age. She killed skillfully and without remorse, something no child should do.

Kantees knew why but that changed nothing. There was little love in Ulina, so Kantees had to provide it for both of them, and she put her arm around the girl and pulled her in close.

The *ziri* were fast asleep now, they could sleep anywhere. She thought about sending Sheesha to see if he could find the others, but Lostimal was still high and any *zirichak* would be easily visible.

Ulina curled up under her *ziri*'s wing and Kantees let herself fall asleep within Sheesha's embrace.

KANTEES LAY on her back in the early morning sun and stared up at the sky. Perfect blue again, she really wished for some clouds. Even rain. They were too exposed here, the *tekrasa* were once more floating around the castle. It would only take a patrol coming out this way for them to be discovered, and there was almost no cover between here and the wooded hills.

Even if she did not like woods, they would be safer there. And if they could get into the hills the *zirichasa* could hunt.

Something nagged at her. She felt as if she needed to be some-where, as if there was something she needed to do, right now.

She climbed to her feet.

"Let's go."

Ulina never questioned her decisions, just obeyed, and she was mounted in moments. Sheesha lifted his head then lay down so Kantees could climb easily.

"We're not hiding," she said as if explaining both to Ulina and their *ziri*. "We're attacking."

CHAPTER 19

The sky had lightened from black to deep blue when Chara woke up. She found some more wood and added them to the embers, encouraging the fire to take light once more. She guessed this place must be kept stocked as a regular stopping point for the patrols.

Then she studied the map, it was not far to the gate that would take them into the main part of the castle. Unfortunately, the map did not show any detail of that, and from Elona's description the place was large, old and a maze itself. There had been a large iron key that they assumed had something to do with the entrance, it did not look like the sort of thing an armsman would carry about normally.

The smell of cooking food roused the others and they ate some of the porridge the armsmen had.

Chara went and looked at the bodies again. She examined the one she had bitten. A bruise had appeared around the place she had ripped out his flesh. She did not recall spitting it out, which meant she had probably swallowed it.

The thought made her stomach turn over and she nearly lost the meal she had eaten. She had been calmer when she had lived with the Slissac, they ate no meat despite having the teeth for it. When she had lived with Usala their diet had not had a great deal of meat in it, she had been calm then too. The humans had fed her raw meat.

She stood and looked at the high walls. What had Kantees called this group? The Dunor? A council of rebel lords willing to help the Tirnian emperor overthrow all the other kingdoms. Why did she even care? Why shouldn't she let these humans fight it out between them? It made no difference to her or her people.

Except Elona had said the emperor—or empress—whether it was the *Kisharuk* or not, had claimed they already knew about the Slissac in the mountains. And it made sense, this person was using the giant *tekrasa*, and knew the patterns of how to control them.

Which suggested they really did know about the Slissac and surely if anyone did, the *Kisharuk* would.

She sighed. No, this had everything to do with her. Her people had created the monster to kill the Taymalin, she should be helping her sister to destroy it.

Did she believe in it? It didn't matter. Elona was certain. And if it was true, and if the deed could be done, perhaps the world could be changed for the better.

"Looks like you took a bite out of him." It was Darrien.

"I did what I had to."

"You killed four armsmen and you had no weapon."

She shrugged. "I had one after I dealt with the first."

"I would like to fight like you."

She turned to look at him. He seemed sincere. "I do not know what I can teach you."

"How to kill four armsmen in a brawl without a weapon?" Then he smiled, and she wished she could smile back. Instead, she nodded her head.

"When we have a chance, we can try it," she said. "But now I think we should move."

Elona has appeared around the corner and was stretching. "Agreed," she said.

~

IIT WASN'T long before they were in the alley where the gate was supposed to be located. The walls looked seamless but Chara saw where the plants that grew in the crevices had been disturbed and the crack between stones into which the key fitted and turned.

The door was not wide enough for a *zirichak*.

Darrien looked back at Tuleesha. "Now what do we do?"

"We go on without them," said Elona.

"They can be useful in a fight."

"They don't fit and we need to keep moving."

"We could fly," said Chara.

Elona turned on her. "I don't want to fly!" She looked as if she was going to cry, then swallowed it and finished quietly. "I can't protect you."

"If we get into the air and move fast, they won't have time to react," said Darrien.

"You don't know that."

"On the back of a *ziri*, it will take barely five breaths to reach the central area."

Chara took Elona's hand in hers. "You know this is the right thing to do."

Elona stared downward and her head gave the very slightest of nods.

"Do you want to ride with me?"

Elona looked embarrassed. "I feel safer with the saddle and the straps." Then she shrugged. "Not that it makes a great deal of difference."

Chara clicked. "You ride with Darrien, can't have you falling off halfway."

"Don't laugh at me."

Chara took a step forward and wrapped her arms around her sister. "I am not laughing at you."

"You were."

"A little."

"Sisters can have fallings out."

"If we did then I, as a good Slissac 'atriarch, would have to send assassins after you."

"And I would send them back to you in a jar."

Darrien huffed. "When you've finished making up, we have a rogue council of the Taymalin to deal with."

"Is your father one of them?"

"Mine? No, he's far too comfortable and lazy, but I do have an uncle who would very much like to be the Lord of Baralain instead. Wouldn't surprise me if he was one of them."

Chara turned to find Sulassa directly behind her, as if she had known.

Darrien strapped himself into Tuleesha's saddle and Elona climbed up behind him. She might complain but Chara could see that she was much more relaxed at least getting into position, even if she was still terrified of the flying itself.

"Where are we aiming?" said Darrien.

"If I remember right there's a courtyard beyond the main tower, the opposite side to the main entrance."

"The fireballs were coming from a 'osition on the ley-circle side, near that entrance," said Chara.

"Are you sure?" said Darrien.

"Yes. I could see the 'atterners."

"At that distance and in the dark?"

"I ha'e 'ery good eyesight at night. Certainly 'etter than yours."

"She does," said Elona.

Tuleesha took a step backwards and Chara saw Elona tense.

"All right, I wasn't disbelieving, just verifying."

"So, we will fly directly to the back of the big tower from here. If they see us at all they will not fire on the castle itself."

"We ho'e."

"I have a question," said Elona. "What are we trying to do?"

Chara stared at her and Darrien probably would have if he could have twisted round far enough.

"Don't you know?" he said. "This was your idea."

"I know, they keep trying to kill me. Or capture me, depending on who it is. And they will have been corrupted by the *Kisharuk* itself." She sighed. "It's possible they aren't evil; they probably think they're doing the right thing."

"My uncle wouldn't know the right thing if it was sick on him," said Darrien. "Self-interest is his only guiding star. Any of the others will be just the same."

"And how are you going to sto' the' trying to kill you, unless you destroy the'?" said Chara.

Elona shrugged. "I just thought it needed saying."

Chara leaned back and Sulassa reared. "You have said it, sister. We ha'e already destroyed most of their 'ower and they 'ust not 'e allowed to re'uild."

Elona nodded.

Darrien took the reins and Tuleesha beat her wings rising almost vertically in the small space. Chara leaned forward and Sulassa launched herself with a great leap. She could hear the powerful wingbeats of the other two as they all rose up.

Moments later they cleared the top of the maze walls. Tuleesha accelerated away with Sulassa tight on her tail. Chara twisted her head round and saw the others nose to tail behind them. She had expected them to form into a diamond but it seemed that geometric patterns were not the *zirichasa*'s only choice.

Then her heart leapt into her mouth as a fireball launched from the walls off to their right. Followed by instant relief as it shot away to the north, another followed it, and another.

"I'll take the patterners!" she shouted to the *ziri* in front of her and leaned to the right. Sulassa veered out of formation. "You keep going!"

She had no doubt her sister's power would keep them safe, but the fireballs almost certainly meant Kantees was on her way. She glanced back to see that one of the *ziri* had followed her while the other stayed with Tuleesha.

Darrien had said they were useful in a fight, he was most certainly underplaying their power. They were meat eaters with formidable teeth and talons. She had no doubt they would be of great help, as long as they knew who to bite.

The platform from which the fireballs were being launched came into sight. It was set lower than the tops of the walls by the height of two men. But she knew they had been guided once in the air, which meant the patterners must be able to see.

Sulassa swerved as an arrow whistled beneath her left wing.

Of course, they had defences. Chara tried to get a picture of what she was attacking in the seconds before they crossed the last wall. The flat roof. Three trebuchets mounted on turning devices, and being loaded with a dense ball of interwoven branches. Fires, one for each. There were at least two patterners at each weapon along with four or five men to load and wind.

Archers at intervals on the wall. And the small tower where several faces were peering out at the oncoming *ziri*.

The trebuchets needed to come first. She had to prevent them from firing. The archers on the walls would not fire into a fight if they thought they might hit their own, though *ziri* made big targets.

She changed her mind at the last moment.

Leaning as far back and to the right as she could, she turned Sulassa as if it was a sharp corner. She back-winged hard as they passed almost directly over the closest archer.

Chara pulled her legs up and as Sulassa came to almost a stop in the air, she leapt out and down. It was further than she expected it to be, but she hit the ground and rolled as she had been taught. It hurt.

The archer had an arrow strung but had not been expecting the feathered creature to stop, nor someone jump down. Nor, she supposed, had he expected to see the demon that all humans feared.

She crashed into him at full pelt and heard something snap. She drove her knife into the soft flesh of his neck. And was up and running before he realised he was dying.

The next archer was a good distance away but a winged shadow sped over her head. Terror froze him to the spot, when he realised his danger and tried to save himself by leaping from the wall; it was too late.

Sulassa caught him up in her talons and lifted him with powerful wing beats. He screamed as he went up, whether it was the pain of the talons piercing his flesh or the fear—it really didn't matter.

She had not climbed far before Sulassa let him go and turned back.

Chara leapt down to the rooftop and ran at the first of the trebuchets. Only the patterners mattered. She had wanted the archer's bow but that was what had snapped.

This was not like the fight last night. There were very many more of them and they knew she was coming. And the shock of seeing a living Slissac was not going to last long.

A blast of sound, like a thousand thunderstorms, rolled across the roof as a fireball erupted into flame. Then an explosion of wind knocked her off her feet and threw her backwards as it was flung it into the air.

Moments later she was on her feet and running back towards the trebuchets as the fireball shot away. The men had been ready for it and had kept their feet. They went back to reloading the machines.

Chara reached the first one. One of the workers tried to get between her and the patterners. His wild punch missed her body but struck her arm with nerve-numbing intensity. She slashed the knife across his chest and he lost interest. She dodged past him before he changed his mind.

An astonished and terrified patterner held up his open hand as if he wanted to talk. But he and his friends had tried to kill them yesterday and were firing on Kantees now.

He looked surprised when she slammed the dagger into his belly.

Another concussive blast of sound crashed across the roof, knocking them down again. She saw one of the burners wobbling on its three legs, and in a moment she was behind it. She grabbed the feet as the heat burned her face, and lifted. It was almost too heavy but she forced herself up until the ferociously hot contents spilt out onto the wooden base of the trebuchet.

Flames erupted and engulfed the machine and two of the men in moments. They did not scream for long.

She turned on the next machine but it had vanished.

She hesitated and took a step forward. And stared at the solid stone roof top in front of her. Solid stone? She glanced at the burning trebuchet beside her. The turning device, what was left of it, was set into the roof. It went down at least a hands-length, there was no such hole where the other machine had been.

Without another thought she closed her eyes and immediately felt the heat of the nearest brazier. She remembered its position in respect to the device itself, and ran forward, with her dagger ahead of her.

She was momentarily distracted as a line of gold seemed to be etched across her mind—then something crashed into the side of her head, knocking her to the floor. There was a laugh just behind her.

In the way no human could achieve, she twisted at the waist, bringing her shoulders and head to face backwards, and slashed wildly at the place she thought the sound had come from.

She made contact—and there were gasps.

She opened her eyes and could still see nothing here. Whatever the pattern was, it affected her alone. They could see her. Another blow came in from her left. They weren't using weapons, perhaps they didn't have any.

She heard a *ziri* screech right in her ear. She ducked beneath the buffeting wingbeats. A terrified scream close to her was cut off by a crunch.

"Get them, Sulassa!" *And the one I don't know the name of.*

She heard feet running, along with additional screams.

She opened her eyes and the view she had been expecting had returned. The bloodied remains of someone in patterner's robes lay in front of her.

Without anyone trying to kill her, she took the time to up-end the other braziers and set the remaining trebuchets on fire.

She wanted to stop but there was no time.

"Sulassa!"

The *ziri* came at her call, leaving a man groaning and twisting on the floor. Chara did not care whether he lived or died.

CHAPTER 20

Elona felt it when Chara veered away—she understood why but it still left her very alone. It wasn't that she disliked Darrien but she barely knew him, and he was not Chara, or Kantees.

Who I also barely know.

She wondered what had possessed her to create the bond between them—or even how she knew the pattern to do it. She had said that her magic did not persist after she had stopped concentrating on it. That was the truth but it did not take into account the effects it might leave behind.

The bond was what remained after the magic was gone.

The creature she was flying on tilted to the left and she forced herself to open her eyes. The central tower was directly in view canted over at a strange angle. Her stomach flipped and she grabbed Darrien even tighter.

She really couldn't decide which she hated more, *zirichak* or *tekrak*.

The only advantage of a *ziri* was that the journeys tended to be shorter. But at least the *tekrak* tended to be more stable. She hated being out of control.

"Archers below!" shouted Darrien.

Elona conjured the blue wall beneath them with barely a thought, and kept her eyes closed. She could see the patterns of the *ziri* and its well of power. How could a creature like this, so perfectly suited to its task, be natural?

Despite her fears she knew she could communicate with it, if she wanted to. This was different to the *sikechak* in the wastes of Tirnia.

"Can I land with this barrier under us?"

"I don't know."

She banished it as the *ziri*'s wings fought the air to bring them down gently. Elona forced her eyes open and summoned a blue dome like the one she had created in the Fastness. But smaller.

Just enough for the four of them.

Tuleesha came to a halt and she couldn't get herself unbuckled fast enough. Darrien got to the ground quickly and helped her down.

There had been an onslaught when they first landed but it had slackened off as the armsmen realised they were wasting their arrows and crossbow bolts.

"You need to go," said Elona.

"I should protect you."

"You make my task harder if you're here, since I'm the one that's protecting you."

Elona appreciated Darrien better when he simply nodded and climbed back into the saddle. Through the blue barrier she could see dozens more men pouring from the buildings, all armed in one way or another.

There was a flash of light to her right and fire exploded against her shield.

Patterners too.

"How do I get out of here?" said Darrien.

He had a good point. They were close to the edge of the court-yard with their backs to a wall.

"Can you go really fast, with the golden light?"

"Only Kantees and Gally can do it."

"Well, fly as fast as you can towards the wall, I will make sure the protection is gone by the time you get to it."

He gave her a look but nodded again. The air convulsed as Tuleesha and the other *ziri* blasted themselves into the air. Elona watched as they headed away, gaining speed.

And she dropped the shield. Raising a new dome much smaller, so that Tuleesha was now beyond it.

As if that was a signal, the massed armsmen charged at her.

She doubled the size of the dome and they slammed into it. She felt nothing of the impact. The ley-circle was close enough that she could draw on its limitless power.

Shadows flicked across the sun-filled courtyard and she looked up. The air was filled with *zirichasa*, flying in tight formation. Criss-crossing backwards and forwards. Nine of them in a diamond pattern.

She put the idea into Sheesha's head that they should come down. She went down on one knee where she stood and shrank the dome until it barely cleared her head.

The pattern of the *ziri* formation was clear in her mind and the moment it was close enough she dropped the shield and recreated a new one big enough to include the *ziri*.

Men screamed as they charged at her, finding themselves suddenly within the blue dome. Perhaps twenty of them. Armsmen with swords and bows.

Elona stood slowly as they raced toward her.

Nine *zirichasa* landed between her and them. Their cries cut off as they saw the razor teeth they now faced.

"Don't kill them!" she shouted.

"Lay down your weapons," came Darrien's voice. "And you will not be harmed." He stood in his stirrups and commanded like the Taymalin lordling that he was. He was right to do it, of course, they would be more likely to listen to a man.

Elona walked forwards, pushing *ziri* tails and necks out of the way as she came. She paused briefly at Chara's side and squeezed her thigh, the highest she could reach, and then moved on.

She reached Sheesha and nodded to Kantees. Then moved up further until she stood with Sheesha's massive head beside her. She placed her hand on his neck.

The men had lowered their weapons but had not dropped them. She was fairly sure she could protect her friends though she wished they had stayed away. Though even if Darrien had told them, Chara for one would still have come. She doubted Kantees was very good at taking orders either.

The air inside the dome trembled as a cannonade of magical explosions thundered against the outside. From three different directions.

These patterners outside were working hard but she did not think it likely they could summon enough chaos to disrupt the defensive pattern long enough to break it. It was distracting but all she had to do was keep rebuilding it.

"Where is the patterner?"

There was a pause and the man in his robes emerged from behind the armsmen. He was young, and no doubt wanted to prove himself against the attackers.

"Who do you serve?" she asked.

"Who is asking?" She wasn't sure where his accent came from, it wasn't Faerholme but from her recent experiences she was sure he wasn't Tirnian, or from Mirriasmia.

"I am Lady Elona of Corlain."

"Lucas."

"And who do you serve?"

"The Dunor."

"He is Otulain by his voice, out of Esternes," said Kantees from behind her. "A nasty family and even if they are not the head of the Dunor, they are its heart. Power is the only thing they value, and the life of a *ziri* means nothing to them."

Sheesha's growl had Elona's own heart thumping with fear even though she knew she was not its target. The man in front of her went pale as he stared at the monstrous creature.

"I have heard of Otulain," said Elona. "Fishmongers."

Darrien and Kantees laughed. The patterner looked uncomfortable.

"But it is not important."

Another fusillade of explosions struck the dome, Elona could feel it crumble and had to rebuild it. If they managed to get more strikes in a short space of time, she was not sure she could maintain it. One of the fireballs, if that's what they were, would get through.

"I have had enough of this," she said. For dramatic effect, she stepped forward and raised her arms. There were slightly muffled cries from outside where armsmen were trying to escape the slowly expanding blue barrier. "You think this is just a pattern for defence, Lucas once of Otu? That is only true in the hands of unimaginative patterners. But for a *fahain* it is also a weapon."

A wall collapsed as the unstoppable barrier bent it out of shape and it lost its integrity. Men were escaping through doors, and climbing walls.

The armsmen inside the dome were staring around but Lucas kept his eyes on Elona as if he thought he might learn something.

Elona stopped when the entire courtyard had been cleared. Sections of walls had collapsed and there were piles of debris around the edges of the barrier.

"We wish to speak with the Dunor," she said. "You will arrange it. Sundown at the ley-circle. We will go there directly, so do not think for a moment there can be any escape."

"And if they do not agree?"

Elona expanded the dome by an arms-length in all directions. More walls collapsed and the main doors of the tower shattered inward.

"Then I will return and destroy everything that remains here. And those who do not die in the collapse will be eaten by the *zirichasa*."

Sheesha growled on cue while the others moved, flapping their wings, snapping their teeth, and hopping side to side.

She turned her back on him and walked towards Tuleesha.

Behind her there was a snap of teeth and Kantees' voice. "I

wouldn't do that. My baby has not eaten for a couple of days and he's quite hungry."

With Darrien's help she climbed up behind him, and was grateful that none of the armsmen, or the patterner, could see her face. She managed to hold the dome until the *ziri* took to the air but then it felt like too much, and she let it go. But Kantees had already instructed Sheesha to move fast and the golden light wrapped them in silence as they shot away from the castle like an arrow.

Elona didn't open her eyes again until the *zirichasa* were approaching the ley-circle. They had left the castle in the wrong direction and it had taken Kantees some time to bring the formation round in a huge loop to target them on the circle itself.

"There are *tekrasa*," she said almost casually, as if there was no danger from them. But Elona remembered that part of the story where they had fought dozens of the huge plants here. Against armies on the ground, they were dangerous, and could bypass fixed defences easily, but against a *zirichak* they might as well be on the ground themselves.

"Can you make winds?" Kantees asked.

"No."

"Fog?"

"No."

Kantees seemed to have a skill in making her feel useless, then again perhaps that was a good thing. She knew she was strange and others would see her as dangerous. It was not a feeling she was comfortable with.

"Can you get rid of them?"

Elona sighed, and felt sick as the world turned beneath them. "Why not just fly past them fast, close enough to scare them then come back and warn them to leave?"

She was tired of being the heavy cavalry. Someone else could do it. She was tired.

"That should work," said Kantees.

"Let me off first, before you have your fun."

Kantees looked round at her then shrugged. Tuleesha and Sulassa broke formation and descended at the place where they had emerged from the collapsed path, near the river.

Chara was there to help her when she had got herself out of the straps.

Both *ziri* launched into the air, Chara looked longingly after Sulassa.

"Sorry," said Elona. "I just didn't want to do it anymore. I need to rest."

"It's all right."

They sat with their backs to a tree, and Elona resting in Chara's embrace. Her scarred face pressed against Chara's shoulder.

"Perhaps Kantees will let you keep the *ziri*," said Elona.

"I don't think it's up to her. Don't worry about it, you just sleep."

"The *Kisharuk* isn't here," said Elona, her mind refused to stop despite the weariness.

"How do you know?"

"I can't feel it."

"What does that mean?"

"I don't know. It can live forever but it's not used to be being beaten—except it told me that *fahain* had always been a pain in its side."

"So, two should be double the trouble."

"Kantees doesn't believe me."

"You don't know that."

There was a flash of gold across the sky.

"I wouldn't believe me either. I don't know why you do."

Chara clicked her laugh. "Who says I do, Taymalin?"

"But you do, Slissac."

Chara gave a very human sigh. "Of course I do. It's not an easy thing to 'elieve, 'Other used to tell 'e the stories of course, though she never tried to scare 'e with it."

"Your people created it. It doesn't want to kill you." Elona gave a short laugh. "It doesn't even want to kill Kantees or any of the Kadralin. Just the Taymalin."

"Do you think it would 'other to tell the difference?"

"Probably not."

"All the 'ore reason for Kantees to 'elieve and work with you."

CHAPTER 21

*D*arrien arrived back with them a little while later, with Sulassa in tow. They had been dozing but the blast of air woke them. It took him a moment to unstrap himself and drop to the ground.

"I need a change of clothes," he said and sat down in front of them.

"Yes, you do," said Chara, sniffing loudly. "And I need some clothes that fit 'e, 'ut we can't all ha'e what we want."

"Everything is all right?" asked Elona. He seemed relaxed so she guessed it was, but she needed to know.

He smiled. "We didn't even need to fight. It seems the Dunor decided to have the *tekrasa* and armsmen withdraw."

"I don't like it."

Chara nodded. "Neither do I."

Darrien sighed. "Kantees doesn't trust it either."

Elona climbed to her feet, though she felt stiff. "They want to get us in one place so they can try to kill us in one fell swoop."

"Kantees wants to make plans."

Chara went over to Sulassa and gave her neck a hug. "Did you 'iss 'e?" Then to Darrien. "Do you think Kantees will let 'e kee' her?"

"You need training," said Darrien.

"I can ride. You ha'e seen 'e."

"But you don't know how to look after a *ziri*." He smiled. "Kantees'll have you slopping out a Ziri Tower for months before she'll let you look after one."

"I ha'e slo"ed out ani'al dung all 'y life."

"But the smell of *ziri* shit is a fragrance like no other."

Chara sniffed. "I do not think you e'er sho'elled *ziri* shit."

"I'm going back to the ley-circle," said Elona.

"I'll take you," said Darrien.

"No, thank you. I need to stretch my legs."

You have no idea how much I'd rather walk.

"I'll come with you," said Chara.

"We can't force Sulassa to do that—I just want a little time on my own. I want to think."

Chara didn't argue.

ELONA WALKED DOWN to the track. It wasn't far to the ley-circle from here, in fact, it wasn't far enough. She was tired of this game with the Dunor. They were not the ones that mattered. Only the *Kisharuk* was important now.

But she had to take away the creature's powerbase.

She slowly worked her way up the incline towards the ridge. She thought about Avalia and Makeela, and the other women in the Widow's Court, had they escaped the city? Had they even needed to?

How many of the Dunor's army had she killed when she had made it cold? Had Drahail taken advantage of it? Was it only yesterday, or the day before?

Between them, she and Kantees had already dealt with a good proportion of the Dunor's forces. Was it possible they had more elsewhere, hidden close to another big ley-circle? She did not think it likely. From what Kantees had said, she had forced their hand in Esternes.

By draining the lake at Canvor, Elona had given them an opportunity they felt they could not resist and organised this attack. Which she and Kantees had foiled.

Elona reached the top of the ridge and looked out across the plain, glimpsing the turrets of the castle in the distance. She could see the dark blots of *tekrasa* against the blue of the sky, floating near to it.

Close to the edge of the ley-circle were a group of seven *ziri* and she could see Kantees talking to Ulina. They were a strange pair. Elona wondered for a moment whether Darrien might be in love with Kantees. If he was, it was not reciprocated, Kantees seemed very single-minded.

Though that accusation could be applied equally to me.

She started down the slope as the other two *zirichasa* went over her.

Elona looked into the ley-circle. It was not as large as the Wellspring close to her home, but it was bigger than the one at Canvor. And that line of thought took her to the strange tower at the Fastness, something that could channel the power of a feeding and was not destroyed by it.

No human patterner could do that, as far as she knew. They would certainly have built their castles around ley-circles if they could. To her knowledge the Fastness was unique. And she had destroyed the tower by opening a path.

She watched as Chara and Darrien circled the others and came down to a light landing. She couldn't deny that Chara looked very confident on the beast and, from this distance, it looked safe enough.

But she pushed away the thought of flying as another idea came into her head. Something that would mean they wouldn't have to deal with the Dunor at all.

SHE CAME up to them as they were laughing, and she had missed the joke. It didn't matter, she was used to being the outsider.

"Enjoy your walk?" said Kantees.

"Better than flying."

Kantees laughed again, but it was good natured.

"How far are we from Faerholme?" Elona said.

"Difficult to say but we are ahead in time by a long way and a good deal further south. It's morning there now."

Kantees nodded and looked at the sun descending. There wouldn't be much time.

"I was the one who drained the lake at Canvor."

"So you said."

"I opened a path. And it was a very short one."

Kantees smiled and Chara clicked.

"I think Darrien should go," said Kantees.

"That's what I thought."

"Go where?" said Darrien.

"Shouldn't you go too?" asked Elona.

"They're unlikely to listen to a Kadralin, no matter how much help I've given them. What about you?"

Elona uttered a humourless laugh. "Me? The crazy woman with the scarred face."

"They won't listen to 'e either," said Chara and clicked again.

Darrien looked confused.

"Where am I going and what am I doing?"

"I'll go as far as the other end," said Kantees. "Then come back so you know when to let it go."

Elona nodded. "That would be best, I don't want to accidentally kill Darrien."

"What are you three talking about?"

ONCE KANTEES HAD RETURNED they settled down. There was nothing to do but wait for the Dunor to make their move. That would be the hardest part of the plan, Elona thought she could hold two patterns at the same time but if her concentration was disturbed, something would go.

Chara had flown off to the cells they had been kept in to see if she could find something to eat.

"She rides well," said Kantees as they watched her go.

"Unlike me."

"When I was a slave in Jakalain, tending Sheesha most of the time, sometimes they would have wives and daughters of visitors wanting to ride. Even they were better than you."

"Thanks. I'm scared of falling."

"The *ziri* won't let you fall."

"It's out of my control and I can't even contemplate it. There are no words you can say that will change the way I feel. I am not happy about it, I wish it was different, but it is the way it is."

"Did you fall out of a tree when you were young?"

"Ladies aren't permitted to climb trees in the first place."

Kantees sighed and plucked a sun-withered stalk from the grass. She stuck an end in her mouth.

"Would you let Chara keep the *ziri*? She has become attached to it."

Kantees laughed. "They do that. Sneaky, I call it."

Elona smiled. "So what do you think?"

"There's a lot to know about them."

"That's not a no."

Kantees smiled and changed the subject. "You never really said how you got the scars, or are they burns? They look a little like burns. Why haven't you had them healed?"

"They won't heal."

She pulled the shirt off her left shoulder and down to show Kantees the hole in her chest. "That is the result of healing. I was dying. And I healed myself."

Kantees looked as if she was about to say something unhelpful, so Elona didn't give her the chance. "This is not the Mother's Milk, this is something else. There's another power, and I can use it—but it does this to me." She covered herself up again. "This side was when Jaymis—" She hesitated realising she hadn't thought of him for what seemed like days. "—Jaymis and I were caught in a ley-circle during a feeding. The only thing I had to protect us was this other power."

Kantees shook her head. "Another power? I've never heard of that."

"The patterners know about it, and so do the Kadralin shamans."

"I survived a feeding too," said Kantees. "But I think it was the *chilafrah* that stopped me from being … whatever happens. Anyway, it absorbed a lot of the power. I would have been dead anyway if it hadn't worked. I had a parasite in me, planted by an abomination in a Slissac tower. It wasn't nice."

Elona's breath caught in her throat. "Slissac tower?"

Kantees nodded. "I've seen a few of them. They built them on ley-circles."

"What do they look like? Tell me." She leaned forwards.

"Black, tapering towards the top, they have patterns drawn everywhere. They gather the Mother's Milk and channel it down the middle. It means you can build right up to them. The power doesn't destroy the surrounding areas so people live round them."

Elona sat back. "The castle in Tirnia where I found the *Kisharuk*, it had one."

And I had no idea what it was. But the Slissac who built them are gone. Do the ones living in the mountains know about the towers?

"You know what they're like then."

"We only saw it from a distance." Elona got out her knife. "This uses that other power. I don't know how it can be contained because it destroys patterns, but it is that power in the blade that means it can cut anything."

Ulina looked up. "The Farahalek know."

Elona nodded. "They must. But the skill needed to draw the other power into the blade and bind it there." She shook her head. "I do not think I would want that power."

"Why not?" said Kantees. "Perhaps if you did know you might be able to do something about your scars."

"Perhaps."

A whisper of feathered wings went over them and Sulassa landed lightly. Chara slipped from her back and walked over carrying a bag. She sat with them and pulled out some cooked meat that had been roughly hacked into pieces and a couple of loaves of bread. She passed round a water bottle.

"Not bad," said Kantees.

"'Ut I found so'ething 'etter." She put her hand into the bag again and pulled out a pack of cards. "And they're all here."

"What shall we play?" said Kantees.

Elona said. "Devil's Bargain? I used to play with Bejeren sometimes. I think it would be better with three." She did not miss the irony, now that she came to say it out loud.

Kantees frowned. "How do you play that?"

Chara's eyes narrowed. "Darrien was told 'e a'out that game you 'layed, Kantees."

She sighed then laughed. "They could never stop talking about how I beat them."

"You were going to pretend you didn't know how to play?" said Elona.

Kantees shrugged. "We're not playing for money."

She still won every hand.

CHAPTER 22

It was much later, when the sun was turning red as it headed for the horizon, that there was movement from the castle.

Chara was first to notice and pointed at the *tekrasa* lifting into the air. They may have sent a good number to Canvor but they had kept quite a few in reserve. There was no wind and the light still sufficient for the creatures to be entirely happy.

The others stood up and stretched, as Chara jumped on Sulassa's back and flew high above the ley-circle.

"Are you sure you can do this?" said Kantees to Elona.

"Of course."

"You're lying." Kantees sighed. "But that's all right. If things go bad, I'll get Sheesha to pick you up."

Just as long as they don't know how to cancel my protection.

Elona went to stand on the ley-circle close to the edge nearest the approaching castle.

She had done this before, even to the same place. She could do it again. She just needed to concentrate.

A fireball launched from the castle and at first it looked as it if was firing upwards vertically but then the arc became clear.

Kantees leapt on to Sheesha and every *ziri* except Sulassa launched with her. She left Ulina behind as well. The child looked grim. Moments later they were a golden arrow spearing through the sky directly at the fireball.

"What's she doing?" breathed Elona.

There was no time for any response as the golden *zirichasa* formation collided with the fireball. It erupted in a huge explosion of flame. The concussion of its disintegration thundered across the plain, bending trees and knocking the *tekrasa* sideways.

Elona realised this was the same thing as had happened in the morning battle. She sighed in relief, Kantees knew what she was doing. Except she had to have tried it that first time, not knowing.

Two more fireballs shot upward, moving across the sky on different lines, one much higher than the other. Then a third launched.

"She cannot sto' them all," said Chara.

"I'm ready," said Elona.

"Take me," said Ulina, she tugged at Chara's arm. "I must fight."

Elona thought for a second. "Yes, take her out of the circle, get beyond the protection. You'll be more use out there."

She eyed the arcing fireballs. The higher one was speared by a golden light and erupted in flame. "Go, quickly!"

Chara ran to Sulassa and as she settled herself, Ulina climbed up behind. The beating wings took them up and away fast.

Elona focused on the incoming fireball waiting until the last minute before throwing out the defensive blue dome.

The power of the ball of flame seemed to eat at her own strength and the dome winked out of existence as a hot air washed over her.

"I need to do better than that," she told herself. But she could not see how she could possibly open a path while she was being bombarded like this—let alone hold it open.

But I must.

In the distance she saw a golden light flashing above the horizon.

And I am not alone.

She raised one hand, and the barrier thickened. Everything beyond it now in shades of blue. Then she lifted her other and held it towards the centre of the ley-circle.

Sometime during the day, Chara had asked her whether she needed to move her hands to make the patterns. She had said no, because perceiving and changing patterns came from inside.

But it seemed to help.

The patterns for a portal were complex, but she had seen them again and again. She knew the patterners made things too complicated, how could they not, they did not truly understand what it was they manipulated with their clumsy symbols.

It was as if she was being torn in two as she conceived the portal to Canvor. Now she could feel the power surging from the ley-circle, pouring through her body and out to be moulded by the patterns she was creating. She was the conduit—limited only by how much she could carry without destroying herself.

At the Fastness, it had been easy to make a hole between the two places. It did not truly matter how large it was, or how stable. And she had not been trying to maintain another pattern at the same time.

She heard the roar of men coming from outside. The *tekrasa* loomed above the trees. A smaller ball of fire slammed against her wall of protection, and dissipated.

The sky behind lit up with tremendous power—another cataclysmic wall of air blasted across them. There had never been a battle like this, she knew because she had been forced to study them.

More missiles of burning fire rained down on her protection disrupting the pattern in a dozen places, forcing her to focus on the protective dome, she pulled it in a little. It required less power to maintain.

Another blast erupted from the castle but there had been none of the big fireballs coming over since Kantees arrived there.

She hoped Chara was staying out of the fight. She had no power.

Flame engulfed one of the *tekrasa* and it plummeted to the ground and exploded as it hit. She could hear the screams of the men as they burned. She took another breath and concentrated on the path.

She had to expand the dome as the portal took shape, she had made it almost as big as the one at Canvor the Dunor had used to send through the flying plants.

Another *tekrasa* went down in flames and screams. Elona caught sight of a dull-coloured *zirichak* skimming in and out of the trees and creatures. Fewer flaming missiles were hitting her shield. She refocused on the portal. The ley-circle she wanted was easy to find in the strange place between patterns.

More power flowed from the ground beneath her feet as she concentrated on bringing there closer to here. She had always been able to do this but it wasn't until they had been trapped inside the collapsed path that she came to understand it. The patterners did not know what they were really doing and thought they needed to make a path.

The place that was there and the place that was here became one.

"Please don't take long," she said aloud as she sank to her knees.

Once in place it became easier to maintain the two patterns but the power coursing through her did not reduce.

The Mother's Milk disrupts patterns, and tears them apart. That is why you cannot be near a feeding. Every pattern becomes nothing.

And that was what was happening to her now.

She could feel her patterns ripping asunder. Then the healing started, almost as if it was other than herself. But it could not work fast enough, it could only slow the erosion.

"Please be quick," she whispered.

Golden light filled the world beyond her closed eyelids.

Her defensive shield disintegrated, and the shouts of armsmen baying for blood became like crystal in her ears.

The portal wavered, but with the dome gone she could focus even more power into it. She had to keep it open for as long as she could.

She heard hundreds of feet pounding past her, metal shod boots crashing on stone. Then the roar of a *tekrak*'s fire-tube.

Horses' hooves clattering past. Rolling carriages, more armsmen.

"Elona," said Chara from behind her. "Let's get out of the way 'efore they see either of our faces."

Two hands grasped her shoulders and helped her into a standing position.

Elona concentrated even more on the portal, flowing it power to keep it strong and solid.

"I can see Canvor," said Chara with a hint of astonishment in her voice. "It's not a 'ath, you made a door."

Elona opened her eyes to see armsmen, in the colours of Faer-holme, with banners of the various dukedoms, pouring through the gate she had made into the sunlit midday of Canvor. The mud of the drained lake, the shoreline, and even a part of the castle was in view. And *tekrasa* lined up and floating through with the banners of Canvor be-decking their sides so that no one made a mistake.

Elona and Chara finally made it to the edge of the ley-circle, close to where the portal started, and sank to the ground. Sulassa was waiting.

"Something destroyed my shield," said Elona breathlessly as if she had run a league and a half. The healing was working in her body but every part of her ached.

"*Zirichasa*," said Chara. "Twenty, thirty. Like a ball of golden power."

"Saved my life."

"Then Kantees' formation joined them."

"Probably shouldn't talk," said Elona. "Need to concentrate."

"I'll just say they are taking down all the other *tekrasa*."

There was something about the way she said it that demanded Elona break the command she just made. "Other?"

"I did the first three, couldn't have them hurting your shield."

"Thank you. Saved me too."

Elona was grateful that Chara continued to hold her. But now they both went silent so that Elona could hold the portal.

"Tell me when I can stop."

IT TOOK a long time for the army of Faerholme to cross through. But there came a moment when Chara said it was safe to stop.

Elona let it go.

IT WAS dark when Elona opened her eyes once more. The shapes of the sounds around her told her she was inside a building, but the sounds of night creatures were not far away. Her body still ached everywhere but she could see, with her inner sense, that the healing was complete.

Death is my companion and if I do not feed him, he will take me instead.

"You're awake," said Chara's voice in the dark.

She tried to say "Yes" but her mouth was parched and though she went through the motions not a sound emerged.

"Here, sit up."

Chara helped her to get upright on the edge of the bed. Then put a wooden cup in her hand. "Water."

Elona sipped at it and felt the warmth of it soothe her dry tongue and throat.

"Try to drink it all, being out in the heat of this place for so long isn't good for you."

She sipped the water for a while and felt her body responding.

"Ready for some fruit?"

"Very hungry."

A bowl was put into her hands and she found it contained some sort of fruit with a furry skin. She knew her sister wouldn't give her something that wasn't edible. The first bite was a surprise and a delight. The skin was quite tough but the flesh inside was sweet, soft and juicy. There was a large stone in the centre which she dropped back into the bowl.

It was when Chara put some sort of shawl around her shoulders, she realised she had nothing on. It didn't matter with just the two of them.

She managed four of the fruits and was feeling considerably better.

"Where are we?"

"Se'eral leagues from the castle, Kantees says it's the northern ti' of the island."

"It's an island?"

"A 'ig one, though not as 'ig as Esternes. She was 'ery clear on that 'oint." Chara clicked her amusement. "There is a 'illage who are friendly."

"I'm glad we're not at the castle, I couldn't face Drahail or my father."

"Kantees enjoys talking to them, she said the look on your father's face ha'ing to deal with a Kadralin was a 'icture."

Elona smiled to herself in the dark. She would have liked to have seen that.

"It is good when you s'ile."

"You saw that?"

"I can light a candle if you like."

"No, it's all right."

"Lots of other *zirichasa* and their riders are here."

"The ones who came through first?"

"The one called Galiko, the only other one that can 'ake the *ziri* go golden."

"What's he like?"

"Strange. He is like a child in a 'an's 'ody, 'ut then he will say a wise thing."

"I suppose he must be *fahain* too." Then she yawned.

"Go 'ack to slee'."

Elona didn't argue and lay back. She felt comforted when Chara lay down and held her. She was asleep before she could have another thought.

CHAPTER 23

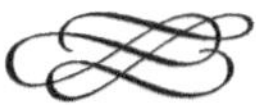

The sun streamed through cracks in the walls, along with a strong but warm damp wind. The aches of the previous night persisted though they had lessened. Chara was no longer there but the bowl of fruit stood on a table. She ate her way through two more of the curious fruit, although she was keen to eat something more substantial.

Some clothes had been thrown over the end of the bed, a shirt and jacket with a long skirt and stockings, which had been darned several times. Her boots stood by the door and it looked as if someone had tried to give them a clean.

She sat on the bed to put them on, lacing them tight.

She looked out of the open door without stepping beyond the threshold. She was surprised at the number of people. A group gathered round a fire, some talking in pairs and threes, others on their own eating or petting the *zirichasa* that were as numerous as the humans. And it wasn't just that, she noticed their faces, from dark Kadralin to pure Taymalin and every shade in between. Those dressed like Darrien, clearly the lordlings who rode *ziri*, and the ones in, not rags, but common dress. Women and men alike.

The only group that seemed to be unrepresented were highborn women like herself. Because they did not ride the *ziri*.

And there was not a single face she recognised.

She knew they had seen her open the door but, apart from surreptitious glances in her direction, no one came towards her—until a woman broke away from the group at the fire. The quality of clothes she wore suggested she was of the merchant classes, but the style was strange.

When she got within ten paces of Elona she dropped into a neat curtsy.

"Lady Elona, you are awake. The Lady Chara asked me to see to your needs, she said you would most likely be hungry and thirsty. We have bread and fresh cooked meat that we can share if you wish."

"That sounds lovely…" she let her voice trail off.

"Oh, I'm sorry, yes, forgive me, I am Marakees from the town of Two Circles on the Isle of Esternes, wife to Galiko and rider of Aratat." Her skin said she was mostly Kadralin, and Elona could see the woman was trying not to look at her scarred face.

"Aratat?"

Marakees smiled. "You know the old story then? Do not worry, my Aratat is not vain, at least no more than any *zirichak*."

Elona nodded.

"Thank you, Marakees. My sister was right, I am hungry."

If the suggestion that Chara was her sister had been surprising there was no sign of it. Perhaps, in such an egalitarian group, it meant nothing.

"Please to follow me, Lady Elona." She curtsied again and turned back towards the fire. At their approach, the people around it moved away leaving just the flames licking the bottom of a steaming pot.

Someone brought a stool and Elona sat down. Then Marakees served her with a bowl of soup, a large mug of something which seemed to be slightly alcoholic, and large pieces of bread. Then she stood by waiting to be commanded.

"I don't need to be treated like this," Elona said eventually.

"But you are the Lady Elona of Corlain, and you are *fahain*. You opened the path from Canvor—"

"Stop." Elona put her bowl down in her lap, despite it being the most delicious thing she had eaten in days—in fact the *most* she had eaten in days. "I am serious. You call Kantees by just her name. I am no different. I may not have been disowned by my father but I have disowned him."

"Please do not upset yourself, La—Elona. We want to give you the respect you deserve. My town had been in the thrall of a monster longer than anyone knows, even now, and it was Kantees who rescued us. She said we should give you the respect of your station. I'm sorry if we have offended you."

The woman seemed on the verge of tears. "I understand, Marakees. Sometimes it is hard to do right without doing wrong."

I know that only too well.

"Thank you, La—Elona. I, all of us, will try to do right, and not wrong." Then she gave a soft smile. "Kantees was the same. I kept calling her Lady Kantees and she did not like it. It was very hard to stop because we are not equals."

"No one is more important than anyone else."

"There are those who bend the World's Pattern to their will, and those who let it bend them." Marakees suddenly seemed full of words that needed to be spoken. "Kantees made the World's Pattern do her bidding, and you are the same. That is what it means to be *fahain*, I think."

"In that case," said Elona. "We can all be *fahain*, it's just a choice. It's just that one road is a great deal harder, and sometimes we are not the one to choose it."

"You sound like my Gally, if you don't mind me saying."

The air went silent between them. Elona felt she should say something but she had not had the right education to make small-talk. Besides they were not in a great ballroom, they were eating round a fire on an island—she did not know where. Except it was south, and warm.

The perfect blue skies of the previous days had been replaced by one with clouds scudding across it at high speed.

"The weather has changed," she said.

"Has it, Lady Elona?"

"It's been clear skies."

"Perhaps a storm is coming."

Not another one.

She finished the food and drink, and let it settle for a while, staring silently into the flames and listening to the chatter around her. She could never make out more than the occasional word but that was not what she listened to. These people were happy and excited.

Closing her eyes, she let her pattern sense roam. She did not pry but she could see clearly there was a bond between them not unlike the one between the *ziri*, and similar to the one she had created between Kantees, Chara and herself.

It seemed the Slissac were happy to copy and refine natural patterns, even among themselves. It was another clue that fed her idea about the Slissac creating creatures like the *ziri* and the *nachasa*. And perhaps the *Kisharuk* was their greatest work. And if that was true, they should also know how to bring it down. They *must* know.

Finally, she opened her eyes to see Marakees watching her, she looked away as soon as she had been discovered.

"Forgive me, Lady Elona."

"Just Elona."

"I'm sorry."

I wish you would stop apologising. "That's perfectly all right. Can you take me to Kantees and Chara now?"

"Oh yes, they are waiting for you."

"Why did you let me waste time?"

"I'm sorry, Lady Elona, but Lady Chara said not to tell you unless you asked. She was concerned that you should rest thoroughly and then eat properly. We know that you performed patternings that no other person in the whole world could have done. I have not walked many paths, but I know they can be long. And you made a path of no distance at all. Everyone is talking about it."

Elona groaned inwardly. "Very well, take me to them now please."

Marakees jumped to her feet. "I can take you on Aratat."

"Walking."

Marakees nodded as if she had been warned about Elona's reluctance to fly, and led the way off the top of the hill and down a slope. The path seemed well-worn and Elona wondered who normally lived in the small low building she had woken in.

"If I may ask, La—Elona."

"My face?"

"Oh, yes."

"It is a magical injury, and it cannot be healed."

"I see."

They were silent for a little while more. The air was filled with flying insects, some of which were quite large. Elona considered putting a bubble of protection around the two of them but it would be draining. She was too far from the ley-circle to use it.

A stray thought crossed her mind. "Does Kantees have a man? Darrien?"

"Oh no," the woman sounded almost shocked at the idea. She lowered her voice. "Kantees does not care for men. I mean she likes them as friends, she and my Gally are the very greatest of friends and have been all their lives."

"I see." Elona thought about what Chara had said about the Slissac matriarchs. "Does she like women instead, perhaps?"

"Women?"

"It can happen."

"Oh, well, yes, I know, Lady Elona, but no. I don't think so." She paused, perhaps wondering if this was not a conversation she should be having. "I think Sheesha is the only creature she truly loves, and he can be as a bad as any husband."

"All the more reason not to fly," said Elona.

"But flying is the most wonderful gift. I never tire of it and I never cease to be thankful to Kantees and Gally for rescuing us."

"I am glad they rescued you, Marakees, but I'm afraid you can't expect me to ever love flying."

By the time they reached the bottom of the hill and the edge of a village, the sky had filled with thickening clouds. A storm seemed inevitable.

It was apparent the villagers agreed and she could see some moving their *lukisa* hurriedly towards a large stone building. They passed a woman with her children chasing birds and putting them into a small enclosure.

Finally, they reached a very old building, overgrown with plants on the outside and tree growing up through one of the walls. But it lacked the patterning she expected to see on a Slissac construction. For that she was grateful, she had had enough of Slissac tunnels.

The path inside was swept clean, and the way lit by torches.

"The people of the village use this place for their meetings," said Marakees

It opened up into a room with more people than she was expecting. Kantees and Chara sat on stools placed on the far side of a large fire, there was an empty place between them. Chara had found clothes similar to the leather she had been wearing when Elona first met her, she wore a hood raised to keep her face in shadow.

Darrien was there and a couple of other clean-looking Taymalin lordlings. Next to Kantees was a young Kadralin man with a round face. She guessed this to be the much-spoken-of Galiko.

A woman stood slightly back from Kantees in much the way you might expect a servant to do, while Ulina stood with her hand on Kantees' left shoulder. The conversations died away as Elona entered, and she felt uncomfortable with all eyes on her.

Marakees guided her to the unclaimed stool, then went to the round-faced man. She kissed him on the cheek before standing behind him, which confirmed Elona's guess.

Kantees stood up. "I would spend time on introductions but I think most know Lady Elona of Corlain by reputation at least. And I could tell her all your names but she will probably forget them and never meet most of you again anyway.

"I have only one thing to say: I'm going away for a while with Elona and Chara. I'm not sure how long we'll be gone."

There was considerable surprise among most of the people in the room but not, Elona noted, Galiko.

"With Elona's help we brought down the Dunor yesterday, finally, and that's something I've been wanting to do for a while. Now the Taymalin lords know who they are, they will be able to deal with them properly."

"Like last time?" said the woman standing behind her.

"Not like last time, Helka. Last time they had no proof. Yesterday they had the enemy on a battlefield, and defeated them."

"How can you be sure things will change?"

One of the lordlings spoke up. "The Concordance is clear enough, Helka, any lord, or their family, found plotting against the rest will be declared dead and his title inherited as appropriate."

"Declared dead? That does not sound very final."

"It's a convenience. They can't outlaw the entire family, only the ones who actually broke the rules. It allows continuity if there are members of the family who remain innocent. So those who are found guilty become *ikenyalin*. They are considered to have died and the line of succession is followed."

Elona thought she was the only one who noticed Chara's sharp intake of breath at the word *ikenyalin*.

"Besides, what succour can you give someone who is dead? You do not give food to the dead, nor clothe them. They cannot speak and so cannot be heard. They may still breathe, but they are dead to everyone else."

"Taymalin rules," said Helka which Elona considered an odd comment since the woman was as pale-skinned as she was herself.

"This was a Taymalin war."

Kantees raised her hand and the room went silent. Elona was impressed at the respect the woman held among such a diverse group of people—especially the high-born Taymalin.

"I have spoken to Drahail and he assures me that this will happen." She turned her head to one of the Taymalin. "And already has, Lord Hendreth?"

"Yes, Kantees. I will be attending the extraordinary convocation that has been called to deal with the results of this situation. My father and older brother are now *ikenyalin*, I never expected to become the head of the family. It is not something I desired."

"I'm sorry."

He shrugged. "They brought it on themselves. And me."

Kantees turned back to the rest of them.

"The Dunor is no more, so now we will go in pursuit of the one who brought this about: the emperor."

"I heard the emperor is dead," said another of the lordlings. His accent clearly of Faerholme.

"He isn't," said Elona.

The look she got revealed her worst fears that, at least among her equals, he thought he knew all about her. She would always be branded as the mad and murderous daughter of Corlain.

"How do you know?" No pleasantries, no politeness.

Kantees sat down and Elona stood, as much as she hated it. She glanced at Kantees, wondering why she had to do this. It was irrelevant what this man thought, since she would be going after the monster regardless of what he said. Kantees had promised to come, she did not answer to them either.

"Because I was there. I was the one who drained the lake at Canvor to destroy the emperor's Fastness in Tirnia."

"I don't believe you," said the man again.

Elona looked at Kantees again, why was she allowing this?

"I vouch for Elona of Corlain," said Darrien standing up. "She froze the advance guard. I saw her defeat a hundred men of the Dunor without lifting a finger. She opened the path—no, the *gate*—between Canvor and this place with one raised hand. While she held off the army of the Dunor with the other. You saw it too. Do you doubt her power, Kline?"

He seemed slightly abashed. "I don't doubt her power."

"Then why doubt her word?"

"We were there in the Fastness of Tirnia," said Elona. "The man I cared for, Jaymis of Betlain, died there."

"I knew Jaymis," said Kline.

"He died and I could not stop it. I did all I could to bring down the emperor, but he had many patterners and I could not do it. All I was able to do was bring down the Fastness."

"And make it possible for the Dunor to attack."

"A step which has brought them down," said Kantees. "They were always arrogant, just as they attacked Jakalain prematurely. Certainly, there have been deaths at Canvor that could have been prevented had the lake not been drained. But, in the end, it was the right thing."

And I will never be able to forgive myself for the death of those innocents.

"Gally believes Elona of Corlain."

The room went silent and no one argued. Elona looked at the smiling man with the round face—was he a man? He looked barely more than a boy. Yet he was married to the woman Marakees. And the way he spoke of himself as if he was talking about someone else. As Chara had said, he was odd.

Elona searched for something to say next. "As Kantees said, I am in search of the emperor now."

"He will be declared *ikenyalin*," said the one called Kline, as if it was an apology for his earlier words.

"That doesn't matter, he is powerful and he has at least a dozen patterners who serve him. He may have more forces, and he is not afraid of employing the Farahalek."

"They require payment, if he has no lands, then he has no money."

"We may hope this is true," said Kantees standing up.

Elona sat, relieved to have someone else take the floor.

"However, Elona is not wrong, the emperor remains a danger. That is why I will be joining her on her quest for vengeance and the righting of wrongs done to her. It is the only way we can be sure he will not return."

"Who else will be going with you?" said Darrien.

"Ulina," said Ulina.

"Of course, and Chara, no more than that."

"I wish to come," said Darrien.

"I will too," said Kline.

Kantees smiled. "No. I need you to stay here. Increase our numbers and be ready in case we have need of you."

"I want to come," said Helka.

"Only the four of us will be going."

"Who is this Chara that you should choose her over me?"

Kantees turned to face Chara. Elona tensed. It seemed they did not know what she was. Why had Kantees even brought her to this meeting and placed her on an equal footing with the two of them? What was going on?

"I was born into slavery," said Kantees as if ignoring Helka's question. "And yet everyone here accepted me as their leader, even when that was the last thing I desired. All I wanted was to find my people in the mountains and hide there for the rest of my life."

As she spoke, she stepped away from her stool and walked around the fire, looking at each person in turn.

"Kline, why do you follow me?"

"You're Kantees of the Ziri."

"I am a Kadralin slave. I am not even fit to speak in your presence. I am a woman who should obey men. I am property."

He laughed as if it was a joke but his humour dried in his throat. "We are not different, Kantees."

"So, you accept me?"

"Of course, I do."

"And you would accept anyone I chose to call daughter—" she nodded at Ulina. "—or sister?" She raised her hand toward Elona.

"Of course."

"Anyone at all."

He frowned clearly sensing some trap but unable to see what it could possibly be.

"And the rest of you are the same?"

There was a chorus of assenting voices.

Elona took a moment to look at Galiko. He continued to smile almost as if he knew what was coming, perhaps he did. Elona did not think this pretty speech by Kantees could somehow cancel out the influence of two thousand years of hatred toward the Slissac, but neither could she interrupt. She prepared to protect Chara, and try not to harm anyone else.

"Look at Elona." They all stared at her making her uncomfortable again. "Her face is scarred black through the use of a terrible power that no healing can repair. And I say she is my sister though her skin beneath is the whitest and purest Taymalin." She gave a laugh. "Is anyone offended?"

The chorus this time was full of disagreement.

"So it is that I tell you now, Chara too is my sister, as much as Elona is, and that those two have been sisters for very much longer, though they were not born of the same mother. Is not the sister of my sister also my sister?"

"Of course."

"And if I told you that Chara was a Slissac?"

The silence was deep, a couple of people laughed. But Kantees was not laughing and most of her audience simply looked confused except Darrien and Ulina.

"Why would you say that?" said the new Lord Hendreth.

Kantees turned to Chara and nodded. She stood up and pulled back her hood.

There was a moment's silence as all those who did not know, rose to their feet and stared.

Elona stood too and stepped back through the ring of people so that she could see everyone, in case she needed to cast a pattern. Kantees caught her eye and shook her head. Elona however did not have Kantees' faith in her people, and she would most certainly defend her sister.

"Sit down," said Kantees turning on the spot with her arms outstretched. "Or make yourselves into liars."

"But a Slissac!" said Kline.

"Tell me, did you even think they were real? I didn't."

He did not answer.

"And if they are not real how can they be a threat."

"She's real," he said.

Kantees laughed. "Yes, she is. Chara tell them who your mother was."

"A Tay'alin wo'an of no'le 'irth, Usala. She ne'er said her fa'ily na'e."

"I don't understand what she's saying," said someone. The words were followed by something being struck and an "ouch".

Another voiced chipped in. "You ever tried understanding a

Tenyan?"

There was laughter.

"She said Usala?" said Kline.

"That was her na'e."

He looked confused. "There was a healer in my family, she was called Usala. She disappeared."

"If it was the sa'e, she found 'e and was the only 'other I knew. It is how I s'eak your language so well." She emphasised the last two words.

That brought more laughter and Elona could feel the tension in the room relaxing. Darrien cleared his throat.

"I will vouch for Chara, she is a warrior and she rides a *ziri* like she was born to it." Darrien smiled to himself and then added. "Before Elona opened the door, Chara brought down four *tekrasa* on her own, so her sister could make the patterning."

"Three," said Chara. "Only three."

"Everyone sit down," said Kantees. And they all did, although most continued to stare at Chara's strange features.

"Now we have that out of the way, I will say it again: The four of us will be leaving in the morning. I need you to continue to recruit riders and to bring in more *zirichasa* from the wilds."

"But who will be in charge in your stead?" said Helka.

"Gally of course, he is the only other that can make the golden trail—"

"But—"

Kantees held up her hand and the woman went silent.

"And you, Helka, will deal with anyone who chooses to disagree with Gally, because he is too kind and gentle."

"Gally can be hard too," he said with an even broader smile.

"But with Helka by your side, you won't need to be, my friend." She sat back down on her stool with the firelight making her skin glow. "Now, be off everyone, there's a storm coming and you need to make sure your *ziri* are safe. But Gally, Marakees and Helka, you stay please. We have some details to go over."

A little while later the remaining seven gathered closer round the fire.

CHAPTER 24

"And that's it?" said Elona.

Chara put her hand on Elona's arm. "It is all right."

"I'm trying to protect you."

"I a' grown up, Elona. Kantees and I discussed it."

"Without me."

"You needed to slee', and what is done cannot now 'e undone."

Elona said nothing more. She listened to Kantees talking to Helka and Gally, but it seemed there was no real reason for them to be there. Until Kantees turned to them as thunder shook the building.

"Are you well enough to open a path this evening?"

"I would need to be at the circle."

"I heard that was not needed, that you can do it from anywhere."

"It takes a lot of power, and only in times of great stress. I need to be close to the ley-circle to do it on command."

"What about the *ziri*?"

"What about them?"

"One of the first things I learnt was they have a huge capacity for Mother's milk."

Elona nodded. "Yes, I saw that in them too, but it's not enough to make a path. Until yesterday, I have only done it when I am in the direst need, and even then I was always close to a circle to draw on its power even if I was not aware of what I was doing."

Kantees looked disappointed.

"Is there a problem going to the ley-circle?"

"We would have to deal with the officials of Canvor, and the rest of the Taymalin. They all think they have a say in what I do. At worst I am still a slave to them, at best I am merely a woman."

Elona nodded. "I understand. Is there no other circle?"

"Only one within fast flying distance, assuming I can find it again."

"Flying."

Kantees shrugged. "We have *ziri*, so we fly. There is nothing strange in that. You are the only person for whom it is a problem."

Elona pursed her lips. "I have no desire to see Drahail, my father, or that damnable Arch-Patterner."

"Florian? No, I have no desire to see him either. He ruined my life."

Elona stared at her. "He destroyed mine."

Chara clicked. "Are you going to argue a'out who's life was hurt the 'ost?"

"No," said Kantees.

Elona took a deep breath. "How far is this other circle?"

"We had to fly for the good part of a day across the sea, but we were not flying fast so as to preserve our *ziri*'s strength. We were escaping the island."

"So we must fly across the sea?"

"The ley-circle is deep within the ocean. We found it during a feeding."

"That must have been interesting."

"Very, but the *ziri* were tired and we did not tarry."

Elona thought. "But if we know it's there, the *ziri* can fly fast to it."

"We only know the rough direction."

"I can sense a ley-circle from a distance."

"I too, and the *ziri*, of course."

"Very well. Since we must have a circle in order to get away from this place, let it be that one."

THE STORM CONTINUED to lash the island for most of the remainder of the afternoon, but then blew itself out in time for a strikingly colourful sunset.

Elona and Chara stood outside the hut where she had awoken and watched the display.

"We do not have to go back to the Slissac town," said Chara as fitful gusts of the vanishing storm tugged at her hood, and she had to hold it in place. It was common knowledge now that she was a Slissac, but Kantees' people kept their distance and tried not to stare.

"We have to re-establish your position," said Elona, "and besides, I have been thinking. If the Slissac created the *Kisharuk*, then they should know how to get rid of it."

"They might, but would that knowledge be in the town?"

"If not there, then somewhere."

Marakees approached them from the side and curtsied. "Lady Elona, Lady Chara, my mistress says they are ready to leave. The *ziri* have eaten and are strong. I can show you the way."

"Thank you."

They followed her across the open space, watched by the curious collection of riders, and down the slope on the other side.

Sheesha's gaudy plumage of blue and gold stood out against the browns, greys and blacks of the wild *ziri*. There were nine in total. She understood why Kantees always flew with riderless *zirichasa*, their combined power was more effective. The bigger the formation, the faster they could fly.

"You will ride Ilith," said Kantees pointing at a large *ziri* with a saddle and reins. "He is used to carrying people of little experience."

Elona's heart froze.

"Alone? You're not serious."

Kantees' anger was not hidden though she did not shout. "Sulassa cannot carry two, and we all have our own. It would be too complex to have you carried, you must learn to at least stay on the back of a *ziri* even if you are never a rider."

Elona held up her hand. "You must understand I may be sick."

"I'll make sure you are at the back of the formation."

Elona glanced round and saw that Chara was already on her *ziri*'s back. Marakees led the way to Ilith, who lay quite flat as they approached, and remained motionless as she mounted.

"It is a lot easier without a saddle," said Marakees as she strapped Elona in and helped her put her boots in the stirrups. "Try not to tell him what to do, and he'll just follow the others."

"Like a horse," said Elona. She could try to pretend it was a horse, except it would be very far from the ground.

"I've seen a horse," said the woman. "From a distance."

"Thank you for your help, Marakees."

"It has been my honour, Lady Elona. Something to tell our children."

She turned away, curtsied to Chara, and then hurried to the edge of the clearing.

Kantees looked round to check everything was ready. Ulina was mounted on her *ziri* and the others seemed restless and ready to fly as if they sensed a great adventure.

Elona could not hold back a squeal of fright as Ilith bounded into the air. His wings beat harder, pressing them upwards. Within moments they were high above the trees. Elona slammed her eyes shut but without anyone to hold on to, that made it worse.

She tried opening them just a little, enough to get a vague impression of Ilith's undulating neck, and the horizon. She told herself that if she could just focus on the distance it would be all right.

But it wasn't.

Her stomach heaved and she turned as far round as she could to throw up, desperately trying not to get anything on Ilith's feathers.

If he noticed there was no reaction.

Her mouth tasted like a sewer and she felt faint as they passed further inland. They seemed to be going in completely the wrong direction, her inner sense told her they were getting closer to the castle ley-circle instead of further away, and passing by it to her left.

She felt confused and brought her hand up to rub it down her face. She had a headache starting as well. *I do not want to fly!*

The *ziri* formation heeled over to the left sharply and their orientation changed abruptly. The ley circle was now directly ahead of them and she could feel the command to the *zirichasa*, making them increase their speed.

In her discomfort, Elona was hit by a flash of clarity that burned away all the doubt and pain—just for a moment. Kantees expected her to make the path while circling a ley-circle over the ocean, even assuming they could find it—after half a day of being on the back of Ilith.

But she could barely focus after this short time.

Plus they hadn't used this circle because they did not want to negotiate with the Taymalin lords. Yet it was a perfectly good ley-circle, and they were flying towards it in a straight line.

She felt the pleasure of coming vengeance. It helped to settle her and focus her mind.

They were coming up on the ley-circle fast now and she could feel Kantees readying herself to drive the *ziri* into their golden light.

Elona settled back in the saddle as best she could and closed her eyes again. It was easier now that she had a purpose. She felt the power of the ley-circle and let it come to her.

She had spent several moon-turns in the Slissac town with Chara and she knew its ley-circle—knew how it felt. This was so much easier when she was not also maintaining a protective shield. She felt through the World's Pattern until she found it.

The *ziri*'s magic light burst around her, penetrating her eyelids with its golden glow.

And she pulled the two ley-circles together.

She heard three human gasps, as she felt them penetrate the boundary and what had been there became here. The golden light vanished and she was instantly chilled to the bone by the icy blast.

She opened her eyes but it was completely black. They were flying through something that stung her skin.

She threw a small ball of light forward, above Kantees' head so as not to blind her.

They were in a snow storm.

A stream of epithets poured from Kantees' mouth, though Elona could barely hear her in the freezing wind but she did not need a pattern-sense to know her sister was angry.

They must have reached a place where the cloud was thinner because daylight came through but it did nothing to help. Except reveal looming crags wrapped in more cloud.

"More light!" screamed Kantees.

Elona obeyed by expanding the size of the ball and drawing more power from the local ley-circle. She knew it was the right one. Kantees turned the *ziri* back towards it then started to descend in a tight spiral.

By expanding the bubble of light even further and moving it below them Elona was able to make sure they could see any problems. But they seemed to be descending into a valley, not that she recognised it. She had never visited the Slissac circle.

She was freezing now, her skin was probably turning blue, where it wasn't already black, and her teeth chattered. She had not been this cold since she had walked over the mountains. She had survived that, she could survive this.

Finally, they saw the ground, very close, and moments later landed in the middle of the ley-circle, though it was barely twenty paces across. The *ziri* all moved closer to one another. Elona unstrapped herself and slipped off, landing face down in the snow because she had lost all feeling in her legs. The impact intensified her headache and she scraped her arm in the process.

She managed to get into a sitting position, leaning against Ilith who lay down beside her. A pair of boots arrived in front of her. She looked up through the swirling snow at Kantees.

"Mother's tits! What did you do?"

Elona closed her eyes, she was tired. Her body needed time to recover.

"There's no need for foul language. You've been spending too much time with those lordlings. Anyway, we're here."

"What about the plan?"

"The plan?" said Elona. "At what point did you tell me we would be flying over the castle ley-circle?"

"It was obvious we should get the power from there for as long as we could."

"To you! Not me. It's equally *obvious* that if you expect me to make a path from the back of a *ziri* after flying for half a day, then I should be able to do it from the back of a *ziri* when I'm not exhausted."

"You all need to get out of the cold," said Chara. "There's a tunnel o'er there."

Elona was so stiff and cold she needed help getting to her feet but Ilith let her lean on his warm feathers as they followed Chara to where a hole gaped in the side of a mountain. If it had ever been natural it wasn't any longer, every surface had felt a chisel and there were patterns worked into its surface. Slissac without a doubt.

Chara ran her fingers across some of the indentations.

"I a' ho'e."

But she did not seem very happy about it.

CHAPTER 25

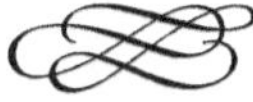

They moved deeper into the tunnel and out of the biting wind, though the air did not get any warmer. Elona fed a little power into the moss and the walls around them glowed with a dim blue light. It was easier than maintaining the light herself.

"Where are we?" said Kantees.

"The ley-circle at Hanna," said Chara. "It is where I was 'orn, where 'y family has its *etukala*—" she hesitated for a moment, "—that 'eans na'e-place. There is no hu'an word for it."

"If the plan was for us to wait outside while you two to do whatever you need in this town, it's not going to work," said Kantees. "The *ziri* can cope with the cold, but we all need food and the name of this place is nowhere."

"You'll have to come with us," said Elona.

"Into a town full of Slissac."

"I can send you back."

"Oh no, princess, you don't get to sacrifice your pasty-white Taymalin skin to save humanity all on your own. You need my help."

"Not if you're just going to complain and present impossible conditions." She counted off on her fingers. "Either you stay here, or you come with us, or you go back."

"Sto' it, 'oth of you," said Chara. "Right now we should rest, it will be dawn soon. Then Elona and I will go into Hanna. You can choose what you want to do then."

The two eyed one another but Kantees turned away as Sheesha raised his wing, and she climbed beneath it. The other *zirichasa* drew closer together and Elona saw Ulina climb under another wing.

Chara looked in her direction. "You slee'. I'll stay on watch."

"Are you sure?"

"I' not tired and the *ziri* are war' enough."

Elona nodded, opening the gate had taken more out of her than she was willing to admit, and she needed to be fresh to face a town of angry matriarchs.

"Yes, all right but wake me if you need me."

Ilith was directly behind her when she turned to find him, she nudged his wing with her foot and he lifted it. It was warm beneath the cocoon of feathers and though she had only woken a relatively short time before, she was soon asleep again.

THE *ZIRICHAK* SHIFTED BENEATH HER, she felt as if she was falling and came awake with a shudder. She wiped her hand across her face, and felt the dry hard skin of her scars.

She had almost forgotten them, and the way her untouched skin pulled against them when she talked, or smiled. Not that there was much to smile about.

With a shove of her hand, Ilith's wing moved out of the way and cold air poured in on her, along with brilliant sunlight reflected down the tunnel. She pushed herself to her feet and looked across the feathered mounds of sleeping *zirichasa*.

A silhouette stood at the entrance.

Elona picked her way between the squash of bodies and then made her way down the passage, her boots making solid thumps that echoed slightly. The figure did not turn though she must have been aware of Elona's presence.

"Here we are," said Chara.

Elona just put her arm through her sister's and rested her head on her shoulder. She had no response.

"I need to tell you so'ething."

Elona could feel her tension and wondered what could be so important.

"You can tell me anything."

Chara shifted and sighed. "Slissac do not make babies the same way as your people."

Elona gave a short laugh. "I was not expecting that."

"What?"

"We don't usually talk about that sort of thing."

"Usala did not know what to tell 'e as I grew up. She was wise enough to understand things 'ight not be the sa'e. Especially as 'y 'ody is not like yours."

"Similar."

"Two arms, two legs, a body, a head. You could say the sa'e for a *nachak*."

Elona nodded and looked out at the stark mountains, crags and slopes highlighted in snow and shadow. She had crossed terrain like this wearing barely more than a shift. Half-frozen. She should have died a hundred times over. Only the healing that lived within her had kept her moving but even that could not last forever.

It had failed in Avakending. It was almost not enough back at the castle gate.

She was as mortal as anyone else.

And Chara was talking about babies.

"What about making babies? Do you lay eggs?"

"No, we do not!" Chara was suddenly hot with anger. Then she forced herself to calm down. "Sorry, that is an insult a'ong the Slissac. Only lower species lay eggs."

"Oh, Mother's milk, I'm sorry. I didn't know."

"Of course, you didn't." Chara reached round and patted

Elona's arm. "How could you? But no, that is not the secret." She paused. "I have been im'regnated."

"And I made love with Jaymis. You didn't say you had met someone here."

"Elona," said Chara very seriously. "You 'ust sto' thinking the Slissac are like you. You've 'een here, you know the 'atriarchs are in a constant 'attle."

"Yes, but—"

"I told you before, we do not have feelings for males. They are mostly useful for just three things, serving, fighting and breeding."

"Did you think that before you came to this place?"

"I did not think of it at all."

The sky was clear save for ragged clumps of cloud tearing across the blue expanse. The sun had not yet pulled itself above the mountains, but their snowy tips were brilliant white.

"What is it you're trying to tell me? Are you having a child? I promise not to interrupt."

"I have been im'regnated. That does not 'ean I a' with child, 'ut I can start it whene'er I choose."

Elona was silent as the full meaning of Chara words became apparent. "His seed is in you now?"

"Yes."

"Whose?"

"It doesn't 'atter. He was strong and healthy, and of a good line. He was costly."

"You make him sound like breeding stock."

And then she understood. They didn't say anything for a while.

"How long does it last?" she said finally. "The seed."

"A few years."

"Does it—does it seem strange?"

"It feels natural to 'e."

Elona squeezed Chara's hand. "I don't know what I should say, if you were with child, I could be happy and congratulate you. This is not a thing I understand."

"I know. You don't ha'e to say anything at all. There is a cele'ration at the time, usually, 'ut I did not have one."

Elona felt lost, when Savi had become pregnant everybody knew what had happened—her friend had told her everything—but beyond that nobody talked about the details. It was not polite. Yet the Slissac had a party when the matriarch was—her mind rebelled against it—impregnated. Then she laughed at herself, she had lost all shame in regard to her own person yet was now embarrassed because Chara was different.

"Perhaps we can have a celebration," she said finally.

"I would like that."

There were footsteps behind them followed by heavy talons scratching on stone.

"Why is no one here?" said Kantees. "Don't they defend their ley-circle?"

They both turned. The woman emerged from the shadows with Sheesha's head looming over her, while the rest of him was lost in the dark of the cave.

"Who 'rom?" said Chara.

"I don't know, other Slissac? Us?"

"It's not the same here."

"You mean Slissac don't fight each other?"

Elona turned to look at her sister, wondering what sort of answer she was going to give. The Slissac families were in a constant battle one with another.

"Custom," was Chara's only response.

"How are we going to do this?" said Elona. "You belong here—I'm barely tolerated but how do we explain all the rest? How do we get in? How do we stop them from trying to kill us all?"

"It's not going to 'e easy," said Chara. "'ut whatever ha''ens you need your hair re'oved, Elona."

She nodded as she ran her hand across the bristles. She had been in two minds, this resolved the question.

"Ulina can do it," said Kantees. "But why?"

"Hair is a sign o' an animal."

Kantees grinned. "I always knew that."

❀

THEY HAD EATEN as well as they could and after the plans had been laid Elona and Chara headed along the tunnel while Kantees held the rest back at the circle.

Elona conjured a light above them which illuminated the patternings along the length of the straight passageway. The place was familiar inasmuch as Elona had been in many Slissac tunnels. It had never occurred to her to wonder how they were made, but now she had perhaps an idea, after she had breached the walls of the Fastness.

Even then the carving of the symbols would have been a mighty task, and she had never seen a Slissac tunnel that lacked them. She shook her head and thought perhaps she would never understand.

The tunnel brought them out on to the side of a mountain and the road immediately split into two levels. The central higher path and two running parallel to it on either side. They stayed on the middle one. A short time later they met another road where a complex arrangement of tunnels and bridges joined the three levels.

As they followed the climbing path, surrounded by mountains, it came around a ridge and the black blocks of the Slissac town, partly buried in a mountainside, came into view and the road split again so there were now three levels.

That they were observed from the walls was not a question. It did not take long before a group of soldiers came through the side gates and deployed along the road. The central gate also opened and a female Slissac figure emerged.

Two people without an entourage using the high caste road and no message sent ahead caused problems: it would have to be established exactly who they were before any decision could be made. Though killing them where they stood was the highest on the list.

Elona brought up her hood to hide her face, the material sliding over her freshly shaven head. She dropped back half a pace. While she had been accorded equivalent status to Chara through the sister-binding, she was not a matriarch. She then reached out to Sheesha and gave him a nudge.

Chara did not hesitate and continued forward at a steady stride.

"I will protect you," said Elona.

"I know, 'ut this is worse than the 'irst ti'e."

"But you know how things work now."

"That's why."

"Kantees will be on her way."

"I wish it was only us."

"Nothing bad will happen," said Elona. If only she believed that herself, with the Slissac everything was a battle. "Who's that on the road?"

"Gate Warden. She only comes out when it's important."

"We *are* important."

It took a considerable amount of time to reach the town but eventually they were within speaking distance of the female Slissac who barred their path. There were over a dozen soldiers ranged on each side of the road, all with crossbows. More archers stood on the walls.

Elona kept her head down and tried to keep her scarred face most visible, since it most resembled Slissac skin.

Chara gestured to her and she stopped. Her sister continued forwards a few steps. Elona relaxed and spread her senses.

There followed a challenge and Elona recognised Chara reeling off her name, giving her family, lands and lineage back through who knew how many years.

As she did so, Elona noticed the soldiers had become unsettled. It wasn't as if they would not know who she was, so why was this a problem?

Elona reacted without thinking even before the twang of a crossbow reached her ears. The shape of the bolt pierced the patterns. It flashed into flame and there was the slightest chink as the metal of its tip landed on the stone of the road. But Elona had already thrown up the blue barrier to encompass the three of them.

The bolts that followed did not get as far.

Chara was now shouting angrily at the Gate Warden, and gesticulating. The Slissac was, as much as Elona could tell, looking nervous and uncertain. She replied to Chara's words. Then shouted through the barrier. The soldiers lowered their weapons. Elona had a good look to ensure they were safe and let the protection drop. The blue wall evaporated. One of the soldiers lay on the ground with two others standing over him.

"What's going on?" said Elona.

Chara did not answer but asked her own question equally short and commanding.

The answer that came was halting, and lengthy.

Chara turned. "I'm being invaded!"

Some of the soldiers were now looking up and one of them called to the Gate Warden.

The crossbows were raised again, this time pointing at the sky.

Chara made another short and pointed statement. Elona was getting back into the rhythms of the language, even though she had barely managed to make herself understood in it, she had been able to follow the meaning by the time she left. Chara was using a particularly demeaning mode of address.

The Warden barked another order, the crossbows were dropped and the men moved at a run back towards the gates—apart from the one that had fired the first bolt. He was not moving at all.

"What do you mean invaded?" said Elona.

"I've been gone too long."

"Less than a five-day!"

Chara turned and waved at the formation of *zirichasa* turning in circles above them. Three broke away from the others and spiralled down.

"Can't they hurry up?"

Elona kept an eye on the town gates and walls as the *ziri* landed. Chara ran over and threw herself on to Sulassa's back. Elona cursed under her breath as Ilith waddled over to her and flattened himself against the road. She climbed into the saddle and slipped her feet into the stirrups.

"Go now!" commanded Chara and all three launched on thudding wingbeats—Ilith slightly behind the others as Elona fumbled with the belt buckle.

They joined forces with Kantees and the riderless *zirichasa* within moments.

"We need to go to my *ichakah*," said Chara pointing into the town.

Home—palace—throne of power translated Elona in her head.

"Where?" called Kantees.

"On the right, the last one before the cliff. They won't be expecting an attack from above."

The *ziri* formation turned just as something rounded rose above the blocky buildings of the town.

"*Tekrak!*" she called.

From her position near the back, she saw the others look that way. And did not miss Ulina reaching for her knife.

"Plenty of time!"

The *ziri* accelerated as one. Ilith might know how to behave with inexperienced riders but he wasn't slow. Elona shut her eyes as they careened towards the city and over the walls then realised she could not protect them like that. The wall guards watched them flying over but none raised a hand or a weapon. The strange roads curved among the buildings and high walkways spanned the gaps between them.

Some functions of the town required cooperation despite the constant struggle for power among the matriarchs. The constant battling made the rebellion of the Taymalin lords look like child's play.

The *tekrak* had barely cleared the buildings when the *zirichasa* were approaching the roof of the building. Ulina and Chara leapt from their mounts before they had even touched the ground. Elona had never seen Chara like this—yes, she was a great hunter but when she had become a matriarch, she had been so uncertain, still grieving the loss of her mother, and begged Elona to stay.

But Elona had her own path and vengeance to enact.

This new Chara moved with purpose. Much had happened to both of them.

Elona undid the buckle as Ilith landed and managed to dismount quickly, as Kantees gestured to Sheesha and he led the *ziri* off the rooftop.

Chara had opened a hatch in the roof and Elona caught a glimpse of Ulina dropping out of sight.

"How will she know who the enemy are?" said Elona as she hurried up.

Chara turned and pointed at the *tekrak*. "Can you sto' that?"

"I'm not letting you go in without me."

Kantees sat on the edge of the hatch space and dropped through.

Chara put her hand on Elona's arm. "I want you with me, sister."

"Should I destroy it?"

"Can you sto' them without killing?"

Elona hesitated for a moment then looked around at the bare surface of the roof. "Give me your cloak."

Chara shrugged it off her shoulders. Elona took her knife and rapidly slit the cloak into lengths. "We need to make a ball."

The *tekrak*'s fire tube was burning and the creature picked up speed. Its gondola was packed with soldiers. Chara tied off two ends and handed Elona the cloth ball.

"I've never done this before. I might kill them all."

"What's the delay?" Kantees' voice floated up.

Elona tossed the ball upwards and pictured the ball of fire back at the castle. The pattern formed in the ball and it erupted in flame. Elona drove it with all her will away from her and straight at the gondola hanging below the approaching *tekrak*.

The Slissac on board had no chance to react.

The fireball struck the patterner in the chest setting him alight, and the flames quickly spread to the ropes and roots.

Elona turned away, sat on the edge of the hatch, grabbed the other side and swung down. She let go with her hands and came to a jarring landing.

"We arranged a table," said Kantees. "You missed it."

Chara landed on the solid surface and was able to pull the hatch down and slid the bolts.

"Just had to deal with the *tekrak*," said Elona brushing her hands.

"How do we know which to kill?" said Ulina.

"'Y clan will 'e hiding 'ehind sealed doors in the … heart-room. All else are ene'y."

A muted explosion rumbled through the walls and yellow light momentarily shone through the gaps around the hatch.

Chara turned and led the way out of the room. "Come on."

CHAPTER 26

The passageways were not dark, lit as they were by ledges filled with glowing moss. The three sisters hurried along the corridors, Chara knew where she was going. Elona and Kantees followed.

Elona was curious about the Kadralin woman, she carried no weapons but did not seem concerned that death might strike at them at any moment. Perhaps she trusted the child to deal with any adversary.

Ulina was not with them.

"There is no one alive on this level," was all she had said when they set off.

And they had encountered no one. Nor any bodies, but there were plenty of rooms they had not checked. Once they had descended the first flight of steps she had gone forward and disappeared from sight.

Unlike in a human building, the Slissac did not build their stairs stacked in one place, but spread them out. It was further confused by the need to have different routes depending on the person's rank. Elona had been lost more than once when they first came to this place, and she barely remembered her way about now.

They headed down some stairs and almost tripped over a pair of bodies. Fresh blood trickled from their knife wounds. Ulina stood to one side, blood spattered across her clothes.

Chara turned one of them onto his back and studied at the symbols on his leather armour.

"Kiyoreth."

"What's that?" said Kantees.

Chara looked distracted as if she was remembering.

Elona responded. "Family name."

Chara said something in the Slissac tongue, Elona caught some of her words.

"Blood feud. This the family that tried to wipe out the Aytrueth—Chara's family—years ago."

"This way," said Chara and headed down the passage to the right.

Ulina darted away and ran ahead.

"How far to this heart room?" said Kantees as they followed Chara at fast pace.

"We need to get below ground level and into the cliff."

"They know we're here. They'll be sending reinforcements. This heart room is a usual thing for Slissac?"

"It is."

"They will know where we'll be going as well then. Ulina won't be able to kill an army by herself."

"She won't be alone."

They descended several more levels without incident and came to a halt in a room that Elona recognised. One of the main eating areas, chairs and tables filled it making it look particularly normal.

"No fireplaces," said Kantees.

"It never gets very cold in here."

"All this stone, it doesn't suit me."

Chara stood in the middle of the room and looked from door to door.

Ulina slipped in through a gap.

"Many Slissac from here onward."

"How 'any?" said Chara.

"Thirty I have seen. More I have heard."

"Shut the doors," said Elona.

Ulina moved fast and did so.

"What do we do now?" said Elona.

"We have to get to the heart-room," said Chara.

Kantees put her head on one side. "Why?"

"That's where my clan are."

"But the problem isn't—"

Her last words were cut off by Slissac shouts from behind the door in the direction Ulina had warned them about. The girl leapt toward the entrance as someone fumbled with the handle.

Elona threw up her arm and a wall of blue covered the door.

"They'll go for the other doors," said Kantees.

"What caste are the soldiers?" said Elona.

Ulina had been creeping around the edge of the room, she pointed at the next door along. The blue barrier extended along the wall until it took in that one as well.

"What do you 'ean?" said Chara.

"Are they above or the same as the servants here?"

Ulina indicated the next door. The barrier encompassed it.

"A'o'e," said Chara.

"And that one's a servant door." Elona nodded towards the almost invisible outline in the wall to one side.

"Yes."

"What good will that do?" said Kantees, as Elona extended the barrier in the other direction as Ulina indicated.

"Because the soldiers won't see it."

"That's crazy."

"No," said Chara with sudden realisation. "She's right. I' 'een here so long I 'arely e'en notice it. E'en the middling rank doors in the 'igger houses."

Ulina was already there and working on finding the mechanism to open it. Moments later it swung back.

"They need to think you're running," said Kantees and headed for the last main door that was not blocked by the protection wall.

"They'll kill you."

"Have to catch me first. Ulina—you stay with Elona and Chara."

"Mama—"

The word seemed strange coming from the child's mouth.

"I will not die. No time to talk. Go."

Chara hesitated at the door then shook her head and stepped across the threshold. Ulina paused a moment looking at Kantees then turned and followed Chara.

Kantees reached the exit and opened it carefully. She turned back and nodded. Elona stepped back into the darkness of the servants' passage and let the protection wall drop as she closed the door.

She heard an angry shout from Kantees followed by the sound of many feet thudding through the room. She wanted to pull all the heat from the room but could not afford to do anything that might give them away. Instead she turned and followed the other two along the dimly lit tunnel.

"She will be all right," Elona said to Ulina.

"I know."

The passageway sloped down steeply then turned and went off into the dark. The moss was not lit. But rather than light all of it, which she knew would leak to other areas and perhaps alert the enemy, Elona gathered some of the moss and held it to herself. Once it was glowing sufficiently, she passed some to Chara and gathered more.

They continued for a while until Chara stopped at a junction.

"I don't know where we are."

"I will look," said Ulina and darted away to the right.

Elona tried to imagine where they were in relation to the main passageways but she felt defeated too.

There was a risk but she sat on the floor.

"I'll see what I can see."

She let her senses go, an easy thing to do in this dark silent place.

Sparks of life were the first things to show. Chara, of course, but also the tiny creatures lurking in the walls. Scared to be seen but looking hopefully for food that might have been dropped.

She found Ulina and her blade. There was something about the walls too, they did not block her perception but they were noticeable, beyond what she would expect, as if they had power gathered into them. Except a short distance ahead where her perception was blocked by a wall of intense and powered patterning.

The Slissac she found too. A lot of them moving around in groups of two and three but there was a crowd of them ahead and down from where they were. It was easy enough to make out the shapes of the corridors there were so many of them—it seemed familiar. She opened her eyes to find the moss glowing gently. She had much better control now but it seemed as if these plants responded to any power.

"I think I found it. We're not far, but there are fifty or more soldiers gathered around a door."

Chara sighed. "I wish I could see what you see." Then she shook her head. "How can we win against them?"

"What do we have to do?"

"This is 'y house, if I cannot hold it then I do not deserve to have it."

"What would happen to you?"

"I do not know."

"I can kill many." Ulina had arrived, despite the light she had managed to do so without them noticing. "But not fifty."

Elona looked at the child, she felt a strange kinship since she too had slaughtered people. It left scars.

"But you could deal with any stragglers if they were on the run."

"Easily."

"We need to get into the heart-roo'."

Elona turned at a sudden sound only to realise Chara was shaking with mirth and the noise of her clicks echoed through the tunnels.

"Is she unwell?" said Ulina.

"Laughing," said Elona but stared in non-comprehension.

"If you can find the way, sister," said Chara gasping for breath. "We shall walk there."

"This passageway?"

Chara nodded then her clicking ceased abruptly. "Yes and no, we can use the passage to get there but I cannot use a servant's door. I will lose 'y rank, they will not o'ey."

"This is ridiculous," said Elona.

"It is our way."

"Is it the passage that matters or the door?"

"It's what they see that's im'ortant.

Elona shook her head. "What if we made our own door?"

Chara looked as if she wanted to protest but finally said. "I don't know."

"That's all we need. You come through a door that isn't the servant's one, and you will still be their matriarch."

"I don't know if that will work."

"It's that or we leave."

Chara held out her hand, Elona took it and was pulled to her feet by her sister.

With hands clasped they continued along the passage. Ulina ran on ahead.

Shortly afterwards they passed over the top of the crowd at the door of the heart-room. Elona could feel the power pulsing through its doors and walls.

"I can 'eel something," said Chara. She stopped and looked at her fingertips. "'Ower. It 'akes 'y skin tingle."

"You can feel it?"

Chara stared at her and nodded.

"It's some sort of patterning around the heart-room. It's strong and is keeping the attackers out, I think. I met something like this in Tirnia."

"Can we get through it?"

"We'll cross that bridge when we come to it."

They kept moving and came up to Ulina who was standing at a junction.

"This way," said Elona and went left. "Stay with us, Ulina, we won't meet anyone now."

Less than a hundred paces later they reached a door. It too was suffused with the pattern.

"That answers that question," said Elona.

"Why the servants didn't leave the roo'?"

Elona nodded.

Chara touched her hand to the door. Elona saw a sudden shift in the pattern and was too late in pulling Chara back before the pattern collapsed.

"It's gone," she said in wonderment and stared at her hand.

"It's all gone, the others will be able get in."

I'm going to hate this, Elona thought as she placed her hands against the wall beside the door. *At least it isn't as thick as the Fastness.*

She focused on the patterns that made up the stones and drew the power from it. She heard Ulina start to cough as the wall disintegrated in front of her.

I hope Chara's people don't try to kill me when I break through.

She took half a step forward, all conscious thought left her as she encompassed only the pattern of the stone and the power she drew from it. Storing it within herself like a *zirichak.*

Another step.

The air was filled with dust and her lungs too, yet somehow she continued to breathe, just as she had at the Fastness. More magic.

Then she fell through, the smell was intensely unpleasant and the air seemed thick, hot and heavy. There were clicks, grunts and voices. She felt Chara step past her as a thunderous crash echoed through the heart-room. The attackers were breaking in. In the background of her thoughts, she heard Chara speaking so quickly it was impossible to follow.

Moments later the servants' door opened and there was the sound of many running feet headed away. Ulina helped Elona into a sitting position.

The door thundered again. They must have some sort of battering ram.

She looked around trying to understand how they might restore the barrier. It was tied to Chara somehow as the matriarch. And she had been able to feel its power, was she *fahain* too, or was it just because she was Slissac?

The door crashed again this time something splintered and she heard a cheer go up from outside.

"Help me to the door."

Elona leaned heavily on Ulina as she staggered across the stone floor.

A line of Chara's soldiers formed up to make a defence when the attackers broke through, and Chara was standing with them slightly in advance.

The final stroke of the battering ram shattered the main bolt. One of the hinges gave way and the left-hand door shuddered open. The first of the attacking soldiers slipped through screaming.

Elona waved her hand and the blue protection barrier lit up in front of them—bringing their charge to an instant halt.

They hesitated, not expecting any real opposition.

Chara shouted something at them. Demanding. Challenging.

Elona felt the power inside her boiling, needing to go somewhere —either that or she would have to sleep. She was not sure which.

The soldiers stood to one side and a senior stepped through. Another male.

Before he even had a chance to speak, Chara spat words at him.

He retreated.

"What was that?" said Elona.

"I told him I would speak with a matriarch or no one, and if he did not remove his forces, they would all die." She turned more towards Elona and spoke in a lower tone as if anyone who heard her words could understand. "Can you do that?"

Elona nodded. "Soon would be best though."

"Now would be good, sister."

Elona nodded again. "I'll have to drop the barrier."

Ulina slipped away as Elona closed her eyes. It was easy to perceive the space behind the door and she let herself soak into the patterns.

She released the barrier as she let the energy within her flow into the air and the stones beyond. Behind her eyes she perceived the soldiers in the room racing forwards, but did not let the sounds of fighting and death distract her.

Elona drew the power she had stolen from the wall and fed it into the air on the other side of the door and, when that was gone, she reached out to the ley-circle. Slissac cried out in fear and pain.

Warm air from beyond the broken doors touched her unscarred cheek.

With her inner sight she watched the patterns of living creatures slump to the floor, and others flee. The air heated up and brought with it the scent of burning leather and flesh.

Then there were other screams and the roaring of monsters.

Someone touched her arm and she opened her eyes to see Ulina standing beside her. "Mother comes."

It took Elona a moment to understand then cut off the flow of power.

"It will take a while to cool down," she said as the girl darted away towards the door through which a trace of smoke drifted.

Elona gathered her thoughts and took in the scene. The Slissac attackers were dead, as were several of Chara's men.

The *zirichak* noises echoed through the passageways again much closer. The remaining soldiers moved into defensive positions by the door as a feathered head snaked round it, pushing in the crumbling doors.

Chara shouted at the soldiers to remain still and pushed through them.

"Sulassa!"

The creature made a curious sound, almost cooing as it pushed its body through the gap, tearing what remained of the doors off their hinges. She was followed by two more *ziri*, one of which was Ilith.

Ulina was gone.

The hall was large but looked strangely small when occupied by three creatures that settled down to preening in the middle of the room. One of them sneezed.

Elona crossed to her sister. "What now?"

Chara looked at the bodies, the damage and the *zirichasa*.

She gestured to one of the soldiers and snapped a series of instructions at him. He passed out further orders to his men and they headed for the main entrance while the other went for the servant's door but did not enter.

"My people will get this cleaned up but I cannot show weakness," she said turning back to Elona. "Will you accompany me to the council?"

"Of course."

Elona had been able to scare the senior matriarchs with the threat of power, but now she would be able to demonstrate it. She already had. If the *ziri* and Ulina had not killed every soldier then word will have got back. She corrected herself, if none had survived that too would be sufficient proof.

They went to the corridor and viewed the carnage for the first time. Heat still emanated from the walls, though the air itself was cooler. Blackened bodies lay on the ground, one in particular looked as if it had died crawling away. Elona touched her hand to her cheek feeling the hard crust.

The soldier who had been sent out was searching the bodies, Chara waited and watched until he found something and proceeded to attack it with a knife. He came hurrying back, went down on one knee in front of Chara and held up what he had found. A piece of cloth, a symbol of some sort.

Chara took it without a word and together they headed out along the main passage, with the *ziri* following noisily behind. The route to the heart room was not too complicated though it involved several complete turns and junctions. And it was not long before they were breathing fresh air and the light of the day stood ahead of them.

Zirichasa guarded the entrance.

CHAPTER 27

There were few windows in the black blocks of buildings that surrounded them in a curiously haphazard arrangement. Snow still covered everything but the ground had been churned up by dozens of Slissac feet and the talons of the *ziri*.

Sheesha was a chaotic splash of colour against the monochromatic town, while the other dun coloured *ziri* seemed to fit in well. Kantees came over, she had stains of blood on her clothes and her arm was bandaged.

"I'm glad you're not dead," she said.

"Much trouble?"

"Not really, once I was out, I'd already called Sheesha so he made sure it was safe."

"Do you want me to heal you?" said Elona.

"Not yet," said Chara. "We will go as we are, battle worn and angry."

"Go where?"

Elona looked up at the cliff. "In there."

"We will fly on the *ziri*," said Chara.

Elona's heart fell. She remembered the audience chamber and the large cave mouth that gave out onto the cliff-face. Flying round to it would be the easiest and fastest way but not something she wanted to do.

"'Ut there's so'ething I 'ust do first."

She walked out into the centre of the space between the harsh buildings. Ulina hurried after her. Elona worried about the Slissac seeing a human girl but it was far too late to be concerned about that. With Chara so exposed, Elona was ready to throw a defensive wall in case of attack.

Then Chara began to shout, it was almost a chant. Elona caught the occasional word.

"What's she saying?" said Kantees.

"It's a demand. I heard the name of the family that attacked. I think she's demanding their matriarch meet her in the council chamber."

"Good move."

Elona nodded and kept her eyes on her sister. "You know they hate humans here. They won't kill me because I'm officially sister to a matriarch."

"You made me a sister too."

"If they acknowledge it, and Ulina is a different matter."

"I'll kill any that threaten her."

"Well, she's your daughter so that will make a difference."

Chara had finished her challenge and stood in the silent snow, holding herself taut. Then she held up her hands and clapped three times in quick succession. Sulassa launched into the air, glided low to where Chara stood and landed neatly behind her.

"That's impressive," said Kantees, "she's only been riding her a two-day at most."

Elona sighed. "She's a natural."

Then Ulina whistled and Halenth did the same. The two of them mounted.

"She has the sight," said Kantees watching Chara thoughtfully as Sheesha waddled up to her.

Elona felt Ilith's breath on her hair and sighed. She had to mount and strap herself in quickly because Chara was waiting for her.

"This should be interesting," said Kantees and watched as Sulassa launched into the air closely followed by Halenth. Sheesha's wings thundered as he went up, Ilith was gentler but they were soon flying with the riderless *ziri* coming up behind them.

As Elona watched Kantees leaned in to Sheesha and whispered to him, she heard him grumble and Kantees slapped his neck. "You don't need to, so let her."

The *zirichasa* moved together effortlessly as if in a dance they all knew, but this time Sheesha was not at the head of the diamond formation. Sulassa took that position with Ilith and Halenth in the second rank. Sheesha was at the centre being flanked and followed by the others.

Ulina was the one who seemed the most surprised and she turned to stare at her mother but she just laughed. "Sheesha needs to learn some humility."

Chara led the formation in a spiralling climb above the town, to make a very clear point. Then she headed out along the valley above the road.

Elona smiled. When you are untouchably high above all others, what rank does that make you?

They flew faster and faster.

And the golden pattern wrapped itself around the formation. The *ziri* pulled their wings in and, arrow straight, they shot across the sky. After a few moments the formation banked as one and pulled around in a great curve with the mountains flashing beneath them. Elona could feel the ley-circle beneath them, and the energy flowing from it to power the pattern.

She glanced over her shoulder to smile at Kantees but the expression on her sister's dark face was unfathomable. She did not look entirely happy. Elona turned her gaze to Ulina next to her—though she still felt the rigid tension behind her—at least Ulina's expression was understandable. She was staring directly at Chara and seemed astonished.

They came full circle and were heading back towards the town.

"How do I stop?" shouted Chara, her voice was shaking.

Elona felt Kantees relax. "They must do it slowly," she shouted back. "Your will controls the pattern that they have created. It is like slowing down after you have been running."

There was a pause. Elona saw the town coming at them fast, but even as she watched, the speed of approach lessened and moments later the pattern collapsed and they were blasted by freezing air.

Chara yelled with delight and relief. The formation turned again before it reached the town, heading along the cliff. With the pattern gone, Elona felt her sickness returning and her head spun as the *ziri* changed direction. The rogue winds and updraughts made it worse, she thought she might throw up again.

Moments later they passed a dark horizontal gash in the cliff-face on their left. Chara pulled the *zirichasa* sharply to the right, almost making a complete circle. But as they came round, they were facing directly at the entrance and she took them in to land just inside.

Elona unbuckled herself as quickly as she could though her hands did not seem to want to obey her, and her stomach still threatened to unload its contents.

Finally she was back on solid ground took a deep breath and stepped forward to where Chara and Kantees stood facing the interior. The sound of *ziri* breathing and their talons on stone echoed between the walls.

The chamber was empty.

On the right stood the thrones for the senior matriarchs, they were carved from the stone of the chamber itself. The walls were engraved with Slissac patternings, as usual. These creatures were nothing if not consistent.

To the left were the places where the supplicants came to present and plead their cases. Complete with the strange barriers that would hide the lower castes from view.

"No one here," said Elona.

"They will co'e," said Chara. "They heard my challenge. They saw us fly. This chamber is never left unguarded."

"But not the cave entrance."

"Only a slow *tekrak* could come that way, and the winds are treacherous so close to the mountain."

Elona remembered how hard it had been to land the *tekrak* near

Aris—they hadn't succeeded, she had jumped when they were close to the ground.

"Did you like leading the *ziri*?" said Kantees.

"I did enjoy it," said Chara as she watched the entrances.

Elona looked at Kantees' face and was not sure how Chara was failing to notice the edge in her voice.

"You took the golden path."

Chara turned to her and clicked her pleasure. "That was very good. I understand why you love to fly."

"Sulassa is not—" Kantees broke off.

"Not what?"

"Capable."

Chara's shrug was as human as her mother had been. "She did not complain."

"You are the third."

This time Chara faced Kantees. "If you want to say so'ething, just say it."

"Nobody can learn to fly a *ziri* as fast as you did. Only two people can make any *zirichak* fly fast, me and Gally. You must have flown before. You *must*."

Chara shook her head. "No, I never have."

"Then how did you know?"

"You know she's not lying, Kantees," said Elona. "Perhaps it's something about being a Slissac." She was about to mention her idea that certain creatures had been created, or changed, by the Slissac to serve them. But marching feet interrupted her.

They all turned to look as the moss in the room brightened and filled the cavern with light.

"Do you know what you're going to say?" said Elona.

"I just have to re'e'er what they did, the words will co'e." She turned. "Ulina should kee' back, Kantees, you stay there with Shee-sha. Elona with me."

"Of course."

Soldiers trooped into the room and distributed themselves along the edge, all seeming to look down but Elona was sure they were keeping an eye on the strangers. Then the three senior matriarchs entered wearing shimmering black gowns that swept the floor.

They were followed by a number of other matriarchs. Elona recognised the elders, they had wanted her dead and probably still did. But the others she did not know at all. The heads of the Slissac houses did not socialise a great deal, it was too dangerous.

Then came one who stood out from the rest. While the elders were stiffly superior, and the others had been deferent though curious as they cast glances at Chara, Elona and the *zirichasa*, this one strutted.

No doubt the Kiyoreth matriarch.

She had been discovered trying to wipe out the Aytrueth clan perhaps for a second time. But she had been stopped and would probably try to bluff it out.

~

ONCE EVERYONE WAS SETTLED, Chara took a step forward and felt rather than saw Elona in step behind her. She wished she fully understood the customs of her people, the time she had spent here without Elona to rely on had been helpful. It had forced her to learn.

Learn or die in the process.

She had not mentioned the number of poisoning attempts, as well as outright physical attacks against her directly. She had only survived through the efforts of her clan.

It was not that the Slissac in the town thought of her as an outsider. On the contrary, she was a matriarch in body as well as name, and that made her fair game. The fact that she did not retaliate probably encouraged them.

She did not want to kill anyone—that was Usala's doing, of course. Her mother had brought her up by the standards of a decent human and had no idea what a Slissac society demanded.

Now here she was, on the dawning of the Feast of Spring, having managed to snatch her clan and house back from Kiyoreth.

This much she understood. The matriarch—Yuntana—had decided she would attack early so that when the feast took place, she was already in control of the Aytrueth property and she wouldn't have to fight for it with any of the others.

Chara's return and routing of the Kiyoreth forces meant she had lost troops, she had lost face, and she had lost Chara's property. Most of all she had lost the opportunity to acquire more fungus chambers.

Yuntana was already approaching the elders. Chara walked forward quickly and took her place, two arm-lengths from her rival. Elona stayed slightly back and to one side presumably so she could keep an eye on the crowds.

Chara did not think anyone would try to assassinate her here, in front of the elders, but it was not impossible. Hopefully with Elona and Kantees here, as well as nine *ziri*, nobody would be that foolish.

After all, if Chara was killed Elona would take over the house.

"The Matriarch of the House of Kiyoreth will speak," said the Prime Elder.

Chara had been expecting that. Technically they were the same rank but Yuntana was older. But what possible argument could she offer?

"Gracious elders," she said, "I demand recompense from the House of Aytrueth."

There was a murmur among the gathering of matriarchs.

"For what?" said the Prime.

"My losses, gracious elders, the House of Aytrueth has killed many of my people—and she has brought more white-skins from the outside, it is a capital crime for which she should be punished."

The elder on the right moved slightly. "Do you think we, the elders, are blind?"

"Of course not, gracious elder."

"Then why do you point out the white-skins?"

"I beg your pardon, gracious one. I felt outrage at such blasphemy."

The one who had spoken sat back and the Prime spoke again.

"And what is the recompense you seek, House of Kiyoreth?"

"Aytrueth should replace my people with her own. Or give property to their value."

The Prime Elder turned her gaze on Chara, though her eyes flicked to Elona standing behind.

"House of Aytrueth, justify your crime in bringing white-skins to this place."

"I see no white-skins, gracious Prime, I see only family."

"We granted sisterhood to the one by your side only."

"And my sister gave sisterhood to the one who stands with the great *zirichak*, but she is not a white-skin as you see."

"Do not bandy words. She is human regardless of the colour of her skin."

"Yet she is also sister to me by the same bond that holds Elona, and the child is her daughter. You may call forth a patterner to test it and it will be found to be so. They are family to me, and I have committed no crime."

"Your word as a matriarch will be accepted for now but your claim will be tested before the feast tonight.

"I am happy to follow your wisdom, gracious Prime."

Chara glanced at Yuntana. She wore a black dress not dissimilar to the elders, as if she was trying to identify with them. Perhaps she intended to be one of them. Kiyoreth was a powerful house—and it occurred to Chara that she had no idea how elders were chosen.

The voice of the Prime spoke again. "How do you answer the claim of Kiyoreth?"

It was difficult to know where to begin since every single person here knew exactly what had happened and why. So rather than explain, she laughed. Her clicks rose high and echoed around the chamber.

How long had it been since anyone had laughed in this place?

Yuntana turned. "You mock the elders!"

"No, Yuntana," said Chara between clicks. "I mock *you*."

"Chara of House Aytrueth, compose yourself!"

Chara ceased immediately and bowed. "I beg your pardon, gracious elders. I was long under the sway of the white-skins and when such a foolish and obvious fallacy exists, they will laugh. I have yet to attain the true temperament of a matriarch. I hope that you can forgive my lapse."

"Then provide your answer."

"Gracious Prime, answer what? It was Kiyoreth who attacked Aytrueth and they lost soldiers in their failed attempt. If those males had been so precious to them, they should have kept them at home."

"She insults Kiyoreth!"

"Aytrueth is insulted by your attack, Yuntana. I have lost clan to you. You should have stayed in your heart-room." Chara spat the words, the meaning was clear enough, only the old and feeble stayed in the heart-room. "You thought to claim Aytrueth for your own in my absence before the feast. And you failed! Just as your mother failed to wipe out Aytrueth the first time."

Yuntana suddenly lunged at her.

It was as if time slowed. Chara saw the knife coming from the folds in Yuntana's robe. Its wicked, slightly curved length flickered in the light from the cave mouth. The gap between them shrank fast but moments later a blue light sprang up and Yuntana thudded into it. The knife aimed at Chara's heart twisted off to the side.

The wall pushed away from Chara, forcing Yuntana to stumble backwards trying to stay on her feet.

Chara turned. "No, Elona, get rid of it."

"She's trying to kill you."

"I must deal with it without help."

Her sister frowned and dropped her hand. The blue wall encircling them vanished. The air was filled with the growls and howling of the *zirichasa*. Many of the matriarchs were retreating while the soldiers moved forwards, weapons out.

"Apologies from the House of Aytrueth, gracious Prime. My sister did not understand, she was only protecting me."

"I demand the Rite of Faraha!" screamed Yuntana. "House of Aytrueth to be forfeit to House of Kiyoreth."

The Prime stared at her. "Only if you win."

"That is not in doubt."

CHAPTER 28

Chara said nothing as they flew back to the rooftop of her clan building and went inside.

When she found her deputy, she gave orders for the rooms close to the building entrance to be given over to the *zirichasa* temporarily, since the rooftop had no cover for them. Ulina was charged with settling the *ziri* in their new home and making sure they went out to feed.

Then Chara headed to her quarters with Elona and Kantees.

As she entered the dark room with the heavy red wall-hangings she sighed in relief. It was good to be home. She invited the others to sit. Elona was familiar with the place and settled on the sofa she had always used previously. Kantees was less sure but found a chair with plenty of cushions.

While they waited for food, Chara explained almost everything that had been spoken of.

"I was beginning to remember the words," said Elona. "But it was hard to follow, everything was so quick."

"They're going to test whether Elona's patterning is a proper sister binding?" said Kantees. "What happens if it isn't?"

"They will try to kill you."

"That's not going to happen," said Elona. "The binding is right, and they will not be killing any of us."

Three servants came through a side door with trays of food and a drink. Chara realised she was already falling back into the traditional ways. It was almost as if the door they had entered by was invisible.

The food was put out quickly and they retreated from the room.

Chara watched Kantees hesitate over the food. "What is this?"

Elona laughed. "Different types of mushrooms mostly, it's the wrong time of the year for fruit."

"Grown in 'y own tunnels," said Chara.

Kantees took something that most resembled a surface mushroom and bit into it.

"It's not too bad."

"After a few months you'll be screaming for some meat. Or just some real vegetables," said Elona.

"This is all you have?"

"There are 'any ways of preparing them."

"But nothing's cooked."

"There are no fires in any room?"

Chara shook her head. "We don't feel the cold the way you do."

"I don't feel the cold either," said Elona.

"I'll sleep with Sheesha."

They went silent as they ate. It had been a long time since they had broken their fast.

"I won't let her kill you," said Elona, and then took a sip of water.

"They will not attack again," said Chara. She had not mentioned the challenge from Yuntana.

"You know I don't mean that."

Chara sighed. "I thought you said you could not understand."

"I said it was difficult to follow."

Chara glanced at Kantees who was sitting back in her chair, paying close attention to the conversation but not saying anything.

"That matriarch demanded a ritual of some sort, probably a duel. To the death, no doubt."

Chara sighed again, knowing that she sounded like her human mother when she did it. The sigh was a human reaction, not something a Slissac did.

"Yes, she has challenged me and the elders have accepted it."

"I think they do not like you," said Kantees.

"They do not. I a' fro' a clan that was declared dead. I 'rought with 'e a white-skin who was 'ound as 'y sister. And now I 'ring another."

"I am not white."

"As far as they are concerned you are. You are not Slissac, you are one of the slave race."

"I am not a slave!"

Both Elona and Chara were taken aback at her reaction. "We never said you were."

Kantees sat back. "I was. Once. Slave to Taymalin."

Elona shook her head. "Esternes. It's the only place that makes Kadralin into slaves."

"I did not 'ean any insult. In the land we ca'e fro' we enslaved the white-skins."

"I know the story," said Kantees.

"That's why 'y 'eo'le left," said Chara. "They did not like the slaves."

"I suppose that's something," said Kantees. "Nice to know some Slissac knew how to behave towards other races."

Chara looked down at the piece of green fungus she held in her hand. It had a particularly spicy flavour which she very much liked.

"You do not understand, sister," she said. "They had no respect for the white-skins. To 'y ancestors, they were ani'als, what they hated was the way the sla'es were s'reading. They 'elieved the slaves were 'aking the Slissac weak."

"You never told me that," said Elona.

"I learnt of it after you left," said Chara. "So yes, they hate 'e for so 'any things. Not 'eing dead, 'eing raised 'y a white-skin, 'ringing you here and 'etraying their entire reason for existence."

They ate the rest of their food in silence.

CHARA PULLED a cord to summon her deputy, but they were at the main door almost immediately.

"Gracious mother," she said, "the patterner from the elders has arrived. She waits in the audience chamber."

"Very good." Chara switched to the Taymalin language. "It is ti'e."

The three of them followed the deputy down through the labyrinth of passages, Chara paused before the door.

"We will need clothing suitable for the feast for my guests including the white-skin child."

"Yes, gracious mother."

"My sisters will need extra material about the chest."

There was a quick glance in their direction. "I understand, gracious mother."

"Will there be any difficulty?"

"No, gracious mother."

"My old clothes, from when I first came here, you know where they are?"

"I do, gracious mother."

"I will need those for the feast."

"Is that wise, gracious mother?"

"I believe it is."

"As you wish, gracious mother."

She bowed to all three and moved away quickly. Just as Ulina emerged from round a corner.

Kantees embraced her warmly and the child returned it. Chara thought for a moment that she might enjoy, perhaps, the embrace of a daughter. Then she roused herself and flung open the doors of the audience chamber.

Six people rose to their feet. The priestess stood in the front holding the staff of her office, through which she channelled her power. Beside her another priestess, younger and probably in training to replace the older one eventually. Three soldiers stood with them, while the sixth was a lithe Slissac woman whose bow was as perfunctory as it was smooth.

The priestess did not bow.

"Matriarch of Aytrueth, I have been summoned to test the truth of your claims as to the sister-bindings."

"I understand, gracious elder."

"Do you understand that if they are found to be false, these white-skin interlopers will be killed?"

"I understand that is the desire of the elders."

"This is Lanala of the Watch. She is charged with carrying out the sentences."

Chara nodded to her, but she did not respond. She looked very dangerous.

"This will not take long," said the priestess, raising her staff to the horizontal. "Chara, place your hand upon the staff. Command your first sister to do the same."

When Chara touched placed her hand on the wood, she could feel the power in it. Like a golden pool, golden and liquid. Now she understood what Elona had talked about.

"Elona, you 'ust 'lace your hand on mine as you did 'efore."

She felt her come close, their arms touched and Elona's hand came down over hers.

The priestess let out a small cry. Chara saw she was staring at Elona's face. But then she looked down and placed her free hand over both.

There was a flash in Chara's head, and for a fraction of a moment she saw a cord of brilliant white that seemed to extend from Elona to her.

The priestess pulled back her hand.

"The sister-bond is strong."

She stared again at Elona before forcing her eyes back to Chara.

"Call the other here."

Moments later Kantees' black fingers rested on hers. And again, as the priestess examined them Chara saw the flash.

"Who made this sister-bond?"

The one called Lanala, moved forwards her hand on the knife at her belt.

"Elona."

"The sister-bond is strong. The one called Kantees is sister to Aytrueth."

Lanala looked disappointed. Humans had difficulty telling the emotions of a Slissac but Chara had no such problem.

The priestess looked across at Ulina. "What about the white-skin child?"

"She is daughter to Kantees, therefore my kin by binding and blood."

The priestess put her head on one side. "These may be the only white-skins I have ever seen but I am not blind, Mother of Aytrueth."

"The child was found wandering, the one called Kantees became her mother."

Lanala stepped forward. "If they are not family, I will kill the child."

Chara looked into the female's wild eyes. "You may try if you think you can win, this one is trained to kill and wields a mystic blade. And whether you succeed or fail in that test, neither I nor my sisters will rest until you become a meal for the *zirichasa*, and whatever remains is spread as manure to grow our food."

The priestess raised her hand. "Enough. I accept that the child is the daughter, even if they are not of the same blood."

"There is a daughter binding is there not? You wanted Elona to be my daughter rather than my sister."

The female nodded. "That too can be done. If they are willing."

"There is no need for Lanala or the guards to remain, is there?"

The priestess dismissed them as Chara summoned a servant to escort them out of her house.

Chara turned to Kantees. "The 'riestess will do a 'other-daughter 'inding with you and Ulina."

"Is it needed?"

"She accepts you have ado'ted Ulina as your daughter."

Kantees pursed her lips. "I hear a *but* in your words."

"Others 'ight disagree."

"I don't trust her. I have been a slave once, I don't intend to let that happen again."

"I can make sure it's similar to the sister-binding," said Elona. "And I can stop her if I need to."

"And it will make things easier for you?" said Kantees looking at Chara.

She nodded. "Yes, but it 'ust 'e your choice."

"I do not fear their magic," said Ulina coming closer.

Kantees turned to the priestess. "We will accept your binding."

It seemed that a translation was not required as the priestess nodded. She turned to her assistant and gave short instructions to prepare a cloth for a pattern. The young patterner pulled a roll of white material from within her robe and a charcoal stick from a small box. They moved to a table and as the priestess dictated the assistant drew symbols along the cloth with the stick.

Once it was done the length was cut off and the priestess examined the symbols carefully. Once satisfied she handed it back to the assistant who put away her things before the two returned to the centre of the room.

"Don't you want to look at the patterns they've drawn?" said Kantees.

Elona shrugged. "I have no idea what they mean."

"Because they're Slissac?"

"Because I have no education in patterning. We are all alike, sister, what we do comes from the heart not the head."

The priestess held the staff out horizontally nodded to Ulina and gestured towards the staff with one hand. The girl put her pale hand on the wood close to where the old Slissac woman held it. Elona drew closer to them as Kantees placed her hand over the top of her daughter's.

The assistant bound their hands to the staff loosely and even Chara could feel the priestess summoning the power of the ley-circle.

The old woman chanted quietly as she held her other hand over the physical binding. Chara closed her eyes. The light from the patterning grew in her mind and she watched the mystic cord form between Kantees and Ulina.

Then all the light faded and she opened her eyes again, to find the priestess looking directly at her.

"You saw?"

"I did."

"If you had lived here your mother would have arranged to have you taught patterning."

"But my mother was not here. She was killed by House Kiyoreth."

"Your mother was an effective matriarch and cared for her clan. I see that in you, Chara ar-Gey Aytrueth. You must tell your sister and sister-daughter their names after I have left."

"I will, Gracious one," said Chara. "But I have to ask. What does Yuntana seek to gain from challenging me to a duel at the feast?"

"Aytrueth, of course."

"But I have sisters, Chara tu-Gey and Kantees ko-Gey."

"White-skins? With you dead no one will honour the bindings that no longer exist. They should be ready to flee if Yuntana succeeds."

And with that, she left.

CHAPTER 29

They had retired to Chara's quarters where they were brought more food and water to drink. Elona flopped down in her chair.

Ulina was looking at her arms in the dim moss-light. "I do not feel any different."

"I think it just magnifies something that's already there," said Elona.

"Even between us?" said Kantees. "We had barely met—even now it is only a few days but you performed that binding"

Elona shrugged. "What she did with you and Ulina is different—similar but not the same. It's more like the bond you have with the *ziri*."

"You can see that too?"

"It's my curse."

"Being with the *zirichasa* is a blessing," said Kantees.

Elona chose to ignore that comment and looked at the food. She had eaten it a hundred times before in different combinations, colours and flavours but it was as if she was seeing it for the first time.

"When we were with the elders, and you were arguing with them—"

"I was not arguing," said Chara. "I was 'resenting 'y case."

"You mentioned food."

"Yes."

"What has food got to do with it?"

"It is power."

"What do you mean?"

Chara clicked in amusement. "You ne'er liked it or questioned where it ca'e fro'."

"I didn't want to know."

"The *ziri* can bring meat for you, mother-sister," said Ulina. "I can cook it."

"Aunt," said Kantees. "Mother-sister is aunt."

"She has it right in my language, Kantees," said Chara. "I like 'eat too so'eti'es, 'ut I a' used to this. I like it."

"Why is it power?" said Elona.

"You should ask where it co'es fro'."

Elona sighed, she was tired of this game. "Very well, where does it come from?"

Chara pointed down. "Fro' the tunnels. You know we do not far' in the sa'e way as you. Lower down the slo'es there are ani'als, 'ut they are used 'or their skins and hair. We do not eat the'. We eat this."

She held up a chunk of fungus cut square and coloured yellow, then popped it into her mouth.

Elona nodded. "So the families grow their mushrooms in underground tunnels."

"Yes."

"Let me guess," said Kantees. "There are different varieties of fungus some of which are better than others? Harder to grow but delicious? You could live on the easy-to-grow ones but the ruling classes want the nice ones."

"That is how it is," said Chara. "The clan I took over…"

She hesitated and Elona knew she was thinking about the poison she had unwittingly given to the old matriarch. It was part of the ritual but Chara had not known the old matriarch would intention-ally take her own life.

"My clan has a good one."

"And Kiyoreth wants it," said Elona.

"Yuntana will try to end what her 'other started, my existence says Kiyoreth failed and that is 'ad for her. If she also gets the Aytrueth tunnels that is a 'onus for her," said Chara. "Kiyoreth controls 'ost of the tunnels even now."

"That we are your sisters counts for nothing then," said Kantees and took a bite out of a red fungus sliced into finger-length pieces.

Chara shook her head.

"We can fight," said Elona.

"If I die," said Chara, "there is no reason 'or you to stay."

Elona took a deep breath and reached out to place her hand on Chara's. "Even if that were to happen. We still need to learn more about the *Kisharuk*."

"Do you really think the information is here?" said Kantees.

"We have to start somewhere. If the stories told about it are true, then it was created by the Slissac so we should be able to find out something."

"The priestess might be able to tell you," said Chara as she put down her plate and stood. "I a' going to rest. You should too."

"Are we safe?" said Kantees.

Chara paused. "Safe enough."

~

"Perhaps I shouldn't come," said Kantees as they looked at the flowing dress that had been brought for her to wear. "Ulina and I need to be on the outside in case of trouble."

"If I die," said Chara, "Elona will need you both."

Kantees glanced at Elona. "I cannot match your patterning, what could I do?"

"I don't know what power they could bring against us," said Elona. "I can only concentrate on one thing at a time." She thought briefly of that moment she had killed the incarnation of the *Kisharuk* in the Fastness, bringing down the building around them. That would not work in a cave where the enemy could retreat into the passageways.

"So we all die?"

"It won't happen."

"You cannot promise that, sister."

Elona sighed. "I probably can." *Even if, through my panic I only save myself. Yet I pulled Chara from another place, I should be able to bring them all. Even the* ziri. "It will be all right."

Kantees looked unconvinced but picked up the midnight blue dress she had been given and held it against herself. "I've never worn a dress. They are not practical for riding."

Ulina had one in the same colour, if anything she looked even less happy about it than her mother.

Elona's dress was one that had been made for her when she was here before, a very dark green. She did not mind wearing dresses, the only problem was that these were designed the way Slissac liked their clothes. Straight from the shoulder to floor with no arms, no volume and no shaping. They were adjusted for both Elona and Kantees' busts but only with additional material. There was no support. The dresses were not flattering and resembled shapeless night dresses.

Kantees put her the belt around the waist which helped. Ulina followed suit while Elona used a tie made from the same material.

Chara's dress was red, making her stand out from her sisters. Though she too wore a belt—the dark brown one from her hunter's outfit, made by Usala.

"Not a very Slissac colour," said Elona.

"I a' 'aking a 'oint."

"What's the risk of poisoning?" said Elona making Kantees stare at her.

"Not high."

"Not high?" repeated Kantees.

Chara shrugged. "It is considered 'ad form to 'oison during a feast. If one starts, e'eryone will do it. So no one does."

"But Yuntana might," said Kantees.

Chara nodded. "She will not 'oison 'e, 'ut she 'ight try to kill you three."

"Are you being serious?" said Kantees.

"Yes."

"So we should not eat or drink anything?"

Elona thought for a moment. "How much time have we got?"

"A little, we can arri'e late."

"Have you got any poisons here?"

"Of course." Chara saw the look Kantees gave her. "I would ne'er use the', 'ut the 'revious 'atriarch had all the usual ones."

"I'd like to see them," said Elona. "I have an idea."

ELONA WAS grateful they did not ride the *zirichasa* to the hall where the feast was to take place but in some ways the route they took was worse.

Freezing mountain air with flakes of snow blew through the open door so high above the ground it made her head swim. They had to cross the bridge with no handrails, just as their escort crossed the one below them.

She stopped several steps from the opening.

"Do you need help, sister?" said Kantees beside her. There was no criticism or scorn in her words but, of course, she would have no problem with heights. She enjoyed flying.

"I can do it."

"Walk behind me, hold my belt and keep your eyes fixed on my shoulders."

"Or close the'," said Chara.

Elona sighed. "Closing my eyes always makes it worse." But she accepted Kantees' idea and gripped her belt tightly. It was dark outside so she could not see far, but the wind buffeted her as if teasing her into thinking it would push her over the edge.

Kantees walked slowly and Elona shuffled behind, afraid to lift her feet too far from the floor in case it wasn't there when she put them down.

It seemed to take forever but eventually they were on the other side and entering the cliff. There was no way in from the building itself—such an entrance would have made it too easy to attack.

Once underground Elona settled. They waited close to a junction as another matriarch went past.

"Yuntana doesn't have any heirs, does she?" said Elona.

"Three daughters. No sisters."

"You'll have to fight them too?"

"They are not old enough."

"What happens to them?"

Chara said nothing and they moved forward once more, turning right into a large passageway. Moss glowed at intervals and, inevitably, the Slissac patterns covered the walls.

"What happens to the daughters?"

Chara sighed. "They die."

"Like the matriarch?"

"I have no choice. It is our way."

"Then change it."

"I am Slissac."

Elona shut down her anger; Chara did not need to hear it.

CHARA FELT NUMB. This was not the first time her life had been under threat. She had never told her mother of the times when she had been faced with villagers who were scared and angry at the Slissac in their midst. They wanted her gone, or dead. But they feared Usala, feared that if they did anything to the Slissac girl then Usala would no longer heal them or their families.

That had not stopped the threats.

It had taken a long time before Chara knew they were powerless. But by then she was hunting with all the risks that provided facing wolves and soaring *sikechasa*. When the Tirnian soldiers had come for Elona, they had both almost died at their hands. Then almost drowned.

After which she had come here with the countless attempts to poison her, and the constant threat of attack.

Her life had been anything but quiet.

But this was different. This time she was walking into the danger knowing what it was, and with no chance to step-aside from it. Yuntana had a reputation as a very capable fighter. There were few rules in this challenge except that the combatants could use a single short blade, no one could interfere until it was done, and that they should try not to hurt anyone else.

They moved along the passage, her two sisters and Ulina behind.

It did not seem fair she might never get to ride a *ziri* again. She had loved riding her horse but the great flying beasts were something else again. And it felt so natural. Chara touched her hand to her lips as she remembered how upset Kantees had been when Chara had the *ziri* fly the golden path.

But to Chara it did not seem very special, it was as if she was born to it.

She glanced at the patterns in the walls as they passed.

It had been strange when she touched the magical barrier around the heart-room. No one had instructed her that such a thing was possible, or that her touch would remove it. Even Elona had no idea about it.

At least Elona, Kantees and Ulina would be safe. They would be able to protect themselves if Yuntana succeeded in killing her.

She flexed her fingers in an effort to bring the life back to them. She felt cold to her core though the passage was warm enough.

The sound of Slissac voices grew as they approached the end of the tunnel and the hall in which the feast would take place—and the arena of her death.

The group in front of them stopped and so did they, a respectful distance back. The name of the family and the matriarch were called out and then the other members of her retinue—daughters only. Killing off potential rival sisters was common enough. Did those daughters even now plot to murder their siblings so that they would inherit their mother's position when she died? Perhaps even plot to kill her too?

The past were full of such things. It made Chara ache with the pain of all those lives unnecessarily lost. Yet if she had been brought up by her real mother, perhaps she would have felt the same way.

The group in front of them moved into the hall, Chara and her family moved forward.

The Slissac doing the announcing was the young priestess who had been with them earlier in the day. She bowed low, as was fitting to any matriarch.

"Aytrueth!" The sudden silence in the hall was astonishing as the woman continued. "Chara ar-Gey, Elona tu-Gey, Kantees ko-Gey, Ulina ar-Tek-la Kantees."

The silence was broken by sounds of anger.

The priestess turned to Chara. "Some of the older matriarchs do not like white-skins being allowed into the feast."

"And you?"

"I do not judge." She hesitated for a moment. "There are many that look to your survival as an omen."

"Good or bad?"

"It depends on whether they fear change."

"Everyone fears change."

"But not all wish to deny those fears." She glanced behind. "You must go in."

Chara stepped forward into the hall. The sound of talking had increased again, though it was more hushed than it had been before their arrival.

"How many here can speak the human tongue?" said Kantees.

"Only Chara."

"That's good."

The question now was where to go. At present all the matriarchs were standing around the edges of the room, in small groups for the most part. Either just clans together, or ones that were allied, or at least friendly. Chara had not managed to establish ties with any other family.

They hugged the wall from fear, to avoid the chance of an assassin coming up behind them. Chara shook her head. This was no way to live. The people of the village might have hated her but among themselves they helped one another. Yes, there were those who wanted to control the others, but for the most part all help was given without any expectancy of reward.

This place was a nightmare of distrust.

"Where shall we go?" said Elona behind her.

Chara strode forwards until she came to a place a short distance from two other families, and a good distance from the wall. Both groups had eyed her as she approached, some had even moved to one side to give her some room to get to the wall. But instead, she stopped and turned her back on them.

"They will see this as either 'ravery or arrogance," she said.

"Or foolhardiness," said Elona.

Kantees looked confused.

"Threat of assassination," said Elona. "Chara has turned her back to potential enemies."

"Your people are crazy," said Kantees.

Chara shrugged. "There is nothing I can do exce't show a di''erent way."

"And, one of them is coming to talk to you."

"Behind me?"

"Young one, hands open and forward, doesn't look like she has a weapon."

Ulina slipped past as Chara turned, and stood in front of her.

The Slissac girl stopped and stared. Then remembered herself and, still keeping her empty hands in view, bowed. She stayed in that position as she spoke.

"Gracious mother of Aytrueth, the mother of Tokueth would speak with you."

Ulina did not take her eyes off the girl, and her hand was on her tiny blade.

"Daughter of Tokueth, I am honoured and will gladly speak with her."

The girl backed away, always keeping the palms of her hands on show. She did not have to tell her matriarch the response since they were just a few paces distant.

"A feast is probably the only time you can safely open negotiations," said Elona.

"You understood?" said Chara.

"Only parts, but it makes sense. If you didn't have events like this how would you even know who the other matriarchs were?"

"We'll see."

The Slissac who came forward was not as young as Chara but could not have been a great deal older. They bowed to one another. Chara was uncertain now, she was expecting to die very soon, and was not in the mood for political discussions.

"May your lineage survive to the end of time," said Chara, there was a great deal of official language she had been taught to say when greeting other matriarchs.

"Let us dispense with that, Gracious one, we do not have much time before the feast. I am Landirna ar-Gey Tokueth and I am taking a great risk in talking to you. May I come closer that we may speak privately?"

"I am happy to but is the risk too much for your family?"

Landirna moved forward until they were within touching distance, it made Chara uneasy.

"What do you wish to say?"

"Should you survive this evening, I will align my house with yours."

"Because if I survive, Kiyoreth will be mine?"

"You think that?"

"That's what happens if Yuntana kills me, isn't it? That's why she's doing it, because no one will accept my sisters as replacements because they are white-skins."

"It is not that simple, Chara of Aytrueth. If a house eats a smaller one, nobody cares. But if a small one defeats a larger one, then the council must decide."

"That makes no sense."

"Aytrueth, a small house such as yours cannot be allowed to jump into prominence simply by killing a matriarch. That way leads to chaos." She paused. "It is enough to know you will have our support if you succeed."

"Are there any others?"

"How can I know?"

The name of Kiyoreth was called at the door. Chara turned to look at Yuntana with her three daughters. And when she turned back Landirna was already back among her family.

CHAPTER 30

*I*t seemed Yuntana had decided to be the last to enter. She moved among the matriarchs acknowledging greetings and giving the impression she was one of the elders. A flurry of activity among servants resulted in tables and chairs being brought in. Another young priestess moved among the matriarchs and brought them to specific tables. One table per family.

Some had only a single person. The Aytrueth one was typical in having four, though in most cases that was a matriarch and her daughters. A few had more but none exceeded eight. The tables were all one size and the matriarchs sat with their backs to the wall.

Chara decided it was worth following that rule, and she had Elona on her right with Kantees and Ulina on the left.

The Slissac stared at them openly. Less at her than the white-skins of her family.

She had not mentioned to her sisters what the derogatory term for humans was among the matriarchs.

Trays of food were brought round and placed on the tables.

"I dislike this," said Kantees.

"We might as well be in a public inn where the owner keeps rude and sullen staff," said Elona. "Or simply eat this food in our own rooms."

Chara sighed. "At least you do not ha'e to fight for your life as dessert."

She reached out to take a large piece of fungus that had been stained blue. "This is one fro' 'y tunnels. It tastes like cheese, you'll like it."

"Wait," said Elona putting her hand on Chara's and then waving her other around the fungus, muttering something. "It's all right now."

Chara hesitated and looked at the food in her hand. "What was that?"

"Magic," said Elona.

"When did you e'er need to wa'e your hand or chant to make patterns?"

"I don't need to, it was for effect."

"Was it 'oisoned?"

"Not that I could tell."

Chara took a bite and hummed as the taste spread through her mouth.

"Unless they used a different poison to the ones you gave me."

Kantees leaned forward to look past Chara at Elona. "Is that supposed to be funny?"

"A little."

"If it's 'oisoned, it's delicious," said Chara.

"What about the rest of it?" said Kantees.

"I couldn't see any poisons in any of it."

"And if you did?"

"I would tell you."

"Could you get rid of it?"

Elona hesitated. "I might but I don't think the food would be edible afterwards."

They stopped talking and ate from the tray, then washed it down with water, similarly tested by Elona.

Chara's skin itched as if someone was watching her, as if one of these might launch an attack against her. She shook her head, that was exactly what was going to happen. Yet the feeling did not go away.

It was difficult just living here. They might be her people but it was too different from her life with Usala. She took a deep breath, well, perhaps she would not have to if she lost against Yuntana. Something made her look towards the far wall of the room, as something was there. Then the tips of her fingers tingled and she stared at them though nothing was to be seen—they looked normal.

"Can you feel it?" said Kantees.

"A feeding," said Elona. "And soon."

"'Y skin itches," said Chara.

Kantees nodded. "That's how it can be." She waved her hand in the direction of the table of the priestesses, one of the younger ones was also staring in the same direction as Chara had. "They're feeling it too."

"They said that I 'ight ha'e 'een a 'riestess."

Kantees placed her hand on Chara's. "That explains your connection with the *ziri*. It's a blessing of the Mother."

"A curse," said Elona.

Kantees nodded. "That too, for the likes of us."

"So you think I a' *fahain*?" said Chara.

"I don't think that word means anything," said Elona. "If you have the talent and it's discovered when you're young, you are trained. If not, they call you *fahain*."

"But anyone can make a pattern," said Kantees. "If they have it written for them."

Elona shrugged. "That just means everyone has some talent."

"'Ut you can do things no 'atterner can do."

Kantees laughed. "But how would they know what they can do? They have their training and it's like putting blinders on a racing dragon. They only see what they are shown."

The Prime Elder stood up and the talking in the room died away.

"There has been a challenge. The House of Kiyoreth has demanded the Rite of Faraha against the House of Aytrueth." There was little response from the watching matriarchs, they must have already heard. It was strange how fast information could travel even in this place. "The House that fails never existed and its name will not be spoken."

She stepped down from the dais to the floor of the cave and held out her hands to the tables of Aytrueth and Kiyoreth.

Kantees squeezed Chara's hand and released it as she got to her feet.

"We're with you," said Elona.

"You cannot interfere."

"I won't."

Chara turned to look into her sister's eyes. "And you 'ust not kill the' if I lose."

"If you were to die, Chara, I would be matriarch by the rules of your people, and I will protect my family in whatever way I see fit," said Elona.

"Sometimes," said Chara placing her hand on Elona's shoulder, "I wish my face was as flexible as the soft skin of yours. And if it was, I would smile."

Yuntana's voice called from the centre of the hall. "Take as much time as you need to say your goodbyes, Mother of Aytrueth. I promise to kill you swiftly."

"I didn't need a translation for that," said Kantees. "Kill the little *jikak*, sister."

Chara clicked quietly then looked up and met Yuntana's eye. "Your mother failed to kill me, Yuntana, but at least she did not die in the attempt. You will fare less well than her."

The Prime Elder waited as she walked to the centre of the hall. The hem of her dress brushing the stone floor with each step.

She tried to remain focused on the two Slissac ahead of her but the surges of the Mother's milk from the ley-circle was distracting, and the feeding had not even started. It felt as if the circle knew what was about to happen.

With an effort she recalled what she had been forced to learn about the Rite of Faraha—which was not a great deal. It had been just a footnote in a document she had to read, and that was only just after learning the Slissac written language. At least her mother had taught her Taymalin script, and there were a lot of similarities.

She glanced up and past her adversary at the walls of the hall, inscribed as always by the ancient script mixed in with patterning symbols. None of the wall writings she had seen had ever made any sense. Some of it was simply storytelling—often repeated—while the rest were patterner script which she did not understand at all.

The symbols were used to help mould the World's Pattern into the form that was desired by the patterner. Which did not explain why they were scattered through every Slissac-made tunnel and room she had ever seen. It was as if they did not dare make a passage or hall without adorning it.

Except the walls around the heart-room had power flowing through them which she was sure had not been true when she left.

She came to a stop a few steps from Yuntana, and faced the Prime Elder.

"Kiyoreth, do you withdraw your challenge?"

"My challenge stands, Gracious Prime."

"Aytrueth, are you ready to oppose the challenge."

"I am ready, Gracious Prime."

I am not ready. I will never be ready. Why am I doing this, why did Elona come into my life and ruin it? I was happy with my mother.

The ley-circle seemed to rumble, and now Chara could feel the power in the sky too. Elona had never mentioned that.

"Disrobe."

Chara stripped. She was aware of the shame that human women had for disrobing in public, their bodies revealed so much. For Slissac, it was very different.

Once upon a time, she remembered, the Rite of Faraha was performed without weapons. They were expected to tear each other to bits with their bare hands and talons. It was more refined now.

One of the attendants to the Prime Elder stepped forwards carrying a tray on which were two daggers, their slightly curved blades reflecting the lights. She offered the tray first to Chara as the one who was defending the challenge.

They should be identical, and they looked it.

She took the one nearest to her, she had no skill in judging or comparing such things. The handle fitted her hand comfortably and she held it by her side.

The tray was offered to Yuntana who picked up the remaining dagger and swept it around as if showing off her prowess. Chara did not need to watch, she knew Yuntana had a lifetime of practice. While Chara had a single year. Her only advantage was her ability at hunting and it did not seem that would be of much use.

"At my word you will fight, each only with the other, until one is dead," said the Prime Elder.

I am naked and she is a nachak.

"Fight."

The sound was barely out of the mouth of the Prime Elder than Chara threw herself sideways towards the ground in the direction of Yuntana, at least where she had been the last time she had looked.

But Yuntana was already gone

As Chara rolled, her opponent went over her head. Chara lashed out with the knife but she was too far away. Now she was on the floor and Yuntana was probably on her feet.

She came to a halt face down and sprung up, dodging backwards as a shadow came at her from the left. A blade slashed in front of her eyes. Chara heard a sharp intake of breath from the Aytrueth table.

Already she knew Yuntana was playing with her. If she had been close enough to attempt a blinding strike, she could have gone for the belly instead which would have resulted in death much sooner.

The proof of her arrogance was right there, she thought as she skittered backwards, not taking her eyes off her opponent.

The opening moves were complete. They both still lived and were unbloodied.

Chara was already breathing heavily and Yuntana was the same.

The ley-circle buzzed in the back of Chara's mind as she took up the standard fighting stance. Legs bent, feet apart, sitting low to the ground, arms held almost casually but the weapon slightly in advance.

Yuntana did the same and Chara seemed to hear people noting how her opponent's position was so much lower, demonstrating her superior skill. If anyone were taking bets, Chara would have bet on Yuntana.

She thought suddenly of Usala, what would her mother think of her? She was a woman of peace and kindness. She would not have approved of this. But Usala was not here and this was the only truth there was.

Chara took a deep breath and relaxed, letting her body settle further into the posture. She met Yuntana's eye. If she had been human, her opponent would be smiling her arrogance. But it could be seen readily enough in her yellow eyes.

Yuntana moved out of the ready posture and stood as if she were waiting for a visitor, arms hanging by her sides, the point of her weapon pointing at the ground.

"There's a tale of Faraha where the combatants waited for days for the other to falter. Until one of them blinked and died."

Chara did not respond but just remained focused. She could feel her sisters, they were not actively helping but their will, their desire for her to succeed, gave her strength.

Yuntana sidled towards the Aytrueth table, putting more distance between them though keeping Chara in view.

"If I were to kill one of your white-skins there would be no retribution. The rules do not apply to slaves."

She had moved so far to the side Chara was forced to adjust her position to continue to keep her in the middle of her vision. As she did so, Ulina stepped to the front of the table, her blade drawn. The Farahalek child looked far deadlier than Yuntana, even with a blade as small as the one she wielded. Perhaps the matriarch sensed it because she moved back towards Chara.

There were sounds of discontent among the matriarchs, as if they had been hoping for something more exciting. The two combatants tearing into one another with the spilling of blood as one of them died.

Something had to be done or Yuntana would drone on and eventually Chara would get tired standing in this position—perhaps that's what her opponent was hoping for, thinking that Chara was scared.

The feeding was very close now and the energies bubbling from both the circle and the sky were plain to Chara in a way they never had been before. Yet it was as if she had always known about them, that she had intentionally kept them hidden from herself.

But it was the *ziri* that had set her free. She could feel the power and sensed how the patterns in the walls channelled it. Just as it had done in her own heart-room.

The walls were protection. And they were weapons.

Pain bloomed in her leg and she collapsed in agony to the floor.

She had taken her attention off the fight and Yuntana had taken advantage from her position a dozen or more paces away. She had thrown her dagger, not to kill, but to maim.

And she clicked her victory, pouring scorn upon her fallen enemy.

Chara pulled herself together. The pain demanded her attention. The heavy blade had sunk a hands-breadth into the muscles of her thigh. It had been an accurate shot.

Outside she knew the Mother's milk lashed down from the moons. The energy filled her mind. Chara grabbed the dagger in her leg and suffered the agony of pulling it free. Her blood flowed in a thick stream and dripped to the floor.

Usala had healed her a dozen times, from injuries that normal living had given her. Now she stared at the gash in her leg and willed it to become whole once more. In her mind's eye the patterns in the walls around the hall seemed to glow. They fed her the raw power of the Mother's milk and the wound closed. Though the pain continued, even if dulled.

Chara climbed to her feet.

The murmurs of the matriarchs were stilled. They simply stared.

Yuntana's face was filled with astonishment. Then she pointed at the Aytrueth table. "They have interfered! Their patterner has healed her. Aytrueth is forfeited to me and they all die!"

The room exploded in uproar, Elona and Kantees were on their feet. Ulina had mounted the table and stared around

The Prime Elder raised her arms, and eventually the room went silent.

She turned to the priestess. "Did you perceive whence came the healing, Gracious One?"

The patterner looked at her companions all of whom nodded. Yuntana looked exultant as she awaited the statement.

"The white-skins did not interfere, Gracious Elder. I and all of us here clearly saw the power emanate from the walls themselves and channel through Chara ar-Gey Aytrueth."

"No!" screamed Yuntana. "She is no patterner! She cannot be!"

Chara thought Yuntana seemed to have missed the point but it was clear the Elders had not.

"The walls?" said the Prime Elder.

The priestess simply nodded.

The Prime Elder turned back to the two combatants. "No rule has been broken. Continue."

The pain in Chara's leg had eased and her wound was now just a thin line. She stood up holding both daggers but Yuntana was not looking at her.

"Gracious Elder, I withdraw my challenge. I cannot defeat a patterner who can heal herself as she is wounded."

The Prime Elder looked long at Yuntana. "You cannot withdraw from the Rite of Faraha." She paused to allow the statement to sink in and as she saw Yuntana about to speak again she added. "Nor do I recommend you yield, since Kiyoreth will be eaten by Aytrueth and you will be required to drink the draft of unbecoming. If you wish to live, you must fight."

Chara had to give her opponent credit. Once she had accepted the word of the Elders, she turned to face Chara and this time she looked deadly serious. And vastly more dangerous now she knew she might lose.

Having both daggers did not please Chara. She had not trained in this, but she needed to try to take advantage at least.

Keeping her weight low to the ground she advanced slowly.

Yuntana screamed and leapt forwards, but off to Chara's right side. Chara lashed out at the unexpected move but Yuntana twisted in the air and the side of her foot slammed into Chara's wrist.

The shock of it loosened her muscles and the dagger clattered to the ground. Yuntana was on it in a moment and lunged forward with the knife aimed at Chara's stomach.

Chara slammed her left hand down. Blade struck blade. Yuntana's attack was deflected between Chara's legs, but the attacker's shoulder struck Chara's lower leg pushing it back and tipping her forward. Some of her training kicked in. She tucked her head in, her free hand hit the ground and she rolled away once and then twice. But her leg was bruised and in pain from the impact.

She spun round on her knees to find her opponent on her again. Chara parried, pushing the oncoming knife to the side, but Yuntana sliced down cutting a long thin line down her upper arm.

Chara could feel the power in the walls but as Yuntana struck with her full body from the side, she was knocked off balance and forced to the ground. The Kiyoreth matriarch was not stupid, she knew the constant attacks kept Chara from concentrating.

It was working.

Yuntana landed on Chara's back, knocking the wind out of her. Chara felt the power in the walls and pulled at it, she had no thought beyond wanting to survive—wanting to ride the *ziri* again.

A collective in-drawing of breath echoed through the room.

Chara turned her head right round to see Yuntana's knife coming down at her face. She pulled enough to the side for the blade to only slice her cheek. She grabbed the wrist so her opponent couldn't pull away. Chara rotated her head forward again then slammed it back into Yuntana's face. Then did it again, just because she could. The power from the walls was hers now, she could feel it filling her up, making her stronger.

Keeping her grip tight on the wrist she rolled onto her side to get Yuntana off and rotated in place. Twisting the wrist and bringing her own dagger into play, she drove it hard into Yuntana's shoulder.

Her opponent grunted with the pain, got her feet under her and drove herself upwards ripping her wrist from Chara's grip despite suffering claw wounds as Chara's talons cut through Yuntana's skin.

Talons?

There were sounds of unease coming from the crowd of matriarchs.

"No," said Yuntana staring in terror.

Chara spun round, tripped over her tail and thumped heavily into the floor. Her arms felt strange and she had lost her knife. But she wasn't concerned, she reared up and looked down at Yuntana, who seemed surprisingly small.

There was a lot of movement in the hall. Matriarchs and their retinues were fleeing for the exits. Only the elders and priestesses remained in their seats, although one of the apprentices was hiding behind hers.

Chara turned her head to see Kantees was grinning all over her face while Elona just stared in what resembled astonishment. The scarring on her sister's face looked surprisingly distinct even at this distance.

Then she saw the tail, covered in feathers and wondered how a *zirichak* had got in the hall and how Yuntana was going to complain that someone had cheated again. Chara followed the line of the animal's back, past the wings and felt her neck getting tight.

Pain hit her in the belly, her head whipped back and she was looking directly down at Yuntana repeatedly stabbing at her. Without a thought, she lunged down and bit her opponent in half.

She felt strangely pleased as she crunched the matriarch's head, though she was bleeding heavily from her stomach, and it hurt a great deal.

She spat out the knife before swallowing then, as Yuntana's upper half travelled down her throat, she swung her neck round to the Prime Elder. She tried to speak but could only produce grunts and growls.

She sat back on her haunches, and burped.

CHAPTER 31

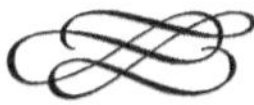

"Mother's milk," whispered Kantees as she got to her feet.

Elona saw it but still wasn't sure she believed her eyes as Chara's body deformed. The tail was first. She was reminded that humans thought the Slissac had tails and how she had blurted it out on the second day she was with Chara and Usala.

Now there was a tail and her legs grew in size while her arms lengthened.

She had been terrified that Chara wouldn't be able stand against Yuntana's frenzied and continuing attacks, that she wouldn't be able to heal herself fast enough. It was all Elona could do to stop herself from trying to save Chara from the knife wounds being inflicted on her. She had seen the power going into her, but it had just spread through Chara's body and seemed to fade out immediately.

The appearance of the tail had surprised everyone including Chara as she turned and fell over it. It left her defenceless for that short time but even Yuntana was staring.

The change in Chara's pattern was not something Elona had even conceived as possible. Feathers sprouted and grew to full size in moments, her neck lengthened as her head changed shape into a *zirichak*.

As far as Elona could tell Chara was not in pain. It was almost as if she had not noticed, the way she had watched the other matriarchs trying to escape and then turned to look at Elona and Kantees.

The part where she had eaten Yuntana had been unpleasant, though Kantees seemed quite pleased.

Chara's body was still receiving power from the patterns in the walls. Elona could see they were channelling the raw energy from the ley-circle even after the feeding had passed.

Perhaps it had something to do with what Kantees had said about the Slissac towers that stood on ley-circles but channelled the power instead of being destroyed.

She looked up again and saw that Chara was trying to communicate with the Prime Elder. The physical change must be total since she could not form words.

"Come on," said Kantees. "She's won."

I suppose biting your opponent in half counts as a win.

Kantees headed for Chara while Elona hurried across to the dais on which the Prime Elder sat. Slissac kept all their emotions inside, their faces were too inflexible to show much but even so, the Prime Elder looked uncomfortable.

Elona bowed low, even though that wasn't a Slissac custom, and tried to make herself understood in a language where she could not produce half the sounds she needed. She tried to keep it simple.

"House Aytrueth?"

The Prime Elder pulled her eyes from the *zirichak* and looked at Elona.

"House Aytrueth has survived the Rite of Faraha."

"Elona! She's hurt and needs healing right now."

There was so much Elona wanted to ask, such as whether this shape changing was something the Slissac knew about. But she just didn't have the words. It seemed the Prime Elder had decided Chara had won, so as long as they could get her back to her proper form it should all be good.

She bowed again and went over to Chara. The stab wounds

were bad but it did not take much to stop the bleeding, and the Mother's milk still leaked from the walls.

"I think we need to get her out of here," she said to Kantees. "The walls are feeding this change with power, perhaps if we can get her out it will stop."

"But what if the change is too abrupt? And what about the part of that Slissac she ate? It won't change size, will it?"

Elona shook her head. "I don't know."

Chara brought her huge head down and perched it on Elona's shoulder.

"Do you understand what we're saying?" said Kantees.

Chara grunted.

"Grunt twice if you understand this."

Two grunts.

"You're still you."

One grunt.

"Was that no or yes?" said Kantees.

"It was yes."

"How do you know?"

"Because if she hadn't understood she wouldn't have responded."

Elona took a step back from the changed Chara, and explained what had happened as best she understood it, along with their concerns about changing back with what she had eaten still in her.

Moments later Chara regurgitated the remains of Yuntana's torso and head on to the floor of the hall directly in front of Elona.

"That's disgusting," said Elona. "And it stinks."

"*Ziri* do that with bigger animals when they eat them," said Kantees. "Chara knows how to be a *zirichak* even though she's still herself."

Elona shook her head. "That's not important right now." She faced Chara with her big eyes and wide mouth. "We discovered our skills slowly which meant we learnt to control them. For you, it's all happened at once. There are two possibilities I can think of, either you have to stop the power flowing into you, or you have to use it to make the change back."

"Which first, Elona?" said Kantees.

"Try to use the power you're getting to change back." She hesitated. "You didn't imagine every part of a *ziri* to make this change, did you?"

Chara's head swung from side to side.

"So that's not how you do it. Try to remember what you were thinking when it happened and do the same, but conceive yourself instead. Does that make sense?"

Chara's head tilted to one side, then nodded.

"We'll step back."

Together they returned to the table. Ulina was still standing on it and keeping her eyes on the entrances, the Elders and the patterners.

Elona saw Chara turn her head and look at them then away once more.

"Don't look at her," said Elona.

"Why not?"

"It might be harder with someone watching."

Kantees gave a short laugh. "Yes, things can be like that."

Elona followed her own advice but she did not need to see with her eyes to perceive the magical forces working in and around Chara. That she had completely changed her pattern to become a *zirichak* was without question, the patterns were there in front of her.

There were stories, of course, legends and mythology that told of individuals that could change their form. No one believed them. They were just tales for children handed down from mother to child.

And yet it was true. She still found it hard to believe though she had seen it with her own eyes. But if Chara could do it once she could do it again, and her skill would improve. That was how it had worked, for both Kantees and Elona herself. All the time learning new ways that their skills could work, becoming able to use more power—well, perhaps that was not how it was for Kantees.

Perhaps it would not be like that for Chara.

But Chara was also *fahain*, if that meant anything at all.

"Perhaps she will be able to change into different creatures," said Ulina.

"Perhaps she will," said Kantees.

Elona could wait no longer and looked over to where her sister stood. Still in the form of the *zirichak*. She had not realised before but instead of appearing as one of the wild ones, with their simpler colours, Chara's feathers were green, yellow and blue. She was the most colourful thing in the hall.

But she had not changed back.

Biting her lip, Elona got up and walked across the hall to her sister.

"No luck?"

Chara shook her head.

"You tried both ways?"

Grunt.

"But you're still in there, all of you?"

The *ziri* put her head on one side and performed a movement with her shoulders that could only be described as a shrug.

The Prime Elder and the head priestess stepped down from the dais as the others departed.

Elona pursed her lips. This was going to be difficult.

"Chara ar-Gey Aytrueth. Elona tu-Gey Aytrueth. Kanteesss ko-Gey Aytrueth," said the Prime Elder. Elona was grateful the Slissac seemed to fully accept that this *zirichak* was Chara.

Every matriarch had seen her change, seen her bite Yuntana in half—the parts of her body still lay in the middle of the room stinking the place, though no one took any notice. Cleaning up the mess was a task for lesser creatures, and they couldn't start until the matriarchs, elders and priestesses had left.

Chara lay down and curled herself round so she was not towering over them, and gave the Elder her full attention. Kantees moved beside Chara's head and sat with her hand buried in the feathers of her neck. Elona saw Ulina stalking around the perimeter of the room as if looking for enemies.

The Prime Elder launched into a long speech which Elona found almost impossible to follow, except that she mentioned the Aytrueth and Kiyoreth names several times, and the words for mother, daughter, and sisters.

When she finally finished Chara grunted and nodded.

At which point the Elder spoke at more length and even faster.

Once she had finished, Chara looked at Elona and gave the shrug.

Elona spoke to her sister directly. "I think there may be a way we can do this. You understand me." Grunt. "And you understand the Elder." Grunt. "If I ask questions which have simple yes or no answers, we could make some progress."

Elona could have sworn the noise that Chara generated from the back of her long neck expressed scepticism of her last point.

"I can try."

Grunt.

"Was she talking about the fact you are now matriarch of Kiyoreth?"

Grunt.

"And that means you take everything they have?"

Grunt.

Elona was tempted to think of it as barbaric, as if the Taymalin were past that stage in their society, but it had been exactly what the Dunor had been planning. Kill everyone who opposed them and take over their property.

This is going to take a long time.

"Let's hope you can change back soon."

Grunt.

Elona looked out of the window in the new quarters they now inhabited. It had been a three-day since the feast and there was no sign of Chara returning to her normal form. She spent a lot of time with Kantees and the other *ziri*, and went out hunting with them because a *zirichak* cannot live on mushrooms.

Getting Chara out of the hall had been hard enough. The place was buried deep in the mountain and there was no easy exit to the outside, as there was in the main audience hall of the elders. If the outside air had been close, Elona would have made a hole herself but it was not an option.

The only way out for Chara, as with anyone else, was through the tunnels and she could barely fit her body into them, let alone her wings which kept getting in the way. Normally a *zirichak* on the ground walked on their back legs and used their wings to support the weight of the front of their body. It was ungainly but it worked.

To get through the tunnels, Chara's wings had to be kept flat against her body and pointing backwards which meant Chara was forced to push herself along the ground with her talons while her head and neck slithered along the ground.

It was slow and from Chara's frequent momentary panics when she could not move her wings, very distressing. Elona felt for her friend but there was nothing she could do to help—though if necessary, she was willing to disintegrate a wall. Kantees stayed at her head the whole time, not intimidated by the dangerous array of teeth. And she talked constantly, telling Chara how well she was doing.

After a while the tunnels widened enough that Chara was not in constant danger of getting stuck, though still not sufficient for her to use her wings to walk. But in the end, they reached fresh air, and then the glow of dawn since most of the night had passed by.

Chara screeched, and launched herself from the high exit into the air below. Elona panicked as she saw her sister fall until moments later, still screeching, Chara shot upwards and across the roof tops. The other *ziri*, on the Aytrueth building, burst into the air like arrows and they flew off into the grey dawn.

"She needs to do this," said Kantees. She put her arm around Elona's shoulders.

"What if she doesn't come back."

"How can she not?"

Elona had still had to negotiate the high bridges to return to Aytrueth. And she stayed awake until Kantees brought her news that Chara was back, and that she had brought food with her.

Only then did Elona sleep.

~

IN THE DAYS THAT FOLLOWED, the High Priestess, her name was Llakassa, became an almost permanent addition to the Aytrueth household. And Ulina was beside Elona too, having been told by her mother to be bodyguard.

Between them, Llakassa and Elona attempted to reach a common working language: part Taymalin and part Slissac. Sometimes they resorted to drawing on the tables to communicate their ideas. And between them they also talked to Chara.

Elona, having examined the top floor, rendered the rooftop into dust so that Chara could at least spend her nights inside the building—the other *zirichasa* joined her. Elona watched the way Sheesha behaved, he had always been the leader with Kantees but now he seemed to defer to Chara. Perhaps that made sense, after all she had led the formation on the back of a tamed wild *ziri* and made them fly fast.

Did that mean Sheesha would want to mate with Chara? Elona found the idea very confusing. It also made her wonder what happened to the Slissac seed Chara held in her body. It was all too complicated and there was so much she did not understand.

She laughed at herself. She had thought she had come to understand patterns and the Mother's milk, perhaps even the strange power of the void that had scarred her. It turned out she knew nothing.

CHAPTER 32

On the fifth day, Llakassa came to Elona saying something about Kiyoreth and daughters. Elona remembered the three of them sitting at their table in the feast, and how they watched their mother being bitten in half by Chara. No doubt they had been joking only moments before about how their mother would kill the stupid outsider and they would take over.

Perhaps they plotted to kill one another too, because each of them would want to be the next matriarch.

Elona shook her head. "We ask Chara," she said in her simple version of the Slissac tongue. It was a phrase she had learnt to use.

The two of them plus the shadow of Ulina went upstairs to find both of her sisters together. Chara raised her head and bumped Elona gently in the stomach by way of greeting. Elona was not sure but it seemed as if there was an air of sadness in her. And why shouldn't there be, she was lost in a body that was not hers and unable to communicate. So Elona put her hands beneath Chara's scaly chin and placed a kiss on her snout. Ulina hugged her mother who returned it with a smile that expressed the love she gave.

"We have to talk about Yuntana's daughters," said Elona.

Chara grunted. She twisted her head to look at Llakassa and nodded in greeting. The High Priestess bowed.

They all sat on the floor as Chara laid her head down.

"You could," said Elona with a glance at the priestess, "have them killed."

Chara growled and the sound shook Elona.

"Good. That would be a terrible thing to do."

Grunt.

Elona looked at the priestess. "No kill."

Llakassa turned to Chara and said, as far as Elona could tell, just what she had and again Chara growled. It was a system they had worked out to make sure they understood and agreed on what Chara wanted. They would ask in both languages, and hopefully get the same response.

"You don't have to go through the daughter binding with them, which I think means they would become servants. But if you do make them your daughters, they outrank any child you have because they're older."

Elona looked at Llakassa and held her hand open then gestured toward Chara. "You tell."

The priestess launched into a much longer description of what it meant to perform the daughter-binding. Elona only knew as much as had been discussed in respect to Ulina.

Finally, Llakassa had finished and looked at Elona again.

"So do you want to perform the daughter-binding with them?"

Chara lifted her head, grunted and nodded at the same time. She did not seem in any doubt which Elona found curious and she wished she could talk to Chara about it properly. Perhaps one day.

Llakassa asked the same question and got the same response.

"Agreeeed," said the priestess, then she clicked to herself as if using the language of the slaves amused her.

THE RITUAL HAPPENED in the main audience chamber on the sixth day after the feast. It had to be witnessed by the other matriarchs, and particularly their patterners, to ensure all the forms were followed.

The day at least was auspicious. The sky cloudless with the sun shining strongly as the year moved into summer. But here the snow still clung to the mountain sides and piled up in shadowed gullies.

Despite the good weather, Elona was not expecting this to turn out well, three young girls to be bound as daughters to a *zirichak*? To an animal? The fact she was going to be forced to ride Ilith again did not help.

Chara had offered to carry her by bending low to the ground and poking her snout towards her back. Elona smiled through her fear.

"No, I can't."

Chara nodded forcefully.

Elona placed her hand on Chara's nose. "I trust you, of course I do. But even if I was brave enough to ride you without a saddle— and I'm not—it wouldn't be right."

Chara turned her head to the side as if querying why.

"What would it look like if the matriarch of Aytrueth, now the most powerful family here, arrived carrying a white-skin like a common *kichek* or horse? You are the one in charge, we must all follow you."

Just as Sheesha and all the other had been doing since she had changed—as they had done that day when she rode Sulassa and made the golden path. She was the mistress now.

Chara paused and then nodded.

Elona sighed and turned to Ilith, with Ulina there ready to help her up into the saddle. She could not help but feel a complete fraud among these people and their *zirichasa*.

She climbed into Ilith's saddle and let Ulina do up the straps.

Then Ulina bounded onto the back of Halenth and they launched into the sky. Leaving Elona's stomach behind. There were just the four of them this time. Chara, Kantees, Ulina and Elona, they did not bring the rest and simply flew along the cliff to the cave and entered.

Chara landed perfectly with the others behind her. Ulina was undoing the straps before Ilith had settled and Elona had solid rock beneath her feet once again.

The gathered matriarchs withdrew as Chara approached the dais. Elona wondered if she had been practising because she managed to make it look graceful, swinging her body and tail as her wings moved to the same rhythm. A real *ziri* wouldn't care how they walked as long as it worked, but Chara knew how silly they could look and she needed to be as regal as possible.

Sunlight poured into the cave mouth and bounced off the stones lighting the room and showing off Chara's dazzling colours.

Elona and Kantees walked forward with her and Ulina stayed at Elona's shoulder. There still might be an attack, or some other form of challenge.

The Prime Elder stood and spoke at length, Elona understood enough to know she was talking about the duel and that Chara had won it. That the two houses were now one, and Chara had agreed to bind herself with Yuntana's daughters.

As far as she could tell there was no mention of Chara now being a *zirichak*.

The Prime Elder stepped forward now, but did not come down and did not wave the daughters forward.

Elona could see the terror written in their eyes. They could not keep still, and a group of Kiyoreth women were preventing them from bolting.

This was a problem.

How could the ritual be performed if the girls were scared? The magic would not work without their consent. They probably thought Chara would eat them just as she had done their mother.

The High Priestess stepped up now and she moved across to where the girls were being held. Then she turned to Chara and said something at which she settled to the floor, curled up and laid her head out towards the dais and away from the Kiyoreth group.

Then Llakassa sat down and talked to the girls. Elona was too far away to hear, but it seemed somewhere between a chant and a song, although the words she heard were not repeated, so perhaps it was just a story.

Elona was certain no magic was cast but the girls did settle and finally sat down too. Although she could not be sure of their ages, Elona guessed the eldest might have twelve years and the others perhaps ten and eight.

In this place where every potential matriarch was in a constant war against her rivals, and where kindness seemed in very short supply, the idea that the priestess was calming children by telling a story seemed very out of place. But as she had often thought, the whole structure of the matriarchs seemed flawed, how could it survive with all the murder?

"If it was me," said Kantees. "I would just tell them they would become the most powerful matriarchs here."

"Just one of them and then only when Chara dies."

"Even so, it's an opportunity when they would have none."

"Perhaps that's what they're being told."

"Taking a long time over it."

"They're just children," said Elona.

Kantees glanced at Ulina then back to Elona. "They know what's at stake."

"They're scared."

Eventually Llakassa stopped talking and stood, the three girls did the same and stared at Chara lying there, her eyes open, but otherwise inert on the floor. The priestess walked across to stand next to Chara's head and the girls followed, the smallest had the boldest step of all three. Perhaps whatever Llakassa had said made the most impression because she was the youngest.

The three stood in a line beside Chara's long neck and instructed by the priestess reached out and placed their hands on the feathers. Elona could not help but smile when the smallest let her hand stroke along the neck.

The priestess took three strips of material already inscribed with the required patterns from her assistant and laid each so it lay across a child's hand and hung both sides of Chara's neck. The only movement to be seen from Chara was her body rising and falling as she breathed.

As the ritual progressed the priestess demanded the agreements of each of them in turn, interspersing Chara too. So Chara did the only thing she could, grunt her agreement. The smallest jumped the first time though the other two managed to hold their positions.

And then it was over.

The voices of the matriarchs all breathing out was a gentle sigh that bounced from the walls. The daughters of Chara stood back as she lifted her head and neck, then using her wings pressed herself upwards until she towered above them.

This time they did not try to run, did not seem to be afraid.

Chara bowed her head once to the priestess, and then the elders. Being very careful where she put her feet, wings and tail, she elegantly walked back to where Elona and Kantees stood. The three girls walked in a line beside her.

They are Chara's responsibility now. And I have three nieces— she caught herself and looked at Ulina. *I already had a niece and I did not even think about it.*

She wondered how they would get them home.

CHAPTER 33

Day by day, the sun mounted higher in the sky, and the snows disappeared except on the highest peaks.

Chara woke each morning feeling the power of her wings and body, wanting nothing more than to fly with the others. Which she did every day for a short time, or longer when she had to hunt for food.

Sheesha's attentions were annoying and she had to keep putting him in his place. She was not an animal. Though she marvelled that he accepted her as his matriarch so easily. Perhaps it was the same as with Kantees, she was in charge.

But still, she could not spend all her time with the air beneath her wings. There were things that had to be done. Whatever else had changed she was still matriarch of Aytrueth.

It was when she had seen her adopted daughters being taught to write she realised she had been a fool. The look on Elona's face had been priceless when Chara had scratched out "How are you today, sister?" roughly in the dust using the writing that Usala had taught her.

Things moved quicker then. Not only could she make her thoughts known to Elona and Kantees, Slissac writing was very similar to Taymalin and with the help of Llakassa she managed to make herself understood in that language too.

She could even communicate with her new daughters.

With Kantees, Chara picked out the three smallest *zirichasa* from the formation and gifted them to the girls so they could ride with her when she flew. Their pleasure was genuine though they were still nervous of her, after all she had bitten their mother in half as they watched. The binding could do nothing to change that.

However, she had also made them heirs to the most powerful house and the only one that rode *zirichasa*. On the one hand that would make them all the more eager to kill her so they could inherit, but perhaps not for a while.

At least in this form there was little anyone could do to harm her.

Elona too was working hard to understand the Slissac language and the idea of writing what she wanted to say—avoiding the problems of her mouth being unable to form the sounds—made all the difference.

"How can we change you back?" wrote Elona when they, Kantees and Llakassa were together. She also spoke the question out loud.

"There are many Slissac tales of shape changing," said Llakassa. "Both patterners and *fahain*."

"And they could change back?" said Kantees.

"Unless they had been cursed into the shape."

"This was not a curse," said Elona.

"I needed to win," said Chara. "It just happened so that I could. I do not think that is a curse."

Llakassa nodded her agreement. "There was no power from the outside that did this. You did it to yourself."

"So, I should be able to undo it."

Elona scribbled her next statement on the paper before she said it. "You are the High Priestess, do you not know how to make the patterns change? Are there written records?"

"We have some histories," said Llakassa, "but nothing that deals with things like this—except the stories themselves and they have no details of the magic."

"But what about you," said Kantees looking at Elona, "with your power?"

Elona shook her head. "I can bend patterns to my will and I can mend them, this is different. The very patterns themselves have been changed."

Chara held up her wing and they waited patiently while she scratched her question. "Who else know?"

"Our people went their own way so many years ago," said the priestess. "We have few records from that time. Our forebears only carried what they could when they left."

"You're saying the Slissac back where you came from might know?" said Elona.

"They might but they are long ago and far away. Perhaps they are all dead now. The way was forgotten so that we could truly separate ourselves from them."

In Chara's mind, the phrase *the way was forgotten* was like a half-remembered chant from before her family had been killed.

"Do the Taymalin patterners know?" said Kantees.

"If they do, it will be a hidden teaching. They are very protective of their secrets."

She went quiet and Chara could see she was thinking about something. Elona's hand went to her face and touched the scarred cheek. Chara understood that her sister had been considered beautiful by human standards. She had spoken of Jaymis a little, how they had been together and how he had died. Elona had never said that Jaymis ever made comment about her scars—though she had not gained them until they had been on the journey together.

Kantees spoke of two men, lordlings, but seemed not to care for them, at least not as husband or even lover. But her story had been as astonishing as Elona's when she finally told it. Perhaps she was not as powerful as Elona when it came to patterning, but her empathy with the *zirichasa* was a remarkable thing.

Chara sighed.

She could laugh at her innocence when she and Elona had

finally gained the house from the old matriarch. It was not Usala's fault, she was Taymalin and brought up in their society, and that was how she had brought up Chara. Along with stories about princes and princesses, love and heartbreak. Even Elona had reinforced it with her story of how she had almost become the queen of Faerholme.

And it was with those myths in her mind that Chara had come to this place, fully expecting to marry a Slissac male. Only to find the best she could hope for was to be inseminated by one that she chose from a list. And paid for.

There was no romance here., unless she found another matriarch not intent on killing her with whom she could share a bed. Or use one of the servants.

It did not seem likely.

"Kadralin!" said Elona suddenly, snapping Chara from her maudlin thoughts.

Elona smiled, a thing she did very rarely, and stepped back to the writing table.

"I can't help you," said Kantees.

"No, when I was with the Kadralin traders—" she sank to her knees. "—this is embarrassing. It was a celebration, not a feeding, I don't really know what it was about. But the shaman, Yolandra, conjured a power and seemed to change shape in the fire."

Kantees frowned. "I have never heard of this, but the Taymalin tried to remake us in their image, to make us forget ourselves."

"Only on Esternes."

Kantees held up her hand. "I know."

"Sorry. But Yolandra changed her shape."

They waited while Chara scratched a question. "You told me it was fire."

Llakassa was looking confused, so they took a little time informing her of Elona's revelation and Chara's objection.

"It was the fire, and perhaps she wasn't really doing it. But it may be there's something we can use in that."

"Kadralin knowledge is not written down," said Kantees.

"We have to find Yolandra."

"Or any Kadralin shaman, I know one on Esternes, there will be others," said Kantees.

"We can search until we find one who knows."

"But," wrote Chara, "I cannot leave here."

ANOTHER FIVE-DAY PASSED and the weather warmed even more. The snows melted into torrents of water thundering down the mountainsides and into the valleys with their tumbling rivers. Green spread from the valleys up the high slopes.

CHARA HAD an audience with the Prime Elder, and Elona went with her as protection. Ulina was forced to stay behind. That the Aytrueth was composed largely of white-skins was officially accepted but not liked by anyone so it did well not to make a point of it. Elona was permitted partly for security and partly because she had been the one who had arrived with Chara the first time.

They went up to the roof and Elona looked round, apparently for Ilith.

Chara grunted at her and ducked her body, laying her neck along the ground.

Elona looked round and frowned. "I can't."

Chara grunted at her again, though this time it was more of a growl. Deep and menacing.

"You haven't got a saddle—and you shouldn't have one. I'm not riding on you, we need to get Ilith."

Chara really growled this time. She was tired of Elona making excuses. Besides if her plan worked out this was how it would be in the future, how she wanted it to be—at least until she could change back. Now that she was able to communicate without help, even if her writing was messy, there were things she could do without Elona knowing.

"You really want me to ride on you, bare back?

Grunt.

"What if I throw up on you?"

Growl.

Elona threw up her hands. "Very well, but I won't be cleaning you. And if I fall off and die, I'll never forgive you."

Chara had found the *ziri* mouth and tongue could produce an effective click when she wanted to laugh. So she did it now, and bumped Elona in the stomach with her snout, making her sister stagger.

"I'm not laughing," said Elona.

Chara watched as her sister stalked to where Chara's neck met her body. She could imagine her thinking how much larger than Ilith she was.

Ulina hurried to her side and helped Elona climb up, putting her legs each side of Chara's neck.

"Tuck your legs under the wings," said Ulina. "Hold on to these feathers but do not pull them out."

"I feel sick already."

"Lean forward and to one side if you are going to throw up." Ulina then thrust a heavy bag at Elona. "Chara said I have to give this to you."

Elona frowned at Ulina then looked questioningly at Chara, but she slipped her arm and head through the strap so it hung safely across her shoulder.

Chara turned her head round completely so she was facing Elona, she did look small against the size of the wings. Carefully she moved her snout all the way along her neck until she was barely a hands-breadth from Elona's face. Then, as gently as she could manage, she touched her mouth to Elona's unscarred cheek.

Elona reached up and placed her hand against Chara's face. "I know you mean well, but this is not something I can control. I trust you. Let's go."

At her word, Chara swung her head back, pushed her weight on to her legs, spread her wings and launched herself upwards.

Elona screamed but Chara could still feel her legs tucked tightly beneath her wings so knew she hadn't fallen off yet.

The joy of flying had never left her over all the time she had been this way. Her wings were strong and the wind had no tricks it could play that would fool her. They twisted over the town and her *ziri* eyes picked up every movement of every person visible at a window, crossing a walkway, or on the ground. She curved around. If she had been alone, she would have gone out across the mountains but she did not wish to cause her sister any more discomfort than she had to.

She turned towards the cliff and flew through the buffeting winds until the cave mouth came in sight. She glided in and came to a smooth landing.

The audience hall was empty save for the elders and patterners, all seated on their ornate chairs.

Lying down, Chara allowing Elona to dismount before moving into the main hall at slow but positive pace. She had seen how the real *zirichasa* moved on the ground—ungainly but effective. It was important that she appear to be more than just an animal and had practised walking a great deal, just so that she would not disgrace her family at times like this, and so she would not be mistaken for an animal.

The two of them reached the space in front of the dais. Chara bowed her head, and saw Elona bow out of the corner of her eye. She was wearing a new dress that Chara's staff had made. Heavy material but shaped to be a better fit for human females, the seamstress was getting quite good at it. Chara liked having feathers but they took a lot of cleaning—although it was not something she had to think about, her body just went through the motions when it needed to.

But now was not a time to be preening.

The Prime Elder stood up.

"You wished for this meeting, matriarch?"

Chara turned her head to Elona and nodded. It took her sister a moment to understand then she took the bag off her shoulder and lifted the flap. There were several sheets of writing skins inside, covered in small handwriting. All of it in the Slissac tongue though Elona recognised some of the glyphs.

Llakassa came down to take the documents from Elona.

"What is it?" said Elona quietly.

The priestess clicked softly. "New 'atterns."

Chara could hear them perfectly, and felt a little unhappy that she had kept Elona in the dark about her plans. But it had been important to do it.

"You have read these?" said the Prime Elder as the priestess handed them over.

"I copied them for House Aytrueth, Gracious Elder. And advised where it was appropriate"

The elder turned to Chara. "I must be certain this is your intention."

Chara nodded and grunted.

"I cannot stop you but I fear for our people."

Chara shook her head. She understood the elder's fears. No one had founded a new town in a thousand years. But that is what she saw as part of the problem, her people were dying out. She had asked the priestess to study the records and had found what she suspected, the population here and in the nearby towns had been decreasing. It was slow which meant no one had noticed but they had become stagnant, and inward looking. The spirit that had brought them to this place had died.

But expansion meant there were risks of revealing themselves to the humans.

Ultimately Chara did not think it was possible to keep themselves hidden forever, but she had not said that and it was not in the document.

Instead she and Llakassa had studied the past. The creatures they used to the make the tunnels were gone, the last one had died a long time ago. And there was no one to resurrect them. But Aytrueth had the *ziri* now, and they could learn to tame them, riding them between towns as needed, just as the *tekrasa* were used to carry cargo.

It was true that she could start this without the blessing of the elders, but it would be easier with their consent.

There followed a great deal of talking among the elders and priestess. This was not something she was supposed to be a part of but the hearing of a *zirichak* is extremely good. So she listened for a while until the arguments seemed to go around in circles and then became bored.

She glanced at Elona who looked both angry and confused.

She wished she were able to talk, she had even tried but it was impossible. *Zirichasa* throats did not seem to have what was needed.

She was getting hungry. It was a couple of days since she had hunted and taken down a *sikechak*. It had been enjoyable in itself because they were good flyers and it had taken effort. But their skin was tough and they didn't have a lot of meat on them. She really fancied a juicy *kelukisa* that she could suck the blood out of and then eat.

Something jammed into her side, and she looked down to see Elona had punched her. She was pointing at the dais.

I have been caught daydreaming about eating meat.

"Chara ar-Gey Aytrueth ko-Tek Tegina ar-Tek Guala Aka Hanna," said the Prime Elder.

Chara bowed her head in response.

"Did Elona tu-Gey Corlain tu-Gey Aytreuth know anything of this?"

Chara shook her head firmly.

"You did not discuss the founding of a new colony with her?"

Again she shook her head.

"I ask a third time by the patterns of your ancestors, does she know what this audience is for?"

Chara shook her head again. There was no reason why this should feel like a betrayal, and yet it did.

The Prime Elder nodded. "Then, Chara ar-Gey Aytrueth, you have the support of the council for the formation of a new home."

Chara looked down at Elona to see her sister looking up with a frown on her face. Facial expressions were something a *ziri* could do, though not with the same finesse as a human. She used her wing to indicate the exit and Elona followed her as she moved close to the opening.

She lay down and let Elona clamber on to her back. Without

Ulina's help it took longer but she settled and hooked her legs under Chara's wings.

By choice Chara would have gone to the edge and simply dropped over the side, the *ziri* part of her always wanted to use the least energy in flying. But Elona would not enjoy that. Instead she launched herself into the air, skimming across cave floor until they burst into the open.

CHAPTER 34

Chara banked to the left, away from the town, and climbed fast. Moments later they were joined by a couple of riderless *ziri*. Once high enough, Chara checked where the town was, and the tunnel she and Elona had used to escape the soldiers—the *zirichasa* had a knowledge of direction unlike anything she had experienced. She drew power from the ley-circle and launched herself on the golden path.

Her *zirichak* body flattened itself into an arrow as they shot across the mountains but the journey was not long. She let the power slip away and spread her wings. They were blasted by the sudden moving air but slowed quickly and descended in a spiral into an enclosed valley with a lake of frigid water and bordered by pine trees.

She wondered if Elona recognised the valley where they had escaped the Tirnian armsmen by swimming into the Slissac cave system.

But this place was not the same as it had been. She could smell the wood-burning fire before she saw the single column of smoke drifting up from the trees. A small boat made from animal skin stretched over a frame lay upside down on the lake shore.

Chara smelled human.

But still she circled down. Someone living in the trees and catching fish in the lake was not going to be a problem. Even if they had to be moved out, perhaps somewhere far away so they could not tell other humans that the Slissac were expanding their territory.

Though this had always been her people's land.

This was where she had been pushed out into the open air by her mother, to save her from death.

The pebbles on the lake shore crunched as three *zirichasa* touched down. Chara had planned to bring Elona here after the audience to explain to her what it had all been about.

Now they would have to deal with the visitor first.

At least with just Elona and her as a *zirichak*, the person would not realise Slissac were involved. This could be very easy.

"You might have told me we were not going home," said Elona as she slid from Chara's back. She stumbled as she landed and Chara turned in concern.

But she was crying.

Chara made a little noise in the back of throat and brought her head right up to her sister. She made the noise again, trying to make it sound like a question.

Elona wiped the tears away with the back of her hand and placed her palm on Chara's snout. "It's all right. Just—I never thought I'd see this place again. It's so beautiful, even if the memories of it aren't. And it's so good to be away from everything else."

Chara's *ziri* instinct was to lick Elona's tears, they smelled of salt. But she restrained herself. She had been licked by a *zirichak* before she changed, and it had not been pleasant.

Instead, she brought her feathered wing around her sister, like a hug. It was the best she could do. Elona cried even more.

Chara heard someone moving in the woods and lifted her head to look.

A human as she expected but just one. With a stick, hobbling slowly down a rough track from the fire to the shore. It was hard to see, the sunlight was strong and it made the shadows unfathomable.

Then that scent again, only more of it. More detail. It was a woman, she knew that now. But seemingly familiar—but how could it be? Her *ziri* nose had smelled very few humans.

Chara shook as the memories flooded back to her.

She tried to say "Mother" but she could only make a curious squeak in the back of her throat.

Pulling her wing from around Elona, Chara launched herself into a short glide that took her from the shoreline to the edge of the woods, landing lightly directly in front of the old woman.

She kept making the same squeaking noise over and over, as if she were a *ziriling* fresh from the egg, and flattened herself against the ground.

The woman stared at her with her single good eye, the other covered with a patch. Chara was panting trying by force of will to make the woman recognise her.

"Good afternoon, Usala," said Elona from behind Chara. "We are very pleased you are not dead."

The woman peered at her as if seeing past her damaged face. "Elona? Elona!"

Then perhaps she realised Elona had said "we", she stared at Chara still trying to express herself and failing, her body trembling.

The woman looked at Elona and back to Chara. Then she gasped and dropped to her knees. "By the Mother, Tek!" Then back at Elona. "It is Tek?" Half statement, half question.

"It is her, but the name given to her by her real mother is Chara." Elona was crying again.

Chara moved her head forward until she touched Usala, and the woman flung her arms across Chara's great head and wept.

At Usala's touch, Chara shook with emotions she could not express but managed not to knock her mother over.

It was a while before they spoke again.

Usala sniffed and looked at Elona. "Her name is not Tek?"

"It means mother—she wanted her mother."

"And I got it wrong."

Elona smiled. "I feel very strange saying this when she's right here but I suppose I have to, because she can't talk—though she can write. She is Chara ar-Gey Aytrueth ko-Tek Tegina ar-Tek Guala

Aka Hanna ar-Ku Jyrna ko-Ku Jyrna Aka Kalenaye. She is matriarch of the House of Aytrueth in a Slissac town close by—as the *ziri* flies."

"But she is…"

"A *zirichak*, yes. She changed her shape though only recently, and she can't change back." Elona came closer and put her hand on Chara's neck.

Usala climbed to her feet with difficulty. "You're a *zirichak*."

Grunt.

"I prayed you had survived, both of you."

Grunt.

"I'm afraid we were certain the Tirnian armsmen killed you," said Elona.

"They thought it cleverer to maim me when I would not give them the information they wanted, and left me to die slowly." She took a breath and lay on Chara's face, stretching her arms around to each side. "It really is you."

Grunt.

"You did not heal yourself," said Elona.

"My wounds meant something, I was unwilling to take that away." She looked at Elona. "You are not unscathed."

"These wounds cannot be healed."

"Cannot?"

Elona shook her head. "I have tried with all my skill, and all the power of a ley-circle at my beck and call."

"You have changed too."

"If you mean I am no longer the sick and frightened child that Chara brought to your doorstep, then yes, I have changed."

"I would invite you into my home," Usala said, "but you will not fit."

Chara lifted her head, slowly so that she did not surprise Usala and turned to move back to the beach. She went down to the sandy stretch before it became pebbles and scratched in the sand. The voices of Elona and her mother were perfectly clear.

"She is coloured like one of the racing dragons."

"We have some new friends," said Elona. "They ride dragons."

"I used to love the racing, the riders were always so handsome."

"Our friend is Kadralin, she rides a racing dragon called Shee-sha, and there's her daughter too."

"A Kadralin? I've been away such a long time, have things changed so much?"

"No, not much."

"She has a story too then."

"We all have stories."

They approached where Chara had been working and Usala made a little noise as she read the words scraped into the sand. "I love you, mother."

"My lessons were not wasted then," said Usala laughing.

"It's the only way we can communicate properly," said Elona.

"But why are you here? Not that I want you to go."

Elona looked at Chara. "Yes, I'd like to know that as well."

Chara sighed, this wasn't going to be easy, at least she could let Elona fill in the background as they went along.

She let Elona wipe the sand flat, it was easier for her.

"Slissac house too big too many daughters."

Elona had to explain then about how Chara was the matriarch of her house, fought a duel, and changed shape to win. It still felt like she had cheated but the rules of the Faraha were clear, any means as long as no one interfered.

"Make new place here split house."

"Really?" said Elona.

Chara nodded and added to her writing. "Best."

"Because otherwise your daughters will try to kill each other."

Chara shrugged and Usala laughed. "It really is you."

"But why didn't you tell me?" said Elona, she seemed hurt and with reason.

Chara pointed at the words and waited while Elona obliterated them.

"Human trick."

Elona stared at the two words scraped into the sand.

"I see."

"I do not," said Usala.

So Elona explained how terrified the Slissac were of humans, how much they despised them and how this group had left the others because they thought the human slaves weakened the Slissac. Chara had kept Elona in the dark so no one could say it was a human idea.

Chara's stomach rumbled. She swept away her last words and wrote "hunting". With that she launched herself into the air, and the other two *ziri* joined her.

CHAPTER 35

The sun was dipping below the mountains and the air growing cold as Chara landed on the shore after her hunt. It might be spring but a clear night would be very cold.

She waddled into the water to clean off the blood. Wild *kelukisa* was delicious and easy to kill—at least when you're a very large *ziri*. She wondered whether she would crave eating raw meat when she changed back. *If she changed back.*

There had to be a solution. If she could change herself so easily when she needed to, how could it be hard to return to her real self? Llakassa had scoured the records trying to find something relevant but there was nothing.

Chara could smell woodsmoke and cooking, Elona and Usala must have gone up the slope and into the forest.

She shook herself dry. The water did tend to cling to her feathers and made her feel heavy, but it was the natural thing to do. There were times she was afraid of losing herself in the *zirichak*.

Leaving the other two *ziri* on the shore, she made her way up on foot rather than trying to fly up and land among trees. She was not quiet as she crashed between the trees. Branches poked at her as she worked her way along the narrow trail. Still it was not as bad as the tunnels, at least she could still see the sky.

The building looked old, certainly the moss covering its timber walls had been there longer than when she and Elona had come through here. But they had not been looking for places to stay, just running into what seemed to be a dead end.

It looked solid enough.

The door opened as she blundered around the outside.

"Feeling better?" said Elona.

Chara grunted and settled herself in the open space in front, where the firelight from the door spread out.

"I spent the time telling Usala our complete history since we left."

Usala came to the door as well, leaning on her stick.

"I know someone who might be able to tell you how you can change back," she said.

Chara raised her head and looked at her mother intently.

"Florian," said Usala.

"The Arch-Patterner," said Elona, her words dripping with contempt.

Chara knew Elona disliked the man, and that opinion had been reinforced by Kantees. She had no particular desire to meet him but if he knew how to make her Slissac again, it was worth a try.

She gave a non-committal grunt.

"He knows more than any other patterner," said Usala.

"He manipulated you just as he did me—and Kantees."

"If he did, then see what you've become."

"My life has been destroyed. The man I loved, and the man I might have loved, taken from me because of him."

Usala tutted. "From what you told me, if it had not happened, this—what did you call them? Dura?"

"Dunor."

"They would have taken over everything, and that would have meant Tirnia in charge."

"He could have found someone else."

Usala said nothing to that.

Elona sighed. "We still don't have to like him."

"Leaders sometimes have to do things that are difficult and uncomfortable, even though they might ultimately be the right thing."

This time it was Elona who remained silent. Chara curled up. She did not feel the cold beneath her layers of feathers but the right position made all the difference.

"And it's not over," said Usala.

"No, the *Kisharuk* has not been destroyed."

"That part is hard to believe."

"You think I lied?"

"No, of course not."

"It's not just a bedtime story to scare children."

"That's what makes it hard to believe."

"We'll see how knowledgeable the Arch-Patterner is, because the question after asking how to save Chara, will be how to kill the *Kisharuk*."

The conversation lapsed. Finally Usala said she was cold and was going to bed but would make up a pallet for Elona.

But Chara lifted her wing and Elona said she would sleep outside.

Chara had no difficulty sleeping as a *ziri* and while she had never had someone sleep underneath her wing, it was one of those things that simply felt right. So Elona nestled in and Chara dropped her feathers over the top, feeling comfortable with her sister so close.

THE NEXT DAY, after Usala had fed Elona a big breakfast, the three of them stood on the shoreline again.

"I will have to move, won't I?" said Usala.

Elona glanced at Chara and she nodded.

"It would be safer. If Chara was here then it would be all right, you're her mother and the Slissac consider that important. But if you're here by yourself someone would decide that killing you would be the best thing to do."

She looked at her sister for confirmation and Chara nodded again.

"But it won't be immediate, it will take time for them to organise it. We can come and collect you before we head in search of Florian and take you wherever you want to go, back to Faerholme?"

"Not back there, no. I'll think about it. When do you think you will come?"

Chara shrugged.

"Perhaps a moon-turn?"

"I'll be ready." Then she laughed. "I will ride a *zirichak*?"

Chara lifted her head and hooted. Then looked down at her mother.

"I can ride you? I thought Elona did that."

"I hate it. You can ride her if you want to. At least with Ilith, I can have a saddle with straps and stirrups"

They made their goodbyes and Elona reluctantly mounted Chara's back.

In a smooth movement, Chara launched herself across the lake, skimming the surface. It was not that she was showing off for her mother, she told herself, but for Elona so that they did not rise too quickly.

As they approached the far side, she banked right and curved in towards the cliff, where the water met stone. She could see the darkness of the cave entrance below the waterline where they had trusted to nothing but luck to escape the Tirnian armsmen. It was ancient history. She turned again and started a steady spiralling climb.

There was no ley-circle nearby and nothing from which she could draw power for the golden path, but she knew both from Kantees and from her inner being that it was not essential. It simply helped.

And she wanted her mother to see.

As they approached the same height as the peaks around them, she headed back down the lake and then turned once more in the direction of Hanna with the two brown and black *ziri* at her side. They flashed into gold.

She did not understand the store of power that she had within her as a *ziri* but she knew it was there, and she could feel it depleting as the three of them shot through the sky.

But then the ley-circle was close enough and, again in a way she did not understand but instinctively knew how to achieve, she drew energy from it.

She managed to slow and return to the normal world in a blast of cold air. This time there was no battle and they circled swiftly down to the new family home. The reds and golds of Sheesha shone and he set up a loud hooting call for her, both as a greeting she understood and as an alert for everyone else.

Once landed, Chara lay flat so Elona could dismount easily, and she could feel the gratitude of her sister as her feet landed on the roof stones—just as Kantees, Ulina and Chara's three daughters emerged on to the roof.

"Where have you been?" said Kantees, looking angrily at Chara.

"Looking at the place the new house will be," said Elona.

"I was worried! I knew you weren't dead, and Llakassa managed to explain what—" she broke off staring past Elona and at Chara who had stopped listening anyway.

Her new daughters had gathered around and were touching her then the eldest put her arms round her neck, the others did the same.

A warmth grew inside as the binding between them intensified. Her *ziri* sensitivity to the magic could almost see it. And for the second time, tears dripped from her *zirichak* eyes. She wrapped her wings around her daughters.

She understood them and the change. They no longer had to fight each other, or plan each other's deaths. Each of them would get their own houses. Two here in Hanna, the old Aytrueth home and the new one, split fairly if not evenly. And the third, would have responsibility for the new home and perhaps become the elder of a new town if the other Slissac families followed their lead, and why should they not?

This town and the ones subordinate to it had been feeding off themselves for so long it had become their way of life, and it was unsupportable. They were dying, slowly but inexorably.

Chara had provided them with a way out.

Just as her name traced her lineage back generation after generation, through all the places they had made a home. So the new family splits would belong to the name of two of her daughters and one of them could add a new place name as well.

CHAPTER 36

Elona woke up in the dark and stared at the ceiling. The smells of a Slissac home were distinct and, although she lived in them every day, they always seemed to be strongest first thing in the morning. Perhaps it was the moss.

She let her power leak out and the room filled with soft light. Not for the first time she looked round for Chara only to remember she was sleeping on the roof with the other *ziri*.

When they had both lived with Usala, she had been the one that was afraid and Chara had comforted her, sometimes holding her during the long cold nights of winter. Then they had come here and again they slept in the same room. And Chara had been the one to crawl into bed with Elona, because the Slissac was afraid—and with far more justification than Elona had.

She had finally escaped the chains holding her to the town— though the one with Chara had not been one she wanted to break.

But Elona had yanked Chara out of her new life and almost brought down ruin on her. Making her an outcast once more, yet now she slept with the *ziri*. Perhaps they curled up together for warmth.

She sat up and poured water into her cup from the pitcher. It wasn't cold but it brought her out of the half-dreamlike state.

The time since Chara had presented her plan to the elders had been busy, mostly for Chara—despite her difficulty in communicating—but even for Kantees, who had taken over the training of the daughters.

Part of the plan had been that the original Aytrueth house would specialise in the training and use of *zirichasa*, every family must have its own skill that it could use to trade with the others.

The youngest daughter, Yalanka ko-Gey-la Aytrueth, was to have the original Aytrueth house and the *ziri*. The eldest, Taricha ar-Gey-la Aytrueth, was designated as Chara's direct heir, and would have what would have been hers anyway if her mother had survived—and her sisters had not succeeded in killing her. It was left to Guteriku tu-Gey-la Aytrueth to take on the responsibility of building the new town.

Except it wasn't really new. It already had the canal and wharf which Elona and Chara had used escaping the armsmen. It had been a way-point for transferring cargo, it was just a matter of reopening it, constructing the heart-rooms and building out from there.

The daughters were not of-age, in the case of the youngest it would be another six years, but the Slissac had legal contingencies for things like this—their way of life made such rules imperative. The Elders became responsible and no one who caused trouble could benefit from their act. They would not be punished, not even for killing a child, but since they reaped no reward there was no point to it—but the elders would still avenge the murders. Two reasons for not committing the act in the first place.

She shook her head. The place was crazy by her standards, but then most of her rules did not apply.

Elona stared at the Slissac writings on the walls.

She knew now they were not for nothing, they channelled power though she had no idea how that worked. Would they have to wait for another feeding before Chara could summon the power to change back? How could you guarantee it would be enough?

And to think Chara had the ability to change the patterns of her own living flesh.

Elona touched her cheek without realising she was doing it. Running the tips of her fingers across the coarse non-flesh.

It wasn't just the power, it was the will to make it happen.

Both were needed.

THE SERVANT DOOR OPENED, a tray of food was deposited on the table, and the one who had served it was gone as if they had never been.

Elona shook her head again.

She was very aware of the difference in class in the lands of the Taymalin. In a different life, if she had not been who she was, she would have grown up barely acknowledging the servants, she would have married the Prince, and if not him then another noble.

Her best friend would have not been a servant girl. She would never have received the education she had. She would have been shallow and vapid. All the things she hated in others.

Perhaps that was something to be grateful for.

She ate from the various fungus dishes. There were one or two that she enjoyed but she did not think she would ever really take to them. Perhaps they tasted better to a Slissac.

She laughed to herself as she thought of how much she would prefer Chara's current diet of red meat. Though perhaps not raw and still warm with life, cooked would be better.

The household seamstress had taken apart her Taymalin clothes and made something similar in structure but of more hard-wearing material for the journey. Not that the journey itself was likely to take very long.

They had had long discussions about their destination, Chara and Kantees had visited Usala more than once and told her the plans, and asked whether she had decided where she wanted to go.

The *ziri* could travel fast but it was still easier for Elona to transport them through a patterner's path, besides the less time she spent on the back of Ilith the better she would like it. She did not know whether they had told Usala just how short that journey could be.

In the end Usala had decided that she would return to Faerholme after all. She wanted to visit Idolain first, just to see her home once more, then she would decide where to go from there, if she did not want to stay.

But Elona did not know the circle at Idolain and so could not take her there directly. She felt, once more, there had been too much time wasting. The *Kisharuk* was free and every day they delayed the monster would reassert its power.

Everything was always so complicated.

The situation with Aytrueth was now under control, and they needed to find the Arch-Patterner in the hope he knew how Chara could change back. Then she had to deal with the creature that wanted to destroy the Taymalin, and that was a task only she could perform—at least, she hoped she would be able to. She would die trying.

"But we can only deal with one thing at a time," she said to the empty room.

The new dress fitted well, with patterns sewn into the seams. She had seen similar things in commoner's clothes. It was not fashionable among the nobility. But now she wondered whether these might have power too. She had always thought the habit of putting patterns on to everything was just superstition. Now she saw it as a tradition inherited from the Slissac when the Taymalin were slaves, and one that had never been abandoned. Only its origins had been forgotten.

Ulina arrived to escort her to the roof.

They were still careful. Other families, including ones from the surrounding enclaves, had decided to follow Aytrueth's example and split so that all the heirs could survive. It meant the newly founded town would be built with several families which in turn made it more viable.

Chara and Llakassa had upset the tidy closed world of these Slissac—and there were those who did not like it. Hence Ulina's presence, they blamed Chara but mostly Elona because she had been the first human to break into their small world. Perhaps they could have tolerated that alone, especially once she left.

But to return with *ziri* and more humans? Becoming the most powerful family with such an astonishing feat of magic, and then going back to the old ways of expansion.

One might expect them to appreciate a return to the traditions on which their home had been founded but that wasn't what they disliked—it was change itself. In that Slissac and human were alike.

Some of us get no choice, thought Elona as she left the room for the last time and headed along the passages and up the stairs towards the roof. Ulina at her side.

THE FRESH AIR was cool but not cold as they emerged, but Elona still shivered as she watched the *zirichasa*. They were excited, knowing somehow that they were about to fly to another place. Elona felt for the ley-circle. It was calm and filled with the energy she needed.

There had been discussions with Chara and Kantees about whether Elona should ride on her sister's back. Chara was happy to do it but Kantees did not think it was appropriate since their departure was going to be watched by all the other families from the safety of their homes. Elona added the fact that she preferred to be strapped in.

Chara had reluctantly agreed, as well as accepting that Usala would also not ride her. Only close family knew who Usala was, and she would go unnoticed if she rode one of the other *ziri*. To have an unknown human on Chara's back would be even worse than Elona.

Chara said that the Slissac did not normally use the tops of the buildings—they were too open and therefore dangerous. But today things were different—not every house but on most there were Slissac watching the departure of Chara and her retinue.

Some of them probably hoped everything would return to the way it was, but Elona could have told them, after this, it could never be the same again. Change was inevitable.

Kantees had taken charge, neither Chara nor Elona objected.

The *ziri* were her responsibility, and that applied to Chara as well when it came to the matters of being a *zirichak*. There had been stand-offs between Sheesha and two of the other bigger males. Kantees said that, since Sheesha had not succeeded in mating with Chara—whose embarrassment in the discussion of the subject was obvious even if she couldn't blush—the others had thought he was losing his strength and wanted to try.

It had not come to any actual fights, Sheesha was so much larger they did not push beyond the opening moves.

Kantees had asked Chara embarrassing questions about how she was feeling in that regard and, with Elona reading out her scratched answers, she had to admit her body did want to do it.

"You're behaving like a *ziri* in heat, even if you don't mean to."

Elona blushed enough for the both of them.

"But you're big enough to dissuade even Sheesha, at least for now," said Kantees. "But it's causing strain in him and the other males. You're not supposed to behave like this, you're supposed to be willing. The sooner we get you changed back, the better."

Elona could only agree.

But that had been days ago. The excitement of the departure kept each human, Slissac and *zirichak* focused on what was to come.

Three of the *ziri* were staying behind, the ones that had been given to Chara's daughters, which left them with three spares. Chara's mount, Sulassa, was carrying Usala and the other two had been given extra baggage.

Somehow they seemed to be leaving with more than they had brought. Every one of them, except Chara, was also carrying luggage. The seamstress and her apprentices had been busy again stitching double bags that could rest over a *ziri*'s back, and strapped in place.

Then there was a stillness. The three daughters who had been with Chara stepped away, as did the other Slissac who had been helping. Everyone was on the back of their beast with Elona properly strapped in place. She had hoped that familiarity would make flying easier for her, but it didn't. The feeling of being unsafe and out of control never went away.

The sun's rays crept over a ridge and bathed them in its light. Chara raised her head and hooted into the morning sky. Then launched into the air in one powerful push. Like a wave the remaining *ziri* followed her.

Elona's stomach lurched. Ilith did not try to make the journey any easier for her—why should he, he was at home in the sky.

Chara turned above the town of Hanna and the *ziri* formed up behind her. Seven was a difficult number for a formation but the beasts instinctively knew what to do. Sheesha, moved in directly behind Chara, then Halenth and Sulassa, and finally Ilith in the middle at the back flanked by the riderless *zirichasa*.

They turned several times over the town gaining in height— making sure that everyone could see them clearly. Kantees described Sheesha as a show-off, it seemed that *ziri*-Chara was the same.

Elona closed her eyes and concentrated on the ley-circle while holding the signature of the one at Canvor in her mind. She felt Ilith fly straight and saw they were heading for the circle.

Drawing up all the Mother's milk she needed, she made the path in the air high above the circle. And focused on it, drawing it tighter and tighter. Pulling the Canvor end through the World's Pattern. Chara accelerated, and the others with her.

She's going to do it.

Elona felt the power of the *zirichasa* forming around her but it did not interfere with the pattern she was making.

The *ziri* flashed towards the opening of the path.

Elona drew the ends together until they were in the same place.

She opened her eyes and for a moment saw the portal ahead of them, a circle just big enough to take the formation, a darkness with a pre-dawn glow against the brilliant blue of the morning in this place.

Then they were through.

And she let the portal collapse behind her.

CHAPTER 37

The blazing golden light subsided and they were hit by the cool early morning air—filled with the smell of burning. As her eyes adjusted, she could see a pall of smoke hanging over the city.

Chara turned as they approached the terraced levels along the sides of the hill on which the castle stood.

The side they were on was in shadow against the dawn but lights shone out in some of the buildings as if people still lived in them. It was when they came around to the other side she could see through the dark haze. The whitewashed buildings were blackened and burned.

It had not been this bad when they had left. Something must have happened.

Chara circled the citadel and climbed slowly.

Armsmen appeared on the walls, weapons readied.

Elona allowed herself to feel the power of the ley-circle and prepared to defend them. But no one fired as they came round once more, rising above the level of the walls, and then the buildings of the castle itself.

The sun was dawning a second time for them and its light made Sheesha and Chara glow.

The place where Elona had brought down the tower was clearly visible. There did not seem to have been any attempt at repairs, but there were dozens of ballistas and other big siege weapons pointing outward, with at least half of them only partially built.

Chara glided now, with the others remaining in perfect formation behind her. Elona understood she was waiting, but wished they could be back on solid ground. On the third pass in front of the main gate, she heaved painfully, but nothing came up. She couldn't decide whether she was grateful or upset about it.

After their fifth pass around the citadel, which did not seem to have suffered much additional damage though there were marks of fires in several places, a group of nobles could be seen in the courtyard behind the main gate.

Their gaudy clothing gave them away, and she recognised Drahail among them.

"Go down now," she shouted.

Chara immediately banked to the right hard with the others following. Elona inadvertently saw down the cliff-face, through the hanging haze to the buildings far below them and her head swam.

Her only coherent thought was that if something attacked them now she was too sick to do anything about it.

But there was no attack. And the *ziri* landed lightly.

Ulina was with her in a moment helping her to unstrap herself and then handing her down to the solid stone.

They had agreed Chara's situation should remain a secret. She would pretend to be a normal *ziri* for the time being.

Elona and Kantees went forward and bowed to the King. He looked tired and worn. The air stank of damp and burning.

"Your Majesty," said Elona.

"Let's go inside, and break our fast," he said, and turned away.

"I beg pardon, Your Majesty," she said forcing him to turn back. "Allow me to present Lady Usala of Idolain."

Usala came up and curtsied. She was dressed in something a commoner might wear.

"I do not know of you," said Drahail and turned to the men who had arrived with him, one of them moved forward. He stared at Usala for a few moments and then whispered in Drahail's ear.

"If Lady Elona says that's who you are then I accept it. You may join us."

Usala bowed her head. "You are very gracious, Your Majesty."

Elona noted how her voice and manner had changed, as if she remembered how things were at court after all these years. That should at least convince Drahail that Usala was at least noble-born.

Before following, Elona went to Chara and patted her neck. "Sorry."

Chara shrugged.

THE ROOM they ended up in was airy, with plenty of windows looking out on to other parts of the castle. It was possible to believe that nothing was wrong—save for the all-pervading smell.

Food was brought and laid out in front of them.

The smell of cooked meat made Elona's nose tingle and her mouth salivate in anticipation.

"What happened?" she said simply before she attacked the fresh bread.

"While we were busy fighting on that island you took us to, the emperor's *tekrasa* arrived in force again and put the city to flame."

Elona watched him. He looked so much older.

"Are the queen and prince all right?"

"They're on their way to Betlain."

"I'm sorry we were not here to help."

"If you had been here, you would not have been there. It is one and the same. We all lose in war."

They ate in silence for a time. Elona had a glove over her damaged hand but she could not disguise what had happened to her face.

"Am I free to come and go from the castle?"

Drahail was in the middle of chewing something and waved his hand. He swallowed. "What are your plans?"

"Lady Usala wishes to return to Idolain."

"I cannot spare an escort."

"I did not imagine you would, sire, and have another arrangement in mind."

"What else?"

"I would like to know where Florian is."

Drahail put his hands flat on the table and looked at her directly, though she could see his eyes drawn to the dark scarring of her face.

"I know there is no love lost between you and the Arch-Patterner."

"That is not why I need to find him, sire."

"He is not here."

"I do not mind where he is, my Lord King, I have need to consult his knowledge on an important matter."

"What matter?"

Elona considered who else was at the table and who would be listening.

"If you will only tell me on that basis, sire, then I must speak with you alone."

"Very well, after we have eaten."

∽

"You're joking," said Drahail.

"Do you really think I would make such a jest?"

They were in a small room off the main hall where the rest of the diners waited for the King to give them leave to withdraw. The open windows let in light and the cool air, though it smelled of burning and death.

Drahail held a glass of something sweet and alcoholic, hers sat untouched on a low table.

"Your Slissac has turned into a *zirichak*? It's like something out of a tale for children."

"My *sister*," she said.

"You helped her escape from my dungeons."

"She had done nothing wrong."

"She's a Slissac, Elona, and that makes her wrong. It was difficult enough preventing the people out there hearing about it. Even so there are rumours—some people think the crown is in league with them. They might gossip and laugh over it but most don't believe it. Do you realise what would happen if they knew a Slissac was here? That they were real?"

"Frankly, Drahail, I don't care. Just tell me where to find Florian and we'll leave. I promise not to bring her back to your precious court."

"Of course you do."

"Of course I do what?"

"Care."

She grabbed up the drink and took a mouthful. It was thick, very sweet, and smelled of flowers. It made the back of her head tingle as it went down.

"What happened to you?" he said after a pause.

She shook her head. "It would be easier to ask what hasn't happened." She sighed. "Jaymis is dead."

"Hope's brother? How?"

"Possessed by the *Kisharuk*."

Drahail stared at her then swallowed his remaining drink.

He went to the door and told the other guests to go. Then he came and sat closer to the fire. Elona sat in the other chair and told him everything that had happened.

"But the *Kisharuk*?"

"That's what it said it was and I believed it. There was something strange and powerful inside. It did not seem to be able to do patterning of its own, but it had an army of patterners to do its bidding."

"You think Jaymis is dead?"

"I have to believe that, though it claimed he was still inside."

"And Myrlask was the *Kisharuk* too?"

"I don't know for certain but it seems likely. Then it took over Lord Nemon's wife, Hilaneena."

"The one you met and killed."

"I killed the body, not the *Kisharuk*."

"I still want to believe this is a jest."

She still held her glass though it had been empty for a long time.

They were silent for a time. Finally he rose and placed his glass on the mantel.

"The Conclave should be informed."

She felt anger bubbling up inside her. "And you think they will believe it? You only listen to me at all because you are you and I am me." She stood and placed her glass on the table. "Tell me where Florian is and we will leave."

"To do what? Face the *Kisharuk* alone again?"

"I will do whatever I have to. Just tell me where he is, Drahail."

He sighed. "I don't know. He received a message a couple of days ago and left. You don't ask the Arch-Patterner where he's going."

ELONA FOUND someone to guide her to the roof where the *zirichasa* were resting in the warm afternoon. Summer had almost arrived though the days were still not as long as they might be.

The *ziri* were sunning themselves with their wings spread wide. Chara was among them, with Sheesha lying next to her. Kantees sat nearby with Ulina.

Chara saw her approaching and raised her head, twisting her neck so she would be part of the conversation.

"Drahail doesn't know where Florian is."

Chara sighed as only a big *ziri* can, blowing up dust between them.

"Apparently he received a message and left."

Kantees looked thoughtful. "I may know someone who can help."

"And where do we find them?"

"Not here, we'll have to go to Esternes."

"But I don't know any of the ley-circles there."

Kantees put her hand on Elona's knee. "I know you want to get to this Florian quickly but sometimes you have to do it the old-fashioned way. We'll get a patterner to make a path."

~

Usala had been given a luxurious suite of rooms in the heart of the castle, as befitted her position as a lady of Idolain. Elona went to talk to her.

"I don't think I could get used to this," she said as she requested a pot of *tasa* from the girl servant.

"Are you sure? You seem to be adapting well enough."

Usala shook her head. "Just because I haven't forgotten, doesn't mean I like it. If you try to do things for yourself it upsets the staff. They're here to serve, and they don't like it when they're not allowed to do their jobs. I learnt to rely on myself and I prefer it that way."

The *tasa* arrived and Usala poured them both drinks. Elona was still feeling a little light-headed from the drink she'd had earlier. Not dizzy but warm.

I should either not drink or build some tolerance for it.

"The Arch-Patterner isn't here," she said, "and I need to go to Esternes where there's someone who might know where he is." She was not sure how much of a long shot this was going to be but she had to trust Kantees.

"And you don't want to be wasting time escorting me to Idolain. That's all right, Elona, I wouldn't expect you to. I'm sure I can ask the King to arrange an escort."

"I don't know if he will want to spare the men. But I do have another idea if you would like to try it. It will probably mean walking, or taking one of the outgoing caravans."

Usala smiled. "I am not afraid of exercise."

Elona nodded. "I have some friends, women, I think that if they are still here in Canvor, you could stay with them and I'm sure they would help you get to Idolain. Probably go with you."

"Stay with them?"

"I think you would like them, and the way they live."

CHAPTER 38

*E*lona gripped the saddle tightly and forced her eyes open as Ilith's long swoop from the castle flattened out. She had no choice because she was the only one who knew what they were looking for.

She had persuaded Kantees and Sheesha to stay behind, because she did not think the courtyard would hold more than two *ziri*, especially not if one of them was Chara's size. Ulina had insisted on coming and was now standing on Ilith's back behind Elona, holding the reins. The *zirichak* didn't seem to mind the extra weight.

Although she had lived at the Widow's Court, she did not know how it looked from above. But she had told Chara to circle round to the lake-side of the city. Her knuckles were going white as she gripped the saddle leather in a death grip, trying to maintain control of herself. The buildings twisted below her. This time Ilith was in the lead with Chara following which made Elona doubly uncomfortable.

She spotted what should have been the street of clothiers but was now lined with burnt-out and collapsed buildings. She told Ulina to follow it down. They swept low over the buildings. Ilith had not beat his wings once since they launched.

They glided down the street. Elona stared at the destruction. And felt a lump in her throat when she saw Kendreth's shop was now just a blackened skeleton. She hoped he had survived.

Unable to speak she pointed further round and they descended to where the city was no longer on the slopes and the ground flat. Elona forced herself to keep looking though her stomach wanted to return everything it had eaten in the past few hours.

There were stretches where there had been no damage to the city, and then they turned into the shadow of the mount and it took a few moments for Elona's eyes to adjust.

There was more devastation on this side. Whole swathes of buildings burned to the ground. She had never had any love for the city, but there were people here she cared about and her eyes blurred with tears. She rubbed them away angrily—she needed to be able to see.

She pointed at what she thought was the correct street running in a slow curve, and under Ulina's direction Ilith turned. And suddenly there it was. One side of the road the buildings were partially burned and on the other stood the Widow's Court, she could see a couple of children in the courtyard and washing draped on lines criss-crossing the area.

She had forgotten the washing.

"There! Land on that roof."

Elona slammed her eyes shut gratefully as Ilith dropped from the sky and left her stomach behind.

They touched down and she could hear screams and crying. There was no way to avoid that. She fumbled at the buckles as Ulina jumped to the ground from behind her. She slithered out of the saddle and into the strong arms of her niece. Had she grown taller?

Chara had landed behind them and Usala was carefully dismounting.

"Hold my hand, Ulina," she said. "Don't let me fall."

Ulina did as she was asked as Elona moved in small cautious steps to the edge of the roof. She shut her eyes.

"It's me, Elona—I mean, Parthia." *Mother's milk.* "It's all right, it's just me Parthia. Is Avalia there? Or Efley? Makeela?"

"Parthia?"

"Makeela! Yes, it's me. It's all right, it's safe. Just a couple of *ziri* and my niece and my … stepmother."

Usala laughed. "Stepmother indeed. I wouldn't have married that father of yours if he had been emperor of the world."

Elona stepped away from the edge with Ulina guiding her.

She opened her eyes. "You knew my father?"

"Oh yes, he was a possible match for me. I thought he was an idiot."

Elona wasn't sure how she felt about this revelation. She had a strange urge to defend her father against Usala's accusation in spite of everything he had done.

She was saved from having to make that decision as the trapdoor in the roof clacked and creaked. The bolts were drawn back and it was thrown open. Out of breath Makeela climbed up on to the roof and then stopped dead, faced with two *zirichasa*.

"Makeela!"

Elona hurried over, Makeela put out her arms and they fell into a hug. Elona was surprised by the tears in her own eyes. Makeela kissed her on the lips, hard and firm.

Makeela pulled away and held her at arm's length. "You're alive and you came back."

Elona shook her head. "I am not back, not really. I am just bringing someone to join you, she is alone and in need of help."

"Riding the back of *ziri*?" She glanced over Elona's shoulder. "I knew they were big, but these are so huge. I don't know how you're brave enough to ride on them. I've never been to a race, but I've seen them flying over the city."

"I can't chat, Makeela. Is Avalia here?"

She could feel the life go from the woman.

"Avalia is dead, Parthia."

"How? When?" *Please the Mother it was not my fault.*

"Come down, we can talk there. Efley is our leader now."

～

ELONA, Ulina and Usala arrived in the room where Avalia had spoken to Elona that last time. It looked the same, but now Efley sat where Avalia had. She had expressed her delight at seeing Elona—neither Ulina nor Usala commented on the fact that Elona was not using her own name.

They went through introductions and sat.

Makeela went off to arrange some drinks and food.

"Makeela is a good person," said Efley.

"She is," said Elona.

"She has not been the same since you left."

"She thinks she is in love with me," said Elona.

Efley smiled. "She is, in her way."

"She seems a person who has suffered a great deal," said Usala.

Efley frowned at Elona.

"I have said nothing. But to my discredit, I have not thought of those who live in the Widow's Court enough in the days I have been away. You were very good to me."

"And did you succeed in finding your sister in the castle?"

"I did, and she was rescued."

"We have not seen Zora."

Elona pursed her lips and looked down. "She was killed by a Tirnian assassin."

She looked surprised when Efley gave a short laugh. "Just like Zora to die in the most dramatic way."

Elona smiled too. "I wish I could say it was a quick death. The assassin died though and in much greater pain."

"That is just. We guessed she was no more. When we fled the city, we saw the fires above the castle. We knew it did not bode well."

Makeela returned with the water jug, some cups and a few sweetmeats on a plate.

"What happened to Avalia?"

Efley sighed. "We had travelled to the river and were forced to wait until dawn. In that time, the number of those fleeing the city had risen into the hundreds, all trying to ride the ferry across the Cormark.

"It was chaos, people were fighting each other. The ferrymen refused to work because they were afraid too many people would try to ride, so the mob killed them. That was when we decided to head downriver, just to get away to safety."

Elona shook her head. "I gave you bad advice."

"The advice was good, Parthia, but others had the same idea. They were desperate and scared. Everyone was saying it was Slissac come to enslave us again." She gave Elona a hard look before continuing. "Avalia thought downriver would be better because most people would head the other way looking for another place to cross. Perhaps she was right, but for us it was not a great deal better. It was only halfway to midday when the bodies floated past. Hundreds of men, women and children all drowned."

"They tried to use the ferry."

Efley nodded. "That is what we heard later. So, we continued and, after a two-day, reached where the south road approached the river. We stopped at the next inn where we learnt there had been a battle, Faerholme had won and Canvor was safe so we returned."

Makeela moved in her chair. "But you did not comeback, Parthia, nor did Zora."

"I couldn't."

"Then the armies prepared for war," continued Efley, "and waited by the ley-circle. Eventually it opened and they went through." She hesitated. "That night the portal opened again and the great *tekrasa* flew in once more. This time there was less defence. They poured fire on the city and the citadel, but left again. The Court was not affected but the city was burning. Avalia said we should go out and help those in need." Tears formed in her eyes. "We made groups of three and armed ourselves with knives, then went out into the city to see what we could do to help." Her voice broke.

Makeela cleared her throat. "She was separated from her group. She never returned. Whether she was overcome by the smoke or something else, we don't know."

"We tried to search but couldn't find her," said Efley.

"So many buildings collapsed. It's like a different place. There are gangs on the streets every night now," said Makeela. "Though the king sends men to watch the streets they are too few."

"We don't try to help anymore."

They fell silent.

Finally, Elona spoke. "I would like you to help Usala."

"Your stepmother?" said Makeela.

"She's not my stepmother, that was the first thing I thought of, I didn't want you to be scared."

Makeela opened her mouth to say something but Elona held up her hand.

"But she has been like a mother to me, at least she was when I was very ill. She nursed me back to health, she's a healer. And wise."

Usala made a sceptical noise. "I can speak for myself, *daughter*."

"And is this child really your niece?"

"She is the daughter of a woman I consider to be a sister," said Elona.

"Both a pretend sister and a pretend mother?"

"Better than any real one I might have had."

Efley smiled. "Of course, Usala can stay with us. I can see from her fingers she's a woman who knows what hard work is. Unlike someone I could mention."

"Do you have to leave, Parthia?" Makeela sounded like a little girl.

"I can't stay."

"I will look after your stepmother."

"Like you would your own?"

"Oh, very much better than that."

So they said their goodbyes. Elona and Ulina mounted the stairs once more and climbed up to the roof accompanied by Makeela.

Ulina went to Ilith to check the saddle and straps.

Makeela took Elona's hand. "I really will look after Usala."

"I know you will, you're a good person."

Makeela looked down. "The others think I am strange because I don't like men."

"I wouldn't think many of the women who come to the Widow's Court like men much."

"It's not the same."

"I know."

"Do you think I'm strange?"

Elona did not reply but stepped up close to Makeela and kissed her, as if she were kissing Jaymis. She did not hurry and let herself enjoy the closeness of another human as Makeela put her arms around her.

Chara breathed in Elona's ear and nudged her from behind. The two of them stumbled, barely managing to remain upright.

Makeela gave a little cry of fear but Elona laughed and batted Chara's muzzle with her hand. "Stop that, anyone would think you're jealous."

Chara grunted and sat back, her head now high above the two women.

"Is it jealous?" said Makeela breathlessly.

"If she is, she has no right." She took Makeela's hands. "I like you Makeela and I don't think you're strange. I know you care for me—"

"I love you, Parthia."

Elona shook her head. "I care for you and you'll find someone one day, who you can love truly and who will love you back. But it's not wise to love me."

She turned away, walked to Ilith and mounted with Ulina's help.

"Why don't you ride the big one?"

"I won't put a saddle on her and I can't manage without one. I'm terrified of heights."

A strange combination of repeated grunts and what sounded like tongue clicking poured from Chara's mouth.

Makeela drew back. "What's wrong with her?"

Elona smiled. "She's laughing."

Chara spread her enormous wings and launched herself. Makeela ducked but Chara was wheeling through the air high above the rooftop already.

"Will I see you again?"

"If the Mother is willing!"

Elona slammed her eyes shut and grabbed the saddle as Ulina launched Ilith upwards.

In the distance she heard Makeela shout. "Farewell, Elona of Corlain!"

EPILOGUE

It was the following morning, in the cold before dawn, with mists covering the damp clay that had once been a lake, that four *zirichasa* landed in front of the ley-circle, among the massed forces of Canvor, Corlain and the other major houses of Faerholme.

Elona on the back of Ilith made sure her face was fully hooded. Ulina rode Halenth, Kantees on Sheesha, while Chara had no rider.

A single patterner was hard at work scratching out symbols in the mud. A circular area around the ley-circle had been flattened, allowing the patterns to be cut into its surface.

The *ziri* and riders waited in silence as he worked. Elona felt the power building. This was not going to be a wide path but Kantees had stipulated it needed to allow the wingspan of a large *ziri* and that was what had been provided.

"Soon," said Elona.

The *ziri* launched into the air as one and circled away from where the portal would form. They flew half the way back to Canvor before turning again.

Elona did not mention that the portal had come into existence because she knew Kantees could see it too. As could the *zirichasa* themselves. Flying nose to tail, with Chara in front, Sheesha second, Ilith third and Halenth last, they accelerated towards the portal.

Moments before they struck, Elona felt the surge of power, the air about them turned golden and they vanished into the World's Pattern.

~ To be concluded ~

READ VEONA (PATTERNER'S PATH 0)

Discover the real beginning of Elona's story...

Subscribe to my mailing list and download the prequel **VEONA** (Patterner's Path 0).

Go here: **taupress.com/vs-veona**

ABOUT THE AUTHOR

Steve Turnbull has been a geek and a nerd longer than those words have had their modern meaning.

Born in the heart of London to book-loving working class parents in 1958, he lived with his parents and two much older sisters in two rooms with gas lighting and no hot water (true!). In his fifth year, a change in his father's fortunes took them out to a detached house in the suburbs. That was the year Dr Who first aired on British TV and Steve watched it avidly from behind the sofa. It was the beginning of his love of science fiction.

Academically Steve always went for the science side but also had his imagination and that took him everywhere. He read through his local library's entire science fiction and fantasy selection, plus his father's 1950s *Astounding Science Fiction* magazines. As he got older he also ate his way through TV SF like *Star Trek*, *Dr Who* and *Blake's 7*.

However it was when he was 15 he discovered something new.

Bored with a Maths lesson he noticed a book from the school library: *Cider with Rosie* by Laurie Lee. From the first page he was captivated by the beauty of the language. As a result he wrote a story longhand and then spent evenings at home on his father's electric typewriter pounding out a second draft, expanding it. Then he wrote a second book. Both were terrible but it was a start. After that he switched to poetry and turned out dozens, mostly not involving teenage angst.

After receiving excellent science and maths results he went on to study Computer Science. There he teamed up with another student and they wrote songs for their band - Steve writing the lyrics. Though they admit their best song was the other way around, with Steve writing the music.

After graduation Steve moved into contract programming but was snapped up a couple of years later by a computer magazine looking for someone with technical knowledge. It was in the magazine industry that Steve learned how to write to length, to deadline and to style. Within a couple of years he was editor and stayed there for many years.

During that time he married Pam (also a magazine editor) who he'd met at a student party.

Though he continued to write poetry all prose work stopped. He created his own magazine publishing company which at one point produced the glossy subscription magazine for the *Robot Wars* TV show. The company evolved into a design agency but after six years of working very hard and not seeing his family—now including a daughter and son—he gave it all up.

He spent a year working on miscellaneous projects including writing 300 pages for a website until he started back where he had begun, contract programming.

With security and success on the job front, the writing began again. This time it was scriptwriting: features scripts, TV scripts and radio scripts. During this time he met a director Chris Payne, who wanted to create steampunk stories and between them they created the Voidships universe, a place very similar to ours but with specific scientific changes.

ABOUT THE AUTHOR

Steve Turnbull has been a geek and a nerd longer than those words have had their modern meaning.

Born in the heart of London to book-loving working class parents in 1958, he lived with his parents and two much older sisters in two rooms with gas lighting and no hot water (true!). In his fifth year, a change in his father's fortunes took them out to a detached house in the suburbs. That was the year Dr Who first aired on British TV and Steve watched it avidly from behind the sofa. It was the beginning of his love of science fiction.

Academically Steve always went for the science side but also had his imagination and that took him everywhere. He read through his local library's entire science fiction and fantasy selection, plus his father's 1950s *Astounding Science Fiction* magazines. As he got older he also ate his way through TV SF like *Star Trek*, *Dr Who* and *Blake's 7*.

However it was when he was 15 he discovered something new.

Bored with a Maths lesson he noticed a book from the school library: *Cider with Rosie* by Laurie Lee. From the first page he was captivated by the beauty of the language. As a result he wrote a story longhand and then spent evenings at home on his father's electric typewriter pounding out a second draft, expanding it. Then he wrote a second book. Both were terrible but it was a start. After that he switched to poetry and turned out dozens, mostly not involving teenage angst.

After receiving excellent science and maths results he went on to study Computer Science. There he teamed up with another student and they wrote songs for their band - Steve writing the lyrics. Though they admit their best song was the other way around, with Steve writing the music.

After graduation Steve moved into contract programming but was snapped up a couple of years later by a computer magazine looking for someone with technical knowledge. It was in the magazine industry that Steve learned how to write to length, to deadline and to style. Within a couple of years he was editor and stayed there for many years.

During that time he married Pam (also a magazine editor) who he'd met at a student party.

Though he continued to write poetry all prose work stopped. He created his own magazine publishing company which at one point produced the glossy subscription magazine for the *Robot Wars* TV show. The company evolved into a design agency but after six years of working very hard and not seeing his family—now including a daughter and son—he gave it all up.

He spent a year working on miscellaneous projects including writing 300 pages for a website until he started back where he had begun, contract programming.

With security and success on the job front, the writing began again. This time it was scriptwriting: features scripts, TV scripts and radio scripts. During this time he met a director Chris Payne, who wanted to create steampunk stories and between them they created the Voidships universe, a place very similar to ours but with specific scientific changes.

But you can't keep a good writer restrained, so apart from the output of Steampunk stories Steve returned to his first love of Fantasy and Science Fiction.

Don't forget you can read VEONA by going to **taupress.-com/vs-veona**